DENISE STALLINS

LAYING IT ALL OUT THERE

A NOVEL

LAYING IT ALL OUT THERE

This book started out as a memoir, but since life does not have a majestic yet compact narrative arc, the memoir became a work of fiction. Names, details, professions, people, pets, outcomes, and characteristics have been changed, events have been rearranged or compressed, dialogue has been created, and stuff just made up. Interactions with the Transportation Security Administration, however, are as accurate as recollection permits. So, any resemblance to actual persons, living or dead, or actual events—except the coronavirus pandemic and the TSA—is purely coincidental.

Nothing in this book constitutes legal advice. At the time of this writing, growing, possessing, and using cannabis is a criminal offense in most places and penalties vary widely. If you are caught with cannabis where it is not legal, this book will not save you from prosecution and may even make your situation worse. Also, nothing in this book constitutes medical advice of any kind at all.

Cover and Interior Design by Damonza

Identifiers: LCCN 2022900739

Hardcover ISBN 979-8-9855580-1-2

Paperback ISBN 979-8-9855580-2-9

eBook ISBN 979-8-9855580-0-5

Published in the United States by Flatbutt Press

flatbuttpress.com

denisestallins.com

Dedicated to my parents, Floyd and Joyce Stallins.

TABLE OF CONTENTS

Part One | 1

Part Two | 121

PART ONE

A NOTE FROM ALENE

I changed all the names. Except mine.
And Nolan's.

He said it was okay.

Also, I'm not calling this a memoir.
Because of all the slight felonies documented herein—Federal and State.

- Alene Adele Sterling

CHAPTER ONE
THREE THINGS

THERE ARE NO fat people in Colorado. Or billboards. The Colorado Department of Transportation actually enforces the Ladybird Johnson Highway Beautification Act of 1965. Colorado lawmakers did not give in to the lobbying efforts of the Outdoor Advertising Industry and do not grant the exemptions that eroded the Beautification Act everywhere else. That's why you see thickets of billboards for lawyers and collision repair looming over roads everywhere else in the country instead of the fruited plains and purple mountains. But the first time you are in Colorado and you're driving around with Nolan in July of 2016 in his beat-up old Jeep and he asks if you notice anything different, anything missing, you can't isolate it even though you feel something *is* different. Then Nolan says there are no billboards, and I am amazed that I didn't realize it and yet I kinda feel like I did. But I didn't. Being able to see the mountains in Colorado matters. Beauty by design. Beauty for everyone.

CDOT is the department keeping billboards out of Colorado. I don't know which agency is responsible for keeping fat people out. Or how they achieve their goals. The lack of fat people I do notice on my own, even without the annual evening news segment proclaiming Colorado the healthiest state in the nation, showing footage of lean kids, svelte adults, spry old people, and smiling dogs jogging on scenic trails. Nolan explains that Coloradans are active and like to get out into nature. He goes on about healthy lifestyles, but I stop listening and develop theories of my own: Perhaps Colorado distributes a choice of a bike, a dog with leash, or a snowboard at the border to anyone moving into the state. Or it gives out a set of Colorado active wear: for men, a faded t-shirt and cargo shorts. For women, a t-shirt and leggings, paired with a waist pack to hold keys, a phone and dog treats. These theories settle in since everyone in Colorado seems compelled to bike, walk a dog, slide on snow, or combine those activities in some fashion every day.

The way that mountains are the backdrop of Colorado, fat people are just a part of the setting of Texas, where I'm from. Where Nolan used to be from.

No billboards at all mean there are no billboards advertising cannabis which is what, five months later in the middle of a catastrophic winter storm, I will come back to Colorado for. It is what I will fly to Denver to buy four times in the next three years so I can sneak it back to Texas, where it is not legal. But on my first trip out there, to visit Nolan, I don't know that yet. On the fourth day of the visit, when I ask why I haven't seen any marijuana shops, Nolan tells me that we have driven past many. He points one out and I still don't see it; that is by design too.

Colorado has 150 pages of Retail Marijuana Advertising Regulations, which prohibit advertising on television, radio, sports events, or pretty much anywhere, other than the store sign itself which can only be a "fixed sign located on the same zone lot as a Retail Marijuana Establishment and that exists solely to identify the location of the Retail Marijuana Establishment and otherwise complies with any applicable local ordinances." Also signs cannot use cartoon characters. What that will turn out to mean in practice is that in the first years of the Green Rush, you couldn't *see* a cannabis dispensary unless you already knew where to look for it, and even then, the odds were off. But that first summer, I didn't care because I had no idea that I would ever need to go into one.

This book is about three disparate things that don't mesh together. Also, it lacks all subtlety. Like Shakespeare or *Star Wars*, the subtext is not too 'sub.' I've taught English and literature at community colleges since the mid-90s and specialize in Freshman Composition One and Two, which is actually an important teaching niche; I pay dues to three professional associations dedicated to just those pigeonholes. My life revolves around getting people in their first year of Higher Ed to be able to read something, figure out what's being said and what's not being said, and explain the said and the not-said thing coherently to someone else. Complicating this life mission is that the nineteen-year-olds I teach don't care, don't want to be in a writing class, won't-don't-or-can't read, have anxiety, work minimum wage jobs, are mad at their parents, and can't see why anything matters. There could be worse jobs, like in a gulag in Siberia, working weekends and holidays. Great literature weaves intricate ideas into a fascinating tapestry of humankind's tentative exploration of itself and the universe. This book ain't that.

So the three disparate things. Cannabis should be super-legal across the galaxy, like it was for most of human history. Don't spank children—or anyone else who isn't *really* into it. And one other thing that I forget just now. It'll come to me.

Before I flew out to Colorado four summers ago, I hadn't seen Nolan in eight years. When we were undergrads at the University of Texas at Austin, his parents lived in Dallas. Then Nolan did his grad school degrees at Caltech, MIT, plus a guest semester at the University of Waterloo in Ontario, before settling down at the University of Colorado Boulder. His parents moved to Corpus Christi because his sister's husband got a job there, which meant their grandchildren—via Nolan's sister—would now reside there.

Once, during his yearly drive to Texas to visit Ma and Pa de Jaager, Nolan swung through San Antonio. He introduced his Chesapeake Bay Retriever named Fia to my parents who were sitting in their usual spot. One was at each end of the big couch against the wall with the life-sized torso-and-head graduate degree photo of me in cap, gown, and hood, next to the studio photo of my sister Tessa with her two daughters. Fia is shy and vocal; she howled and Nolan translated: Fia was happy to meet us but a bit nervous.

Nolan and I went to dinner at Macaroni Grill and talked for hours. My back was to the restaurant and only when it started getting chilly did I look around and realize that all the other customers had gone and the staff was cleaning the room. When we got back, my parents gave a report of Fia's evening including how long it took her to relax after Nolan left, and how many times she went outside to lay in the yard.

I call Nolan every year or so to say hi and keep in touch because I don't have many friends and I need to maintain some tenuous connection to the few I've got, and because this time, I actually needed to talk to him. My best friend in town, Mitch, was too ass-bustingly busy to meet for lunch and I was agitated. I had yelled at a Comp One class. It was mid-semester; the class was at nine in the morning and full of students with new high school diplomas whose parents had told them to either get a job or go to school. The class was headed for massive attrition, which is professor talk for flunking out.

It was a dead class; that's actually what teachers call it when we have a roomful of unresponsive people. Dead. In high school, students can sometimes get away with not turning in some assignments; in college they can't, but this group hadn't figured that out. I'd tried eight weeks of explaining that high school was over, college was different, time to grow up, come on, get your essays in, I'll give you an extension. Cajoling didn't do shit. So Monday morning at 10 a.m. I cussed out the entire class.

As a professor, I'd done this many times. By now, I even know when a blowout will be needed during the semester and secretly schedule it in. The I've-had-it-with-this-shit and I'll-flunk-all-of-your-asses-out spontaneous rant is entirely planned. The sad thing is that it worked, like always. Missed papers materialized and the early morning dullards coffee-ed up enough to keep my Productive Grade Rate from diving off a high-rise. The one man in the class who was over forty watched my performance indifferently. He'd already had a career, having worked up to being a manager in a local warehouse while he raised kids, and now he was pivoting his life around to become a nurse. He saw through the dramatics and sipped bottled water. He had also kept up with his assignments and knew that none of the threats applied to him.

Then I cussed out my Composition Two class, it wasn't

planned, I genuinely lost it, and it did not work. Two students dropped the class, and my world went to shit, so I called Nolan.

The Comp Two classroom was a horseshoe set-up: students' desks were lined up to form three sides of a large square or horseshoe, open at the front of the class. In the middle of the horseshoe, is a rectangle of tables. Students sit around the outside of the horseshoe and also around the rectangle in the center of the horseshoe and I move around the horseshoe or around the inner rectangle or stand up front near the white board, the drop-down screen, and the instructor's desk.

The room was on the side of the building that did not get hit by the morning sun and the class had been erratic all semester, participating some days, and some days acting as if their presence was doing the world a favor, which always strikes me as strange in Higher Education. There's no law that people have to go to college; you actually have to sign up and fill out forms to come, so why act like an ass once you get there? That morning they were sleepy and sullen and the one who set me off was Ivy Ruelas.

She came in late, sat down at the front of the rectangle, did not take out the literature book and did not take notes, just stared into space, stared at a student across the table who started to squirm, and stared at me. I had disliked Ivy since the third week of the semester. In twenty years, I've only had four students that I have truly disliked. One of the four was eventually executed by the State of Texas for kidnapping, raping, and murdering at least three women over eight years.

During class, two years before they caught him on surveillance camera dumping his last victim's body in an alley, he told me not to call on him in class again: he didn't like to be questioned; I better leave him alone. One of the four broke her toddler's leg, did not get him medical care, and then dropped him off at her sister-in-law's so she could claim that the sister-in-law had injured him after the in-law rushed the child to the hospital. During a conference with me, that student complained that Child Protective Services should stop taking her kids away. One of the four was a compulsive liar.

Ivy was number five on my list of students that gave me the creeps. She had long dark hair and a porcelain doll pallor and made me clammy for two reasons: she had a completely flat aspect, her face always expressionless, but not vacant, and she wanted to be a nurse. She was not interested in medicine or patients and suggested to students around her that patients were kinda gross, she didn't really want to touch them or help them, but nurses made a lot of money. There was a bonus when you got hired. She had a cousin who was a nurse who had a sporty car, a condo, and partied at all the choice places. You had to go to college to be a nurse, and nurses were rich.

I got the same vibe from Ivy that I'd gotten from the serial killer and the child abuser. But Ivy hadn't done anything; she had never caused a disruption in class other than having her phone out when she wasn't supposed to. I would ask her to put the phone away, and without a word, she would do so, sliding it into her purse, staring at me. I would turn to the board, and when I turned back, the phone would be out again, while Ivy sat immobile, with a face that was not smug, not challenging in any way, just expressionless.

Twenty minutes after she came in that morning, Ivy opened her backpack, spread out a book and spiral, and started working on an algebra spreadsheet, taking up most of her table. I was in the middle of a lecture-discussion-PowerPoint combo. It took a while for the slow burn to rise. Half the students had not read the comments on the papers that I'd spent four days grading; half were watching Ivy work on a spreadsheet unrelated to the class she was sitting in. The third half was struggling with sleep; a guy in the corner of the horseshoe carefully worked a donut out of his shirt pocket.

"Get your shit together on the rewrite!" came out at volume. Heads jerked up, donut-guy paused, mid-bite, and I spun into a ten-minute tirade starting with how there were "people all over the world who are desperate for an education, who risk death just trying to get an education, and here the government will give you money to learn, to improve your life, improve your ability to contribute to society, and all you have to do is to pay attention, pay fucking attention, write three fucking coherent papers in four months, which I tell you step-by-step how to write and . . ."

Somewhere in the middle of this I caught sight of Ivy filling in a square on her spreadsheet. I took three steps toward her, stood at the head of the rectangle and asked the entire class, "Why the hell would a student in college come to a class and spread their work for some other class out across a table and not pay any attention to the class that they were actually in? How in the hell does it not cross that student's mind that it'll piss off their professor?"

Without a furrow in her brow or a flush of her pale cheek, Ivy packed the book, spiral, and spreadsheet away. After class, a few students mumbled that they would turn in their rewrites and the guy in the corner apologized for trying to eat a donut. He'd had to work till two in the morning, closing a fast food joint the night before, had overslept, missed breakfast, and grabbed a donut while running to class. He was just so very hungry.

The next morning when I got to my office, the light on my phone was blinking. Ten minutes later, my department chair looked uncomfortable as I took a seat in front of his desk. He's a young guy, early thirties, preternaturally nice and sporting faux tribal tattoos on one arm and a Dallas Cowboys star on the other. Delicately, he asks if there is any chance I may have used some foul language in my Comp Two yesterday. Immediately I say 'yes,' too slow to realize that a storm's a-brewin'. Surprise squats on his face, though whether it's because I used foul language or because I'm readily admitting it, I can't tell. "I told them to get their shit together," I explain. "A lot have missed assignments, blown the first major paper, or tanked the midterm last week. Those grades have got to come up—"

"Two students came to me yesterday and complained," he sighs.

"Two?" Even as I sit there, the idea of blowback has not occurred to me; I'd already reassured the guy with the donut that it was okay to eat in class if he needed to. "For saying 'shit'?" I ask.

"They said you yelled at the class."

"I did raise my voice."

"Is it possible you used the F-word?"

He's kidding right? "It's possible," I postulate, "I may have dropped an F-bomb." Or eight.

He pauses; the conversation has gone foggy for him. "The students said that you made them feel uncomfortable and concerned for their own safety. They dropped the class."

Now it's my turn to pause. "Who dropped the class?" He gives me their names. The girls—Tina and Daphne—are friends; both sit on the horseshoe directly behind Ivy.

"They actually seemed pretty upset, Alene. The tall one,"

he says, unable to remember which girl goes with which name, "was on the verge of tears. She struck me as quite religious. I don't know what religion, but pretty strict, whatever it is. Anyway, she seemed offended, and, uh, verbose. She might pursue the complaint further and go to the dean."

Back in my office I actually do feel contrite, not because the tall religious one might complain to the dean—she never does—but because the girls dropped the class. As a student, I loved learning; I loved being in college, feeling new ideas, the sharp polyhedron shape of them in my mind. As a professor, being able to place concepts, shiny and unexpected in the reach of students who may never have suspected such fresh realms of thought existed was the payoff for trudging through piles of tangled essays and fusty young adult angst. Both girls were both passing—B students—and now I had set them back in their educational journey. And the educational journey thing is what I truly cared about.

So I had cussed out my Comp Two class, and my inner world went to shit, and I called Nolan.

He listened and didn't say too much, but he never says much anyway. I had already read the first of what would eventually be six anger management books plus *The Art of Happiness* with the His Holiness, the Dali Llama, looking serene in red and saffron robes on the cover. And I was trying to get back into meditating every day; I had decided I would never flip out in a class again. I talked to Nolan for 70 minutes and started to feel a little steadier, less like an ogre, then thanked him for listening to me unload and asked him again how he'd been over the last year, had he done anything fun, maybe traveled somewhere.

"No," he said, then stopped. Nolan didn't talk in fits and starts. He spoke in complete sentences, thinking through what he was going to say before he said it, instead of rambling in the dark like the rest of us. "So. I suppose I should tell you or else you will probably be mad at me later if I don't."

My first thought was he was about to reveal that he'd gotten married and hadn't invited me to the wedding. And yes, I was going to be mad about that.

"I was in the hospital for a month being treated for non-Hodgkin's Lymphoma in a sterile isolation ward while they took down and rebuilt my immune system, but I am home now and have been in remission for six months. You need to be in remission for two years before they say you are cured. Well, it is not cured exactly, but two years means the lymphoma is less likely to recur."

I processed a bit. "When did you find out?"

"A year ago. About a month after you last called."

"Why didn't you call and tell me?"

"What, just call and say, 'hi, I have cancer'?"

"Yeah."

"Come on now."

We'd already talked longer than usual. Nolan sprinkled in a few more details: he was working from home because his immune system was still weak and he couldn't be close to too many people yet, and even with health insurance, he had $90,000 in medical bills to deal with. As we were wrapping up, I told Nolan that I was going to come to Colorado for a visit and asked if I could stay at his house. He said yes, which was convenient since I had just invited myself.

At the end of the semester, Ivy Ruelas cheated on the final exam. I was not the one who caught her. At the start of each exam, I direct the class to turn off their phones, stow them away and place all bags under the table, inaccessible. During the final, Ivy worked her purse onto the chair next to her, got her phone out, and searched for answers; she cheated quite skillfully and, even though I scanned the class, I didn't catch her. But the guy sitting next to her did and got pissed off. He was in his late twenties, had already done a stretch in the military, including nine months in Iraq, and still had army hair. He had worked hard all semester for an 'A' and planned to be a surgical tech. When he finished the test early, he slipped me a note ratting out Ivy. I nodded, thanking him for his 'service' as he left.

Ivy still had the phone in her hand, opened to a 'Free Essays' web page when I did a walk-around a few minutes later and zeroed out her test. I graded it that afternoon just to see how she had done, but her writing and analysis was a mess; it would have failed anyway. I flunked her on the last day of the semester and thought about the two girls who would have passed if they had stayed in the class instead of taking a principled stand against my berating the lot of them.

When I first started teaching in the mid-nineties, community colleges still had room for an esoteric class or two on literary theory. I used to cover the Hero's Journey: In story traditions around the world, heroes are suddenly thrust into adventures where they have to master self-control in order to gather skills, weapons, companions, and magical gifts to bring home and lead their tribe. Before the journey begins, that person, unnoticed, spends his life preparing, unawares, for the trials he will face the day misfortune tosses him out of his mundane routine. Some small twist triggers the rockslide, like yelling at Ivy or calling Nolan or sitting in front of Mitch in seventh grade.

Stupidity is bad, so be less stupid. That's the third thing the book is about, along with cannabis should be growing on everyone's patio and don't spank kids.

CHAPTER TWO
NOTHING AND EVERYTHING

So I CUSSED out my Comp Two class, and it didn't work, and I called Nolan.

And then I called Mitch.

When I was growing up, students sat alphabetically, in rows. So, from the first day of seventh grade in junior high school and for the next six years until graduation from Hasseltin High, at some point each day, Mitchell Benjamin Teller sat right behind me, Alene Adele Sterling, because we were both GT. Inevitably, we became best friends.

In seventh grade, Hasseltin Independent School District tested its students for general smartness so it could herd us into groups of what we would someday become: car mechanics for the blue-collar boys, cosmetology for the blue-collar girls, farming for the 4-H ranch kids, and GT: Gifted and Talented, the college-bound kids. In the 1970s, this was not considered oppression; the boys in shop class wanted to be in shop class just like their dads had been. The ranch kids wanted to win 4-H ribbons and sell a prize steer in the San Antonio Stock

Show covered in Technicolor detail each year by the local news. At the time, Hasseltin High owned more land than any other grade school in the state. There were stock pens behind the 700 building, which, at three stories high was the tallest building in all of Eudah, Texas; still is. The dirt track that circled the football field turned to muddy slosh when it rained, and the track teams had to time their workouts so they wouldn't coincide with the aggie kids, who ran, holding long sticks, to run their pigs around the track to keep the pigs in shape.

The college bound GT kids were almost exotics. By the time we were in high school and taking calculus, advanced placement English, and foreign language, there were only enough of us to fill two classes, so we ended up spending all our time together.

After Hasseltin High, Mitch went to Harvard, then bicycled across Europe for a year, ending up in a cheap flat in Madrid with three island girls who shoplifted from department stores to supplement their way through the Universidad de Madrid. Mitch was teaching English as a second language to make rent. I went to the University of Texas at Austin, and, during a year off, after graduating from UT but before starting grad school, I flew to Spain to hang out with Mitch for a month.

The trip was a mixed bag. I learned pretty quickly to lock my luggage so the Ibiza girls would not pilfer a twenty when Mitch and I went out. The apartment was in a building that had been grand in Franco's heyday, with a magnificent marble staircase winding its way up the floors, but by the 1980s, it was low rent. Other than the opportunistic petty theft, the island girls were genuinely friendly, especially after I made a big American dinner for everyone, complete with loaded baked potatoes. The girls were shocked by the amount of food I thought necessary for a single meal.

The problem was that the apartment had no heat—or not enough heat. Whatever the reason, it was cold. The Ibiza girls' solution to a cold flat was a large bottle of cheap spirits passed around throughout the evening as, wrapped in blankets and wearing mittens with the finger tips cut out, they studied on the floor of the narrow living room. Also, they slept huddled together for warmth, and the apartment's cat huddled with them. Mitch had mixed feelings about the cat. Once, he had awoken to find that the cat, which was in heat, had backed up onto his nose to pleasure itself.

Even before he'd graduated from Harvard and reached Spain, Mitch had realized—while screwing his second girlfriend and simultaneously calculating his spring tuition payment plan—that he was gay, but he hadn't come out yet, figuratively speaking. Also, literally. Anyway, Mitch and I traveled across Spain together: the Prado and the Palacio Real, Toledo, Granada and the Alhambra. But there was a vague tension during the trip which, in the third week I was there, finally culminated one afternoon in a massive argument about nothing and everything as we were sitting at a little bistro table in the sparsely occupied cafe at El Escorial Palace outside Madrid.

The argument started as a heated under-our-breath exchange—did he really want me to visit, he's not talking to me like he used to, there's something he's not sharing with me, and what's with these island girls he's living with, I think they stole money out of my luggage. The exchange gradually escalated to a tearful shouting match. It was all in English, but, for the benefit of the Spanish speakers in the restaurant, a man at a table in the corner helped out and began a line-by-line translation of the fight, like living subtitles on a TV show.

When the argument was over and reconciliation achieved

and the tears wiped from my face and the tea that the waitress had kept serving us—unordered—was drained, the patrons in the restaurant began debating who was right. Every table in the cafe was now full; families with children stood against the wall waiting for a place to sit; the waitress was sweating. Behind the counter, the wife of the cook-manager had materialized, eyes as bright as Christmas morning; we were, apparently, amazingly good for business. The ringside translator had told everyone that obviously we were having an American lovers' quarrel: Mitch secretly lived with three beautiful Ibiza girls who modeled for a department store, and Mitch insisted that he was not sleeping with them but I, deeply in love with him, had spent all my money to fly from the United States to join him, only to find I was no longer the flame in his heart, which Mitch denied was the case, but my heart was broken—see my tears? I did not know what I would do now, and for some reason, Mitch was giving me a sexy cat.

The lunch crowd divided along gender lines with women backing me and men seeing Mitch's view as perfectly reasonable. Yet, since I was a woman, the men felt that he should have conceded to me earlier to avoid so much trouble and emotion. Over time, they decided, he would learn to handle women with more finesse. My Spanish wasn't good enough to follow all of this, but Mitch complained later of the translator's embellishments; he also found that we'd been given a small bag of cookies without charge. After the fight, Mitch and I toured the chilly castle, descending into the crypt holding dead Spanish royalty in black lead coffins.

Two years later when we were both in grad school, I flew to Madison for a long weekend to visit. Mitch was earning his PhD at U Wisconsin. By then he was openly gay, and, not as openly, cheating on his 45-year-old soon-to-be ex-boyfriend with a 22-year-old farm boy who had moved to the big city and become a male model, UW-Madison student. After finishing his doctorate, Mitch got a professorship at Crockett State in San Antonio in the art department. I got a master's in writing from the University of Southern California, then moved back home and started teaching in the Bexar County Community College District and paying off thousands in student loans, eventually becoming tenured faculty in the Bexar District at Mirador College.

Over the last ten years, Mitch's life would make a good Movie of the Week. As a Crockett State art professor, he had a career track that meant teaching classes; curating museums at two of their campuses; securing grants; and schmoozing at art show openings, galleries, conventions, and the living rooms of rich donors who feel it's just polite to offer you some of the cocaine they are snorting off their Serengeti reclaimed wood coffee table as you explain why it's important to fund more fellowships for Crockett State's graduate students.

As a lifestyle, this does not actually sound too shitty except when you have to do it for years: days, nights, and weekends. Mitch declined the cocaine but not the scholarship donation. He spent weeks in the New Zealand Outback with Aborigine artists; attended conventions in Oaxaca, Mexico before the rebels rebelled and set Oaxaca on fire, forcing Mitch and five grad students to hide in a ditch overnight as they fled to the airport; and he had to conference with Yoko Ono who, it turns out, is really a handful.

On Friday nights, I went to art shows with him. I was working downtown at the time, and Mitch had just bought a historic house, because it had true character, about a mile from my campus. Twice, exterminators had to evict raccoons out of Mitch's attic, because *they* had true character.

Mitch wanted kids. Actually, just one kid, boy or girl, between five and eight, with or without a history of issues. When you apply to foster children, you have to specify, up front, what you are willing to take. It saves time, and Child Protective Services is a busy outfit. Mitch figured that he had become stable enough in life to give back to, if not the world, then a kid. He figured he was patient enough to benefit a child who had suffered and needed understanding. He figured a five-year-old would be past all the potty training stuff and would also be in school all day while he worked. Mitch was all grown up now, and grown-ups had kids and a house and took their five to eight-year-old boy or girl to cultural events and music lessons on the weekend.

In fact, according to Child Protective Services, Mitch was nearly too grown up. They have an age limit for being able to adopt and, crossing forty years old, he was about to age out. So, to get foster certified, Mitch spent nights attending parent training for months and found that some of the people there were not acting on humanitarian impulses. They were calculating profit, like a human trafficking racket where you could stay at home and the state brought the children to you. When he told me this, I didn't believe him because kids are expensive; clothes, food, deductibles at the doctor's office, shin pads for soccer games on Saturday morning, it all adds up. Regardless of the stipend that the state gives you, serious money has got to come out of your own pocket.

Jana York was in the office to my left in Estrada Hall. She was seven months from retirement and she and her husband had just adopted a six-year-old girl through a Christian agency.

Like Mitch, they wanted to 'give back', to provide for more than themselves, and the day after her last semester ended, she and her husband would be moving to a house in Port Aransas to raise their daughter.

Jana confirmed what Mitch had told me and she summarized the numbers: foster kids are under Medicaid, so the doctor's covered. Now, say a couple had a spare room with some old furniture, a mattress or extra couch, and they fostered three or four children or a few of their own grandchildren who the state had custody of because the kids' parents were in prison. Then, if you just do the minimum—some food, thrift store clothes when absolutely necessary—month after month you could make a couple hundred dollars. For people on the margins, predictable money can be a predictable motive. Jana and her husband had also done foster training and sat next to couples who saw fostering as a way to balance the family budget.

After doing a home inspection, the woman vetting Mitch as a potential foster parent called me for a reference. She clearly had a form in front of her with dozens of questions: had I ever known Mitch to take illegal drugs, did he have a gambling problem, a history of violence, criminal activity, substance abuse, alcohol abuse, threatening behavior, sudden outbursts, animal cruelty?

I called Mitch after the interview and told him it seemed to go well. Mitch sounded resigned and tired; the social worker had carried a clipboard when she inspected his house, ticking off boxes. She spent time looking at the plumbing, commenting that it was old but must have been replaced at one point and was still acceptable. Mitch confided that he did not think he would get to foster. He was single, gay, aging out, had weird Aboriginal art, worked more than full time and lived in a house that, to a social worker, was not historic, just old. And even an eight-year-old would probably take up more time than he realistically had to give. Anyway, he had a catalog to put together; there was a show coming up.

Three days after he was certified the social worker called and asked Mitch if he would consider fostering a child younger than five. "Hhm, yeah," he said, "I guess a little younger than five is fine."

Would he consider two children instead of just one? She did not like to separate siblings.

"Well, ah, sure, I—" he started to say.

She was on the way over to his house, in the back of a cop car.

Mitch called me at work. There were two babies in his living room. Brothers. One was five days old, the other eleven months. Their mother had already lost custody of two previous children, had just given birth with drugs in her system, then fled the hospital two days later with the infant. Bexar County spent three days tracking her down, then kicked in her door. Three sheriffs entered, took both babies, arrested the mother, and called the social worker, who called Mitch. It was Friday, and every shelter was full. The social worker needed to do an emergency placement after the sheriff's emergency removal. If she couldn't find a foster, the babies would spend the weekend in her office in a playpen on the floor; it had happened before.

When I got there after work, Mitch's mom was sitting in the living room watching the eleven-month-old toddler toddle around in the late afternoon light and the five-day-old infant asleep on the couch, one cushion over from her. She kept staring at the infant. Mitch was wandering around with a cell phone in his hand, unsure what to do but doing things nonetheless. He had already spent seven hundred dollars at Target, assembled one crib, a changing table, and part of a second crib, bought diapers, bought formula, called his mother, called women friends with kids to find out what else he needed, had gone back to Target, bought car seats, and called me.

His eyes were glazed and doing a focused-unfocused thing; his gait was a little jerky. He was talking non-stop, telling me what had happened while also saying out loud the mishmash of thoughts careening through his head: he needed to go back to Target, where was that list, he was making a list of all the things he needed to get, he had nothing, this morning he had absolutely nothing for a baby, and now two babies, he'd make another Target run in the morning, he didn't have any baby clothes, Allison's kids were past baby clothes, he needed to call her.

He turned, eyes trying to settle on me while he paced. "Look at this. There's babies in here. Two babies; never thought I'd ever get a baby. They're impossible to get 'cuz that's what everyone wants. Don't even ask for a baby. Everyone said so."

I could tell he was in a daze, but also really giddy. Mitch's mom, Miriam, was also talking steady, to herself, to me, and to Mitch. She spoke in an undertone that created a rambling white noise counterpoint to his rambling monologue. Mitch's dad had died while we were in grad school and part of the reason Mitch had sought a job at Crockett State was so he could move back to town to be near his widowed mother as she got older. His mom still lived in Stone Landing, the subdivision Mitch grew up in, which was next to my subdivision, Winter Forest. After her husband had died, Miriam had moved to another house in her same neighborhood and decorated it all in white, which was a dream she'd finally been able to fulfill, now that her kids had grown up and moved out. The interior was lovely and sterile as a snowscape. When I visited, I'd tiptoed across the white carpet and perched on the white couch, afraid I might fart and leave a mark.

Mitch introduces me to the babies; the eleven-month-old is Fernando Egan, and the infant is Mackey Fernando. I grimace.

"Yeah," says Mitch. "Awful names."

The boys both have the same father, Fernando, and I register that two siblings both having the same father is a thing.

"So, what do you think?" Mitch grinned.

I think I expressed how happy I was for him, but my mind had shifted into assessment mode. He's a single man who's never taken care of small children and who, when he got up this morning, had no idea how much baby food cost. I looked around; the social worker must have shifted into assessment mode too when she was here. He has a restored house downtown with pricey artwork on the walls; an extensive network of well-educated snoots that'll have his back; and a widowed mother living in the 'burbs who spends her days hanging out with her lady friends at the Hebrew Community Center, which has a heated outdoor saltwater pool that's just glorious, plus a renowned daycare with an eighteen-month long waiting list. So what if Mitch had never changed a diaper before, the social worker must have calculated, he could contract that out.

Peripherally, I hear Mitch's mom say that the toddler is hungry again. "He just finished a bottle, Mitchie, not ten minutes ago."

The infant needed a diaper change. I volunteered and carried him to the one hundred dollar changing table which was hardly wobbly and stripped off all his clothes. He had jaundice. I'd noticed it in the living room and now, close up, I looked him over and wondered if Mitch's mom had also realized it; Mitch had not. The baby's arms were drawn up against his body. I moved his arms and legs around—they worked—then turned him over. He had a dark red welt the length of my finger across one butt cheek.

By the time I redressed the baby and took him back to the living room, Mitch was rattling about how to warm up formula. A phone was in his hand, but he wasn't talking into it. I pressed him for more details about the sheriffs, the emergency removal, and the social worker.

"I went in to work early, even though I don't have a class today," he said. "Student exhibit coming up. Not the graduate students, but still, I take it seriously, when Leah called." Leah was the social worker who had interviewed me about Mitch's fitness. "So I head back home thinking, thinking what? That there's going to be a four-year-old who needs a place to stay over the weekend. I barely get home when two cop cars race up to my house."

"What do you know about the mother?"

"Not much. Leah didn't stay long, which surprised me."

"You said that the mother previously had kids removed?"

"Yeah," Mitch suddenly looked at the phone he was holding. "The state permanently terminated her custody to her first two kids. She has a drug problem and prostitution, I think. Mom, did you hear that part? Were you here yet when Leah was talking about all that stuff?"

Miriam's eyes flicked away from the toddler for a moment. "She was leaving when I got here. She hardly said hello."

"Yeah, well, she left two babies in the house. Did you notice? See that? Wow."

"Mitch," I start, but the toddler has managed to pick up something he shouldn't have off an end table. Miriam doesn't move. I take the knickknack thingy away from Fernando One and put it back. He grabs it again and I put it up higher, out of reach. His eyes follow it. It strikes me that Fernando One is unperturbed by the sudden change in his circumstances. He's been expecting this turnabout? "Mitch," I start again, "the baby has a red mark on his behind."

"Yeah, I saw that. Diaper rash maybe? Mom, did they have automatic bottle warmers when we were little?" He means himself and his brother. "I should call Kaori; she's in Chemistry. I don't know her that well, but we served on that search committee together last year and she'd just had a baby girl. Talked about it during our meetings; kinda annoying at the time, but now."

I pick up the toddler, set him on my lap, and gaze into his face. He stares back, chestnut brown irises against sclera that glow bright white. His baby fat is not distributed evenly and instead, he's oddly pear-shaped. Then he squirms, wanting to be set down again. He continues inspecting his new belongings and I realize there are no toys in the house. "Mitch, you need to take the babies back to the hospital to get checked out."

"Yeah, sounds like a good idea," he says, trying to bring up the Crockett State directory on his phone.

Nothing I say is landing. Miriam is rocking back and forth a bit, arms folded in her lap.

When I get home that night, I go into my parents' room and sit in the blue swivel rocker next to their bed. After he retired from the Air Force, my dad earned a degree in counseling. Wanting to 'give back to the community,' he worked for the County Mental Health Hospital because he felt everyone should have access to mental health, not just people with money and insurance. The job was stressful. At two in the morning, he got calls from police who needed him to talk one of his clients off an overpass or out of a barricaded room. Seven years into the job, a co-worker, a younger man in his forties, had a stroke from stress. My mom decided that it was time for my dad to retire again, before he was the one having a stroke; she did not want to spend their hard-earned retirement years spoon-feeding him.

When I finished explaining the babies in Mitch's living room, my parents agreed with me that the social worker saw his house, realized that he had resources and decided she could score a double. My dad had worked with social workers and knew they carried excessive caseloads, were underpaid, and had to do scary home visits in even scarier neighborhoods, just as he'd had to as a counselor. Nevertheless, he was scandalized; two babies to an unmarried man with no experience? Crazy. Suspicious even.

I hold off calling Mitch until Sunday afternoon, by which time he'd spent another five hundred bucks. He starts listing all the things he'd had to buy on his Saturday Target run, when I cut him off by asking what the doctor said about the infant, Fernando Two.

He hadn't taken the baby to the doctor yet.

Why?

Well, he'd had so much to do, he hadn't slept, hasn't been able to sleep, and the baby's really healthy, and he's gotta figure out the Medicaid paperwork; they explained it in the foster classes but it's complicated, and Chemistry Department Kaori brought over a load of baby clothes. And not just her. Niema too. She's staff and really nice. Some of the clothes are pink, but he's grateful to have them and the babies won't know the difference. And—

"Look Goddamnit!" For the first time in twenty years, since a little cafe on the side of El Escorial, I raise my voice to Mitchell Benjamin Teller. "That kid's got a welt on his butt as thick as a fucking pencil! He's seven days old. His drug-addict mother escaped from a fucking hospital and abducted him, and he was out of official custody for three goddamn days. Who the hell knows what she did or where he's been all that time? That social worker went straight from wherever three sheriffs did a no warning entry and kicked the damn door down at whatever low rent hourly motel room drug den they were at, to a lights-and-siren drive straight over to your house. The social worker didn't have time to do a five-point inspection on that baby. She stayed at your place less than half an hour because she had a half dozen more cases to settle before the weekend hit and every shelter in town fills up and stops doing intakes. That kid might be sick. He might have other injuries. Right now, a doctor's gonna be able to determine how old that welt on his butt is and that it occurred before you took custody of him and that it's days and days old. You wait any longer and they won't be able to figure it out. You're a single man with two babies that you haven't even had for a full weekend. Who do you think'll be blamed if that kid is hurt? I told you to take that baby to the doctor. Where's your head? What are you thinking?"

By the end of the tirade, I had been yelling without taking a breath and needed to suck in air. The flat silence that followed thickened and then remorse jumped on my back. "Mitch—"

"My mother's here. I'll call you back."

"Mitch?"

"I'll call later." He hung up.

⁂

When the phone rang, I was doing my Sunday night, post-*60 Minutes* getting-ready-for-bed routine. Mitch had taken both babies to San Lucas Children's. It was their first trip out of his house: two babies, a diaper bag, bottles, a folder full of foster parent and Medicaid documents, and Mitch's mom had to fit in his car with two newly installed baby seats. He'd had both of the kids examined and they were both good, healthy mostly. Fernando One was eleven months old but had not eaten solid food yet, just formula. He needed to be 'introduced' to baby food so he would not be so hungry all the time. Fernando Two had some very unusual diaper rash, the doctor said. I didn't believe the welt was a rash but didn't say anything; even Mitch sounded tentative as he explained it. Anyway, the doctor gave him a cream to put on it. Also, Fernando Two had newborn jaundice, so the doctor gave Mitch a pamphlet on home treatment and proper sunlight exposure.

The giddiness was gone from Mitch's voice, replaced by a massive wave of exhaustion. There was some stuff about accessing state and city services he needed to know, so he asked to speak to my dad.

While Dad was on the phone, I caught my mom up on what Mitch had said. Mom had begun her career as a nurse. Back then, working women were teachers or nurses, and with my father in the military, nursing meant that she could get a job wherever they were transferred. However, once we were stationed in San Antonio, my mom went into hospital administration in the Medical Center. She told me what to tell Mitch about jaundice, that it was common in newborns, and she gave pointers on how to treat it.

I started listening to Dad wrapping up with Mitch. "That social worker should be up on charges," Dad said. "She should never have just left two infants on you like that; it's ridiculous. It's too much for one person to handle. She has to know that. You need to call her in the morning and give them back." Dad handed me the phone.

"Hey, Mitch."

There was a deep silence, then, "Hey, it's been a long day. So. I'm gonna get some sleep while I can. I gotta call the University in the morning and take the day off. I don't know how long I'll have the boys, so I gotta look into arranging child care like right away. Your dad was telling me what kind of places to stay away from. The state will pay a certain amount but not enough for anything top-notch, or even middle-notch. I don't know; just have to call around I guess. Mom just drove home; she slept on the couch last night."

"You okay?"

"Just really tired. Going to bed now. Night."

"Night."

The foster care classes teach foster parents that the kids they care for will be taken away and that it will happen over and over: Foster parents are the holding station that's needed until the children's parents get their lives sorted out. The only reason I hadn't told Mitch to give the boys back was because I knew he wouldn't. The moment I had walked in and saw the boys and saw him, I knew he was lost; they'd sliced inside him like an arrowhead. If they were taken away, it would destroy him.

Monday, after work, I swung by. The infant, Fernando Two, was lying in diapers in a shaft of sunlight in the living room near a pyramid of unsorted baby clothes that stood four feet high surrounded by a lake of toys; Crockett State's faculty, admin, and staff had answered the bugle call. Methodically, Fernando One inspected his baby toy bounty, glancing at me, unfazed.

Mitch lost twenty pounds the first year. For the first few months, he had too much already booked on his work schedule to suddenly cut back, so our Friday nights of going to art shows serving trendy amuse-bouche and three flavors of vodka, turned into Friday afternoons of Mitch picking the boys up from daycare, and Friday nights of Mitch going to art openings while his mother and I babysat, until he was able to leave the show early so I could drive home. Mitch's mother simply moved into his house; she was there for six months, checking on her own house with the pristine white furnishings on the weekends.

ꕥ

Late in the semester, Mitch had to oversee a set up at the museum on Crockett's downtown campus. I was still working at Bexar Colleges' downtown campus at the time, so after my last class for the day, we had a late lunch, and then I rode with him to pick up the boys. The best daycare he could find was miles away, halfway up Nyla Drive. After copious research, he had chosen it because it was clean, had no red flags against its reputation, and, posted on the wall of the toddlers' room, it had a clear schedule for taking the toddlers outside to play several times a day.

All the parking spaces at the daycare were angled, as though parents needed to make a quick get-away. Inside, every person who worked there had visible tattoos. Andre, the manager behind the front desk, wore a sleeveless muscle shirt over his sculpted torso. Mitch greeted staff members by name, made friendly conversation, and asked questions about the progress of their ongoing personal pursuits. His million-dollar art donor schmoozing skills had been smoothly grafted onto the minimum wage daycare worker set. He had an agenda: he wanted Fernando Two to have the best crib location in the six-months and under room. Mitch had worked out that there were more diaper changes for the baby immediately to the left of the room's door. He'd looked at the bottle feeding and diaper change chart that the six-months and under team member had to keep and had noticed a pattern.

As we headed back out, Mitch declined my offer to carry Fernando One or Fernando Two and scooped the boys up, sliding them into their carriers. It was easier for him to stick to his system. By then, he could carry both boys, the diaper bag, and car keys; if he stuck to routine, nothing got lost.

Initially, Mitch felt sorry for the boys' mother. She'd had a grim life; her father had abandoned the family when she was small, her mother died of heart disease when she was thirteen, and she'd been passed around from one relative to another until she ran away at sixteen and ended up homeless. Drugs, abuse, prostitution and pregnancies followed. But by the second year of fostering the boys, Mitch felt less sorry; their mother kept missing court dates and missing the social worker's supervised visits with her boys. She had walked out of rehab twice then left the state.

After months of second, third, and fourth chances by the court, his tone about the boys' mother started sounding vaguely adversarial, and he had already changed the boys' names. The older boy was now Lewin and the baby was Archie, and Mitch moved to adopt. That cost money. The boys' biological father had to be tracked down so he could sign away his parental rights, which, once he was located in Michigan, he immediately did. The boys had had a year of doctor visits to ensure that they had not been affected by their mother's drug use, and miraculously they were both perfectly healthy. When the doctor gave them the all-clear, Mitch could not leave the office because he was crying so hard with relief. The doctor just watched quietly till Mitch was done.

San Antonio does not have enough Jews to fill up the daycare at the Hebrew Community Center, so most of kids there are non-Jewish locals whose parents recognize great amenities and, just like Mitch, do their research. Mitch's mom pulled her Jew-card and managed to get the boys into the HCC after nine months, jumping the queue in the eighteen-month waiting list. And Mitch realized, now that he was raising kids, he had to think ahead, to soccer and swim lessons. He needed to be part of 'the community' and to do that, he had to establish a sufficient Jew cred reserve of his own. The process could have been awkward: The last time he had been to temple was years ago, and the antique old lady next to him said she knew he was just mouthing the words. His Hebrew was that bad, and he was not in any position to respond: she had the whole survived-the-Holocaust thing on her side, so he just sat there while she scolded.

Over lunch at the Korean place that always ran the AC too cold, Mitch told me how sharply it had hurt when my dad told him to give the boys back. After Mitch's dad died, Mitch had switched to asking my dad for advice in the same way he had once talked to his own father. But a year after getting the boys, when Mitch was regaining some of the weight he'd lost, he understood why my dad had said it. The first year with the boys had been the toughest of Mitch's life.

When the boys were two, the adoption was approved. Texas was about to eliminate its tax benefits for adoptions, and there were only a few days left to get before a judge. If he missed the deadline, it would cost thousands more to adopt Lewin and Archie. So, on December 31st, my parents and I sat next to Mitch's mom in the old Bexar County Courthouse while the judge swore in Mitch and the social worker, Leah, asking them questions and filling out papers.

The judge wore heavy black robes and the lawyers, a tall man at Mitch's table and a slender woman in spike heels at a table for the State, were dressed in stylish black clothes. Leah, not yet middle-aged, had a permanent hunch in her shoulders, wore orthopedic shoes like a nurse on a trauma ward and tugged on the rumpled jacket she saved for court days. The indigenous art Mitch had collected from around the world had come down off his walls and gone into storage. He had ditched the house downtown and moved into a gated neighborhood closer to Crockett's main campus to cut down on driving time. Pictures of the boys covered the new living room. I looked across the courtroom at Leah as she watched the judge stamp and countersign the adoption papers. He smiled at Mitch, announcing, "You are now the parent of Lewin and Archie Teller," and the courtroom broke into applause as Mitch hugged the boys who were sitting on his lawyer's table, hugged his mom, me, my parents, and even his lawyer.

Leah smiled, her social worker calculations paying off: two for one. Mitch hugged her too. We invited her to join us for cake at Luby's Cafeteria, where we were all headed, but a holiday weekend was about to hit and she had to get back to work before the shelters filled up.

CHAPTER THREE
LIGHTS OUT

I DON'T HANG out with jerks or jackasses, so the people I know tend to be incredible somehow or other. My own social skills are inconsistent: parties are so exhausting I have to lay down the day after going to one. Instead of going out in the evenings, I read books. I hate to drive at night, find that most people get on my nerves, and that stupidity is infuriating. I've never made lots of friends, but the ones I do make, I keep.

Here's where it gets strange: My friends are all more successful than me in various ways: smarter than me, more highly promoted than me, doing various types of volunteer work, gorgeous, warmer, more engaging than me, married with children, single with children, single without children but having more sex than I will ever catch up on. More focused and self-disciplined, or more unfocused and creative, they light up the room; others gravitate to them, find them welcoming and open, or find them lofty and mysterious. My friends are richer, taller, energetic, closer to God, closer to Buddha, closer to atheism, closer to their family, slightly famous, slightly infamous, very infamous but still doing volunteer work on the weekends under supervision, more balanced, more crazy but okay with that, no longer taking Prozac for that, no longer under investigation for that, more comfortable with themselves, more comfortable with others, great with pets.

My friends all have some common traits. None are dumb, none are mean, all want the best for human beings throughout the world. And all, except Mitch, drive like maniacs, which is something I don't understand. My friends speed, tailgate, go around slower drivers. Nolan denies tailgating. Several of the others say flat out, "They should get out of my way." Two of those friends are deeply religious; one cursed another driver to hell. None has caused accidents, but I'm a cautious driver and can't figure out how I'm repeatedly connected to people so different from me in that one specific way. Also, my friends tend to be popular; they have lots of friends, which makes sense if you think that someone like me would probably only end up with friends who make vast numbers of friends. My anger management books refer to friends as 'contact circles.'

This book is an ode to my parents, who managed to get out of rustic Arkansas, earn multiple degrees, travel the world, and buy a house in Texas. They raised daughters who did not have to grow up in the 'hollah' at the base of a mountain in Hot Springs. And since my family was stationed in Germany when I was a child, my big sister Tessa and I saw the half of Europe that was not in the Soviet sphere. My parents persevered through all the crap life threw at them; they're both out of their minds now, but I can understand why. That's what your thirties are for: realizing why your parents are the way they are and getting over it.

When I showed this book to friends and asked them to choose their own fake names, two of them asked about the book's title. Decades ago, when I was working on my Master's thesis, my University of Southern California writing professor, Tom Maslin, said that the thing about writing, real writing that's actually worth anything, is that you've gotta risk something. You have to put yourself right out there, expose what you don't want to expose, reveal what you're afraid to reveal. Otherwise, there's nothing new and it's no good. Tom fought in World War Two and brought a war bride back from the Pacific. He was an alcoholic, wrote TV shows for Hollywood, stopped drinking, and became a popular professor. He had an honesty that was hard to believe until you witnessed it: when you get old, he said, you stop talking around reality and just face it head-on because you learn that hiding your inner life is a waste.

It had taken war, alcoholism, and decades of life for Tom to decide there was no point to pretense. He'd had cancer for years even before he was supervising my graduate project. After I graduated and moved back to Texas, I wrote him every few months, supposedly to ask his advice about my writing or my life plans, but really just to keep in touch. I loved him; he always wrote back. The responses were never more than a page long, banged out on his old manual typewriter, but they were sincere and encouraging. Eventually, one letter let me know he was in the final stages; he was dying.

Okay, so here's how my social skills are cringable. I wrote him back, asking if he had anything, a doctor's prescription so that he would not be in terrible pain, so he would not have to suffer. I had no business asking that, but I did and then realized I shouldn't have, but the letter was already sent. The next letter came from his wife; she told me Tom never read my last letter. He died before he could. She did not mention if she read it, and I hope no one ever did.

Tom said that to be a writer, you have to lay it all out there. He did not say if you have to lay your friends all out there too. And he didn't say whether your family would still talk to you after. So, here we go.

৵

Even with my parents' help, I owed thousands of dollars in student loans after grad school—I still love you USC. I struggled, living in Los Angeles for a couple of years, then moved home so I could pay off loans and save money. It took over a decade to become a tenured, full-time professor and earn enough to wipe out all my debt and buy a new car. By 2016, my days are a formula: Work, grocery, home. Work, library, home. Work, gym, home. Or work, work late, home. And when I get home, I change into a t-shirt and shorts and flop on the bed, too tired to move. One night, when the PBS News Hour is half over, I prop my head up during an interview with Ted Koppel.

We're doomed, he says, but not in those words. Instead, he says 'Cyber Pearl Harbor' and talks about what will happen when the electrical grid in the U.S. goes down due to a cyberattack, which Russia and China already have the capacity to launch, and Isis, North Korea, plus numerous disgruntled individuals are developing. Calmly, he mentions the lack of government preparedness and the subsequent consequences of an attack, such as the inability to run water, treat sewage, distribute food, or run air conditioning, heat, elevators, or respirators. A few million will die.

In passing, Koppel notes the need to have three to six months of food and water stockpiled and finishes up with an eighty percent estimate that within a decade, the grid will go down. Gwen Ifill thanks him for the interview. They smile. I see him on three other shows that week, order his book, read it in one weekend, then wish I hadn't because of the anxiety it gives me.

His book talks about 'preppers,' people who prepare for the end-of-the-world, not spiritually, but practically by stockpiling food, water, medical supplies and board games. Preppers are different from 'survivalists' who stockpile bullets and conspiracy theories. In the weeks that follow, I read *Survival Mom: How to Prepare Your Family for Everyday Disasters* because the reviews say it's written for people who don't know anything about prepping, and it has easy to follow lists of what to buy for the end of the world. Lists and retail: two things that I do understand.

I read a couple more prepper books, watch *Emergency Preparedness: Awareness and Survival* and Season Two of *Doomsday Preppers*. Then I make a list of supplies for a bug-out-bag, which is the Sterilite tote full of stuff you either throw in the trunk of your car as you flee before the zombie hordes, or hunker down with in your safe room when fleeing is not an option. I am woefully un-preppered—I don't even have the tote—and decide that I'll put together my supplies in the summer once the semester ends and I have the time. According to the prepper books, I am already doing one thing right, for a completely wrong reason: I'm growing food—not to get ready for the grid-goes-down apocalypse, but because I like pesto.

Basil costs $2.50 for a cellophane package that's barely a handful of leaves, and really good pesto takes three packages, so one spring, I threw some seeds in an old pot on the patio that had dried out dirt in it. Seed. Dirt. Water. How hard could it be?

Harder than that; nothing grew. So I got a bag of decent

potting soil, tried again and ended up with more basil than I could use and pesto whenever I wanted. The next year I added oregano, parsley, thyme and sage, and two years after that, I had two dozen herbs stretched across the back of the patio. Alongside recipes and growing tips, my herbology books touted the health benefits of each plant: French thyme for coughs, red clover for hot flashes, basil for anxiety, garlic for just about everything.

The one herb the books never mentioned was weed.

CHAPTER FOUR
DEEP HEDGES

In the 1940s, mining was big in Hot Springs, and a narrow brown road coiled around the mountain at the back of the hollah behind my Grandmother Ella's house. Coming down the mountain, a truck carrying dynamite exploded one Saturday afternoon, sending out a concussion wave that disintegrated windows, pushed houses off foundations, and toppled my grandmother's refrigerator onto my aunt Gracie, who was sitting at the kitchen table. Gracie was eight at the time. Since everyone affected by the blast was poor, the mining company never even admitted that the truck had blown up and did nothing to help anyone who suffered injury or lost property. Aunt Gracie would have back problems the rest of her life and finally had to have major surgery for it in her late fifties.

Grandma Ella still lived in the same house. Aunt Gracie lived next door, and while Gracie was recovering from back surgery, my dad flew to Arkansas, picked up my grandmother—my mother's mother—and flew back to San Antonio all in one day. My grandmother had Alzheimer's. Ella still recognized my parents but had to be reminded who I was, often referring to me as "the nice girl across the hall who brings her ice cream." Even though she watched soap operas each afternoon on a big color TV in the living room, Ella thought it was 1950 and constructed a complicated scenario to explain why she wasn't in her own house: she was on vacation, perhaps at some kind of resort, and would catch a bus tomorrow or the next day that would take her back home. At the same time, she helped wash up the dishes and gardened in our back yard.

Aunt Gracie recovered after six months, and Dad flew my grandmother back to Arkansas. Ella died years later, at ninety-six years old. Even with Alzheimer's, she stayed active until the last three weeks of her life, moving slowly, pruning the rose bushes growing around her front porch as they had for three-fourths of a century. In her very last week, she was bedridden, eventually unable to swallow, unable to breathe easily. A hospice nurse and Gracie and Gracie's husband sat next to her bed, but Ella no longer recognized her own daughter.

I'm fifty and live at home; my parents are now in their eighties. Mom has pill organizers for each of them and Sunday night is when she counts the pills out for the week, placing each one in its morning or nighttime organizer slot, closing the lids on the row of little boxes with a snap. Two years earlier, Dad had gone in to get a small hernia treated and, by chance, the doctor noticed a shadow on one of the scans, which turned out to be a fast-growing tumor on Dad's kidney. Laparoscopic surgery removed it— "Clean. We got the whole thing," the surgeon said—and Dad was home in two days.

In addition to the hernia (repaired) and the kidney tumor (removed), Dad also had spinal arthritis (getting worse), COPD (causing him to wheeze when he walked), and Alzheimer's.

All of which results in Dad randomly groaning, especially at night, when the quiet of the house makes the sound singular. His groan sounds like an off-tune oboe: ahn-uhn. I found out about the Alzheimer's when I came home from work one day. Mom was searching for something in the garage, slamming around piles of paper towels and laundry detergent that could no longer fit in our over-stuffed pantry. She held a can of soup.

"Your father has Alzheimer's," she said. "We worked all those years, decades so we could have this time to relax and take trips. And now I'm gonna have to spend my golden years taking care of an old man. He goes and gets sick, after all we've been through. Now for this to happen. I just can't stand it; maybe I'll just take off on my own. I don't know."

Dad had been getting forgetful more and more; then he got lost while driving in San Antonio, where we'd lived for forty years. They'd gone to the doctor several times, tested and retested. And when they went to the doctor that day and got the diagnosis, Dad told the doctor that he did not believe he had Alzheimer's. He would know. After he retired from the military, he got a third master's degree, this one in psychology, then he worked in family counseling, crisis intervention, and drug rehabilitation. Mom was still working in hospital administration in the Medical Center when Dad finally retired from counseling. So when Aunt Gracie was laid up, and grandma Ella with Alzheimer's stayed with us for months, my dad had taken care of Ella.

For a week after Dad's diagnosis, Mom was seething and bitter. She sat on the patio for hours, staring across the yard, tapping her foot while the locusts tymbaled in the heat. Then, after that first week, she got up, bought books on dementia, joined two support groups, and started watching Alzheimer's documentaries. She attended day-long local conferences, reviewed their long-term health insurance, and contacted senior citizen organizations to find out what she needed to do now to take care of Dad in the future. She had grab bars installed in the bathroom so Dad could get in the tub safely since his balance would eventually get worse. The documentaries showed the brutal progressive decline of people with dementia, and she watched the shows sitting on the bed, taking notes, right next to him.

And actually, the forgetfulness didn't seem all that bad. Dad could still drive to the most familiar places, to the commissary on base, to church, to the barber. Most of life was within five miles of the house, and for anything beyond that, Mom could take him. The bigger problem was the belching.

Of all the ways your body can betray you, uncontrolled belching is a peculiar indignity. Sudden and severe, it started a week after the successful kidney surgery. The doctors labeled it idiopathic; they did not know what caused it. They offered no treatment beyond telling Dad to avoid soft drinks and gum. Belching wasn't fatal, but it was life-altering; he would have loud, extended belches, sometimes several times an hour. He could feel them coming on and in public places, he tried to suppress them, which was painful, or could not suppress them, which was embarrassing. As a family, we stopped exchanging gifts a decade ago. No one needed anything and the house was already full of trinkets. Instead, we went to restaurants for birthdays or Father's Day, but as the belching got worse, Dad stopped eating out and soon stopped going to church on Sunday morning with Mom.

By the time I left high school, I had stopped going to church every week, and after college, even major holidays did not stir me. My parents' social lives, however, still revolved around Redeemer Baptist. They had been members of the church for decades, and after retirement, they spent a year taking evangelism classes and worked in the outreach ministry that served meals to the homeless each Wednesday under a bridge downtown. For years, Mom had been an usher for Sunday services and funerals, dressed in a white skirt and wearing cotton gloves. Dad was a trustee, attending strategic planning meetings, reviewing the budget, and always on call to rush out to the church when a major bill needed to be co-signed by at least two church officers.

Now, because of Alzheimer's, he could no longer review spreadsheets and had already stepped down as a trustee. But they were both in the church's Seniors Ministry, which organized trips to scenic destinations that were easy to walk for the 60s-and-up crowd. They took tours of the Texas wine country, saw the historic Sunday Houses of the early German settlers in Fredericksburg, sampled the less risqué enjoyments of New Orleans, and even went on a trip to The Holy Land Experience theme park in Florida where Jesus speaks to the Pharisees in the Temple, resurrects Lazarus, and walks on water every day while wearing a wireless mic. As the belching got worse, Mom and Dad stopped traveling.

I already added fresh sage to soup and oregano to pizza, and I had several books on growing herbs, including a big one on medicinal herbs full of recipes for warming salves, cooling tinctures, eye-washes, tonics, and joint liniments. I slogged through the books and found treatments for hiccups, bad breath, flatulence, and diarrhea, but nothing for belching.

So I tried online and not all of the remedies were crackpot. Many explained the chemistry, pharmacology, or folk history behind how a certain root, leaf, seed, or flower affected the human body. I made a list of herbs that helped digestion and came up with a herbal tea. It tasted like hot dirt. The reformulation was too sour to drink, puckering my face like I was sucking a lemon. I added honey, but it was not enough. Another reformulation required both honey and maple syrup to tame the tartness, but the complex mixture also reminded me of mulled wassail and holidays. It took fifteen minutes to make. I gave it to Dad.

"What is this?" Putting down his newspaper, he took the drink and inspected the cloudy umber color with tiny bits of stuff floating around in the mug, even though I had put the concoction through a strainer.

"Herbal tea."

"Okay." Dad took a sip. "Oooo-whee!"

"Too tart?"

"That'll clear my sinuses."

"It'll help with your digestion."

Dad put the mug down saying, "I'll have to drink that slowly," and I wondered if that meant he would pour it out, but when I checked later, he had finished it all. At the end of the day, I asked if the tea had helped.

"Well, it didn't hurt," he offered.

I made it each morning for the rest of the week, tweaking the proportions so it wouldn't wallop his palate so much, but the tartness was unavoidable because of the ginger, apple cider vinegar, and lemon. Three days in, he was belching less, and after a week, the belching was reduced by eighty percent. On Sunday morning, Dad went to church.

On the weekends I enjoyed making the tea. Chopping, crushing, and steeping the herbs is vaguely sorceress-like. But waking up extra early to get it all done before leaving for work turned into a grind, and some mornings, about once a week when I was running late, I slacked off. It was another couple of weeks before I thought to add in saffron and sage for the Alzheimer's. Dad never got used to the taste, but I did and eventually started making enough for two. Some days I would have it instead of my usual black oolong. Mom looked on and never wanted to try any.

❧

On Saturday morning, I hit the gym: jog-walking on the treadmill, lifting weights, remembering to Kegel on the incline leg press. When I get home, both garage doors are wide open and I see my parents rooting around the tool rack. After I shower, I hang my bathrobe on the back of my door and wander around my bedroom naked. In front of my dresser mirror, I de-turban my wet hair, enjoying an odd vacancy inside my head. The lack of conscious thought must have been due to two subconscious brain activities. One, I was hearing my parents in the front yard, a few feet from my window, behind the blinds and curtains. And two, I was processing the sounds as they prepared to trim the hedges that ran the length of the front right side of the house. I started combing my hair in front of the mirror, looking over my body for pudge.

I grew up on Bugs Bunny, Daffy Duck, and Wile E. Coyote, a huge fan of that 'ka-boing' moment in the cartoon when eyes suddenly bug out in shock or fear. The big electric hedge trimmer. Alzheimer's dad with a power tool. My eyes were moving past my boobs as I heard Dad tell Mom to move the cord back, then the brr-whir of blades. The equation suddenly tallied up. And Boing! My boobs did that—Boing!

I can now deduce that what actually happened is that my pectorals suddenly tightened at the same time my shoulders lifted, creating the illusion that my boobs had jumped up and out and a little to the side all on their own. I was still naked as I ran out of my room, grabbing my robe and pulling it on as I sprinted down the hallway.

Dad was taking off the front of the hedge nearest the porch, careful to avoid the shrub rose and gardenia. He always trimmed the front face of the bushes before he lopped off the tops. Mom stood on the driveway playing out the long orange extension cord they had unspooled from the cord organizer. I stood still. Visions of arms tumbling into the lavender or impaled on the potted Aloe vera batted my mind. I ran over emergency procedures: stop the bleeding, call 911, get help from the neighbors when they run over to see who's screaming. I went over to Mom, serenely surveying the falling hedge front.

"Is this really the best idea?" The snicker of the trimmer hid my voice from Dad.

"What do you mean?"

"Dad with the hedge trimmer?"

"He's fine." She flicked the cord a bit. "You could help."

I watched for a while, flinching at every adjustment, but Dad knew what he was doing, always making sure he could see exactly what he was slicing through, where the cord was, not getting tangled up. I went inside, the comb hanging down my back, still stuck in my hair, and yanked my hair into a ponytail, got dressed, and went back out to do yard work all afternoon. The sooner Mom and Dad were done, the safer it would be.

After the hedge was finished, my parents cut back the oak tree's lower branches which had gotten so long they were hitting the side of the house, the limbs—ka-boing!—springing up as soon as the extra weight fell from them.

I needed another shower once the trimmings were bagged.

CHAPTER FIVE
A STILL GLASS OF WATER

In the final weeks of second grade, when they still lived in Rockford, Illinois, my niece Callie got off an unmarked school bus, her little sister Lauren right behind her. They went to a private Catholic school and the bus, intentionally, looked unremarkable, like a large plain van. The van-buses came in non-yellow colors, so the Catholic school kids would not appear affluent, which most weren't anyway. Mrs. Kerns had been babysitting Callie and Lauren since they were infants.

Callie knocked on the door, expecting 'Mama Kerns' to already be in the process of opening it since she knew when to expect the bus, but there was no answer. When Callie looked through the front window, she could see the toddler Mrs. Kerns also babysat, wandering around in the dining room, but the baby, called La-la, was too young to follow directions and could not unlock the door. The bus driver had more kids to drop off but was not allowed to pull away until he saw each child enter a home. Knowing Mrs. Kerns had to be there, Callie banged on the door. A minute passed, and Callie shouted. The driver, by now, had climbed out of the bus. Callie yelled and banged harder as he approached. She tried to explain and did explain, but the bus driver forced her and Lauren to get back on the bus.

And then he continued his route.

After all the other kids had been dropped off, the bus returned to St. Eusebio. Phone calls were made from the school to my sister Tessa, Mr. Kerns' work, one of the Kerns' sons living across town, and to emergency services. By the time Tessa got to the school, picked up the girls, and pulled up to the Kerns' house, the police had forced the door, Mr. Kerns had rushed from his car, running across the lawn, and EMS was doing chest compressions in the living room where Mrs. Kerns had collapsed, just out of sight of the front window. Callie went inside, and three things latched onto her eight-year-old memory: La-la standing in the playpen holding red over-sized plastic keys, the huff-huff from the emergency tech as sweat slid down his temple, and Mama Kerns' false teeth—taken out of her mouth during CPR—laying abandoned on the carpet next to her.

EMS estimated that Mrs. Kerns had been on the floor for two hours before they got to her. She died that evening at the hospital. Callie cried for hours, wailing about the bus driver: "I told him something was wrong. I told him she was in there." In one night, she shrieked her voice raw, "He wouldn't listen!" Twenty years later, my niece Callie was a physical therapist in a rehabilitation center off I-35 in Hegelville, working with stroke patients.

❧

Callie's little sister, Lauren, who had been in kindergarten when Mrs. Kerns died, had no direct memory of that day and very few memories of Rockford, of her father passed out in the basement one winter day where Callie covered him with a blanket so he wouldn't freeze to death on the concrete floor, of calls from bill collectors, of Tessa at the kitchen table crying as she filed for divorce. She and her husband both worked, but he had snorted their finances up his nose and hadn't paid the house note in months. Mrs. Kerns had been Tessa's last lifeline. The babysitter had not been paid for half a year but still babysat the girls out of love, and the night she died, Tessa called home. Rockford was her husband's family seat, not hers, and when she moved back to San Antonio that summer, she had two small girls, four suitcases, and a car that would last another year, if she was lucky. Her body was skeletal from stress.

Tessa got a small house that needed drywall repair about a mile away from us in Winter Forest. My mom bought the girls new clothes and took them to swimming lessons while Tessa worked as a paralegal. Dad picked my niece Lauren up from choir when she was young, then drama club as she got older and Lauren, popular and gossipy, thrived. By the time she got her diploma, she was engaged to Wyatt, her high school sweetheart.

She and Wyatt started at Crockett State. Lauren lived in a dorm on campus with three other girls and after two years, she got certified as a payroll and bookkeeping clerk and dropped out of college. We told her not to. And she got married. We told her not to. And she was happy.

Her husband stayed in school while Lauren paid their bills. The plan was for him to get his degree first, get a good job and then support her while she returned to school. For five years, she and Wyatt took trips to cities where the night life was trending: New Orleans, Miami, a string of others. Then they got a house in Eden Park, a subdivision on the other side of Treece

Road, across from Winter Forest. The yard was full of burrs and itch mites. Lauren still had not completed a bachelor's and neither, amazingly, had her husband. Wyatt worked odd jobs to make ends meet, then started working full-time in lower middle-management at a glass company, until a sharp rise in the cost of lumber slowed down home and building construction and got him laid off, so he went back to odd jobs. Baby Jovi was born in year seven, and they hadn't saved up a dime.

Lauren stayed home with Jovi for a year then abruptly said she had to start working again. It caught my attention because I remembered that years ago, she'd said that when she had kids, she would stay home until they started kindergarten. Maybe that had been their rationale for Wyatt needing to get his degree first. The logic didn't hold, but we had not been able to convince her that, love notwithstanding, she needed to get her own degree and be able to support herself. Mom and Dad were both retired by the time Lauren returned to work, so Jovi was dropped off every morning by seven and was picked up at six or seven at night. Sometimes at eight, if Lauren had to work late and Wyatt had a study group. Mom and Dad were still in their seventies and Dad had just been diagnosed with Alzheimer's, but so far, nothing had changed. He could still get around, make dinner, and work for the church.

Jovi began having stomachaches when she started kindergarten, and possibly before that as well, but in kindergarten, if she got sick, she was sent to the school nurse, who sent her home. Since Lauren was at work, what that actually meant was that my mom picked Jovi up and took care of her for the rest of the day until Lauren came to get her. The stomachaches increased, with Jovi throwing up at school once or twice a week. Once the other kids had seen her throw up a few times, they started making fun of her, and she developed a fear of getting sick at school, which made her stomachaches worse. Lauren said that Jovi was just adjusting to kindergarten, but it was February, past the time needed for adjustments, and my mom, who had started in nursing before she went into hospital administration, thought something else was wrong. "Maybe it's the food at school," Mom wondered. "Jovi is used to home-cooked meals, not processed food." Lauren ignored the suggestion.

࿐

Even a year after I had yelled at my Comp Two class, I was still reading anger management books and meditating each night, trying to retrain my brain. Slowly, my reactions shifted, becoming less volatile. Some days good, some not, then more good, a few not, and I wondered if I could feel the synapses rewiring. Then came the test, Thursday, mid-semester, right after lunchtime, cold, gray, and humid. A Comp One class was unresponsive and late with assignments, but I remembered The Techniques this time. Deep breathing? Yes. Calm mind? Yes. Mantra: Emotions are just emotions, floating away like balloons—or like clouds, depending on which anger management book I referenced. Anyway, I let my emotions float and threw in some pseudo-zen for effect: My mind is a still glass of water.

Nice. Then I added, "The moon rests in a dewdrop on the grass," which went one koan too far since I couldn't remember what the point of the moon, dewdrop, or the grass was.

I looked at the students and started the recommended "I feel" statements: "Class? Let me pause here. I feel like I need to ask you all for your help; I feel that you are not contributing to a learning environment that would be the most ideal for our progress today and also, I feel that—and I may be wrong on this, so I'll need feedback from you—I sense passiveness and perhaps a lack of effort. You *could* answer questions in our discussion, but instead, you are choosing not to actively participate in your own education. What do you think? Is that accurate or do you feel you're being judged too harshly?"

Eyes blinking, tension tightened their bodies as they sat up. If a pack of coyotes was prowling the room, my students could not have become more wary. Satisfaction wrapped around me as I went on, "You have chosen to be in college, and yet it *feels* as though you are waiting for someone else to put knowledge in your mind instead of having the drive to seek it out yourself. Why? What do you think?"

Students raised hands, speaking over each other, interested in anything besides the curriculum. Instead of letting them answer, I explained that last year when I'd had a class as dead as they had been, I got upset and chewed that class out, but I had read several self-help books since then and decided to share my feelings instead of cussing. How they adjusted was up to them. I went back to the assignment discussion and, at the end of the period, asked, "How did I do?"

There was applause.

Moon, dewdrop, blade of grass. My mind is a still glass of water.

❧

When a kid throws up these days, the school sends them home, and by March, the school nurse was not just speaking to Mom when she came to pick up Jovi, she had called Lauren directly. We don't know what the nurse said, but Lauren finally took

Jovi to the doctor, who diagnosed her with gluten sensitivity, but the doctor needed more tests to determine if she had Celiac disease.

I drove to Whole Foods and bought $140 worth of gluten-free cereals, pasta, cookies, and bread, loading them into Lauren's trunk when she came over. Then I got six books on Celiac from the library. Over the next two weeks, Mom sat on the end of the couch and read them all, then bought the best two.

"I don't have time to read," said Lauren when Mom offered her the books. The next day, Mom printed out an article on Celiac she found online. Lauren folded it over three times before stuffing it in her purse.

I make it to the end of the semester without yelling at any of my classes. The attrition level turns out to be about the same as it was when I chewed classes out, but the students are no longer giving me headaches, Lauren is. Since the gluten sensitivity diagnosis, neither she nor Wyatt had taken Jovi back to the doctor since the gluten sensitivity diagnosis.

After school, Jovi helps Mom make a batch of gluten-free muffins from a box mix and I take a picture of them in the kitchen since it is one of those super cute kid moments: Jovi wearing an apron as she stands on a stool so she can reach the counter and stir the batter. Mom puts muffins into two bags, one for our freezer so Jovi can have a muffin with her breakfast when she stays overnight, and the other bag so Jovi can take half of the muffins with her. Explaining how they can be frozen, Mom lets Jovi hand the second bag to Wyatt when he comes to pick her up.

"I helped Grandma make them," Jovi says. She explains their gluten-free-ness using phrases from *The Gluten-Free Kid* book I'd gotten her. I'd gone over it until she had memorized all the wheat type foods that she shouldn't eat: bread, pasta, cakes, cookies, and crackers.

Mom and Dad are sitting on the long couch, and I'm standing in the middle of the room beside the coffee table. Wyatt is on the short couch. "Oh, nice," he says and takes one muffin out of the bag. We watch as he eats it: Bite, chew, swallow . . . bite, chew swallow . . . When he reaches in for a second one, I pick up Jovi and take her into the backyard to play soccer, kicking the ball into the net under the massive pecan tree. She asks if any of the trees in the yard are Mountain Cedar, and I tell her no.

"Good," she says. "I'm allergic to snakes and mountain cedar. So don't give me either of those."

Ten minutes later, Wyatt calls Jovi in. Mom has her tight smile on, but it's starting to snap back like a rubber band that she has to keep re-stretching. "We're just concerned is all. We don't want anything to happen to that little girl," she's saying as she walks them to his car. "Useless," she says as the car pulls off. "He's absolutely useless."

In the living room, she gives me the recap. She talked to him about Jovi's stomachaches, that Jovi needs additional testing, that her diet has to be adjusted. Even if Jovi doesn't have Celiac, being gluten sensitive still puts her at greater risk for other problems like stomach pain, headaches, anemia, even behavior changes. Mom showed him the books and asked about their plan, their timeline for treating Jovi.

"And?" I say.

"He said that he doesn't want to be too aggressive about medical testing and he'll have to talk to Lauren about it." She shakes her head. "They're idiots, both of them."

Even Dad comments, "Doesn't seem to have much of a spine, does he?"

❧

Mom is the first to notice Lauren is no longer wearing her wedding ring and calls my sister Tessa, who lives on a ranch in Arizona with her second husband. She gives Tessa an update on Jovi's stomachaches, which have slowed a little but not stopped. Tessa is not sure what is going on between Lauren and Wyatt, but she does report that whenever she calls, Lauren is always over at Callie's house, which is ten miles up I-35 in Heinrich. Lauren always claims that she is doing laundry or visiting or having dinner, but now that Tessa thinks about it, every time she has called Lauren for a couple of months now, Lauren has been at her sister Callie's, never at her own house with Wyatt.

When Mom hangs up the phone, she whispers under her breath as she often did after a phone call with Tessa, "I'm so glad Tessa's happy, married to a good man now. She deserves to be happy." Mom says this like a prayer before turning back to her speculations about Lauren's situation.

During the last week of Jovi's first-grade year, Lauren, not Wyatt, picks Jovi up each evening. Lauren has changed her hair from the style she'd had since high school, cutting it to shoulder length and adding alternating bands of highlights. Mom tells her flatly that Jovi needs to be treated for her gluten intolerance.

"She's pretending," Lauren responds. "She says she has a stomachache, so she can get picked up at school and come over here because she knows she can lay around and do whatever she wants."

"Germs are a myth invented by the governments," a student happened to mention during a conference in my office once.

"Which governments?" I asked.

"All of them. In renaissance, which is in Germany, I think."

Sometimes a student will say something so bizarre, it sends me into a two-step process. First, scan their face for signs they are telling a joke, being ironic, or just went insane. Second, assess how to answer in a way that will not set off the just-went-insane ones. Mom's face tells me she's doing the same sort of thing with Lauren, but on a deeper, clinical level.

Mom's tone stays abnormally even. "Lauren, I'm a nurse. I worked in hospital administration when you were growing up, but I have been in the medical field my entire adult life and I know when people are in pain. She is not pretending to have a stomachache to get attention, and she is not pretending to be constipated two or three times a week. She is vomiting at school. She frequently runs a low-grade fever. Jovi is in distress."

"I am her mother. You don't respect me; you don't follow my rules. I tell you she can't have a bunch of sweets and you give her all the treats she wants. You don't know your boundaries."

"Lauren, she is losing weight. I weighed her last year and—"

"She is not!" Lauren stands up, hefting an oversized purse with one arm and motioning for Jovi to precede her with the other.

The next evening starts exactly where the last one ended, as though Mom had been mid-sentence when Lauren left the night before. "And Jovi has always been skinny. When children lose weight it means that something is wrong."

"Don't start this again," Lauren sighs, then snaps at Jovi. "Come on; we're going."

"It is dangerous," Mom's tonelessness slips. "You can see she's lost weight. Do you know how much weight she's lost? She needs to be treated for gluten intolerance and she needs better medical supervision. You need to stop giving her food with gluten in it."

"Get your things," Lauren yells at Jovi, then at Mom, "You are not going to bully me."

Jovi was moving slow, picking up the sweater she wore at school, a coloring book, a sock.

"You are in denial about how sick she is," Mom persists, and I know she must have been rehearsing this in her mind, planning out the step-by-step reasoning she would go through. "Lauren, she weighs thirty-one pounds. Last year she weighed thirty-five. A six-year-old should not be losing weight like—"

"The doctors haven't proven to me what is wrong."

"They shouldn't have to prove what is wrong for you to realize that something is wrong and want to do something about it!"

Lauren opens her purse and pulls out an old wooden spoon so big it looks theatrical, the kind you use for serving salad in a fork and spoon set. She rounds on Jovi, "I told you to be ready to go when I got here." She grabs Jovi's arm and drags her to the bathroom. We hear the click of the door locking. "Listen to me—"

My head turned as she dragged Jovi in there. Mom was trying to bring up children's weight tables, and yet Mom is the first to realize what is about to happen, what is happening—There is one plaintive "Mommy" before we hear Lauren wailing away and Jovi scream-crying—and Mom knocks her shin getting around the coffee table to rush to the bathroom door and start banging, and I notice my butt has not left the couch, and suddenly I pop up just as the bathroom door opens.

When they come out, there's a stiff dumb moment; then everyone is yelling: me and Mom at Lauren. Lauren at me and

Mom. Jovi is breathing hard, eyes wide, but she's not making any sound. Dad is standing behind the scrum of voices, not saying anything but watching, his jaw set.

Whatever statements Mom had rehearsed are shattered and her voice gets edgy as a saw. "Lauren, you really need some counseling. You need help. Don't you see that?"

"Stop butting in," Lauren is grabbing Jovi's school bag and walking out.

"She's demented," I say. A general observation to the universe? Then directly to Lauren, "You're demented. You're abusing your child."

"She got a spanking because she is not listening to me."

"She's six. You're not. What is wrong with you?"

"Everyone's been spanked. Grandma spanked you. It's traditional."

My brain flashes white. As part of freshman comp, I've been teaching logic and reasoning for more than twenty years, and suddenly in that moment, I am unable to articulate the weakness of using tradition as a justification. I use the word 'fallacy' a hundred times a month in my classes, and yet I'm unable to locate the word in my brain or the definition of the Fallacy of Tradition or the half dozen examples I have ready on any given Tuesday afternoon.

Apoplectic: adjective - overcome with rage.

We're in the driveway. Apoplectically in the driveway. Apoplectically watching as Jovi is strapped in her car seat, as Lauren gets in the driver's seat, as she waits for me to take a step back. Unaware of how I got there, I'm standing right next to the driver's side door, too close for Lauren to back the car out.

"What is wrong with you?" I take a step away from the car's side mirror. "What is wrong with you?"

Stone-faced, she pulls away.

One summer, I sat down and calculated how many students I had taught, so far, over the years of my career: a couple thousand. They had taken notes as I lectured that the belief that a behavior is good, correct, or justified because it has been around for a long time is a mistake in reasoning, a fallacy called the fallacy of tradition. "A belief that has been around a long time is old," I explained to a couple of thousand students, "not right, and not right because it's old." None of the couple of thousand were Lauren.

After I go inside, I take a hot bath, get a bad headache, make my room as dim as possible, lay down at 7 p.m. and do not get up again all evening.

In both my parents' families, boys were spanked by their fathers, girls by mothers. Since Mom and Dad did not have any sons, Dad didn't have any spanking to do. Mom had spanked me when I was a kid, but very rarely, partly because I was not especially rebellious, but mainly because if I did do something I was not supposed to, I usually thought it out well enough to avoid being noticed. And spankings by Mom were not spontaneous: she told me to get a brush, slipper, belt, ruler, or whatever she was going to smack my butt with, whatever came to mind that was flat and she could get a grip on. My grandmother, Ella, was famous for telling her kids to, "Go cut her a switch off the tree out back." They were then to dutifully return so she could swat the back of their thighs with it.

The last spanking I ever got was disturbing enough to stop my mom from giving any more spankings, ever, to anyone. I can't remember what I was getting a spanking for, but I do remember being unrepentant and unafraid. I asked her why I should bring her something so she could hit me with it. She said it would be worse if she had to get up and get it herself. She was sitting on the couch and I brought her whatever she had asked for, though I can't remember what it was, maybe a ruler. She swatted me hard several times, paused, and swatted me again, but I stood there, not crying, not moving. She tried again, breathing a little heavily. I looked down at her and asked if she was done yet.

"Yeah," she said and handed the ruler back to me, smoothing her hair. "I'm done."

I was about ten years old. I still feel bad for creeping her out.

Mitch, of course, had never spanked the boys. He couldn't. Lewin had been a little over ten months when Mitch got him, and he had clearly been neglected. There were no signs of abuse on Lewin, but his birth mother's previous children had been removed because of a pattern of child abuse, and Archie had been handed over to Mitch with a welt on his tiny behind at just five days old.

When the boys acted up, Mitch yelled. He harassed but never hit them, no matter how tired or stressed out he was. That doesn't mean it was pretty. When Lewin refused to swallow one tablespoon of medicine for some outbreak of a serious kid infection he'd caught, Mitch made him stand in the kitchen. Lewin was feverish, crying and shaky and just wanted to lie down in bed. Mitch had already tried bribes and begging, plus a deranged attempt at reasoning with a cranky child by defining 'antibiotic.' Finally, Mitch nagged, telling him to just swallow it, one spoonful, and then he could lie down, just swallow the medicine, over and over until Lewin did. It took eight minutes, then Mitch carried him to the bed.

And I had spanked Jovi once while babysitting three years earlier. Mom and Dad were on a trip with their Church Seniors, and I'd had her all day for three days straight. That day, I'd played with her: chase games and little kid board games, read alphabet books, cooked breakfast and lunch, then put her in the playpen in the living room and told her to lie down and take a nap. I needed to clean the kitchen and house, start laundry, and then do prep work for the upcoming semester, and I wanted her contained. She'd worn me out, but she still had acres of energy, plus a little girl's mischievous grin as she climbed out of the playpen. I put her back in; she climbed back out. I put her back in. The fourth time, she stared at me as she swung her leg over the top rail, and I smacked her butt. I was holding her at the time, trying to put her back down, and she recoiled from me as much as possible, drawing her thin arms up against her body, horror on her oval face. She lay silently in the playpen, watching me rinse pots and pans like you would watch a loose panther pace by. The guilt climbed all over me the rest of the evening, and I took a vow: Never spank.

I had started having insomnia months before the shouting match with Lauren, back when Jovi was throwing up every week at school. I lay awake for hours or fell asleep, my mind racing, jaw tight as I argued with Lauren in my dreams, and then suddenly awake again, eyes open in the darkness.

Lauren didn't spank Jovi in front of us again, but she still carried the ridiculous spoon in her purse, which said everything.

After the blowout, we assumed Lauren would stop bringing Jovi over, but Eden Park Elementary had a random power outage the next morning. Lauren had to bring Jovi over or miss work. She called on her way over, then when she arrived, rang the bell, opened the door and pushed Jovi inside without speaking. Jovi held a single serving box of Apple Jacks that I took away while Mom fixed her scrambled eggs and grits. An hour later, she got a stomachache anyway, telling us that she'd had pizza the night before for dinner. I read the back of the cereal box, and the first ingredient was wheat.

"Jovi needs a medical diagnosis," Mom tried again when Lauren came to pick her up.

"She's making me miss too much work."

"If you don't take her to the doctor, Lauren, it's neglect."

For a few days, Mom would not say anything; then it would replay again. Eventually, Mom said something every time Lauren came by, and within two weeks, when Jovi's school year had ended and she was out for the summer, Lauren would enter the house, get Jovi, then leave without even looking at us.

Once summer started, Mom babysat all day, taking Jovi to swimming lessons each morning, making her lunch in the afternoon. Finally, as Lauren was getting Jovi from her room, Mom blocked her way in the hall.

"This has got to stop," Mom said. "You are disconnected from reality if you don't see that that child is sick."

"We are leaving."

"When are you going to take her to a doctor?"

"Get out of my way."

Dad was in the living room, watching. "Let her go," he told Mom. "It's her child."

Mom stepped aside and they left.

I start having days of free-floating anxiety. Hours would go by when I couldn't focus. The core problem was multi-layered and somehow contradictory: I could study, train and philosophize to control my anger about someone who was annoying me or about something cruel happening to me, even an injustice done to me. But I could not extend that same discipline to a wrong done to another, to a child. Plus, I had been furious at myself for not being able to conjure up a definition of the fallacy of tradition when I needed to explain to Lauren how her thinking had twisted. After a year of meditation and reading books on inner peace and self-control, I had just lost it: I could not think straight and had devolved into yelling.

Violating another person's physical integrity was fundamentally wrong. That was my deep personal truth. Intentionally causing physical pain was illegitimate. Surely I knew the world was swarming with wrongs that were worse than spanking a child, and yet it was not. And those greater harms were not happening in my bathroom, to Jovi. I had once spanked Jovi and could not undo that. And still, my mind throbbed with grinding frustration at Lauren.

The biggest distraction I had from thinking about Lauren was working through the list I'd made from my end-of-the-world prepper books and buying the emergency supplies and dried foods for the Grab-n-Go tote. In June, I spend three days shopping, crossing items off the list, and storing liters of water in the tops of closets, the corners of cabinets, and under sinks around the house. On one Saturday, I pack Mylar bags with rice, beans, pasta, and other dried goods, add a desiccant and oxygen absorber packet, and use a curling iron to melt the top of the bag. I needed Mom's help to seal each bag as quickly as possible so the desiccant and oxygen absorber would still be effective when they were closed inside the Mylar.

Mom stared at the pile of supplies. "What do you think is going to happen?"

"Hopefully, nothing. But if something does happen, we'll be ready. We'll have the basics covered at least."

"Ready for what?"

Maybe because she doesn't have time for two crazies in the family, she doesn't argue as I arrange the silver Mylar bags into the Sterilite totes. By the time I'm done, the emergency supplies have filled two containers, everything from matches, spare socks, toothpaste, face masks, shampoo, water purification tablets, Advil, multi-purpose tools, batteries, and flashlights, to freeze-dried meals. The supplies cost three hundred dollars, but, according to the prepper books, they should last ten to twenty years. I close the lids on the totes, stack them inside the closet in the bedroom that Jovi uses when she spends the night, and I go lay down. Done.

On Monday morning, Lauren sends a text saying she no longer has confidence in Mom and will not bring Jovi over anymore. Jovi has lost a tooth over the weekend, and Lauren attaches a picture of Jovi grinning and holding a dollar from the tooth fairy, to soften the message, I suppose. Mom sends a text back telling Lauren to take Jovi to a gastroenterologist.

We don't hear anything else.

I dig the good luggage out of the luggage pile in the garage, so I can pack to go visit Nolan.

CHAPTER SIX
BLUCIFER

Mitch calls Saturday morning. The boys are headed to some kid's birthday party at a Laser Tag arcade on my side of town. Mitch, Lewin, and Archie drop by for half an hour before heading to the arcade and, predictably, Mitch talks about the boys. He worries they are over-scheduled, then absolves himself of his own accusation: they don't complain, they love piano lessons, he's taking piano lessons too, he always wanted to learn and now he can practice with them, fifteen minutes a day, and maybe they'll all learn the cello next, and they usually have Brazilian drum dance class on Saturday mornings but not today, it's good for their coordination, soccer's over for now, but swim lessons during the week.

Incredibly the boys excel at everything they try. Mitch's face is free of irony when he says this; this is his genuine assessment. I let it go.

I haven't seen the boys in a couple of months, and I give Archie and Lewin, now six and seven, belated birthday presents that I'd never delivered. They look good; Mitch has them dressed in identical outfits; he does that sometimes. Archie is lean, smiles easily, and is nearly as tall as Lewin now, and he's gotten in trouble twice for being a class clown and not doing his homework.

After they leave, I get my luggage zipped and secured with the little Transportation Security Administration approved lock, then wait for the Airport Shuttle I'd reserved. Mom and Dad stand in the driveway and watch the driver hoist my bag into the blue van. I'm the only passenger and he doesn't pick up anyone else on the way to San Antonio International. He chews on a toothpick and says business has fallen off sharply because of rideshare companies, yet he mentions Uber without bitterness.

Once I get through security, I buy a bottle of water for four dollars and start tracking how much I spend on everything and saving every receipt, a habit I have whenever I travel. I must have boarded Southwest and flown to Denver, but honestly, I don't remember a thing from the flight, so I assume it was unremarkable in every way. Denver International Airport, however, is not.

Denver International is the size of a Death Star. Gates A, B, and C are lined up in three long parallel strips. Trains, agreeably called People Movers, run underground between the gates to the vast terminal. When I de-plane, I don't know any of this; I just follow the flow and end up, sort of magically, at a very clean subway station with an upbeat disembodied voice giving instructions on riding safely. Everything is crowded and orderly; the train is smooth and fast. When the train pulls into Gate B, I look out the window and see an astronaut—just standing there, in full outer space gear, holding his helmet, which is odd. On a pedestal. Okay, a statue of an astronaut. He looks like he's about to dance around. The train picks up speed again and soon dumps me out in the terminal. I find a bathroom, have a post-flight pee, then wander in the only direction that makes sense, looking for Baggage Claim signs.

A few yards away, Nolan is standing in a big open space on one side of what looks like a giant area that has collapsed from an earthquake. There is a huge rectangular sunken depression with terraced concrete walls reaching up toward the level that we are standing on. The pit looks like it is still being constructed or being reconstructed after a missile strike, but there are no 'Pardon Our Dust' signs. Straggly plants are dying on each terrace. I hug Nolan and he introduces me to Kinsley, a girl Jovi's age standing next to him. Neither notice the huge earthquake sinkhole. In the lead-up to the trip, I had asked Nolan which shuttle to take to get to his house, but he said, "It doesn't work like that in Denver," and added that he would just pick me up, but that I would definitely take the bus back to the airport when I flew home.

Okay, so here's the deal. We are walking to baggage claim and the murals on the walls are psychotic. They are so crazy I wonder if they are some kind of joke. One painting has a World War Two soldier in a gas mask and trench coat, holding a machine gun in one arm and swinging a sword with the other, while, at his feet, is a crumbling cathedral and swaddled children lying on bricks. Another mural shows buildings on fire while a blue whale leaps out of a sea of red, above a dead jaguar, a mounted bison head, and children lying in coffins. The colors are festive, but who the hell votes *for* the Apocalypse as an airport theme? A city council on LSD?

Baggage claim is as efficient as the People Mover train and in minutes, we are strolling to Nolan's old red Jeep. In typical little kid fashion, Kinsley hasn't said much since muttering hello, but she stares at me a lot and piles into the middle of the back seat. A thirty-foot tall, cobalt Blue Mustang rears on its hind legs in the grassy median as we head away from the airport. It has glowing red eyes.

"It's caused a little controversy," Nolan offers about the Mustang. "Some people say that it looks demonic."

During construction, when part of the steel and fiberglass structure fell in the design studio, it killed the artist who created it. Its nickname is Blucifer.

Welcome to Colorado.

CHAPTER SEVEN
SONORA HOUSE

THE FIRST TIME I met Nolan, he was not wearing shoes. I was looking for housing close to the University of Texas for the fall '85 semester, and I had waited way too late. It was two weeks before classes and I was scrambling. I'd driven up to Austin for the day and looked for one-bedroom apartments, singles, then efficiencies within a few blocks of campus, and they were full, over-priced, or decrepit. Then I checked out student co-ops.

Sonora House was two blocks down in the West Campus area and had two two-story buildings that framed a green area considered the co-op's back yard. One building had a red wooden deck on its second level. A sandwich board in the co-op's front yard announced a vacancy, and I walked into the main building, the one with the kitchen and dining area. The lights were out, but it was mid-afternoon and the room was full of pearl gray paleness. Cafeteria chairs were flipped up on the tables and Nolan was mopping the floor in a shirt and khaki shorts but no shoes.

I told him I was looking for housing. He stopped mopping, straightened up, and said nothing for several seconds while he looked me in the eye. Maybe he was translating what I said into his native language? Scandinavian exchange student, perhaps? When he spoke, his words were not sloppy, blurring into each other like most American English. Each word was completed before the next was begun, so he spoke a fragment too slowly, and he drew out his vowels slightly more than typical. It was noticeable, but it was not a discernible accent. So, a special needs custodian, maybe?

He told me the co-op had one room left, asked if I wanted a tour, put the mop back in the mop bucket, and showed me around, narrating the basics of co-op living well enough for me to realize he was a college student and co-op resident. Each building had single rooms with a simple bathroom: a toilet and shower. The main building had a TV room with old soft couches that you had to flail to get out of, an industrial kitchen, a walk-in refrigerator, and a common area like a small cafeteria. That's the area that he had been mopping when I came in.

Sonora House was a mid-sized co-op, about fifty people lived there, half men and half women. They kept the ratio even because if there were too many men, the place got filthy, and if there were too many women, it got catty. This was not a sexist generalization, just an observation of the co-op's history. And since women applied to live in co-ops less frequently than men did, Sonora House still had one woman spot left.

Everyone in the co-op was assigned to do five hours of work each week. That kept the rent low and, since the people who lived there planned and cooked all the meals, it also meant the food was good. When I walked in, Nolan had been doing one of his work hours, which was cleaning up the dining area after lunch. If I wanted, he told me, I could stay for dinner, and then the House would call a meeting and vote on whether to accept me. There was an interview. The people in the House could ask me questions and I could ask questions back.

After I was accepted that night, I found out that I asked more questions than any other applicant they could remember. My room was on the first floor of the main building; Nolan lived in the building with the deck on the other side of the back yard and came to meals barefoot, but he put on shoes to walk to class because you had to wear shoes in university buildings.

Over the next two years, Nolan and I would be elected officers in the House. He became the Labor Czar, assigning everyone the work they would do for the semester, and I was the food buyer, overseeing the cooks and ordering all the food and supplies to be delivered twice weekly. Nolan was also president of the UT Camping and Hiking Club, which five people from Sonora House, including me, joined. The Hiking Club's trip to Mexico that Spring Break was epic: we got caught in a blizzard while hiking in Copper Canyon, and Nolan and another hiker had to haul me up out of there when I got altitude sickness.

At a bar back in Austin, at a table full of co-op members who had all gone out together one night, Nolan and I would kiss each other, on a dare, just to see how it felt. It was a good kiss, but no sparklers went off for either of us, plus I was already half-drunk. Two Long Island Iced Teas later, on my hands and knees on a sidewalk on 6th Street, I barfed on Nolan's feet. Luckily, he had put on old sneakers so he could get into the bar. The next morning, I woke up with the first hangover of my life, so brutal I didn't drink again for the rest of the year.

That was thirty years ago, before Nolan had three PhD's, held eight patents, lived in a house officially deemed a work of art, and had a mountain in his back yard.

CHAPTER EIGHT
MOLTEN GOLD

Boulder is only thirty miles from Denver, and Nolan narrates along the way. Several long wooden slatted frames are propped up at forty-five-degree angles in a dry grassy field next to the highway. Coming from Texas, I think they are some kind of fancy wind-breaks. They're snow fences Nolan says. I glance at them, fantastically unaware that five months later, I'll see them again, buried in drifts.

When we slide into Boulder, Nolan turns into a shopping center parking lot with a couple of free-standing fast-food restaurants and an L-shaped row of businesses dominated by a Goodwill Thrift Store. We park across from Noodles and Company. My luggage is in the back of the car and Nolan leaves the windows half-open. After we stand in line to order, I pick a table where I can watch the car through the front window while we have a life-over-the-seven-years-since-I-last-saw-you conversation. I don't mention Lauren, Jovi, or Celiac disease.

Kinsley stares at me across the table while she's eating,

eventually mumbling out a question for Nolan. "Can we go to Rocky Mountain Park tomorrow?"

"We'll go sometime this summer, but we can't go tomorrow. Alene needs a couple days to adjust to the altitude." Nolan puts his fork down, already finished with his spicy Korean beef. His face is angular, thinner than ever before. "I usually take Kinsley to Rocky Mountain National Park once or twice during the summer, so I always get an annual pass." Kinsley is picking at her spaghetti and meatballs, and Nolan spoons half of what she has left into his bowl to finish it off.

While Nolan talks, I survey Kinsley. Lower class. She's wearing shorts and a sleeveless top, mismatched and over-worn. She has cinnamon hair that hasn't been cut in a long time, if ever, and that shapeless shape that poor kids have when everything they eat comes out of a bag, box, or can. I know from talking to Nolan over the years that Kinsley is his goddaughter.

Eight years ago, Nolan decided to rent out his basement, thinking that, since he lived within walking distance of CU-Boulder, some student would find that a one-room basement apartment worked well for him, and a little extra rent money coming in for a room that wasn't doing anything, worked well for Nolan. The first person to show up was a frat boy who expected to be drunk on weekends and who had been kicked out of his previous place for excessive noise. Nolan told him no. The second person to show up was Megan, a cashier at Home Depot. Her ex-husband was in prison, doing a long stretch this time; she'd heard that her semi-abusive mother was keeping clean lately; her father had last been seen nine years ago after a bar fight where two men had been stabbed; her brother worked construction outside Greeley, but she wasn't sure where. Megan was five months pregnant and homeless. Nolan let her move in.

We run by Nolan's house to drop off my bags, which have not been stolen out of his unlocked car. Nolan's house sits in a small, five-house cul-de-sac. The house has a main level and a basement, but the house is on a hill that is so steep, one long side of Nolan's basement is exposed, and the rest of his house sits on top of it. The house has two driveways: a short one on the main level and a narrow, curving driveway that stretches in front of the basement's garage, laundry room, and what used to be the old coal cellar that Nolan converted to a bath and bedroom efficiency apartment, with its own entry. He unlocks the door to the basement bedroom and hands me the key as I pull my bag in.

The bed is pushed into a corner of the room, with an overstuffed bean bag chair next to it. One entire wall, floor to ceiling, is a built-in bookcase with inch-thick wooden shelves, about a third of them loaded with books on chemistry, biology, human anatomy, metallurgy, and industrial toxins. Nolan points to the opposite wall covered in horizontal shiplap, pitted black from when coal was dumped down here for storage over the winters. Other than the color in the pitting, there is no trace of coal. I want to run my hands over the smooth cedar but don't just yet. A desk and austere Shaker chair are up against the old coal cellar wall. There's a tiny kitchenette and a short hallway leading to a bathroom with a sink, toilet, and a glassed-in shower.

"Kinsley spent her first three years here," he says, and I picture how it starts: cashier mom comes back with a newborn; Nolan helps her navigate social services, but, inevitably, childcare breaks down, she'll lose her job, can he babysit just this once?

We pile back into the Jeep and, with one quick swerve out

of the cul-de-sac, immediately we are driving up a mountain. Boulder rests in the foothills of the Rockies, 5400 feet above sea level and Green Mountain Park is Nolan's back yard. As we wind up the road, we pass cyclists with thick knotted calves and other people who are just walking up a mountain. For fun. Because that's what people in Colorado do.

He stops at a small scenic lookout point with a short trail to a jumble of boulders the size of baby whales, poking out from the side of the mountain. The city of Boulder sits like a saucer in the basin below us and Nolan points out the city's features. As he speaks, Kinsley disappears around the front of the rock projection that we are standing on, then reappears on the other side of the jumble and I'm wondering what just happened. She left on one side of some rocks sticking out over nothing, then returned from the other side of those rocks sticking out over nothing, and then we are piling back in the car and heading higher up to the top.

We park past a line of cars filling a narrow parking strip and start hiking over to an area that is a mix of forest, park trails, and scenic overlook. Still in my travel clothes, I am not dressed for mountain walks. For the flight, I had put on a fancy pair of turquoise jeans, a leather belt with an engraved silver belt buckle, and a dark gray V-neck. People in Texas wear jeans when it's a hundred degrees because it's often a hundred degrees and because Texas is flat. My jeans are too bind-ie for this. Then I notice the air because it doesn't smell, and yet it's also fresh and sweet, the best air ever, and I tell Nolan about my discovery.

"Yeah," he says, "it is still pretty good. After a while, you stop noticing how clean the air is anymore until you take a trip and come back. It used to be even better ten, fifteen, even five years ago. But Boulder is getting an influx of people. More are moving here all the time. The air is not as pure as it used to be. Smell this." Nolan is pointing at a tree. "This is a good one." He sniffs it, then steps back.

The trunk is so thick that my hands would not meet if I wrapped my arms around it. The bark is warm in the sun as I inhale deep. God, it's fantastic. Lush, like a bag of butterscotch bits. The second inhalation is not as intense, as if the scent has scooched away from me. "Ponderosa Pine," he says and starts walking again, calling out, "Kinsley, wait. Don't get too far ahead," before turning back. "There are some Ponderosas, they're pretty rare, that are super-scented. They are really prized. When you come across one, you know it." I get obsessed with finding a super-scented pine tree and sniff every tree with the same pattern of Ponderosa bark that we pass.

The lookout on the top of the mountain is popular. Families roam around, smiling absently, staring across the abyss to a mountain range beyond. And the mountains beyond them. My heart slides out of my body a little, the beauty almost painful. People are relaxing on the piles of boulders as I teeter to a good spot and carefully sit down in my too tight, garish pants that looked stylish just this morning and 900 miles away. Everyone else is dressed in Colorado de rigueur: bicycle shorts or dun colored, loose khakis with a half dozen pockets. Kinsley, wearing flip-flops, walks to the edge of the rocks then climbs down. There is an unfathomable drop below her, a thousand feet to the bottom, as she swings around a tricky section.

"Don't go further than you are comfortable going," Nolan says to the place she was a moment ago. "If you get stuck, I'm not going to come get you. You will just have to come back the same way you got there."

My butt's all clenched up. Will I go to jail too when this kid plummets to her death? How does being an accomplice work exactly? Or maybe this falls under depraved indifference? Negligence?

The woman on the rock next to me wants me to take a picture of her, her three kids, and her old college chum visiting from who-the-fuck-cares, back east. She hands me her cell phone and they all lean heads together while I click off three photos which the woman enthuses over. No one is showing concern that a seven-year-old is free solo rock climbing. There is a delay, then Kinsley moves back into sight, having worked through the stuck part.

Trees grow along the top of the mountain ridge and down the side of the drop. People are in them, the mountain teeming with University of Colorado Boulder students who are getting set up for the evening, securing hammocks, staring at cell phones and textbooks, listening to music through headphones, arranging blankets at their feet. It happens slowly and instantly: the sun, sinking, reaches an aphelion and the normal earthly end-of-day sky sublimates into an iridescent ocher sheet of molten gold. Black silhouettes of students hiking, climbing trees, laying in hammocks, and chatting in small groups, move against the flat, icon painting backdrop. A black cut-out of a student pauses, not looking at the shimmering sky framing the world but at her tablet. Then the sun settles another inch, and the sky blurs into evening, cerulean with slate gray clouds lit from below in pale pink and fading mauve light, but the black silhouettes pasted in front of that space hanging between mountain ranges remain. We spiral back down the mountain as night pours into the basin below.

Nolan lives in a glass house designed by McKyle Becker, an

architect with tremendous promise who died young, so there are less than a hundred of his works. The Heaney House was built in the 1960s in a neighborhood where every house is different. Each house was built by someone—who spent time at the Sorbonne or was featured in Architecture Digest—for someone, like the Heaney family. My Grandmother Ella's neighborhood in Hot Springs is like that. But Ella's house and many others were built by my grandfather, Lennox, a carpenter who'd never dreamed of the Sorbonne.

We go up the stairs from the driveway to the main level, and a pillar on the front porch has a silver plaque proclaiming the house a 'Building of Artistic Value' by the Colorado Architectural Preservation Registry. The front door is a regular front door, wooden, but I can see directly through the front wall into the entryway and, from an angle, into the living room. Inside, Fia wags her tail. She's gotten skinny with age and feels bony when I pet her. The walls inside the house are not made of glass which means the coat closet in the entryway keeps me from seeing straight through to the back yard until we move into the living room.

Being inside a glass house is pretty cool, especially this one which uses lots of tricks to make inside and outside meld into each other. There's an overstuffed couch where you can sit and look straight into Nolan's front yard. The glass living-room walls have a sliding glass door. In one corner, a fireplace sticks out into the room, just floating, unsupported, jutting out from a narrow column of cinder blocks that must be the chimney. Basically, the fireplace looks like someone invisible is holding out a big dinner plate that you just might want to build a fire on. Nolan follows my gaze.

"It's cantilevered," he explains, but the only thing I picture is a drawbridge, which requires some adjustment to fit the context here.

There are rocker gaming chairs around the fireplace, but Nolan does not have a television, so I know the chairs are not for playing video games. The walls inside the house are also doing clever things. Rather than extend straight up to the ceiling, the top of the walls have a recessed shelf about two feet from the ceiling and the shelf is full of ferns and other plants with vines trailing down over the edge. This makes it look like the plants are growing out of the walls or, like the fireplace, just levitating.

The kitchen, on the back side of the coat closet, is a museum piece untouched by time. Other than the modern refrigerator, the kitchen has been lifted straight out of the '60s. There is no dishwasher. The farmhouse sink is aged porcelain, and the stove has a panel of push buttons on it that I could not even guess how to operate, although, since boxes of cereal and crackers are sitting on three of the four eyes on the stove, using it might not be an option.

Nolan builds a fire on the floating brazier and we sit on the rocker chairs while Kinsley stretches out on the couch behind us. The fire grows, flares up, and dies away all in about thirty minutes, by which time it is dark outside and the glass walls look ghostly translucent. Tall hedges surround the front yard, but there are gaps, so someone standing on the sidewalk, at a gap, can watch us watching the dying fire.

Nolan pulls a pillow and blanket out of a closet. When Kinsley spends the night, she sleeps on a fold-out sofa-bed. Nolan's bedroom is attached to an office with a large wooden desk and a wall covered by a built-in bookshelf, full of paperbacks, mostly science fiction. Behind the bathroom is a family room with Kinsley's sofa-bed, a 1970s era dresser, and a staircase to the garage leading to the basement apartment. We say our good-nights.

There are three-way light switches on the stairs and in the basement. At the bottom of the stairs, I turn off the stairwell light and turn on the garage light. Across the garage, which is packed with junk just like my garage at home, is another switch to turn off the garage light as I pass the laundry room and turn on the light for the basement apartment.

I meditate and read *Art of Happiness* before I get into bed. The pillow is pancaked; the striped sheets look prison-issue; and the comforter, with a faded nautical theme, no longer has any puffiness yet seems a tiny bit familiar.

Not long after Nolan and I graduated from UT, two friends of ours from Sonora House got married in Dallas. Nolan's parents were still living there, and I stayed at their house overnight after the wedding, planning to drive back home in the morning. I slept in Nolan's brother's old teen room, which was cold. The whole house was, since Nolan's family is cold tolerant. Nolan's mom had put Jessica Hunan, Nolan's ex-girlfriend from Sonora House, in Nolan's sister's old room. Jessica had graduated a year ahead of us and gotten a job in Laredo, which she hated—the job and the town—and driven seven hours to Dallas for the wedding. Inconveniently that night, my period started two days early. I had two tampons rolling around in the bottom of my purse and a folded-up panty shield in a spare pocket. Quadratic equations clicked in my head as I worked out how long I could go without a run to a drug store. When I tip-toed back from the bathroom in the middle of the night, I could hear Nolan and Jessica. She had tip-toed too, and they were both in Nolan's room, moaning quietly in sync.

The nautical comforter with anchors, steering helms, and seahorse had been on Nolan's brother's bed. I'd slept under it in a different city, in a different decade, anticipating, at twenty-one years old, a more dramatic future than the one I was now living. And in five months, in a catastrophic snowstorm, that dramatic future, unwanted, would descend on me.

CHAPTER NINE
HALOUMI

THE CARPET IN the basement smelled faintly of baby pee when I sat on it the next morning to go through my luggage. I had two pairs of long shorts I brought for hiking, one black while the other was passable as khaki. It's the best I can do to blend in.

When I come up, Nolan is setting bowls on the dining table between the living room and the open end of the T-shaped kitchen. The table is covered three inches deep with piles of papers and envelopes, and I clear space around my bowl as I sit down. Kinsley has gotten over the quiet phase of being around an adult she doesn't know and is debating what kind of cereal she'll have for breakfast. Deciding on a combination of corn flakes and krispies, she cups her hands to show that one-third should be flakes and two-thirds krispies.

The papers on the table are insurance letters, incomprehensible multi-page forms, medical reports, bills, and payment plans. This is what a month in an isolation ward looks like.

"So, here's what I thought we might do today," Nolan says. "I usually take Kinsley to a movie on the weekends, so I thought we would do that this morning after Fia's walk. Orange juice or lemonade?"

"Juice. I've been wanting to see *Zootopia*."

"Me too, but Kinsley already saw it. She wants to see *The Secret Life of Pets*. How does that sound?"

"The commercials look funny."

Nolan sets cups of juice in front of Kinsley and me and puts a liter bottle of lemonade in front of himself. "And later, we should go to Pearl Street Mall."

But first, it was time for Fia's morning walk. Kinsley does not put on shoes. As we leave the house, I point out that the door is unlocked. Nolan holds Fia's leash but doesn't clip it on her. "I don't usually lock the door unless I'll be gone for a while," he says. "I have never had a problem. Also, I think because the walls are see-through, burglars would be uncomfortable coming in and rummaging around. And I don't have anything of value anyway."

"You have a laptop." When I was inviting myself up for a visit, Nolan let me know that he would have to spend a few hours a day online, working.

"It's pretty old and small. I doubt that it is worth much, but I can get the internet on it to use for work. And I use it to check the news every day."

We reach the cul-de-sac outlet and Nolan's hand goes down and flat. Fia freezes as he checks for traffic, then he motions and the dog dashes across the street, turns and trots down the sidewalk. "She's going deaf," he says, "so now I mainly use hand signals instead of voice commands."

We head down the hill, then down Broadway, and cross onto the sweeping greens of CU-Boulder. All the buildings match, Collegiate Gothic in sandstone brick. Fia runs ahead then tracks back to us as we cross the lawns, pausing on a bridge over a pond with turtles sunning themselves. I inspect a bronze statue on one side of the field as Nolan throws a Frisbee, which Kinsley and Fia chase.

The statue is of Robert Frost sitting on a bench as he writes a poem, but the statue's plaque honors a university professor. I'm not sure how you honor one guy by putting up a statue of some other guy; plus, how long do you have to be dead before *you* are actually public domain and anyone can just go and erect a statue of you? As I turn back, Nolan is getting up off the ground and Kinsley is running over to him, her mouth making an 'O' in surprise.

"Wow," he says, examining his cargo shorts, one leg of which is ripped near the bottom of his behind and dangling like a leer. "I was running and Fia brought me down like an elk."

"I saw it," says Kinsley. "She started chasing you and jumped on you. Why did she do that?"

Fia dances back and forth, partly abashed, knowing she did something wrong but also wanting to chase the Frisbee again. "Are you bitten?" I ask.

"No. She almost ripped my shorts off though." Nolan picks the disk off the ground and sends it sailing. "She's getting pretty old. She gets confused. When she saw a shape running, her instincts kicked in. She thought I was prey." Fia brings the Frisbee back and we head through a courtyard. I'm wondering when I'm going to tell Nolan why I'm really here. I've flown nine hundred miles so I can talk about Lauren and Jovi and Celiac, but you don't do that right away to a friend you haven't seen in years after he's just gotten out of an isolation ward.

You save it up, then spring it on him the third or fourth day in, with lemonade, when he least expects it.

We walk back to Nolan's house, steep uphill, watch Kinsley methodically don shoes, and let Nolan change from his torn cargo shorts into a pair of different cargo shorts. The movie is packed with wriggly kids and it's cold in the auditorium. I curl up in a seat the size of a recliner. Nolan and Kinsley laugh a lot; I laugh a little and after the movie, we walk over to 29th Street Mall, a long piazza surrounded by high-end stores.

When we get back to Nolan's, we take Fia for another walk, and this time head further into Nolan's neighborhood past Buttress Road, where the more modern houses are. They are large but not mansion-sized, and the architecture on each one says, "Hi, I cost a million bucks." Most have compact lawns with trapezoidal flower gardens or abstract sculptures strolling across the grass. Fia craps in a yard and Kinsley and I keep going for half a block while Nolan draws a plastic poop bag out of his cargoes.

Then it's down time for the late afternoon. Kinsley takes a nap; I get out my e-book reader, and Nolan gets in two hours of work online. At 5:30, we drive over to Pearl Street Mall. Boulder seems to be an incredibly compact place, with everything less than five minutes away from everything else. I know that can't actually be the case, but it feels that way.

Pearl Street is a broad pedestrian walking mall, four blocks long, with stores, restaurants with outdoor tables, street performers, and people: families with kids, college students, couples out for dinner. Benches are everywhere, along with beds of tulips down the center of the boulevard, and a bronze elk, bronze bison, bronze bear with cubs, bronze frog, bronze woman on a swing, and a boulder that's been cleft in half with a 'Do Not Climb On This' sign on it, that children Kinsley's age are ignoring.

Kinsley leads us to an ice cream parlor and already knows

what she will order while I look over the choices under the bowed glass display case and pick rum raisin because I've never had it before. The idea of choosing a flavor for that reason seems to throw Kinsley, who ignores her own ice cream to watch me eat mine.

"You want to try some?" I ask. She takes a spoonful of my ice cream, then another. And another. While I eat my ice cream, Kinsley also eats my ice cream, which is not what I had in mind, but I don't know how to tell a kid to push off. Once my cup is empty, she turns to her own neon sherbet.

From Pearl Street Mall, we're a one-minute car ride to the edge of CU-Boulder. Nolan parks next to Boulder Creek, which runs through the east side of the campus. People sit on the bank in the shade under narrow trees, and we watch a man in a kayak practice complicated moves, paddling up and down little rapids in the middle of the babbling creek, before Kinsley and I take off our sneakers and wade in. The water is frigid—meltwater, Nolan says—and I re-sock and re-shoe pretty quickly. Kayak guy shows off, rolling his kayak over, yellow helmet disappearing then popping back up until he rolls again.

I tell Nolan I need to go by a grocery store to pick up ingredients so I can make dinner and ask if there's someplace I can get nice cheese and organic grapes. He looks at me.

"This is Boulder, Alene. Even car tires are organic. There's a Sprouts in that shopping center we passed."

The woman behind the cheese counter points me to the Haloumi; then I head off looking for arugula, get grapes and a small watermelon, plus everything for a vinaigrette. I also get bottles of water since, even without the prepare-for-disaster book advice, the habits of a traveler kick in and I know better than to be anywhere without water.

Nolan is walking down an aisle calling Kinsley's name. "She wandered off," he says.

Already checked out, I'm loitering past the registers by the time he rounds her up. He puts six bottles of fruit juices on the conveyor, plus milk, bananas, and nectarines.

So the problem with cooking in a kitchen from the early 1960s is that the stove with buttons has three eyes that are covered in flammable boxes of snacks and less flammable pots and pans. The counter, where I need to cut up the fruit and arugula, has a full dish rack on one side and a red Sharps Disposal Container with a dramatic biohazard symbol on the other. Nolan pulls out a skillet and a cutting board and I get to work. Haloumi is a cheese from Cyprus that you can fry, so it gets crispy on the outside and gooey on the inside. I use this is a high-end salad to impress: hot, meaty, salty Haloumi against sweet, cold, juicy grape and watermelon. It blows minds. I know that, in a few minutes, I will be praised as a cooking genius.

I fry the cheese without setting the kitchen on fire, assemble three bowls of salad, add vinaigrette, and sit at the table waiting for the praise to roll in, but it does not.

Halloumi-arugula-grape is not a hit with Kinsley. She eats the melon chunks and picks at the rest, watching the arugula with suspicion. I see on Nolan's face that he's already calculated he'll have to get her something else to eat. He finishes his salad—there's no meat in it, which I realize is a strike out with Nolan—then he pulls a box of mac and cheese mix out of a cabinet next to the stove, turning on the one free eye, and serves it to Kinsley in less than four minutes. Americana Perfectus.

In addition to not impressing anyone with my cooking, I've also managed to clog Nolan's sink, which wasn't expecting to have to choke down escaped leaves of rinsed arugula.

"So," Nolan returns to the table and pulls what's left of Kinsley's salad in front of him, "I thought we would talk about the plan for this week."

"Plan?"

"Yeah. So we'll drop Kinsley home in the morning and Megan can also take Fia for the week. Then I thought we would tour Celestial Seasonings. They give you tea tastings after you go through the factory. And then drive through Rocky Mountain National Park."

"Yowza. That sounds great."

Kinsley looks up. "I want to go."

He turns to Kinsley, "I'll take you up there before school starts. I'll ask your mom tomorrow when is a good time for you to go." In addition to having a National Parks pass, Nolan also has a timeshare that he got years ago to force himself to travel beyond Boulder and not get complacent. He says that the time share is a sunk cost for him. "We'll cut through Rocky Mountain National Park tomorrow and come out the other side near Steamboat Springs where we can stay at a resort. Then we can go to Beaver Creek and stay at another resort, and after that, we can go by Red Rocks on the way back to Boulder. How does that sound?" he says, looking at Fia lying patiently nearby.

"Very cool. You know I can't help with the driving." Nolan's old jeep is a stick shift.

Kinsley yawns. A little mac and cheese is left on her plate, congealing into a plasticized mass.

Okay, so here it comes: Nolan puts her plate on the floor. Fia comes over wagging her tail, eats the remains of the pasta, and licks the plate making slurpy sounds. Then my empty bowl joins the plate. Fia sniffs the vinaigrette for a moment then licks the bowl.

“I didn’t expect so,” says Nolan. “The drive is not bad.”

Dishwashers heat water to 160 degrees, sterilizing every crevice. Nolan carries the plate and bowls to the sink, splashes water and dish liquid in them, swirls the dish cloth over each one once, then props them in the rack on the counter.

In the chair next to me, His Holiness the Dalai Lama beams me a smile. Nice of him to show on such short notice, and we are both amazed by how I haven’t squawked at all.

“What did you think we would do this week?” asks Nolan.

“Oh, I thought we would just go for a hike or two during the day, and I would make dinner to say thank you in the evening.”

“Well, the timeshares have a kitchen, but I usually eat out every day. I take a cooler with juice and milk and cereal for breakfast though.” Nolan runs a little water. “I don’t think the sink is clogged.” He looks back and smiles, “It’s just draining really slow.”

CHAPTER TEN
LAKE IRENE

WE GOT TO Celestial Seasonings a few minutes late. After breakfast, Nolan dropped Fia and Kinsley at her mother's apartment and returned in less than fifteen minutes. I'd gone down to the basement to zip up my luggage and when I went back up, Nolan was in the kitchen, his shorts pulled down to his hip, giving himself an injection of G-CSF in the side of one butt flank to boost his immune system. When he first got released from isolation, he had to give himself the shots three times a day. Now it was down to just once a week, and we would be back in Boulder before he needed another. He dropped the needle into the biohazard container on the counter and hiked his khakis back in place.

The factory's rectangular screening room had rows of benches with an aisle down the middle, and by the time we took a seat, the Celestial Seasonings Tea Story had already begun and the lights dimmed. The summer tourist season was underway and, at 10 a.m. on a weekday, the place was full of of nuclear families, some with grandma in tow, plus one punk couple dressed in black and wearing eyeliner. The Tea Story was family-friendly but cleverly done: the factory workers in the video were real people who worked in a real tea factory, not actors in a tea factory.

Video over, we were shepherded to a hallway, then through a series of exotic smelling rooms stacked floor to ceiling with hundred-pound bags of spices, until we reached a room that was sealed off with a red warehouse door, twenty feet wide. The tour guide paused while we pooled around her, then she gazed at the red metal door, and paused some more. We gazed at the red metal door, then back at her.

Mint, she said, was stored inside. If the mint wasn't isolated, the scent would permeate all the other spices, seeping into everything. In a moment, the door to the room would be lifted, just enough for us to step in quickly but safely without jostling, where we would have a mint experience unlike any we had ever dreamed of. And if anyone experiences dizziness or feels faint, the tour guide was to be informed immediately so that the door could be raised and that person let out. "Ready?" she asked and looked at us.

She's laying it on a bit thick I thought till I realized it was not a rhetorical question. She was actually making sure that we were prepared. Mentally? Spiritually? Two men arrived and raised the clacking steel door, pulling a chain on either side. Obediently, we marched inside, and the door clunked shut as soon as the last person ducked in.

And Holy Shit. Mint filled my lungs, ran its fingers through my hair, saturated my pores; the tour guide had not oversold it. A little girl let go of her mother's hand and twirled in place, arms out wide, trying to embrace the scent. People laughed. "Oh my," an old woman put her hands to her cheeks. She inhaled deeply, but you didn't have to; breathing was enough. The punk couple grinned and intertwined fingers.

Seventy-five seconds later, the tour guide clicked her stopwatch and rapped on the door. We followed the lines on the floor out of the mint room and into the factory, which may have been the loudest place on Earth, full of machines all turned up to eleven. On top of the din, old school head-banger music was blasting. The factory workers were rocking out to the heavy metal, desensitized to the sounds of actual metal. We walked around machines folding little boxes, filling them with tea bags, closing boxes and wrapping them in plastic, then putting lots of little boxes into larger shipping boxes.

The tour ended when it funneled us into the tea tasting shop. Nolan and I picked out our samples, tasted them, then headed to the cafe for lunch, and my vegetarianism collapsed when faced with roasted turkey and lettuce on a large croissant. The dining patio faced a broad green field that ran out to a line of tall trees, and we sat outside, watching wind rustle the grass. Nolan had a turkey sandwich too and talked about when he'd told Kinsley that he had cancer and might die. He wanted her prepared, just in case.

"What about you?" I asked. "Were you scared?"

"No." The trees swayed in unison. "I'm going to die some time or other. We all do eventually. What is the use of being afraid of that?"

Halfway down the breezeway, we headed to the parking lot when I doubled back to the cafe and bought pastries.

Nolan crossed Diagonal Highway, heading out of Boulder. The scenery started out as flat grassland, but we soon meandered through curving back roads, deep in the trees. Rocky Mountain National Park is an hour northwest of Boulder, but

Nolan did not take the simplest route. We drove through isolated enclaves of one or two dozen houses with maybe a general store. The tiny communities were clustered along the offshoots of the two-lane logging roads. I couldn't imagine how people made a living out here.

"Crafts," Nolan answered. Some of these places were art havens.

Nolan pulled off a logging road onto a gravelly indentation. He got an empty milk jug out of the trunk and walked to the tree line, ducking under a branch. Down an embankment was a rippling stream, but we didn't need to go that far. A tube jutted out, and water, clear as glass, flowed from it; the tube was angled so the little jet fell back into the stream. "A guy built this so people could come here and fill up their water jugs." Nolan cupped his hands and drank. "I forgot to put more jugs in the back of my car."

The water was silky cold, clean-sweet like the air in Boulder. I got my bottle of water and poured out what was left so I could fill the whole thing up with the stream water.

The streets leading to the national park entrance were a tourist black hole, seething with people swarming the restaurants and trinket stores lining the blocks. Nolan drove slowly, passing into a neatly maintained neighborhood. He flashed his pass card at the park gate, and we were through. We started the drive up I-36.

For a neophyte day-tripper, someone who is not about to sling on a backpack and hike into the untouched wilderness, Rocky Mountain National Park consists of roads winding through sub-alpine forests, windy tundra, mountains, and unending sky. These vistas are punctuated by long narrow parking lots crowded with people in a hurry to jump out of a rover, be awed, take a selfie, and dash to the next scenic pull-off. The main circuit is Trail Ridge Road, the 'highway to the sky.'

I don't know the name of the first overlook we stop at. We hike up the sidewalk, approaching an area with a waist-high stone wall, and then I spot him. Actually holding an ice cream cone. A fat man in Colorado, walking down the sidewalk, but he doesn't count. God help him, he's wearing lederhosen, without *ein unze* of irony. All smiles, a fat yellow-haired son, fat wife and fat mother follow him and clamber into an SUV as big as a bus. The people along the wall lean over the edge with odd excitement and a woman tosses a handful of Cheerios onto the rocks on the other side of the barrier.

"Oh!" pops out of my mouth. Scrambling across the rocks, not even an arm's length away, chipmunks have already grabbed the cereal. They run so fast they blur, small bundles of greedy adorableness. The woman with the Cheerios wears black sunglasses and thick gold rings. She says something in Japanese and hands cereal to her six-year-old, who pelts the chipmunks like they owe him money. Farther on, tourists speaking English in Australian are feeding their chipmunks Cheetos. White Cheddar Puffs.

"Look right there." Nolan points at the pile of rocks to the left. A plush marmot suns itself on a rock speckled with pumpkin-colored lichen. A broad meadow bowls out below the tumbled moraine that the frenzied chipmunks play on.

A couple of stops on, Nolan pulls off at Fairview Curve above a thousand-foot valley where we look at snow-draped mountains and I pull on my windbreaker. Then he parks below Forest Canyon Overlook that juts out atop a 2000-foot canyon, a basin so steep that no trails scar it. Nolan is in walking shorts and sports sandals but even he dons a hoodie as we join the line marching the long path to the top of the overlook. The gradient is not steep, but, from the exertion of walking slightly uphill, I'm huffing by the halfway mark, aware that the air has gotten thinner. We are well above the tree line and twenty degrees colder than when we were looking at chipmunks. A sign tells me I'm 11,716 feet high. At the far edge of the circular overlook, a middle-aged couple are motionless, entwined in a kiss in front of the mountainous dreamscape while their picture is taken. Newlyweds.

The Trail Ridge Store and Cafe, elevation 11,796 feet, has glaciers. One promontory of ice, several feet thick, radiating cold air, reaches like a hand toward the walkway. Nolan stares at the ice, a crease between his brows and he goes extra Nolan-quiet for a while. The glacier, no longer as thick as it used to be, is receding.

When we start driving again, we gradually start a winding decline. I look out the window and see a mountain, an entire mountain, just standing there, a temple in the blue air, from its base gripping a valley floor to a peak, streaked white with glaciers.

We corkscrew down and down.

The traffic thickens up. "So, we are coming up on a lake that it might be nice to get out and see here," Nolan says. On the left, a few yards off the road, between two pine-covered hills that come down in a wide 'V' reclines Lake Poudre, shiny as a mirror, full of reflected clouds, and swarming with people as frantic as the chipmunks were. Adults are running, children jumping, a man is kicking his legs out from one side to the other like he is dance-kick-skipping in place, and Nolan explains that we are crossing the Continental Divide. "It is pretty popular."

Every parking space is taken, and more cars hover around the edges. "Actually," he adds, "there is another place I have been curious about but never actually stopped at."

Two minutes later, we take a right onto a nondescript turn-off. Unlike Lake Poudre, Lake Irene is not visible from the road, and the dozen spaces in the small lot are empty. At the end of the parking lot, a trail leads into the pines, which close behind us and muffle the noise from the road. An eighth of a mile in, an oblong lake, stretched along the bottom of a forested meadow, has waited for us, maybe for a thousand years. Wind furrows the tea-colored water stained by wood tannins. Young pines are emerging at the water's edge, and no one else is here. No *when* else is here. The air is crisp yet full of the smell of resinous trees, and we walk the path around the edge of the lake, listening to wind in the boughs, lapping water, and gravel crunching underfoot.

The sunshine feels like it is pressing against me, using its thumb to smooth that inch where my eyebrows knit together in anger or when a headache starts. A bench is on the side of the lake under the pines, and I open the take-out box from the cafe. Nolan picks the cherry turnover and I have apple, the cracked glaze sticky on my fingertips. Then we each get a Danish and eat slowly.

About one of every seven trees is dead, and most of the dead ones are still standing bolt upright, like gray telephone poles, but I see several that are tilting at untenable angles. Nolan talks about the mountain pine beetle outbreak devastating Colorado since 2000, pointing out patchy brown areas in the sun-soaked arena. The epidemic of pests started when a drought weakened the trees. "But the forest is starting to recover," he says. "It is better than it was five years ago. If you come back here in twenty years, it will look like it never happened."

When we get to the parking lot, I head for the restroom and enjoy the big Rocky National Park surprise: the smallish, open-air wooden building has a stall, and inside that is a toilet seat screwed onto a long wooden box over a pit. I feel so pre-industrial. The weather is cool, so it's only a little stinky. When I pee, it takes a couple seconds to hit the bottom, fifteen feet below. I'm in a latrine, a big outhouse. No flushing required.

The sunlight is slanting as we hit the most winding part of the pass, a series of curves so severe they switchback on themselves, repeatedly reversing directions half a dozen times between Farview Curve and the Colorado River Trailhead. Then the road straightens out along the Kawuneeche Valley. Trail Ridge Road is only forty-eight miles long, but with all the stops along the vistas, we've taken all day. The air is a diffuse yellow. Traffic slows and starts to stack as we start passing cars that have pulled off to the edge and parked, bumper to bumper.

"I know what this is," Nolan says, looking for a gap, and we luck out: a car pulls away from the shoulder and Nolan slides into the spot. "I guess we are walking."

A long clearing in the trees reveals a low meadow dotted with three shallow ponds, thick grass, scattered stands of trees, and elk. Like movie stars, the elk are unconcerned with the people watching them as they graze, drink water, lay down. Several are cows with gangly legged calves nearby. "Elk are fairly common," says Nolan. "I was hoping to see a moose. They are rare and more solitary."

Rocky Mountain National Park: Dead trees, receding glaciers, kick-dancing Continental Divide enthusiasts, Cheeto-fed chipmunks, and marmots sprawled out like stuffed toys. And yet it has cured me, deeper than a year of meditation. Rocky Mountain National Park has unraveled the knot inside me.

Shafts of light pierce down through clouds and pines, looking like a cathedral turned inside out.

Outdoor Gothic. That's gotta be a thing.

CHAPTER ELEVEN
STEAMBOAT SPRINGS

BY THE TIME we get to Steamboat Springs, it's dark. Nolan drives just as fast at night as he does during the day, but in the dark, it is really disconcerting: Colorado is all mountain roads, so logically I know that the combination of a sudden skid plus gravity will mean plunging to our deaths. Also, deer in Colorado are oddly small, and the rabbits, which are freakishly large, stand straight up on their hind legs all the time. As we zoomed through the night, solitary deer or rabbits would suddenly loom into the headlights and I waited for the quick smack, hard brake, squeal of wheels. But they never jumped. Just stood there, spooky, on the edge of the road, watching the car speed past like skeevy hitchhikers.

Nolan parks under the hotel, and we load up a bellman cart to go to the lobby to check-in. The condo is on the third floor, and it's more than luxe enough with a kitchen, a living and dining room combo, and two bedrooms, each with their own bathroom, plus a washer-dryer in the hallway, near the room Nolan takes. I've got the room on the opposite end, which has a king-size bed with a thick white comforter, and a bathroom in gold and white. We transfer the food in the ice chest to the fridge. Nolan gets a glass of the fruit juice he drinks to regain the weight he lost battling lymphoma, opens his laptop at the dining table and says he'll be up for a couple of hours, working. I sit on the comforter in my room and meditate, get a nosebleed that's mostly dried red mucous, and read till I get sleepy.

The kitchen cabinets have a full set of dishes, and in the morning after breakfast, I follow Nolan across the street, where there is a wetland preserve with a boardwalk meandering through it. The local Rotarians have been pretty industrious. The boardwalk has placards explaining the Yampa River Wetlands ecosystem at each lookout point. Nolan identifies the fish below us that he can see but that I keep missing, and I ask him how he first realized he was sick, before he was diagnosed with lymphoma.

"I wet the bed," he says. "I mean, I knew that one day that sort of thing was bound to start happening, but it seemed pretty weird for it to start this early in life, so I went to the doctor."

"What was it like to be in an isolation unit for a month? I don't know the right way to say this, but I would dream of having thirty days, basically locked up with nowhere I had to go and no one I had to go meet. I know you didn't want to get sick, of course, but the chance to read and catch up on movies and read books and articles and more books for thirty days. It's like jail without the prison gangs."

"I know what you mean and, yeah, you would think that it would be pretty enjoyable, but it turns out you can only watch so many videos before you get tired of watching them, and you can only read so many books for however many days before eventually even that no longer holds your interest the way you imagined it would. A month in an isolation unit actually gets pretty boring, and that's a problem in itself."

I take a swig out of my water bottle. It's early in the day, but it feels humid, and I don't know if that's because it's a humid day or because we're standing over a wetland. "So, when you got out, were you able to take care of yourself, or did you need like a home health aide?"

A fish pops out. Nolan points, but I don't turn fast enough to see anything except a glint of silver, and I stare at the water as he answers. "They don't let you out if you're still pretty sick or completely helpless. My dad came up to stay with me when I was released, and he tried to be helpful, but that got on my nerves pretty quick in a counterintuitive way. I would be lying in bed, and he would ask if I wanted him to bring me something to drink and I'd say 'No, I'm fine.' Then I would be lying there thinking, 'You know what? Come to think of it, I would actually like a glass of water.' Then I'd have to call him back. That kind of felt like I was bugging him, even though that's what he was there for, but feeling like I was bothering someone annoyed me. I don't like having to ask for help, so after a week, I had him leave and go back home."

"Were you up and around by then?"

"Well enough. It was just too annoying having someone ask me if I needed help, even if it was sincere, which I knew it was."

"I got shingles five years ago and I was flat on my back, in bed, in pain for days." I finally see a fish glide past me. "Actually being sick, really sick to the point that I needed to ask my mom to bring me a drink, to ask for help, it weirded me out. She wasn't annoying; she started her career in nursing, so she checked up on me at intervals but otherwise just let me rest, but I'd never been confronted with the idea that I might need help on such a basic level. It shocked me."

We walk a few blocks back into town, the bottle of water that I've crammed into a pocket bonking against my leg with each step. The resort has a brittle artifice stalking it: The town is immaculate. Sloping lawns have manicured bushes, flowerbeds and, just about everywhere, bronze statues. Many are sit-by-me statues, those benches with a revered historical figure sitting on one end, looking amused: Mark Twain with bow tie, Ben Franklin with bifocals, Winston Churchill with a bowler hat. Street urchin children in 1800's period clothes, playing marbles or holding puppies are also popular, and the urchins are not quite impoverished enough to create any thoughts about social justice. Occasional statues of generic Native Americans, mostly women holding a basket and gazing at the sky while some Great Plains wind blows through their metallic hair, show up too, and of course, lots of statues of elk. None of the statues are of specific Native Americans: no Red Cloud, no Black Elk, no Sitting Bull. Also, no Elizabeth Cady Stanton or Rosa Parks.

We eat pizza in a strip mall. In the middle of the parking lot is a five-foot bronze bust of an Indian Maiden—lots of beads, two feathers. Then we head back to the hotel. Nolan puts in two hours of work on the computer while I read on the balcony, where branches from a willow brush the railing.

A five-minute drive from the hotel is a wooded park, with a hard-packed dirt trail lined with waist-high grasses and stands of white trunked aspen fluttering their leaves. Nolan says the aspen leaves are quaking. He digs around on the floor behind the passenger seat and hands me a waist pack that'll hold my water bottle and cell phone.

We hike an easy trail, two yards wide. The park is busy. Three women push strollers up the part of the path that turns from tan dirt into pebbles and then into fist-sized rocks for a stretch, jostling their tough Colorado babies in order to reach higher ground. I tell Nolan about my dad's spinal arthritis, early-stage Alzheimer's, and COPD and how my mom is getting hard-of-hearing and won't admit it. He replies that his parents are also getting old and when he calls home, his mom tries to guilt him into visiting more often by dropping phrases like, 'we won't be here forever.'

"Does it work?"

"Yeah," he says, stepping on a thin green snake crossing the dirt. "I make plans to see them at least twice a year now."

"Snake Nolan," I say as he marches on. I don't know that snakes have expressions, but this one manages to look aggrieved as it slides into the foliage, uninjured but clearly having a 'day.' Matching the color of summer grass perfectly, it vanishes in the underbrush. Nolan turns back just as the snake seems to no longer exist. "You just stepped on a snake," I say, "A pretty one."

"Did I?" He looks about.

The tree-lined trail into Strawberry Park Natural Hot Springs that afternoon passes massage huts and men's and women's changing cabins, before you get to the multiple upper and lower pools. They are fed by scalding water pouring from a pipe at the base of the topmost pool, where chipmunks are chasing each other around in what looks like chipmunk playtime, but what is probably chipmunk fist fights over territory. Cute.

The pools are divided into several basins by gray stone walls, water flowing from one to another, stepping down pool by pool. Nolan points out which ponds are hot or medium hot and which one is Very Hot as we dump our towel bags on steamer lounges on the deck. Glare bounces around as I ease into the one hundred degree starter pool and the water smells of sulfur. Some people are swimming around in sunglasses. Others loiter under the waterfalls where the pools step down to lower levels. The pools have a slow, constant migration. For no clear reason, even when you are situated comfortably on a low bench against one of the walls with a little whirlpool swirling between your shoulders, you feel the need to move to a different area to see what the water over there is like.

It's hot. Like the water you just left. Eventually I try the Very Hot pool and muscles melt off my bones. I feel jellied and unjointed. The sun becomes too much, water flashing in a way that seems noisy, and I drag up the stairs and lay limp on a steamer lounge. For a moment, drained by the thermal water, I'm able to think about Lauren without a cloud of emotion. I can see my anger apart from myself, but, sensing that I can't sustain the separation of myself and my emotional reaction to thinking about her for long, I turn my mind away. We've been here for hours but haven't felt the time passing. I have a slight headache, realize I'm dehydrated and wonder who I should suggest some needed signage to: "The Water is Hot. Stay Hydrated. Take Frequent Breaks."

Nolan brings me a cup of slushy Coca-Cola from the concession and lays on the lounge next to mine, and when the air dries us off, we drive back to town.

CHAPTER TWELVE
THE DEADFALL

AFTER WASHING UP the breakfast dishes in the morning, we load the car. The idea in a timeshare is to leave the place as neat as it was when you arrived. The day's plan is to drive to Glenwood Canyon, where we'll hike a mile up a steep trail, Nolan warns me, to get to Hanging Lake, a clear green lake holding on to the side of a cliff, with multiple waterfalls pouring into it. We're parked behind the hotel, a few spaces over from a dumpster that Nolan tosses a trash bag into.

So here's what happens. While Nolan's dumping the trash bag, I riffle around the waist pack that he let me borrow. Besides the main pocket and water holder, I find other pockets, one with change, another with mesh netting, and a last little zippered gem with a Ziplock bag inside that I take out, inspecting in the morning sun. Looks like poop. Fia poop.

Nolan gets into the car and I hand him a Ziplock bag of dog poop. He looks at it. I see every cell in his body pause. He gets out of the car and walks back to the dumpster. The car is angled just enough so that in the passenger rearview mirror, I see the back side of Nolan as he stands at the dumpster after he has dropped the poop into it. He seems to be staring at the side of the dumpster, but I'm sure his eyes are not actually focused on it. The stillness in his posture tells me that even Nolan can have a "What was that?" moment.

Over-thinking is not adorable, endearingly insecure, or laughably needy like in a romantic comedy. It's the pointless confusion of the human condition made visibly awkward.

This is Over-Thinking: So I open the last pocket on the waist pack and pull out a flattened Ziplock bag full of Fia dog poop. Immediately I start to throw it away, thinking that, ages ago, Nolan walked the dog, picked up after her, put it in the zippered pocket and for whatever reason—the phone rang, the rain came down, he got a better waist pack—completely forgot about it and hasn't used the waist pack again since then. There's a garbage dumpster seven car spaces away, behind the resort where we are parked. I should throw this out before we drive a couple hours to a lake on the side of a cliff. But wait. Is it actually dog poop? I mean, I thought it was, but maybe not. Maybe it's something else that he wants to keep. Or maybe it is dog poop, but Nolan carried it for a reason. I stare at the dashboard; perhaps it's some kind of special wolf poop. In case you run into a wolf? That makes no sense. Or, in case you run into an aggressive elk, you throw it at the elk. That makes less sense. Maybe it's just Fia's dog poop that Nolan cleaned up eons ago while walking her and forgot about after he put it in a waist pack that he doesn't use because he got a better camel-back pack and the poop fossilized and I just handed him a Ziplock bag of fossilized dog poop and he is lingering by a dumpster behind a ritzy resort wondering why I just handed him a bag of dog poop instead of just quietly throwing it away myself without saying anything as *He* over-thinks it.

Ancient cultures embodied intelligence in a great variety of gods, demons, titans, and elves. Normally, when Nolan over-thinks things, he invents new medical instruments that gleam in a surgeon's exquisitely skilled hands, saving the lives of the just and the unjust alike. When I over-think, I hand out bags of dog poop. You're welcome.

Nolan buckles his seat belt and starts the car, "On to Hanging Lake."

࿐

We drove through the Colorado mineral belt, highways carved through deep striated canyons, clusters of mountains dark and jagged, and lonely spires jutting out of surrounding plateau.

Hanging Lake's parking lot was far too small for the mob of cars prowling through it. "I've never seen it this crowded," Nolan said in his most shocked-for-Nolan tone of voice. He circled twice, skirting cars stacked three deep at the head of each aisle. "This is the first time the lot's been full." More cars were trying to come in, horns honking. We left without getting out and went across the road into Glenwood Springs for lunch at Tokyo Taipei.

Nolan had yet to glance at a map, and his car was too old to have GPS, but he knew where every good restaurant was in the state. Without the hike to Hanging Lake, we made it to Beaver Creek Resort before the four o'clock check-in time at the Sheridan, so we left our bags behind the front desk and walked over to the Westin for drinks at the outdoor bar by the double-Olympic-sized pool.

Nolan doesn't drink. Even in college he didn't, and way

back then, I asked him why. He said it just never appealed to him; he'd had drinks, but never found the experience interesting, so he stopped. Nothing more. No overriding philosophy or religious stricture.

Me, however, felt that drinks at bars, especially mixed drinks that were fancy, were huge treats. No one in my family drank much. Dad couldn't. He was an alcoholic the whole time I was growing up, getting loaded on weekends and lying on his back on the living room floor, next to the high fidelity stereo with headphones on, listening to jazz: Miles Davis, Dave Brubeck, Count Basie. The next morning, he lay on the couch while Mom berated him, his head splitting from the hangover. However bad his drinking got though, he never missed work, hangover or not.

He stopped drinking the year I left for college, accumulating sobriety chips from Alcoholics Anonymous that were stacked up on top of his dresser. While I was home the following summer, idling in the afternoon in the living room, he walked in and apologized for any harm his drinking had caused. He paused, then walked back out; that was it. Years later, it crossed my mind how much it had cost him to humble himself to his daughter like that. Once or twice a month, Mom had a glass of wine in the evening, usually after a bath when she was in pajamas and relaxing before bed. Sometimes I would have a glass too, but that was the extent of the drinking at home.

Nolan and I sat at an umbrella table. I had a margarita and was surprised by how tame it was compared to how they are served in Texas, where the rims of the neon drinks are crusted in flavored specialty salt. Bikinied bodies walked around, men with hairy chests lay on loungers, the atmosphere was vacation festive. At four o'clock, we took our bags up to the room at the Sheridan, then walked to the corner outside the hotel and caught a shuttle to the ski resort at the top of the mountain; the rich people's resort, Nolan called it.

The rich people's resort had an even higher density of historical figure statues than those that populated the lowlands, with a relaxed Albert Einstein, an Abraham Lincoln with his stovepipe hat on the bench next to him, an ice-skating child, a bear, an eagle, a beaver, and more Native Americans, including an Indian Brave, which can't be the right way to refer to him. The ubiquitous statues, showing up every few yards in some areas, must be reference points so that people can meet up with their party: "Be back at Einstein at five, so we can all head to dinner." Set right at the base of the ski run, the rich people's resort was a maze of hotels, restaurants, and shoppes, all set in a bulked-up Alpine village architecture. I loitered at the storefront of an art gallery full of modern works, including, near the large window, a fiberglass sculpture that looked very Jeff Koons.

We heard music and wandered over. Hazel Miller, Colorado's Soul Queen, was giving an open-air concert. Nolan and I picked our way around people on blankets and lawn chairs to some unclaimed space and sat down. The music, mostly covers of hits from the '70s and '80s, was upbeat, and the spectators' dancing around the front of the stage was serviceable. We listened until the first shadows of evening stretched across the grass, then started hiking back into town. A wide sidewalk ran along the road, separating the traffic from the back yards of multi-million-dollar homes. A spiced mint scent was wafting around, and Nolan pointed to a tree draping over a fence, "Eucalyptus."

A barefoot woman in a cotton djellaba drifted slowly,

not quite in a straight line, up the sidewalk, followed by a man wearing flip flops, jeans, and a shirt unbuttoned down the front. We smiled and nodded; she smiled and nodded; the man following did not bother. She looked familiar and several sidewalk squares later, I realized she was a TV actress from the seventies but couldn't remember her name or what series she'd been on. A motion ahead of me blurred near the ground.

With his sport sandal, Nolan kicked the snake in the head, just like in the sport sandal ads. The snake was curving down into the indentation between two squares of sidewalk. Brown and an inch in diameter, it was much bigger than the petite Smooth Green Snake from yesterday.

"Snake Nolan!"

He turned and jogged back just as its back-end disappeared into the sidewalk. I looked down. There was nowhere it could have gone, no hole, no crack penetrating the ground, just white concrete, but it was gone. Nolan looked where I was looking. "I missed it."

"Nolan, you kicked it."

"Yeah?'

"It was big."

"Yeah? I'd have liked to have seen it."

We ate leftovers in the hotel, then walked over to the Westin's Riverfront patio and sat near the fire, propping our feet up while I waited on a cocktail, the second mixed drink in one day. A hum rose all around from clumps of vacationers chatting over appetizers and beer. Four boys, aged eight to ten, ran past us, then sat on the other side of the fire debating a trip to the arcade that the resort had stashed downstairs somewhere. Two of the boys were brothers and had each brought a friend along on the family trip. Families treated the resort as a 'free range' area, letting kids run around unwatched yet contained at the same time. My guess was that mommy and daddy were in the hot tub, tossing back a few.

My drink arrived. The stars and the crisp smear of the Milky Way were sparkling bright in the evening chill and the drink was marvelously strong.

&

The parking lot in front of the East Lake Creek Trail is tiny. The next afternoon, when we park, it takes less than ten steps to go from Nolan's car to the sign on the trailhead that says, "Private Property. This trail exists as an easement by agreement between the U S F S and the Property Owners. No access or travel off of trail allowed." There's more on the sign, but it's obscured by tree branches. Towards the end, peeking out behind leaves, I see the sign's last word: ". . . risk."

The hike starts off pleasantly enough, a comfortable tree-lined trail, then it starts to climb. Just as I'm getting winded, it levels off, even dips down for a few yards, then climbs again. Gradually, looking out when there is a break in the trees on the left side, I see that we are gaining some real altitude. Forested land lays out below us in a curved valley, then the trees fold up around us again, straight white trunks of aspen in deep stands. On the right, the mountain slopes up, trees upon trees, aspen and pine. The narrow path climbs again, but this time it keeps climbing, and, getting winded, I need to catch my breath. Unfamiliar plants line the trail; something fern-like and Paleozoic is at my feet, with spiky purple flowers.

As we ascend, we come upon a deadfall on the hill sloping above us. Two trees have fallen, or one has fallen and taken down its neighbor. A pond of yellow-white light floods where the canopy is broken by the missing pillars, and a tangled frenzy of green life crowds the forest floor. Already the dead trunks are disappearing under matted brush; and bark, half-sloughed off, is decaying back into soil. One new pine, eight feet tall, is winning the fight for light, growing faster than another, half its size, a few feet below it. Shafts of light come through a shaggy fir behind the sapling and spear it at intervals. In a century, it will be 70 feet tall, claiming the sun at the top, like the trees all around. Three hundred years after that—a hundred thousand sunrises—it will topple onto the slope, opening a twenty-foot radius for the fastest seedling to claim its space.

We climb further and then the path finally levels off again, and the temperature drops suddenly, twenty degrees lower in the span of a few steps as we enter a thick, shadowed canopy. Insects are flitting around, and a cranberry colored one darts past. We're in a micro-climate; there's even a change in humidity in here. It lasts about thirty feet, then we're through it and back into dappled sunlight and warmth, where ahead, two massive trees create a sun cross, a disk of light forming where their branches almost touch with a compass of beams radiating off it.

The view opens up again and looks out to yet another stunning study of infinity contained: vistas of lush and rugged painted mountains and valleys. On the left side, the tops of a forest of trees do not quite reach up to the trail, as if that side of the mountain, in a giant stair step, has dropped down a level. Beyond it are sky and peaks stacked behind peaks. I notice the upcoming dark patch of ground before I think of its implications and follow along without adjusting my stride.

In retrospect, sliding backwards down a narrow cliff-edge path was interesting mainly because it reassured me that my inner reptile brain could still kick in. The dark patch was mud, slick and on an incline just steep enough to dump me over the side. There was no actual thinking involved, just widening eyes, windmill-arm flailing panic, clawing at the air. One foot sensed the beginnings of empty space, and a flat flash of consequence—air, gravity, plunging—smacked several layers of brain all at once—reptile brain, amygdala, future planning pre-frontal lobe—as my brain realized my ass was toppling backwards off a scenic cliff into a sea of aspen and pine.

Nolan grabbed me. Three of my fingernails managed to rake him above his bicep, before he wrested me back onto solid footing, followed by a moment of stillness and an odd patient look on his face. My nails were still digging in. I un-dug them. A serene breeze stirred the high clouds, quaking the leaves.

❧

The next morning, we check out of the Sheridan and drive to Red Rocks Amphitheater. If ancient gods ever created a stage for themselves, it's Red Rocks. In Greece, I saw amphitheaters carved into the sides of mountains, and in Rome, the Colosseum. This was different; this is magnificence. The walls, massive slabs of red sandstone, are sentinels, standing red megaliths forming three sides of the concert venue. On the right is Ship Rock. Forming the stage and rising behind it is the tilted disk, Stage Rock, and on the left, Creation Rock. Trees and bushes grew along the edge of the stairs running up the sides of the bleacher seating.

Someone blew a whistle. Across the bottom row of bleachers spread a line of teenagers in shorts and sun visors. Dozens suddenly started sprinting up the 70 rows of seating, neatly avoiding the tourists wandering around. A trio of beardies were sitting in the middle of the 9000-seat arena, playing guitars and singing. Farther down, closer to the stage, where workmen were setting up for whoever was performing that night, women were doing yoga, their mats laid out across two bleacher levels.

From the top of the bleachers, you could see hills, green and tan, a blue lake in their midst, and in the distance, Denver, fifteen miles away. We had lunch at the Red Rocks Grille and sat at a table out back with a twenty-mile view and a hawk whirling against the cirrus. Even after we finished eating, we sat sipping water, listening to the hills.

Three decades ago in Mexico, I got altitude sickness while hiking in Copper Canyon. The top of the canyon sits at 7600 feet, so the canyon is really a mountain, sunk into another mountain. An unforecast blizzard poured over the canyon lip while Nolan and Eduardo, who was also in the hiking club, struggled to get me up the path, only ten inches wide in places. The altitude sickness meant I could breathe or walk, but not both at the same time. The sudden blizzard meant that if the club did not hike out fast enough, the dirt road back into town would be invisible. Nolan held my arm and pulled from the front, while Eduardo, his hands on my ass when the trail was steepest, pushed from behind.

When we reached the top, everyone scrambled into the truck of the hotel manager's husband, just as he was about to leave us. He'd been hired for the day to drive the UT hiking club to the top of the canyon but had explained earlier that he wouldn't risk losing his truck if the weather turned; he couldn't afford to replace the axle if he went off the road. We made it back to Creel as the blizzard, in a great spasm, covered the road, the forest, the town itself, and then the Hiking Club warmed up with mugs of hot cocoa in the hotel bar, watching the snow sift down, and I promised Nolan that I'd get him a sweater to thank him for the life-save. The sweater would be green, I said, since he looked best in green, and he said I didn't need to thank him. I said I would anyway. When we got back to Texas, I remembered my promise but just never got around to it.

We took another look at the amphitheater, and when Nolan headed to the bathroom, I went to the basement of the Visitor Center. In the gift shop was a green-and-gray Red Rocks sweatshirt hoodie. Thirty years late, but perfect.

The crease between my eyebrows was gone, smoothed out days ago by the hikes, glorious views, and easy company.

Then we drove back to Boulder and sat in Nolan's living room watching the dark flow in through his invisible walls while I told him everything, about my niece Lauren and her daughter Jovi and Celiac disease and the aging American electrical grid, for hours into the night.

PART TWO

CHAPTER THIRTEEN
AUGUST 2016

In San Antonio, the heat in August has weight, coiling underneath the breeze, pushing back when you move. Automated calls from City Public Service declare an official Peak Energy Demand Day and tell us not to turn on major appliances in the afternoon to avoid rolling brownouts; the demand for air conditioning is causing a load on the system. I close the blinds to keep the heat out of the house. When Mom gets back from Thrift Town, she has news.

Bryn is Wyatt's grandmother, so she's Lauren's grandmother-in-law, and like Mom, Bryn began her career in nursing. But after ten years she started working for a pharmaceutical, providing drug samples to doctors, getting them to switch brands and avoid generics; later, she supervised other pharmaceutical reps. She worked a lot of years, raised her kids, buried her husband, and decided it was time to enjoy life, free of obligations. She lived in a building for adults over sixty and had a clique of girl friends that liked to have lunch downtown on the Riverwalk and take bus trips every couple of months to the casinos in Eagle Pass. She also liked to shop at Thrift Town.

Bryn and Mom got caught up near the blue jean racks. They hadn't seen each other since last Christmas when Jovi sang in the Eden Park Elementary Holiday Choir, and Mom finds out that during the spring, Bryn had often gone over to the school to eat with Jovi because Jovi would sit by herself to avoid other children who had gluten in their lunches. Now that school was out, Jovi was in 'Purple Kid Squad', the school district's summer camp, which was summer school without the actual schooling part. Kids, wearing the school's purple t-shirts, were dropped off in the morning and given activities such as arts and crafts, which meant a coloring book; then recess, meaning an hour on the school playground; then entertainment, which was a movie they had seen before, usually involving a Disney princess, then lunch, and more recess.

Purple Kid costs six hundred dollars for June and July, and while that was six hundred dollars more expensive than Mom's house, it was half the cost of regular day care, assuming you had six hundred dollars to spend on child care, which Lauren and Wyatt didn't, but had to pay anyway. The kids in Purple Kid Squad had to be picked up in the afternoon, and that's where Bryn came in. She had been picking up Jovi at two o'clock and keeping her at her senior-living, toy-free condo until Lauren got off from work.

But by September, Lauren started running out of childcare options. Bryn was the babysitter of last resort, not only because she wanted to get back to her long lunches and aqua-aerobics, but because she too had noticed Jovi's weight loss and complained to Lauren and Wyatt that Jovi was ill. Lauren didn't want to hear it, and, once the school year started, Bryn refused to let babysitting cut into her schedule anymore. So Lauren had started to miss a lot of work because now, instead of Mom picking up Jovi, Lauren was the one having to pick up Jovi every time she threw up at school.

A doctor visit was scheduled.

Weeks earlier, Mom had loaded up on school supplies for Jovi and sent a text to Lauren that she could come pick the supplies up anytime. Lauren called. Jovi had been diagnosed with Celiac disease. If Mom was not too busy, she and Jovi would drop by after school.

I was already home from work when Lauren pulled into the driveway and rang the bell, waiting for Mom to answer the door before entering. Jovi hugs Mom, sits on her lap and prattles about all the things first graders do and about her new homeroom teacher, Mrs. Rodriguez, who keeps a guinea pig named Herman in the classroom. "If you're the best behaved all day, you get to pet Herman and change his water. I came in second on Wednesday." She tries to explain the convoluted system for picking the best-behaved winner.

I talk to Jovi for a bit, say nothing to Lauren, and go to my room after a few minutes where I can still hear Mom and Lauren's conversation, which is as formal as an armistice. There is no mention of the recent troubles. Lauren leaves after an hour, Mom helping her load the school supplies into the car and the grocery bags of gluten-free foods that I had again slogged over to Whole Foods to get. When they're gone, Mom tells me that Lauren said 'thank you' for the groceries. She has started testing which gluten-free pasta Jovi likes best. Mom sits on the end of my bed. "You should have stayed and talked."

"I'm sick of Lauren."

"She's family."

"Then she should have listened to us."

"She's doing the best she can," says Mom.

"No. She's not."

When I had talked to Nolan that last night in Boulder, the one thing that I did not tell him about was the spanking. Admitting that in the twenty-first century, my great-niece was spanked while I just sat and listened to her scream was too damning to say out loud.

My family is very private, even amongst ourselves. Those families that share everything and call each other best friends, hugging each time they lay eyes on each other, seem artificial as tinsel to me. Towards the end of September, my sister Tessa calls and reports that Lauren and Wyatt have been separated for most of the year and that they were getting divorced, papers signed already. Tessa doesn't know or won't tell us the reasons for the divorce and doesn't know who divorced who. She says she just found out herself about it because when she called Callie's house and Lauren answered, she demanded to know why Lauren was doing her laundry at Callie's house all the time instead of in her own house since Lauren can't be visiting her sister Callie that often. Lauren had finally told her the truth, that she and Jovi were living at Callie's. Lauren had sounded increasingly distraught on the phone—Tessa used the term 'batty'—and Tessa wanted us to know why. My guess is that Jovi must have been told not to say anything, ensuring that a new generation of hoarding secrets was begun. Tessa lays out the rest of the divorce details: shared custody, Wyatt gets the house.

So, no house, no college degree, and a part-time kid. If I ever find Lauren's lawyer, I'll kick him in the knee.

I try to think back to when Tessa divorced Reid, Callie and

Lauren's father, but I was in graduate school in Los Angeles at the time and mainly remember that when I came home for a holiday that year, Tessa looked mournful and underweight. Tessa was eleven years older than me and had lived her life like it was a pop song until she hit her thirties. At least twice, that had caught up to her with grim, exhausting, or depression-inducing results, including when she divorced Reid and had to move back to San Antonio and work out how to raise two daughters as a single mother.

During the brief time that I was in the living room for Lauren's detente visit, I noticed that Jovi was relaxed, and Lauren had a smaller purse, too small for a wooden spoon spanking implement. So spankings and the threat of spankings had stopped, but I was still simmering. Emotionally, I could not let go of the anger in the same way that I could now move past trivia, such as problems with my students.

My parents take Jovi to the Hasseltin football game on Friday evening, and she spends the night. With a little wheedling, Mom gets Jovi to tell all she's seen: "Last Saturday, Mommy drank a big glass of wine, cried and cried, and had to lay down all weekend."

The divorce was finalized.

I sleep through the night, my insomnia no longer chronic like it's been all year, and I start reading *Zen for Beginners.* I was taking a break from the anger management fare that I hadn't been able to focus on for months anyway because I was so angry about Lauren. Perhaps a more holistic approach to a calm mind and generous outlook towards humanity might pay off better. I'd already re-read the Dalai Lama's Art of Happiness.

On Thursday, I come home early from work, thinking that I'll spend Friday grading at home, then start the weekend early by reading on the patio. The house is quiet; Mom and Dad are out, and I sit in the stillness thinking about Mom's comment that I need to start talking to Lauren again, but I can't even visualize it. The urge to tell Lauren off is overwhelming, and the best move is to go in my room and shut the door whenever she comes over, to minimize the stress for both her and me. After her first formal meeting with Mom, Lauren slid back into her usual frivolous conversations with endless stretches of trivia: how slow the waitress was at Ding How that afternoon, how incompetent one of her co-workers had been, what fashion show she'd watched on TV. Mom would listen and interject appropriately, using conversation as an end in itself, a vehicle to establish bonds even when the conversation lacked all substance. I'm a dreary mess at light conversation, but Mom and Lauren are chit-chat masters, dancing with the details of daily life.

I hear a car pull into the driveway but stay on the couch with the hum of the air conditioner clicking on, then the bang of the front door opening. Dad immediately goes down the hall to their room. Mom turns on the kettle and clatters some mugs out of a kitchen cabinet for tea.

"Your dad has prostate cancer," she says, dropping her purse on the coffee table. "They'll put him on the schedule and start chemo in December, then radiation treatment in January."

CHAPTER FOURTEEN

NUG PORN

I TAKE *ZEN for Beginners* back to the library and, excluding books on the legal history of the plant or social justice issues, I check out everything the San Antonio Library system has on marijuana. Even Mirador College's library has the six-hundred-page *Encyclopedia of Cannabis* just sitting on a shelf, waiting for me to lug it home. For a long time, I had been thinking that I should research weed in order to help Dad with his back pain, but I had never gotten around to it. Now, I read eight books in six weeks, taking notes and spending every evening and weekend like a good academic, immersed in information.

Books over three years old are out-of-date already. The information on weed was evolving that fast. One book, *Green: A Field Guide to Marijuana*, has page after page of high-quality close-ups of different strains of marijuana flowers, framed against a black background. So, buds, just buds. The pictures are called 'nug porn' and, admittedly, weed has a complex variety I was not expecting, with a dozen shades of green accented with purple, frosted white, red, orange, and yellow. The buds are as tentacled as a space alien. I buy *Brave New Weed* and *Cannabis Pharmacy*, then spend days highlighting information, typing up notes on which weed strains are best for cancer treatment, nausea, Alzheimer's, pain, and anxiety, and studying terpenes, sativas, indicas, and the human cannabinoid system.

Mom and Dad's weeks become a haze of trips to doctors and clinics to get tests done, interspersed with babysitting duties. By November, Jovi, on a gluten-free diet, has gone a month without getting sick. Grade schools are closed for an entire week for Thanksgiving, but parents still have to work. The split custody means that Jovi stays with Lauren from Sunday evening through Tuesday, and she stays with Wyatt, Wednesday through Friday. They alternate weekends. Mom says the child is being passed around like luggage, but Jovi seems calmer, no longer talking incessantly as she had a year earlier.

I start focusing my research on the Texas legal code. More than four ounces of weed is a felony, with the potential for years in jail and high legal fees. If I get caught with less than four ounces, I'll face a fine and less than a year in jail. Plus, I'll be unemployed. Bexar County Colleges requires that any faculty who has any run-in with the law must report the incident to the District within three days so the situation can be assessed. And losing my job would be catastrophic: on the rare occasions that we hire new English faculty, seventy people apply for the position, so even when you hit all the right bells and whistles, it's hard as hell to become a tenured English professor even once. No one would hire an English prof formerly fired for interstate weed.

I tell Mom I'm gonna go visit Nolan for a few days over the holidays. With all she's juggling with Dad and his doctor visits, she mutters that I deserve to have some fun and asks if

I'll need a ride to the airport, but beyond that, she doesn't really pay much attention. The plan, of course, is not to visit Nolan but to go to Denver, buy weed, and get back to Texas without being detained. Mitch flat out tells me not to go.

"It's too risky," he says when we meet for lunch, and I tell him I'm going to bring marijuana back to Texas for my dad. "Seriously Alene, if you got caught. Your job. Plus, you don't even know if your mom will let him take it, even if you do bring it back. You should ask her first."

"If I did," I say, "she would automatically tell me not to do it." The decision to get weed for Dad was never a decision. It was simply what had to be done. Dad might suffer during chemotherapy and there was cannabis out there that could prevent that, that could make such pain and anxiety unnecessary and therefore totally pointless. Who allows that? What would I think of myself in January, when he would be undergoing treatment and I was sitting on the couch wondering if the day could have gone so much easier on him?

Mitch is still listing the dangers of my weed acquisition scheme. He has never seen the inside of a prison but starts vividly imagining the trauma that even a brief detention in a Texas jail would cause me. To shift his focus, I ask him about the boys, then zone out as he details how smart they are and how well Lewin can read and Archie can draw, count, and balance on one foot for some reason.

Once I decide to bring back cannabis, the semester goes by amazingly fast. To have a looming goal—a project with a countdown as firm as the date for a rocket launch, a project that within a few weeks could blow up my intricately constructed life—that goal made me immune to the trivia of delinquent assignments and poor grammar. My students could pass or not pass, spell or not spell. Screw it; it's their life, and I've got my own issues to deal with like staying out of jail. Marijuana may be recreational in Colorado, but this is Texas.

I look at the calendar. The last day of final exams is December 10th, and all my grades and reports must be turned in by the 13th, plus, I'll need a day to pack. I go online and look up Southwest Airlines' schedule and super-saver airfares to Denver. I want to land early enough to get from the airport to my hotel downtown while it's still light outside, and in December in Denver, the sun goes down at 4:40 p.m. Then I'll need a day to shop, plus a day to hang out with Nolan would be nice. And then my weed and I will catch the bus back to Texas.

Choosing a hotel is more complicated. I print out a map of downtown Denver—the City Center—complete with hotels, bus stops, Union Station, and the Greyhound Terminal. It takes all afternoon to figure out what hotel to book. I'm paralyzed by the idea that I might pick the wrong one, that there's a better one that's closer, nicer, safer. Any hotel with 'Grand' in its name is too expensive. I steer away from the cheap places too. Under a hundred dollars a night is too seedy to stay in with my anticipated room full of cannabis, meaning slightly less than four ounces of edibles. I'm expecting four ounces of edibles will be pricey, but I don't really know.

By the time I pick a good hotel, close to several bus stops, at a good price of about a hundred and change, the room is taken because I was so slow about booking it. Over-thinking is expensive. I book a different room at the same hotel but at a higher price and eat the cost, turning my mind away from the expense of the airport shuttle, the airfare, the hotel, and the Greyhound bus fare, which, at $120, is steep enough to surprise me. The plane ticket to Denver is $170, but a mantra,

"My parents paid more for my education than they paid for their house," rolls through my mind. A trip to Denver to make sure Dad can get through chemo is a reasonable return on their investment. And yet, as I'm going through all the planning, there's that thing where you don't sweat exactly, but nervousness gives you that real sharp armpit smell.

By the time I'm done typing in my credit card for Southwest, Greyhound, and the Residence Inn Marriott, the armpit smell is ripe. And I really am feeling too hot; I go to the living room and find that Dad has inched the thermostat up to 80 degrees. He's been lying on the couch watching a football game, wrapped up in a tattered old blanket. I stare at the thermostat. My mom notices and says, "What did he have it on?"

Dad responds, "It's on seventy-seven degrees like it always is."

"I saw you turn it up to seventy-eight."

"No, I didn't."

"You did."

"When?"

"Just a while ago."

"I don't remember."

"I watched you do it."

My head is light. Mom looks at me. "Is it too hot in your room?" then back to Dad. "I told you the house isn't cold. It's that medicine making you feel too cold or too hot. The house is fine."

I turn the setting down to seventy-eight, thinking that I'll drop it to seventy-six for the night after they are in bed. There's no weed that can solve this though, I'm sure.

I am not as brave as I wish I was and not even as brave as I used to be. When Nolan and I were undergrads, the University of Texas Hiking Club had about fifty students, and on any given trip, fifteen to twenty-five would sign up. I went on some day hikes and short camping trips with the club to Lost Maples, Hidden Falls, and Enchanted Rock, but the trip to Copper Canyon over Spring Break in '86, the trip where I got altitude sickness and had to be rescued, required a lot of preparation. The club would drive to Presidio on the Texas border, cross into Ojinaga in Mexico, then take the Pacífico Railroad through Mexico to Copper Canyon, Creel, and Topolobampo on the coast in Sinaloa.

As an undergrad, I was still a military dependent, and the week before the trip, I took the bus from UT's campus, seven miles out to Bergstrom Air Force Base, for travel counseling and booster shots. I sat in a doctor's office, across from the fattest person I had ever seen in the U.S. military, a major, with a bald brown head that had ripples on it like the back of a pug. He sat there for a while behind his desk, a 1960s industrial metal hulk, without saying anything, head at an angle, leaning on his fist, his eyes closed.

I waited.

Without opening his eyes, he said, "So, you're going to Mexico."

"Yes. The UT hiking club is gonna caravan to Presidio—"

"Ah-ah-ah." He stopped me. "How are you getting back?"

Okay. Odd. "Well, we're taking the train back from Los Mochis to Ojinaga, where we will cross back to Presidio on the American side and pick up our cars for the drive back to Austin."

"And what if that doesn't work?"

"We have it all planned."

"Yes," he said, "that's the plan. That's plan 'A.' But what if something goes wrong and you can't get back home that way? What is plan 'B'?"

"Plan 'B'?"

He was awake now, using a slow melodious voice, still slumped forward against his desk, still inexplicably fat for an Air Force officer, but his head was off his fist, and his large amber eyes were considering me. "Plans fall apart all the time. Trains get missed, or trains don't run. Money gets stolen; people get separated from their group, and they get stranded. What is your plan 'B'?"

"If we couldn't take the train back?"

"Not we. You. What will *you* do? What is *your* plan 'B' for getting *yourself* home?"

I came up with a plan 'B.' It involved buses and getting back to the border, to Juarez or Nuevo Laredo, places I knew how to cross.

"And if that doesn't work? Whenever you travel you start with plan 'A.' And you always have a backup plan 'B.' And then, you need a backup to the backup. Plan 'C'. And no matter how crazy or desperate or improbable it is, when everything else falls apart, plan 'C' will save you. Plan 'C' will always get you out. Plan 'C' will get you back home. But you have to think it through before you go." He shifted and ran a thick hand over his scalp, crowding the pug-ripples against each other.

A file cabinet was behind him, and without looking, he reached back, opened the top drawer, pulled out a map and spread it across his desk. "This consult is taking longer than scheduled," he said to himself. He traced my itinerary across Mexico with one finger, telling me what diseases were in each region, what boosters I needed, and what drugs I should have started taking six weeks ago to prevent malaria. He wrote down the shots I required in long squiggly lines with no discernible letters, then waited: My plan 'C' involved a credit card, a bus, a taxi to an airport, and a flight back to Texas. As I closed the door, I saw his head back on his fist, eyes closed.

The young tech in the clinic looked at the prescription and said, "Okay, three shots; two in one arm and one in the other. Do you care which arm gets two?"

I got two shots in my left arm. As he was putting the last Band-Aid on my shoulder I asked, "Is this gonna hurt a little?"

"No," he swiped the Band-Aid again with his thumb, "it's gonna hurt a lot. Take a couple aspirin as soon as you get home so it won't be as sore."

I should have considered that an omen for how the trip would go. Plan 'A' did work, sort of. While driving to the border, our caravan hit a deer forty miles outside Fort Stockton, and we almost chain-reaction wrecked. The lead truck's grill got pushed into the engine by the deer carcass.

On our second day, the Pacífico Railroad train had a small crash; then, one by one, everyone on the trip suffered some kind of injury before we got back to Texas a week later. One guy got hit in the eye by a rock that the train kicked back while he was leaning out, looking at the scenery. One girl suffered minor hypothermia during the freak blizzard while we were hiking out of the Canyon. Another guy, taking a short cut back to the hotel in Los Mochis, accidentally trespassed on a drug dealer's land and got chased by a dog that was so large he thought it was a wolf as he started running. The dog did not get him because he scrambled through a barb wire fence to get away. Arturo, a Sonora House co-op friend of both me and Nolan's, lost his epilepsy medication and started having a seizure every day. And two days after I got hauled out of Copper Canyon by Nolan and Eduardo, I dropped a hiking pack. The aluminum frame landed across the bridge of my foot and I limped for weeks.

Nolan was the only person that seemed to have gone unscathed during the trip until Arturo, Nolan and I camped on the beach in Topolobompo on the Gulf of California, and Nolan got a sunburn. Before realizing the score, he ran into the ocean and stayed bright pink for days.

The whole time though, as the trip slid into eddies of chaos, I knew reasonable plan 'B' and desperate plan 'C' had my back. Now I was facing a different trip. Fly to Denver. Buy some weed. Get on a bus. Bring it back to Texas. Don't go to jail. That's plan 'A.'

That's it. That's all I got.

CHAPTER FIFTEEN
SIGNS

THE MORNING OF the flight to Denver, I woke up early and laid in bed. The night before, I was up till one in the morning googling travel safety tips: put a 'Do Not Disturb' sign on your hotel door; don't put cash in checked baggage, keep it with you in the carry on; lock your luggage even when you leave it in your hotel room; watch where your luggage is stowed under the bus, notice which compartment; don't look at a map on the street, duck into a store instead. All of this was on the 'Women Traveling Alone' site.

Usually traveling involves a vacation tour, visiting a friend, or going to a conference for work, but never going to buy weed by myself. In the days before the trip, I develop a weird nervousness and my intestines decide to offload like a cargo ship in port. While I'm sitting in the bathroom, a horrible thrill of fear courses through me, and an electric current holds steady and sharp in my fingers. Three fingers on my right hand feel lit up, needle cold for thirty seconds. I suppose thrill-seekers live for this palpable energy. I just wait for it to abate, then open up the Fresh Wipes.

The shuttle to the airport is thirty dollars, and I click on the button for the eighteen percent tip. Darius, my driver, is from Pittsburgh. He loves S.A. Been through two summers here. But the heat. My god. But there's jobs here; San Antonio is a good place. He's starting at Bowden, the Bexar Community College on the East Side. Wants to go into engineering, something with math. He's good at math.

The shuttle drops me off at San Antonio International, and the Southwest guy helps me out at the kiosk, then the Southwest lady takes my checked luggage. The TSA guy tells me to drink up and dispose of my water before going through security, and the bin is full of plastic bottles.

Three dollars for donuts, four dollars for new water, six dollars for a slice of veggie pizza, and I'm not even on the plane yet. I do defensive eating when I travel, eating even when I'm not hungry to fend off any unexpected privation later in the day. I also accumulate snacks as I go, knitting together a security blanket of nibbles. I stash a ten-dollar club sandwich in my carry-on then wait at the gate.

At Dallas Love Field, I spend four dollars on a candy bar as I wander around the concourse. On the second leg of the flight, I sit in the emergency exit row next to a man watching a foreign movie on his laptop, where lots of people, mostly well-dressed Asians, punched and kicked each other in ritzy nightclubs with blue lighting. The women punched also. Sunglasses spun off faces in slow motion, bodies flew backwards through etched glass walls, ceilings collapsed. Maybe it was a load-bearing glass wall, and I can only hope the gangsters never drop by Nolan's.

I sip ginger ale, thinking that I'm on this plane because I

don't know any drug dealers, and my nerd friends don't know drug dealers, and, more than that, I don't actually want to interact with drug dealers. So flying to another U.S. state, buying marijuana (a drug) from a store (a dealer) and schlepping it through draconian Oklahoma and back to Texas is as close to following the law as I can get. It is the least illegal option, I guess. The books on cannabis touted ditch weed's neuroprotective, pain reduction, anti-nausea, anxiety-relieving qualities, and its lack of toxicity, how, unlike other drugs—cocaine, heroin, meth, even alcohol—it was impossible to overdose on weed. But it caused euphoria. So something that stopped pain, protected your brain, alleviated stress, and could not kill you, was illegal because it also made people feel good. It increased happiness.

Be less stupid. That's the third thing this book is about. And marijuana used to grow for free in ditches along U.S. highways. It still can.

We land in Denver.

Five months earlier in the summer, when I'd left Nolan's to fly back to San Antonio, Nolan, Fia and I walked blocks down from his house to an RTD stop, a Regional Transportation District bus stop on Broadway, so I could catch the AB Boulder to Denver Airport bus. An hour and nine bucks later, I was at Denver International Airport, accidentally standing in the TSA line for five minutes before going around the corner to Southwest's check-in, then getting back into the line for screening. "New to Our Airport? Step One: Check-in with Your Airline. Right This Way." A sign like that, with a friendly arrow, would have helped.

I'm a huge fan of signage. The problem with airports is that each one is designed as though every passenger already knows how to use not only airports in general but also that specific airport. When we disgorge into DIA, I follow the herd, make it to baggage claim and grab my bag without a hitch, and then I end up like a desert wanderer. I need to get from the airport to my hotel in downtown Denver, and a hotel shuttle is the cheapest way. Except I can't find one. The Ground Transportation sign directs me, vaguely, in a general outside direction. But there is lots of outside, and the airport has multiple levels inside and out. I end up looking at a long line of concrete islands, some with chartered buses, others with cars picking up relatives, none with a clear "Hey, stand here for a shuttle to take you to the hotels downtown" sign. There are also no taxis, so I go back inside.

Maybe I'm on the wrong level. I go down a level and find underground parking lots. I go back up and look at the not-helpful signs again. Going outside in a different direction is even worse since this time, there are not even concrete islands in sight. It's already dark, so I've missed the narrow window when I could reach the hotel in the daylight. I go back in and sit down to rest; the spaces here are so big that each wrong jaunt means a lot of walking and dragging bags.

Finally, I flag down a guy in an airporty-ish uniform and explain my downtown hotel goal. He points, waves his arms to add flourish to his directions, and adjusts his airporty hat. I head back out. I had come out this way earlier but missed a huge multi-story escalator going down, to the left, that is not immediately visible if you don't know it's there. I reach a platform with train tracks and ticket vending machines. Nine dollars.

The A-Line Train glides smoothly through the streetlight speckled dark, twenty-three miles in thirty-eight minutes, right to the back of Union Station in LoDo, lower downtown Denver's historic district. Union Station is full of voices, restaurants, bars, shops, Christmas trees, and chandeliers hanging from the vaulted ceiling. It smells of warm food and coffee. I ask a cop for directions to the Free MallRide and also if it's safe to walk around at night.

"You should be fine. Six-fifteen, it's early yet. Lots of people on the street till nine, ten. After eleven, then you want to be more careful, not walk around alone, but right now, you're okay."

The sidewalks outside are just as energetic as the train station inside. Three guys on Lime scooters whish past and one of them wipes out, hops up, and gets back on the electric scooter, laughing. I get to the corner and thirty seconds later, the 16th Street Free MallRide pulls up. It's crammed full, but people make room and I hoist my bag in. I had looked at my map of downtown Denver on the train from the airport, so now, all I have to do is count the blocks till we reach the right stop. I drag my luggage off, spend a minute getting oriented, then head down Champa. Half a block on, I pass a bar, door closed, windows blacked out, and a heavy smell of marijuana wafting onto the street. I walk through the scent, which dissipates a few steps on, then pass a hair salon where the same thing happens. One more block and Residence Inn Marriott looms up.

The room is an apartment in the sky, as plush as the resorts I stayed in with Nolan in the summer, and I lay down just to de-frazzle before eating the sandwich I got at Dallas Love Field. I call Nolan around nine and complain there were no taxis or shuttles at Denver International.

"Yeah," he says. "So it doesn't really work like that here. Buses and light rail are more environmentally positive."

"The airport could have given me a clue." We talk for half an hour and I let him know that my family thinks I'm in Boulder to visit him, not in Denver to buy weed. I hope he doesn't mind being my alibi. He says it's okay, and he'll call me tomorrow. He has to put in his daily two hours of work.

After the call, I lay back down thinking, while trying not to think: Tomorrow I'm going to buy weed. Tomorrow, I'm going to buy weed. Tomorrow. I'm going to buy weed.

CHAPTER SIXTEEN
THE ATTIC

Deep breathing exercises don't help when I wake up and lay in the dark, feeling those weird little shocks of nervous energy. Sunrise in Denver is at 7:15 and the room grays up. Worried that it will be depressing to eat by myself, I go down to breakfast, but most of the people there are sitting alone at their own table, occupied with the newspapers scattered around or watching a television on the wall. The morning buffet is extensive with a crock pot of soupy oatmeal and steam trays of scrambled eggs, sausage, fruit, cheese, and biscuits. Breakfast feels a bit like a Height of Civilization moment while I flip through the paper and sip orange juice and Earl Grey.

After breakfast, I sit at the kitchen table in my room and search 'cannabis' on my phone's Google Maps. Two dispensaries are pretty close. I study how to get to them, laying out the blocks, route, and street that the Free MallRide travels. More deep breathing. I'm about to do this, this thing that is perfectly legal here, but still. Zing. And anyway, the real worry should be the whole getting-it-back-to-Texas thing. Right now, everything's cool. But also, I'm doing something new, by myself, not sure what to expect. Zing.

Money, ID, room key card, maps, and tissue go into various pockets in my jeans and my big suede coat, and by 10 a.m. I start walking the blocks down Champa Street to 15th to get to the closest dispensary. I didn't even note the name of the place, just its location. I'm starting to get close, a block away, half a block, in a quick, steady stride.

I get a sense that the store has a big glass storefront, but I'm not focused on it because there are two sketchy looking guys on the street, or rather, one sketchy and one disabled. Sixteenth Street is a busy pedestrian mall. But right now, I'm going down a wide sidewalk one block off 16th, past a sparsely filled parking lot. Hobbling away from the dispensary with crab-like awkwardness is a man using aluminum walking canes, the medical kind that cuff onto your arm. His coat hangs too loosely on a body too thin for a grown man, as though he'd been shrunk from some previously taller height. One shriveled leg is stuck out and yet folded under him at impossible angles; it never comes near the ground. His back is curved, and his head is locked at a thirty-degree angle. He has a glossy white bag looped over the hand grip of one of the crutches. Slowly, he makes it across the street to the parking lot.

I take a mincing step to the left. Food's been spilled on the sidewalk and smashed where someone has stepped in it; at least I hope it's food. Farther up the sidewalk, in front of the dispensary, is a guy gliding back-and-forth on a hoverboard glowing blue. He has those rare eyes that are so wide open you can see the entire circle of the iris and dread locks that are too short to lay flat and stick up on his head like antennae. He's looking past me, glide, glide, then looking up the sidewalk in the other direction, glide. His jacket is so puffy it looks inflated and much too light for the forty-degree weather. The morning news had warned that a massive snowstorm was headed this way and set to slam Denver overnight. The guy glides in a circle, not toward me in any way, but the downtrodden disabled man and the hoverboarding local have put me off, and I don't break stride. I go another block, turn right, back to 16th Street, and catch one of the constantly circling Free MallRides up to Market Street and walk a block and a half over to the second dispensary that I had mapped at the hotel room's kitchen table.

The area on 18th Street suddenly looks dingier than the area I just left, as though pictures taken here might turn out in sepia tones without a sepia filter. I close in on where the dispensary is supposed to be, but there is no big glass storefront. Instead, several people are loitering in the street, and one bulky bald guy stands in the middle of the sidewalk, looking alert, actively scanning the street, up, down. I spot the entrance to the dispensary because he is right across from it. His jacket is puffy and a faded olive, ready to blend into concrete and grime. In contrast, to keep my ears from feeling cold, I was wearing a pink wool knit cap from Scotland with ear flaps and a puff ball pom on the top, just to make sure I can be spotted from a distance.

This guy's bare hands were out, balled up in fleshy pink fists at his sides and I relaxed a little. He's security, working the job, and now that I think on it, so was hoverboard guy. I go into what looks like an old apartment building converted into offices. The hallway is unsettling, with thick wooden stairs off to the side in partial shadow, rising up into deeper shadow, and yet, unlike the well-lit Denver Airport, this place has plentiful and effective signage: "Check in with our Security Guard. Wait to be Buzzed In. Do Not Disturb our Neighbors. Be as Courteous as We Wish to be To You."

I pause at the end of the snug hall in front of a door with a keyless digital keypad and multiple deadbolts. There's a soft buzz and I go in. The guard does not look like a guard; he wears a dark guard uniform and a square-ish baseball cap like a hip hop artist on stage. "Hi," he smiles, "Recreational or Medicinal?"

"Recreational."

"How did you hear about us?"

"Google maps."

"Sweet." The easy-to-read signs had already told me that I need to show my ID. He looks it over while giving me directions to the 5th floor. When I go back out, the hallway does not seem as creepy. The wall next to the elevator has good signage too: "Take the Elevator to the 5th Floor. Please only use the Restrooms on the 1st Floor. Do Not Disturb Other Occupants."

The small elevator looks like the 1940s and sways on the way up, but it is clean. The fifth-floor landing has inadequate lighting, two doors with keyless keypads and more signage: Medicinal: 18 years of age. Recreational 21 plus.

I try the handle. The door is so locked. I wonder if I should knock, when a guy—I've no idea where he came from—is at my side, "Let me get that for you." He punches in a number, and the door un-clicks.

Inside, the lighting is better, but it is not the super bright fluorescent lights that you get in department store retail. The floor is a dark polished wood, and there is medium loud music: reggae, hip-hop, rock. A Natty Rems logo is painted on the wall, and hip-hop caps with Colorado logos on them are arranged on display boxes. Similarly themed T-shirts are for sale next to the ATM machine, and I smell something, but it is not weed. The woman at the reception desk checks my ID and hands me a laminated card with 'f19' on it, explaining that there'll be a short wait, not too long, and I can have a seat. There are plastic chairs along the wall and a young couple with 'f18' sit in the corner. I sit down and stare at the framed abstracts of Jimmy Hendricks, Run D.M.C., and Lucille Ball.

Five wooden doors are all closed. Two say, "Do Not Enter." Clear enough. The third is for medical marijuana patients, the fourth is the entrance to the recreational shop, and one lacks signage. This is not what I was hoping for, and I feel twitchy, my posture oddly stiff. Another receptionist, holding a stack of paperwork, comes out of one of the 'Do Not Enter' doors. Everyone is relaxed but me; I'm trying to have a neutral face. The couple in the corner talk in soft tones, anticipating an afternoon of enhanced bliss. Shopping together, choosing the right bud, the walk home, the languid high, was all over their faces, already glowing with deep eye contact and gentle smiles. The young woman had a gap in her front teeth that emphasized how adorable she was.

Two college guys come in and a receptionist looks up, "Recreational or medicinal?"

"I'm medical," one says. "This is my buddy; he's just hanging with me. He's from out of state and has never seen a place, so he came along. They don't have anything like this in Kansas."

"Okay." They get buzzed through the medical door. A trio comes in just as the couple with 'f18' goes into the recreational area. "It'll be a little wait. I've only got one budtender per group and there's max customers back there right now."

Then a guy comes in after the trio, clearly a regular. "How's the wait?" he asks.

"Not bad. Starting to get a bit longer, but it's still early."

"Lots of tourists?"

"Kinda."

My number is called, and the door opens with a click.

Wow. They really like wood. Three budtenders stand behind a long wooden counter, and the woman in the middle, between the two men, is available. "Hi," she says brightly, "I need to check your ID one more time." I hand it over, she looks, hands it back.

Below the counter is a display case with plastic containers of what I think, from the pictures in the books I've been reading, are waxes, dabs? I don't know. And on the brick wall behind the budtenders is more product display that reminds me of a cross between a candy store and an old-timey apothecary: chocolate and gummie edibles, tinctures, and creams. There must be actual flower cannabis here too, but I can't take it all in.

High up on the wall is a narrow window which, even from this angle, looks thick enough to resist a hurricane, but it is letting in natural light that is hitting the brick and wood and casting an amber warmth in the room. In my mind, I label this place as the Attic. The budtender-ess woman is mid-twenties, with straight hair going down her back and a face that is a blend between wise graduate student and motherly best friend. "What can I help you with today?"

Finally. The question I've been waiting for. "Hi. Okay, my dad has spinal arthritis, and I—" I never finish the sentence.

Her eyes flick wide for a fraction of a second, alarmed. "Uh, no." Immediately, and I mean instantly, she is reciting

Colorado legal code to me, ". . . and purchases of cannabis products can only be made for the use of the person making the purchase. No purchase can be transacted for another individual. You are only allowed to buy product for yourself, yourself only. Not for anyone else, so . . ." She has, apparently, memorized the 180-page Department of Revenue's Marijuana Enforcement Division's Sales, Manufacturing, and Dispensing of Marijuana Code of Colorado Regulations, just for her own quick reference. Her head tilts a tiny bit. "So, *you* have spinal arthritis?"

My mouth is still hanging open from where I stopped talking mid-sentence. "Right. Yes. I. I have spinal arthritis. And I did some research but was hoping you'd be able to tell me what edibles would be best for chronic pain, like daytime pain, and I did some research, so I think I'm looking for CBD edibles and also something with a long shelf life." I put in the bit about long shelf life because cookies that go bad in a month won't be useful. Whatever I get needs to last through Dad's chemo and radiation treatment. "So, I was looking for something that can help—me, manage the pain but which is not psychoactive at all. My da-, I would not be interested in any high type of effects."

Crisis averted, she reaches for items in the display case. "What's most effective for chronic pain is flower and combinations of CBD and THC, which does create a high."

I shake my head no.

"Okay, we have this tincture." She slides a bottle less than three inches high out of its little carton. "It's CBD. It's something I use for my own gastric problems. It doesn't work right away. It's something that . . . You take it every day and then, after a few days, it really helps. It makes such a difference, so a drop a day. I take two drops a day because I can get severe pain, and that way, my stomach doesn't hurt. That way, I can get through the day, I can function just fine." A slightest sallow gauntness that I hadn't noted before thins out her cheeks. "Before I started using the tincture, my gastric problems would just leave me," she gestures with one hand at her intestines. "I couldn't work; I would just be on the couch all day, curled up."

"Is it glycerin based? No alcohol?"

She reads the ingredients out loud. No alcohol is listed, and no glycerin either, and I think one of them has to be used to make a tincture. She hands me the bottle; the print is tiny silver lettering on a black label. Stylish, but not easy to bring into focus. She opens it up when I hand it back and shows me that the top of the bottle is an eye dropper.

"So your dad can take, you can take a drop or two under the tongue. It's individual. You have to determine what works for each person."

I ask how much. It's $165. Youch. "And that's not psychoactive?"

"No. This is CBD. There's no high with this; it's just a body effect. Then we also have a CBD body lotion cream. That's a topical. So your dad can just, if you can put this down your own spine, it also has a body effect but no high at all. It's absorbed through the skin; it's sixty-five."

I take both the CBD tincture and the topical ointment. Two-hundred and thirty dollars. While she prints and sticks a label onto each product, I have time to look around a bit more. There are acrylic jars of buds under display lights, and only now does my brain translate the 'Natty Rems' name painted on the wall into Natural Remedies. So this is the funky, low-down branding. The budtenders and staff are all clean and neat, dressed in their own street clothes. The guys have on jeans, and the budtender woman who worked with me wears a long skirt and a faded button-down top. Tip jars are on the counter, one for each budtender, and the one in front of my budtender is full to the top with singles, but I cram a couple more in. She puts the lotion and tincture in a white paper bag, just like a candy shop, that fits nicely in my suede coat's big right pocket. We do the mutual thank-yous.

Back on the street, I'm not quite paranoid. I have drugs in my pocket. Two-hundred-and-thirty dollars' worth of non-psychoactive, pain-relieving, ancient drugs. I catch the MallRide back to Champa and I'm back in my hotel room by 11 a.m. I sit down. I've been sweating, from walking or being nervous, I'm not sure, but I sit. I did it.

One thing I realize is that there is no chance that I will be carting home ten, eight, six or even three ounces of edibles. Two hundred and thirty bucks just evaporated for two little containers, and the cannabis on the packages is measured in milligrams, not grams, and 157 grams was the four-ounce limit that qualifies as a felony in Texas. As I sit there, I'm sure I will never come near it. I am absolutely sure that I will never have anything close to a felony's worth of weed in Texas.

One day, I will be absolutely wrong on that point.

CHAPTER SEVENTEEN
THE BASEMENT

An hour later, recovered enough to try the first store again, I get more cash from where it's hidden in my luggage, then walk the blocks to the dispensary. The temperature has been steadily dropping, and I'm hoping the cold will have driven off any folks prone to loitering.

Sure enough, there is a little more street traffic when I get there, but no one is standing idle or hovercrafting around. This time, I go right into a spacious lobby, which is empty. Further in, a woman with a soft voice and a headset greets me and the three women who enter behind me. There are no dark wood enclosures here. Light floods in through the storefront glass, and the walls are white, tossing the light around. The woman, dressed all in black like a restaurant hostess, checks our IDs, mentions, "The wait is not bad today," and then there's a soft click.

Down a broad set of metal stairs, underground, is a wide, deep space. I don't reach the basement floor because the line to reach the budtenders stretches halfway up the stairs that seem to be suspended effortlessly in the air, like Nolan's fireplace. The women behind me are chatting, wearing coats, scarves, and gloves that are fashion magazine new. The woman in line in front of me has long pepper hair in a ponytail, and the two men below her, standing together on the same stair level, are handsome and look like linebackers for Colorado State. One has medium length, glossy dreadlocks; the other has a fade haircut with a curlicue shaved into the side. Either could fit on the cover of ESPN as the hot new NFL recruit.

The glass counter here is long and curves into an 'L' shape and half a dozen budtenders, all male, are stationed at intervals. They have matching T-shirts with the store's logo: Native Roots. This is the motherlode.

The counter is a generous glass display case with black framing, and, running along the black wall behind the budtenders, are cubby boxes full of products, more than I imagined existed. Like the other dispensary, this place has branding, but it's not reggae-grunge. This is glossy and slick. Upstairs was stark white; down here is black, and yet this is the fluorescent-lit retail I understand. I don't have to neutralize my face. The music being piped in is rock mixed with soft-core heavy metal, but it's not as loud as at the morning dispensary. Jars full of labeled marijuana buds are in the bright display cases and the smell in the air is not weed, but some combination of air freshener, gender-neutral perfume, and an industrial strength, weed-smell absorbing 3M chemical.

Already I recognize patterns: The *wait* is a big deal in dispensary evaluation. When I had googled for cannabis stores, I read the reviews, and the big points of comparison used to judge the stores were price, selection, knowledgeable budtenders, and wait time, which often took precedence over everything else.

The regulars here know the budtenders by name, and two middle-aged buddies that have reached the floor go up to their favorite budtender at the bend in the 'L' shape, banter a bit, then listen to his recommendation for this week's flower. Though the budtender is speaking to the two customers in front of him, he pitches his voice so the whole basement can hear as he extols a much-desired OG that they just got in, that won't be around too long because it is so hard to get, even on the West Coast. He teases out a little of the strain's hybrid lineage, manages to work 'landrace' into its history, and assures them that no one in Colorado has tried it yet. His cadence has the sound of a carnival barker, starting out strong and then getting stronger in a quick delivery. "This flower is loud," he praises, "So loud."

Everyone in line listens to him, pausing their own conversations, turning to watch. It's a premium bud, he says, a little pricier than usual, but for those who can appreciate its great citrusy notes and mellow finish, the experience is worth it. Dramatically he opens one of the jars, so the people on the stairs get the briefest glimpse before the jar is raised in front of his two regulars, who each sniff deeply, like a sommelier. The budtender proclaims the virtues of the bud's strong high then explains the body-feel that it creates—a deep analgesic muscle relaxation but without couch-lock—and how that combines with a hallucinogenic effect that starts out cerebral, yet not overwhelming, with a slow tapering off at the end. He asks his regulars if they would be interested in this rare flower, but they are already nodding; he had them from the jump.

The folks in line are not sure whether to applaud at the end of his pitch, so they don't, but the appreciative chatter that breaks out mimics applause. Even customers already with other budtenders had paused what they were doing to watch the show. The future NFL-ers and pepper ponytail lady ask their budtenders for a look at the vaunted OG.

Somewhere during all of that, I've reached the floor.

My budtender is a study in bohemian hip. He has a foot-long beard, untrimmed yet neat. The budtender next to him has the sides of his head shaved and one-inch ear plugs. The guy next to him has a goatee. All the budtenders are counterculture but safe, telegraphing hipster personality and a personal knowledge of weed, but the whiff of corporate America is buffing the scene, normalizing the cannabis.

The display case is full of precisely arranged chocolate bars and candy, and the cubbies behind the budtenders also show off a riot of choice: lotions, salves, ointments, oils, transdermal patches, tinctures, flavored vape pens, jars of flower, extracts of shatter, wax and resin, and edibles—cookies, brownies, granola bars, lollipops. Here and there, I see a blank space and a card saying "Out of Stock." The music now is a country-rock fusion with lyrics that can't be distinguished between the instruments and room noise. And in the corner, logo-branded T-shirts and caps.

"Can I ask how you heard about our store?" Long-beard checks my ID.

"Google Maps."

"Awesome."

I ask what edibles he recommends for spinal arthritis without mentioning Dad, but I do mention the need for a long shelf life, which knocks out the cookies and brownies. The guys behind the counter must get a blur of customers, hour after hour, week after week, most asking the same questions, and nothing seems to throw the budtenders off. He tells me that the edibles are well packaged, and he's sure that unopened, they'll easily last a year at least, even the cookies too if I freeze them. He starts pointing and naming the products under the display case, in the pyramid stacks on the counter and in the alcove boxes behind him. I had wondered if these guys have some kind of required customer turnover rate, but he doesn't seem bothered by an out-of-town newbie taking up a lot of his time. The information is not rushed, but there is so much, I can't line it all up in my head.

I point to the row of chocolate bars under the glass counter. "Are these all the same thing, just different flavors?"

"No. Only the Cherry Chocolate is non-psychoactive. This is CBD with just a little THC to activate the CBD but not enough to create a high. This," he points to the next candy bar in the row, Black Cherry Chocolate, "is fifty percent CBD, fifty percent THC. This will have a psychoactive effect, but also a stronger analgesic effect." He explains the Cheeba Chews next. "Have you ever had a Tootsie Roll? The Cheeba Chew is CBD, tastes like a Tootsie Roll, ten milligrams per piece."

I think back to the books I read and their cautions about starting doses and edibles. "Can you cut them in half?"

"Sure, they come in blister packs. Just pop 'em out as you use them and you can cut one in half."

Then I remember the question that I had forgotten to ask that morning in the Attic, "Oh, and do you sell seeds?"

He too has committed the 180-page Code of Regulations to memory and goes into robot mode, reciting without inflection, "By statue, no dispensary can sell seeds to anyone who does not have a Colorado residence as indicated on an approved form of government-issued identification such as a valid Colorado driver's license. That is a law throughout the state." He'd checked my Texas ID when I first walked up to the counter.

It had occurred to me that growing my own cannabis plants would save a lot of airfare and other hassles in the future, and between the *Encyclopedia of Marijuana* and the cannabis cookbooks, I was sure I could manage a grow closet and enough organic cannabutter to take care of Dad. Apparently, the state of Colorado knew where their bread was cannabuttered and had taken basic steps to keep the tourist mill churning.

"Okay, I'll take two Cheeba Chews and two Black Cherry Chocolates." The chocolates were the fifty-fifty CBD-THC combination that might have a slight psychoactive buzz, but I also knew that THC increased appetite and decreased nausea better than just CBD. And it was on sale. The card next to the chocolate bars read fifteen dollars.

So. I'm expecting a bill of $130. The total is $218. I dig in my pocket for another hundred. "How much are—"

"The Cheeba Chews are fifty dollars each and the Black Cherry Chocolate are forty each."

I look back in the display case and notice that the card next to the chocolate bars actually says, "Starting at $15." Hhm. Figures. But that still doesn't tally. My face scrunches. "What is your tax rate?"

"Twenty-one to twenty-three percent throughout the state at all recreational dispensaries." Ka-ching.

He puts two Cheeba Chews and two "High-quality hand-crafted infused edible; contains marijuana; Keep Out Of The Reach Of Children; lab-tested Black Cherry Chocolate" bars into a bag. But not a plain white bag; I am seriously alarmed.

The budtender is loading my purchases into a glossy bag, like you get from a fashion boutique. The bag is stark white with bold black lettering featuring Native Roots' logo along with an artistic calligraphy of cannabis strains and weed slang: wax, dab, shatter, indica, sativa, Grand Daddy Purple, Pineapple Express, Diesel, Lemon Kush, Tangerine Haze, plus silhouettes of bongs and cannabis leaves. The bag is roomy and stiff and will not fit into any suede coat pockets. I look at Long-beard, who has been so very patient. "Do you have any plain bags?"

He freezes in the middle of filling the bag, startled into making genuine, budtender to newbie eye contact by a question he hasn't gotten before. "No." He pauses. "These are the only bags we have."

I exit to the left. One set of grand stairs takes you down to the basement and another set of curving stairs takes you back up. The walls around the 'up' stairway are wallpapered in the same stark white and black pattern that is on the store's bag. I stand on the landing near the front door as three young preppies come in, two girls and a guy. The girl in front says, "Oh, I so love the way it smells in here."

"Me too."

And the boy, "So do I." They head to the hostess.

When I go to a grocery store, I'm annoyed if they don't bag the wine or beer, and the idea of walking down a public street, openly swinging a bag that obviously has marijuana in it, is beyond me. Uptightness grips me like a straitjacket. I redistribute the Cheeba Chews and Chocolates into various coat pockets, then neatly fold the bag along its seams so it can fit into a pocket as well. It sticks out. I cover it by tucking my puff ball pom cap and gloves around it and now, street-ready, step onto the sidewalk. Outside, the handsome guys that were ahead of me chat in the shimmering air.

An electronic bank sign says it's thirty-six degrees. The temperature has dropped some more and my ears are cold and stiff before I reach the hotel.

CHAPTER EIGHTEEN
DAM

I SPREAD MY purchases on the table and lay down for a few minutes, but I'm not tired; I'm energized. I've done it. I've added the CBD Cheeba Chews and the CBD/THC chocolate bars to my little stash, and I take a moment to admire the dispensary store bag that I could not walk down a street with. Man, it's sharp. Then I put everything back in my luggage, fold up the bag and zip it into the luggage lining, map out how to get to the Denver Art Museum, finish the sandwich left over from yesterday, and re-bundle up. I had decided before the trip that I wanted to see something in Denver besides the inside of a cannabis shop.

As I'm taking the elevator down, a family gets on. I say 'hi' and they don't reply. The eight-year-old boy seems surprised at the greeting, and Mommy, boy, and Grandma talk about the Denver Mint they are headed to and how it's different from the Philadelphia Mint. They quiz the boy about coins. I walk behind them for a block down the street, and Daddy draws the boy closer as though I might do a grab-and-run with the kid, then they turn at the end of the block.

The MallRide lets me off on one side of the Civic Center, which I have to cross to get to the museum on the other side, so I start walking. And walking some more. The Civic Center looked smaller on my phone. It's a massive public space with a promenade wide enough for a marching Roman legion and the top of the promenade ends in a Greek amphitheater with a quarter-circle colonnaded archway. So, not subtle on any level. The gold-domed Denver Capital building is directly up the hill from the end of the promenade-amphitheater.

I round the end of the Civic Center and see the Denver Art Museum, which has a gigantic chair out front with a sculpture of a horse standing on the seat. The horse is a full-size horse. So, not subtle on any level. Art, sculpted large.

The 'Glory of Venice: Masterworks of the Renaissance' has a shadowy gallery of paintings in the sumptuous pigments of the late 1400s. The exhibition is full of annunciations, Madonnas holding improbably large baby Jesuses, plus a few portraits of elaborately dressed women staring blankly at some middle distance to the right of the thick gold frames that hold them. It's a good enough exhibit—a Titian, a Bellini—but everybody and their museum dog have a Renaissance wing and I've done the rounds before, twice in Italy.

Nolan calls while I'm sitting on a bench in the hall, going through the museum map. We firm up our plans and he talks me through which bus to take to meet him tomorrow at McCaslin Station, which is midway to Boulder.

One morning when I was staying with Mitch in Spain, we took a day trip to Toledo, walking the cobblestone streets of the ancient city to the church of Santo Tomé. Before I went in, to me, the works of El Greco were just those hallucinogenic, stretched religious paintings. Inside the church is *The Burial of the Count of Orgaz.* There is a moment of lost time when you stand before it, of entering the mind of another that held this image and willed it onto canvas. El Greco is in the painting, eighth from the left, looking at you from the 1500s.

Winged totem poles frame the entrance to the Indigenous Arts Collection in the Denver Art Museum. A Pacific Coast kayak hangs suspended from the ceiling between the floor and a second level landing, so while walking up the stairs, you can see the kayak close-up from every angle, underneath and above. Rich pigments decorate clothes, cradles, and saddles. But it's the four-faced Hamat'sa raven mask that radiates. Like the El Greco, genius flows off it. The faces of the black, white, and red masks are set at different angles, in different directions, so you cannot see all of them at once. As you orbit around, one mask disappears as another—the black-beaked raven, the crane, the red raven—shifts and rises through two, three, four dimensions. Not every museum dog has that.

I want to see more of the exhibit, but my thighs are talking back, and I have to walk to the MallRide and reach my hotel before the afternoon light fails. When I hoof it across the Civic Center again, I see grim signals that I did not notice earlier: trash blown into piles, plus bottles and bags suggesting that a down-on-its-luck population hangs out here. On the MallRide down 16th Street, I see two dispensaries that didn't show up on Google Maps and try to remember where they are for later reference, then go past the stop for my hotel and get off near Panera Bread and P.F. Chang's.

The bear claw and cookie from Panera's is going into my carry-on for the bus ride back to Texas, and, while waiting at the bar for my carry-out order at P.F. Chang's, I wonder about a day in the life of a budtender. How long are their shifts? They seem to be on their feet all day. When they clock in each morning, do their corporate overlords assign them a hipster personality trait—a beard, an ear plug, or porkpie hat? But mostly, how many of their customers are like me, describing illness and symptoms? Are budtenders filling the same role as a medieval physic, local monk or village healer woman when they are asked what works for nausea, cancer treatment, gastric problems? And the same from those customers who are just after recreational: I'm looking for a mellow high, creativity, the giggles. I want to sleep, watch Pink Floyd, detach from my body. What do you recommend?

I make it back to the hotel with fifteen minutes of orange daylight left and eat with the living room TV on.

The newscasters are ominous yet thrilled about the winter storm named Decima: icy roads, dangerous travel conditions, and canceled flights lie in its wake as Boise, Salt Lake City, Jackson Hole, and Billings at minus three degrees have already been hit. Coming from the Gulf of Alaska, Decima's snowfall will be concentrated in central and northern Colorado; expect major disruptions, blizzard conditions, rapid temperature drop from thirty degrees to below zero Friday night into Saturday morning. It's going to move from coast to coast; it's a monster, it'll clobber us, it's coming, it's coming tonight, here it comes. Up next, sports.

The image of iced-over planes stranded on a tarmac blasted by gale-force winds fades as they go to commercial.

I spend the evening applying my end-of-the-world prepper skills, using a curling iron to seal the tincture, topical, and edibles into Mylar bags, then washing the exterior of the bags in soap and water, which, even at the time I think is overkill, then storing the bags in my luggage. When I change into pajamas, I notice my t-shirt smells like weed, but the suede coat doesn't. It makes no sense. Even though the coat was unbuttoned when I was in the stores, the t-shirt was still underneath it. I store the odor anomaly in a 'Mysteries of the World' column and move on.

Satisfied with the day's work, I meditate, turn out the light, and look out of the window. My room is on the fourteenth floor, and Denver looks cold and still and alive the way cities at night appear even more lux than they do in the day. A few forlorn flakes of snow drift down like feathers past my window, and I'm in bed by nine-thirty.

I wake up at two in the morning and stand at the window in the living room with the curtain back, the cold washing off the glass in a cascade. Snow was plummeting out of the deep black sky, thick and silent and everywhere.

Decima had come.

CHAPTER NINETEEN

THE GREEN RUSH

At five in the morning, I wake briefly. Iridescent porcelain covers the world. Fourteen stories below, a team of men shovel the walkways around the bank tower next to the hotel. Later, I lay in bed with the quiet and darkness and warmth, then go down and eat a huge breakfast near the big plate windows. Two inches of snow fell in San Antonio on January 11, 1985, and shut the city down for two days. We don't have any snow plows and Houston was using theirs, so they wouldn't let us borrow. The mayor came on TV and told everyone to just stay home. And we did.

I go back to the room and dress for the day ahead: Bra and underwear. Thermal stockings that stretch up to my stomach and a camisole down to my panty line. My thickest socks. Flannel lined khaki pants and a t-shirt. Thickest winter sweater and heaviest brown leather shoes with rubber tread. Suede coat with inner zipper and a button flap on top of the zipper to keep breezes out. Gray scarf that Mom knitted years ago when she re-learned knitting so she could make booties for baby Jovi.

My pink Scottish wool pom hat and leather gloves. I get all this on then walk around to see if movement, with so many layers, is feasible. It is. I take off the coat, arrange money, ID, credit card, and hotel key card in various outer, inner, and zippered pockets, put the cross-strap purse on, put the coat back on, zip it up, button it up, and head for the lobby.

Across the street, a woman without gloves is digging out her car, and she hasn't even buttoned up the front of her coat. The moment I step out of the hotel, the air smacks my cheeks hard, then does it again to make a point. I turn onto 16th and people are everywhere in the bright, minus three-degree air. Snow has been trodden into slush and pushed off the sidewalks. A woman jogs past in leggings and sports shoes, and a postman in a bulky USPS jacket and walking shorts is on his route. A man walks a boxer wearing an ill-fitting dog-cape, and each time they stop, the dog lifts one paw out of the slush then switches it up, lifting another paw for a few seconds before they continue.

I catch the MallRide to Union Station, where, once inside, I have to ask a uniform guy where to catch the Flatiron Flyer. This is not due to bad signage but to a total lack of signage. The place to catch the bus is out the back of Union Station, then downstairs, then under the station where there is a broad bus tunnel. I meander back and forth until I figure out the right gate because of the increasing clump of people waiting there and a few minutes later, I'm on the 9:58 a.m. Flatiron Flyer headed down US 36. A massive blizzard overnight? City streets and highways have been cleared and traffic is humping.

McCaslin Station is on the edge of an outdoor mall parking lot, and Nolan and his red Jeep are waiting. When I get off the bus, I feel the familiar embrace of the 'burbs, then Nolan's bear hug crunching my bones before we drive halfway across the parking lot to a donut shop where I get hot cocoa, and Nolan gets hot coffee and a cruller and listens as I detail the dispensary shopping adventures of the previous day. He's wearing the sweatshirt I got him at Red Rocks. An hour later, I still haven't finished my story, but we have to get going to catch a movie.

Before we get back in his car, I stand on a low hill piled in snow, while Nolan takes a few pictures of me in front of a virgin field of white. The snow is deep and fluffy, disintegrating when I kick it, but even standing just long enough to take a picture, chills my feet and ankles, and my mind tings in prescient alarm: my thickest socks, my warmest shoes, and my feet are cold. Nolan parks at the multiplex in the middle of the strip center and, two tickets to *Rogue One* later, we're cushioned in the big recliner seats near the front row because the theater is so crowded.

After the movie, we eat Italian. Before I continue telling Nolan about the dispensaries, I have to do a huge backtrack and tell him how I got to the point of suddenly flying to Colorado to stock up on pot products for my dad. I recap Dad's hernia, the shadow on his MRI, the fast-growing tumor on his kidney, the successful laparoscopic surgery and then the uncontrollable belching. "What kidneys have to do with belching, I don't know. Even the doctors didn't know why it was happening."

Nolan has a way of looking so that his eyes are suddenly gazing, not out at the world, but in. It only lasts a moment, then snaps back. "The way we are taught in school, most schools, the information is, well, incomplete. What they teach us about the human body and what organs do is too simplistic, too dumbed down to be real information. Organ systems are all interconnected and much more complex than we are taught. They do multiple things that affect other organs and the whole body."

"Well, the belching was constant and severe and he couldn't suppress it, and the doctors didn't do anything about it. I asked my mom what they said about the belching and basically, the doctors said if it wasn't cancer, they didn't care."

"That sounds about right," Nolan commented under his breath, which sort of surprised me. During conversations, sometimes I interrupt people, even though I have tried to break the habit. Nolan doesn't.

"Belching wasn't going to kill him, so it was not on the doctor's priority list, even though it affected my dad's daily life. We used to go to restaurants, especially for birthdays, and he stopped going, so we all stopped going. It's too embarrassing to be in a restaurant and belch out loud. Eventually, he stopped going to church on Sundays, and also to his committees and seniors' meetings and all that." I pause long enough to take a bite of pasta. "So, I thought, you know, I grow all these herbs. So I went through my herb books and none of them had anything about belching. They had recipes for everything else under the sun: depression, warts, cramps, dandruff, whatever, even gas, but not belching. So I got on the internet and looked for herbs that help with belching and damn, I found a dozen. And I came up with a tea with some of those ingredients and started making the tea for him every morning, and it worked. And I don't mean maybe it *seems* to help or there's a bit of a difference. I mean that it reduced the belching by almost ninety percent."

"Wow."

"And my dad was able to start going out again. So, I figured if herbs clearly work for that, maybe other stuff would work as well. I started watching documentaries on marijuana and read eight books on cannabis and took notes on various strains and did research, half of which was useless because it's all edibles now. Why light up when you can eat chocolate?"

"When does your dad start chemo?" Nolan asked.

"Thursday."

After discussing the ingredients in Dad's herbal tea, I explained the crazy prepper stuff that I was into now: the gallons of water stashed in closets, storage totes full of supplies and freeze-dried meals, the grab-and-go binders, and now, in my hotel room, the hair curler sealed Mylar bags full of cannabis edibles. By the end of it, I realize I've screwed up the chronology of my storytelling but just assume that Nolan's super brain will assemble it into a workable order.

When I stop talking for a while to really eat, Nolan gives me a run down on the Green Rush that happened in Colorado, not so much when medical marijuana was legalized but more recently with recreational legalization. "Every pothead in the state suddenly believed that they could open a business, but being potheads, they were bad at it, and their businesses failed as the corporations and businessmen who had never smoked marijuana moved here. The potheads tried theft, knowing there was a lot of money around since it was a cash business, but being potheads, they tried to rob the grow or suppliers or ancillary businesses with less security, not the dispensaries where all the hard cash exchanged hands. The ancillary businesses didn't have currency and the bad business potheads got busted."

So here's the thing. Nolan's teeth did not look great. Between his teeth, he had tartar buildup along his gums. Nolan had never talked much, and when he did, he didn't open his mouth much, so I doubt many people had noticed. I saw it last summer when I came to visit, and when I went home and looked up information on lymphoma, I found out that after treatment, patients have to guard against infection, against cuts, colds and germs, and especially injured gums. Which, I figured, explained his Waterpik instead of a toothbrush when we went to the resorts. And it took two years to build a person's immune system back to pre-lymphoma standards.

Once we finish lunch, iced tea, and going to pee, just moving from the restaurant to the car, the cold works into my clothes. I don't understand it. Nolan's hands get a bit rosy in the air, but he clearly isn't suffering and doesn't bother to put gloves on. That can't simply be acclimation; it's seven below zero for fuck's sake.

It's the puffy jacket. Apparently, the cold regions of the world are rejoicing because new technology is producing low cost, light weight, incredibly warm, down feather puffy winter wear. He reads the skepticism in my eyes as we reach the Jeep.

"Here," he takes off his jacket, then, "Wait, the keys weigh more than the jacket does," and he slips the keys out of the pocket.

"No way!" The jacket is light as a bag of feathers. I squeeze it, get no resistance as it smooshes up small, then puffs right back out when released. Fifty of these things would not equal the weight of my suede coat.

"So, down coats used to be really expensive," Nolan says, "cost hundreds of dollars, and then, a couple years ago, a new manufacturing process made it easier to collect the down and eliminate the rachis."

"Rachis?"

"The rib, the hard quill part, and leave just the fluffy, insulating feathery part that traps all the warm air against your body. That brought the price way down." He eyes my heavy coat with pity. "Now everyone wears puffy down." I hand back the jacket, floaty as packaged air.

~

McCaslin Station is in Louisville, the epitome of suburbs, and Ajoya, the dispensary we go to, is not even two minutes away. If Nolan hadn't parked right in front of it, I never would have noticed it. Underneath the store name and stylized, multicolored cannabis leaf, it has the obligatory green cross and 'Recreational and Medical Cannabis' sign, but all the buildings in the strip mall complex have the same brown brick neatness, so a random pot store does not stand out.

"Just like a phone store," Nolan says when we go in, and clearly, it used to be an AT&T store, but it's been upgraded so that it looks like a mid-level space station. As the hostess checks our IDs, Nolan tells her, "Oh, I'm not buying anything."

The hostess smiles. "I still need to see your proof of age just to enter the store."

With all the budtenders busy with customers, Nolan and I are free to wander about. No hallway, no Attic, no Basement. Just tepid suburban retail in white Formica and glass. Display cases distributed about the space port area stand on thin posts so that they are floating stomach-to-chest high. And, since rectangles would be too severe, the cases are oblong and set on their side so that you are not looking down into them, but across and through them as you move around. One oblong case is full of glass pipes and many varieties of bongs, from artistic, whimsical, clear, tie-dyed, and animal-shaped, to sleek modernist. Each one is hand blown.

The music is new-age granola funk, and the perfume mixing with the cannabis is lighter, though Nolan points out the cannabis smell is still there underneath. At Coffee and Donuts that morning, he had effortlessly explained that my shirt, but not my suede coat, smelled like weed because the cotton shirt was more porous than suede, so the shirt easily picked up the scent.

A budtender is free before I'm done admiring the ornate bongs. The five budtenders are a mix of men and women who speak in quiet voices and have no hint of personality, hipster, grunge or otherwise. The hostess guides Nolan and me to our budtender, a lady with gentle, relaxing mouse-brown hair. The display on the counter is not crowded, not pushy; it's just there, you know, available. No one is loitering out front. No street-scanning heavies nor security are visible, though I assume there is plenty. At the far end of the counter is a door I had overlooked because the white door, in the white wall, barely seems to have a frame around it. It does have a big metallic key code pad. I don't bother to look around for the cameras. They are probably hidden in the ceiling, the carpet, the mouse-brown hair.

"What can I help you with?"

I go through my spiel: edibles, spinal arthritis, chronic pain, and also, what do you recommend for nausea? She has the same topical cream that I bought in the Attic, but also an extra strength cannabis-infused lotion, eighty-five dollars. She shows me Cheeba Chews that I got in the Basement and also points out some CBD capsules.

"So that's the same as the edibles but in a capsule form?" I ask. It's in a pill bottle with a child-proof cap, but Dad already takes ten pills a day. A toffee chew would be more like having a treat.

The store's products are color coded with a blue, green, orange, or purple marijuana leaf on each box. The budtender suggests a smokable strain would be best to control the nausea, and when I shake my head no, the matter is dropped. No pressure. Why would there be pressure for a product that sells itself? People walk in; product walks out. I work out that the blue label is for pain and get the eighty-five-dollar lotion.

Nolan and I get back in his car. When he was first being treated for lymphoma and dispensaries were not selling recreational marijuana yet, just medical, and his friends said, "Man, Nolan, you're gonna be able to get all the weed you want," he never tried it. And now he's been in his first dispensary for the first time. Still didn't buy a thing though.

The sun was sinking as we drove to Boulder. Boulder's mountainous skyline is shaped by the Flatirons, the five red sandstone rock slabs, raised tens of millions of years ago to a fifty-degree angle and now jutting one thousand feet up. The city is decorated for the holidays, and lights in the shape of a giant star stretch, suspended in the dark, across one of the mountains. I ask Nolan about the Flatirons, how they look at different times of the year, and he describes various visions of the Flatirons when the light is under rare conditions and the rock is jet black streaked with white snow, pure black and white, or the tilted slabs glow in a haze when the shafts of sun in winter dive through mist. Nolan turns the heat up, but the car is too old and drafty to get warm.

“My hands are on fire,” I say as we pull into an apartment complex. “That can’t be good.”

“Your gloves are crap,” says Nolan, then invites me to go with him to Megan’s apartment to pick up Kinsley, but either I overthink or don’t think enough and opt to wait in the car while he runs upstairs. He takes ten minutes, chatting with Megan and her new fiancée, an HVAC technician she met while working at Home Depot. My feet are frozen by the time Nolan and Kinsley pile into the car.

We stop at a red light at a major intersection near a tree with a big spherical canopy. The tree trunk has been wrapped in Christmas lights, and ornaments hang in the branches: white balls of lights, some small, some ten inches across. The tree is thick with them, like a vision lifted out of fairyland.

Spontaneously, Kinsley starts to narrate: “My last teacher, Miss Kincaid, she had a Christmas tree like that but bigger, and in the tree she had different animals that sat in the tree for seventeen days. She adopted the animals because they were orphaned. Some she found and took home from the forest and the side of the road, and a couple she got from the pound and took home, and she fed them and then they were happy to sit in the tree in cages with silver doors and birds. Some of the animals were birds, and some were dogs and cats and guinea pigs. The birds had perches in the cages, but the other animals just sat on the branches. And at Halloween, it was the same, but the lights were orange, not white.” Her story went on, fabulous and dramatic. “One very large bird in the Halloween tree, like a peacock but with black feathers and orange teeth, sharp long teeth, would open and close its mouth. It’s scary.”

Jovi used to tell complex and creative stories, and I realized suddenly that I hadn’t heard them from her in a year or two. She's more quiet now, drawing a lot and coloring all her pictures like a Moroni textile.

I thawed out at Nolan's house. His dining table was still covered in hospital bills, but they had been organized into neat stacks. When Fia laid her head on my leg, I remembered the dog in the cape, lifting its feet off the sidewalk.

"The chemicals they use to de-ice sidewalks can irritate their footpads," Nolan says. "I tried to get Fia to wear dog shoes, but she won't walk with them. She just stands there shaking her paws."

After an hour, Nolan and Kinsley drive me to the RTD stop to wait for the Flatiron Flyer, but it's running late, and we sit in the car for five minutes. Clothes that are plenty warm in Texas are not warm at all in Colorado, and I feel tricked by my Luddite coat. Kinsley doesn't even button her puffy jacket until Nolan tells her to, just as the bus looms into view. Nolan and I get out and hug as the bus approaches, coming down Broadway. It's packed.

The ride back to Union Station is the warmest I've been all day, and the comfort gives me time to think: Tomorrow, I'm going to take weed back to Texas.

CHAPTER TWENTY
GREYDOGGIN'

AT SEVEN A.M. I am at the Residence Inn Front Desk. "I'm checking out."

"Oh no," the Front Desk Clerk feigns grief as I hand over my credit card.

When I woke up that morning, I felt antsy and did not eat as much at breakfast as I had the last two mornings. Then I had gone back up to my room to get my luggage and arrange my carry-on with the sealed Mylar bags of goodies pushed to either end, while the center of the carry-on was filled up with my make-up kit, water, snacks, a paperback, MP3 player, and travel necessities.

The Desk Clerk asks where I'm from, and when I say San Antonio, he tells me about a friend of his in Fort Worth where it's seventy degrees. "I guess you'll be able to put away the scarf for a while."

"Forever. It never gets this cold in San Antone." I zip up and button up and wrap my scarf around, then sling my carry on over my shoulder and step outside where my lips flash dry in the icy air. Breath steams with each puffing exhale as I pull my luggage down Champa, away from 16th, and my feet slide twice before I adopt the rhythm for walking on slushy sidewalks. One block over and one block up is the squat rectangular Greyhound Station, indolently taking up an entire city block on its own. Large "No Loitering" signs are outside.

Inside, the Station is a blur of motion and noise. A man in a muscle shirt, black puffy jacket and Timberlands lets his pit bull wander around. It doesn't threaten anyone, but it *is* a pit bull just wandering around. Wrapped around one hand, he holds a leash, which is not attached to the dog. People, despondent, exhausted, or overwhelmed by boredom, are sitting everywhere, some on blankets on the floor. Others mill aimlessly in a large middle area. I stop as I enter, get my bearings, then walk to the serpentine Ticket and Information line.

The man behind the counter will be busy all day and knows it. He's un-flusterable, working with the perpetual line of people the way a postman works with the infinite mail.

In line, two guys compete with each other for the most miserable travel story, punctuated by as many variants of 'fuck' as each can wedge into a sentence. "I've been four fucking days on what was supposed to be a two-day fucking trip, man. I missed my brother's funeral. Fuck. They owe me a fucking hotel room. They haven't even fucking offered me a fucking food voucher. Man. Fucked if I'm putting up with this. I'm gonna tell 'em that." He details how he works for a furniture moving company and his boss drove him to the bus station and then he had an eight hour wait for the bus as a series of delays and missed connections began. Now he's broke.

The other guy's story is equally convoluted, involving a ticket reservation mix-up and "Just one multi-fuck fuck up after another." The point is it's the bus company's fault. With a little more eavesdropping, I realize with dumb shock that all this chaos is because of Snowstorm Decima. Travel routes have been getting snarled for the last four days and the bus schedules are only now regurgitating travelers back to where they were supposed to already be. And as the storm rolls east, the effect will keep pulsing out like a chunk of ice hitting a pond. The Denver Greyhound Station is jammed with the backlog.

Working the counter are a half-dozen people, all African Americans in Greyhound uniforms. The man who is clearly the Final Authority pushes a button on an old-style microphone, his voice booming over the intercom throughout the station. "If you want to play with the dog, then take it outside. It seems to be a nice friendly dog, but you can't have a pit bull running around in here even if it is a friendly dog. When it's in here, it has to be on a leash, under your control."

When it's in here? So it's a service pit bull? The damn thing is big enough to saddle.

I get to the front. The area behind the counter is elevated, so everyone working there is looking down on the customers. I hand the ticket I printed out before leaving San Antonio to Final Authority Man. "Oh," he lowers the mic, taken aback. "Okay." He scrutinizes the ticket. Then scrutinizes me. Maybe I'm a witch? How else to explain an organized and quiet passenger? I look dangerously compliant. Whatever the case, I'm paid in full, and he hands me slips of paper. "This is your baggage label, and this is your baggage claim ticket. This goes on the checked luggage. Right on there. Keep your claim ticket. You'll use it to claim your bag in San Antonio. And there. Right there. Right."

I fumble around with the baggage label and the precious

claim ticket. Next to me, F-bomb guy gets to the counter and speaks so softly, the woman behind the counter hoists her massive bust up-forward-down-forward to hear him better: "I was wondering if, see I've been traveling for four days, and I was only expecting the trip to take two days, so—" My heart twinges as he pleads his case. With his eyes staring to the left of his feet, he explains that he's run out of money, "I need a food voucher."

A Greyhound Uniform guy appears and takes my labeled checked baggage. I follow him to a door with a large "Gate 5" painted over it. Very clear signage. Mhm. A dozen people have already lined up, but he takes me to the front and says to stand there, then throws my baggage onto a luggage cart that he pushes outside, next to an MCI Greyhound "Big Brother" Coach idling in the bus bay.

The woman I was directed to cut in front of complains, "We've been lined up. We're lined up here." But I don't move; I'm trying to watch my bag get loaded, when the bus driver steps in front of my view and, in a gravelly voice, starts asking the passengers for their final destinations. He has a two-day stubble and works his way down the line, glancing at tickets and then rearranging some people to the end of the line. He opens the Gate 5 door and leads us out. At the bus, he examines the tickets again before letting each passenger board.

A wooden step box is in front of the bus stairwell, but I still need to grab the handrail to heave myself up the over-size stairs and suddenly, all the noise outside falls away, like a mute button has been pushed on the world beyond. I take a seat several rows past the driver and watch as everyone boards. Towards the end of the line, the bus driver starts examining the passengers' tickets more carefully, taking longer to clear them.

Once everyone has boarded, it's clear there is enough room for each person to have two seats, meaning everyone is in their own comfy two-seat row. The bus pulls back, gets to the end of the bus tunnel, makes a left onto the street, and gets half a block down when a man sprints out of the station after us, holding a piece of paper—a ticket? —high in the air. Passengers shout at the driver, "There's a man trying to catch us; he's chasing the bus." The bus keeps going, and so does the pursuing passenger, but he's losing ground.

"We've already departed," the driver responds. "It's just like the airport. When you pull away from the gate, you have departed. The schedule is we leave at eight twenty, and we left at eight twenty-three." The driver turns left again and heads to Colorado Springs.

The woman in the row ahead of me gives a tremendous, phlegmy sneeze. Then another. I look around and spot two empty rows of seats. One is near the bathroom at the back of the bus, and I do not want to sit near that, but the other is in the center. I pick up my carry-on and move to the empty row. Five minutes later, the guy in the row behind me gives a small, dry cough. Then another. Apparently, multiple people riding on Greyhound are required to have an upper respiratory infection. It actually seems odd that we haven't had another 1918 type pandemic if this is the petri dish of the masses. The guy behind me will cough all the way to the Texas panhandle, but the woman never sneezes again.

In the meantime, I drape my coat across my seats and take a bottle of water and *Ready Player One* out of my carry-on, but don't start reading yet, because I'm watching Colorado slide by in the morning glow. A hawk rises from the side of the highway.

The bus stops about every hour-and-a-half, and we have

a thirty-minute stop in Lamar at a Mexican restaurant, so I'm able to avoid the dreaded bus toilet, which was a goal of mine just as important as not getting arrested.

⁂

Late in the afternoon, we hit the Oklahoma panhandle and barrel through it without slowing down, then enter the Texas panhandle under a slow sunset. A man in the seats across from mine gives the coughing guy a throat lozenge, and he stops coughing immediately. Okay. So, was the guy across from me hoarding an extra lozenge the whole day? I decide not to fret about it.

We roll through a countless series of small Texas towns, and every town manages to look just like the last town and also like the next town: half-dome tin buildings, one-story houses, grain elevators, Presbyterian churches, and First Baptists churches with Sunday school hours posted. Places have personalities. Small towns in England each have a distinct character, but here, the character is hard functionality and that's it. Fences, some with gates and archways, separate the middle of nowhere from the middle of empty, and the stores in the last town are the same as the stores in the next: Sonic, Dollar General, always a Dairy Queen, a Mexican restaurant, a Chinese restaurant, loans and taxes, vape stores, a furniture store or an H&R Block, courthouses, hair salons, tires, boots, a VFW Post, Subway, Taco Bell, McDonald's, Kentucky Fried, State Farm, Valero Gas, a Best Western next to Econo Lodge next to a Super Inn with two 18-wheelers stretched across the parking lot, a Walmart, a cash store, and then open prairie and wind farm turbines turning above dun colored grassland.

We pull into the bus bay in front of the Amarillo Greyhound Station at 6:40 for a seventy-five-minute stop. The Sports Channel blasts on two mounted televisions and two of the four vending machines need restocking. At the row of sinks in the restroom, when I unfold my toiletry organizer and brush my teeth, the woman at the sink next to mine stares at my makeup case as though she never knew they existed, watching me go through a minimized end-of-day hygiene routine.

In the station's waiting area, I eat leftover P.F. Chang's at a seat in the corner as two buses offload and the station crowds up. Conversations float around:

"I know one thing. If they shut this station down, they gonna have to put people in a hotel."

"How long you been sitting here? All day?

"Since eleven. No, ten. That's nine hours now. Hours to go before my transfer."

The bus shows up in the bay at the back of the station, and everyone that's continuing on lines up at the labeled doors. Not one seat is left empty. I get the window and the rumpled man on the aisle seems to have been traveling for a couple of days, wafting a little stale body odor. The sun has gone down and no one on the bus turns on an overhead light, so I drape my coat over myself, perch my feet on the edge of the seat and go into a half-sleep.

We reach Dallas at five in the morning and the streets are barren. My ticket from Denver to San Antonio was actually two tickets: one from Denver to Dallas and a second ticket from Dallas to San Antonio. Dallas is a major Greyhound Station just like Denver, and everyone gets off the bus. I've got ninety minutes before the last leg of the ride. The station is large but less chaotic than Amarillo and more subdued than Denver, and when it's time to board, people get in line according to the boarding number on their tickets and only now do I realize that the boarding number is a specific thing.

As we head to Waxahachie, the bus, again, is nearly full, but it is freezing. Frigid air streams off the edge of the window, and everyone is bundled up, even shivering. Shit. The A/C is on. I wait. No one says anything. They seem to think the bus is supposed to be sub-arctic as if random, pointless suffering is their lot. In Waxahachie, a few get off, a few get on, and I ask the driver if he could turn the heat up a little; the bus feels pretty cold. He looks skeptical, mumbles that the heat is on, but on the way to Waco, warm air starts to pump out and passengers take off their mittens and relax.

By the time we get to Austin, where I get off to pee, Texas feels like Texas again, sunny and comfortable, six days before Christmas. I don't even get off the bus during the brief stop in San Marcos since it's only an hour before the ride will finally be over. After the passengers who did get off re-board, the bus driver walks up the aisle, counting by twos. Then he does it again, looks down the row of seats and points at a thin young man in a gray hoodie, talking low and intently, or pretending to talk, on his phone, with his head down. The man doesn't argue; he just gets off and walks away.

"He snuck on the bus?" A woman asks.

The bus driver settles into his seat, "That's why we do the count."

The bus arrives in San Antonio at 12:30 in the afternoon, exactly on time, and the driver and a Greyhound worker unload the baggage compartments incredibly fast. I grab my bag moments after they shove it into the bus bay, take a few steps to the sidewalk outside, and flag down a taxi that's driving by. With tip, the taxi ride home cost forty-five dollars, about a third of what it cost to take a bus all the way from Denver. I eat the cost of the taxi and decide not to think about it. I'm home. I'm not arrested. Battalions of cops are not swooping down on the property. Mom and Dad are not going to lose their house to asset forfeiture. I got a carry-on bag with products that I need to unpack and de-Mylar, and I have to make Dad's herbal tea, do laundry, and take a post-bus ride bath.

I don't realize yet that this is just my first and smallest weed run to the Rockies.

CHAPTER TWENTY-ONE
WEEDMAS

I SHOW MY parents the picture Nolan took of me in the snow and tell them about freezing my butt off in Colorado and how Nolan had a puffy jacket that kept him warm. Part of the reason Dad chose to retire in San Antonio from the military was because he never wanted to shovel snow again. Before San Antonio, we'd been stationed in Arizona where he'd twisted his ankle sliding on an icy sidewalk, and before that in Germany, where, in the spring thaw, they find people missing for months, who'd fallen over walking home from the bar.

"The yard is full of leaves," said Dad.

Mom looked up. "Raking leaves is good exercise."

"Leaves? Who mentioned leaves?"

Mom frowns. "You think you're funny now. Wait until you start radiation and haven't built up your strength."

Dad goes to bed as early as 7:30 sometimes and, once he's laid down for the evening, I catch Mom when she heads down the hall and call her into my room to show her the stash.

"You brought this all back from Colorado?" she says, looking at the spread laid out on my bed. "Alene, that's risky. They can open your bags at the airport. What if you were arrested?"

"It's fine. It's done," I say. She pauses while reassessing my trip. I pick up one small box. "So this is a CBD tincture. CBD is non-psychoactive so it doesn't get anyone high, but it reduces pain and stress. One drop under Dad's tongue each night, or one drop during the day and a drop at night before bed can be helpful," I finish vaguely.

"I know that it's medicine. When Uncle Hugo stopped treatment for his cancer, his nephew got him some marijuana and it helped keep him comfortable. I know it works. Uncle Hugo said as much."

"So, you'll give it to Dad?"

"Well, he can't take anything right now. The doctors don't want him to take anything except what they prescribe while he's undergoing chemotherapy because they have to monitor everything carefully so they can determine the effects. They have to track dosages to figure out what works without additional variables." Mom takes a step closer to the bed, surveying all the neatly packaged edibles, tincture, ointment, and lotion. "But I'll talk to his doctors. The radiation treatment starts in January right after the chemotherapy is done."

"This helps reduce nausea."

"I've heard that," she says, then adds, "That's a nice bag. Stylish. Where did that come from?"

The Native Roots bag stands upright in the middle of the bed. I don't think she's read the pothead slang that covers it. "From one of the shops."

Mom straightens up. "Give this to Dad for Christmas. It'll give him something to keep his hopes up during radiation therapy. He won't be so worried about side effects if he knows he has this. This will make a good present. I'll speak to his doctors at his next appointment."

I feel deflated after Mom leaves. I had already pictured Dad's pleased reaction and the satisfaction I would get as a little triumphant reward for braving dispensaries, Decima, and Denver International's lack of a taxi bay. Now I would have to wait, not quite impatient, but stalled.

I go through my full routine to get ready for bed which includes not only the usual face washing and teeth brushing, but also irrigating my sinuses. The dry snot nosebleeds from Denver's mile-high air had started the second day I was there but irrigating my sinuses was the worst choice I could have made: Tuesday morning I bring up pale yellow phlegm and feel the first prickly scratch in my throat.

Mom finds that Macy's has ultralight puffy down jackets on sale. Normally, I hate to shop, but even I think the sale is good timing. Experiencing real cold awakened a primal fear in me, and I want to get some Nolan-level warm clothing. Mom drives us to the mall, talking the whole way.

"The problem is not really the cancer treatment, though that's bad enough. It's the dementia. He won't follow what the doctors say and can't remember if he's taken his medications. He thinks he's taken his morning pills when he hasn't. I'm doing everything I can do. It's his stubbornness that's the problem." She parks the car and digs around in her purse. "Plus, he's lost so much weight. He used to have a butt, a firm round butt. Now it's gone. Just flat. Your father's completely lost his butt. Have you noticed?"

Have I noticed my father's butt? "Open the door," I tell

her. As a boy, my dad had wandered alone on the mountains in Hot Springs, eating wild blueberries and swimming in the natural pools hidden up there. When he was a young man in the military and had a weekend off, he and his friends would rush up to New York. He'd told me what it was like to be in the room when all the horns came in during *Take the 'A' Train* and Duke Ellington's big band blew the roof off the place. Dad had a piece of the Berlin Wall that Tessa, at the start of her impetuous teens, had chipped off in 1968 when we were stationed in Germany. Tessa had eventually forgotten about it, but Dad kept it. What crept into my mind about Dad's dementia was my loss of access to his worlds of experiences. Mom looks over at me and I add, "You have the child lock on."

I buy a puffy jacket and, as a Christmas present, Mom buys me a puffy coat since, "The jacket won't keep your butt warm."

When we get back home, I send Nolan a long e-mail about my bus trip back to San Antonio, detailing how boring Texas towns look, then go online and order winter sports gloves, thermal socks and the Sorel snow boots everyone was wearing in Denver. My primitive fear of the cold eases off.

The bus acquired plague progresses predictably. By late Tuesday, I have a sore throat. Wednesday, a little cough, and, though I still feel fine, I know what's coming. It hits on Thursday with fatigue, a low fever that comes and goes, and a hacking cough that ends in a long hard gasp for the air. I sit on the bed, too tired to do anything that requires walking and spend the afternoon assembling a hydroponic Aerogarden so I can grow herbs on the kitchen counter. I warn Jovi, who has started winter break, not to come near me, but she sits on the bed anyway and watches me assemble the kit. After a while, she gets bored and climbs under the comforter, trying to play, then climbs out again when she gets too hot. I can feel the infection settle into my chest. Sunday is Christmas.

⁂

Getting to the presents on Christmas day takes forever, even though it's just me, Mom, and Dad. Most of the presents are for Jovi, and she was spending the day with her father. Next Christmas, it would be Lauren's turn to have her. Callie had to cover a shift for one of the other rehab therapists, and Lauren said that she just wanted to rest. She had been working late every day for a week.

Mom makes dinner by herself since I wake up feeling worse than the night before, and though dinner is good, the cold has taken my appetite and I don't even finish all the food on my plate. After dinner, Mom clears up while I lay on the little couch at the far end of the living room to avoid sharing germs.

Mom hands the presents around, passing the black and white gift bag to Dad. The weed slang and bong silhouette go unnoticed. Dad takes out the Cheeba Chew first and turns it over. "Oh," he says, pretending to be pleased with the gift, whatever it is. "Thank you," he looks at the tag. "From Santa. Well, that's nice." The Cheeba Chews go back in the bag and he pulls out the lotion next. "I need some lotion." Then the ointment and the CBD oil tincture are up. He turns the box of CBD oil all the way around before putting it back in the gift bag. "Well, that's all very nice."

"Dad—" I organize the information in my head before I explain—Colorado, edibles, CBD, non-psychoactive, for pain and anxiety, for nausea, for the radiation treatment.

When I finish, he stares down into the gift bag again. "Oh-ho. Now that is something. That is great. Thank you."

Mom puts the gift bag of cannabis products on the top shelf of their master bedroom linen closet. I suggest a more covert location, but, Mom reasons, Jovi never opens that closet, so it's fine. I lay around the rest of the day and finish reading *Ready Player One*.

On Monday, I wake up with conjunctivitis and a right eye so crusty it is glued shut. My eyelid is swollen. I scrub my eyes out three times that day with hot water and baby shampoo. Then Tuesday night, my world gets amazingly gross when my left eye gets infected as well. It goes like this. I'm lying around in bed and feel something weird. My eye feels weird. Not quite like something is alive in there but weird enough that I go to the bathroom to look in the mirror under vanity lights. God. Damn. Thick, white, stringy mucous oozes down out of my top eyelid and up out of my bottom eyelid. I squeeze my eyelid and snot comes out. Of my eye. Beyond just the aesthetic horror show, it is also really uncomfortable. I wash my eyes out, and ten minutes later, I'm washing them again. It's like my eye keeps blowing its nose, all evening long.

On Wednesday, I get up and both eyes are gluey and disgusting, but not as bad as the night before. I'm on the road to recovery.

ঌ

Days later, Dad knocks on my door. Standing in the hall, he's wheezing, short of breath, one hand on the door jam. "Go help your mom. Outside," he says. He's wearing yard work clothes. "She's raking those leaves up in the backyard. I'm not feeling well."

He's already heading to the living room, using the wall to

steady himself. He lays on the couch and closes his eyes, one hand on his chest, one on his forehead.

"You want me to call Mom in?" I ask.

"No, I'm fine. Had enough for now though."

I put on shoes then get water in the kitchen. Jovi is on a blanket on the living room floor. "He's not gonna rake leaves anymore?" she stares at Dad.

"No."

"So he's sending you out to rake instead?"

"Yes."

"And you're going?"

"Yes." I drink the water, unsure what she's trying to work through.

"Because he doesn't want to?" She turns to Dad. "Why send Alene out to rake?"

He keeps his eyes closed, "I need to catch my breath."

"You just want to lay down?"

Dad's breathing is steady, no longer wheezing, but he doesn't answer. Under her breath, Jovi says, "Whatever."

"Jovi!" I snap. "Don't say 'whatever' to your granddad like that. You understand me?"

"Yes."

"Do you understand? You don't talk to your grandfather like that."

"I understand."

I go out the patio door. Mom has the leaf blower going, but our yard is big. Our house is on the corner of an intersection, and the yard is a 1970s yard plus half of another. She's got about a third of the leaves blown into a pile past the pecan tree with its skeletal branches. I start raking leaves into the pile. It's 78 degrees and the sun is weaker than in the summer, but soon I'm turning my face away from it, realizing I should have put on a hat.

Mom puts down the leaf blower and uses a snow shovel that has not shoveled snow in decades to scoop up the leaves and toss them into a trash bag, then she paws at the ground with her shoe, and a snake, the hue of dead leaves and pathetically small, tries to wriggle. Mom steps on it, then carefully angles the edge of the snow shovel. I feel bad for its brief moment of terror, but I knew it was doomed: To Mom's mind, there cannot be a snake, even a tiny one, in a yard that Jovi can venture into. Mom leans her weight. I don't watch to see if she shovels both pieces into the lawn bag or not, but clearly, there are worse things that can happen to a snake than being concussed by Nolan.

Three hours later, the yard is free of leaves and lawn bags. When I go inside, Jovi is still on the blanket playing, and Dad must be in his room.

"Grandpa's laying down again." She rolls over, holding a doll above her. "Because he's lazy. He lays down a lot."

"He's not lazy." This time there's no heat in my response. "Your grandpa is in his eighties. He doesn't have as much energy as you do. When people get older, they have less energy. Do your teachers run around like you do on the playground?"

"No."

"Grandpa is actually your great-granddad. And grandma is your great-grandmother. Your grandmother Tessa is my sister. Okay? That means grandpa and grandma had Tessa and me. And Tessa had Lauren and your aunt Callie. So Lauren and Callie are Tessa's daughters. And Lauren had you." I count off each generation on my fingers. "Grandpa gets tired more easily because he's old and doesn't have as much energy." She looks skeptical but doesn't say anything, and I wonder where her thinking is coming from.

By evening, Mom's elbow is sore, and she decides it's from swinging the leaf blower. "It's a little heavy and you move it from side to side."

"Your elbow hurts?" I say, standing by the side of her bed. "Luckily, I have sore elbow ointment."

"Really? Let me try some of that." Mom sits on the bed, propped against the elaborate headboard. My parents' bed, king-size with a headboard that pyramids up to a crest, would work well in a small palace.

"Mom, the ointment that I brought back for Dad's back? You can use that on your elbow." I find the ointment jar and hand it to her.

"How much do I use?"

"Just enough to cover your elbow."

She digs into the semi-translucent, pale-yellow paste and scoops out a fingernail size amount, then rubs it over her elbow. Dad leans up off the bed to watch.

I repack the gift bag and put it back in the linen closet. "It takes twenty minutes to two hours. It takes different amounts of time depending on the person. It is not immediate like an anesthetic. So people need to realize that so they don't think, 'Oh, it is not working—'"

"And use more."

"Right." Forty minutes later, I come back. "Did it work?"

Mom is rolling her hair, a comb in her hand and a plastic pail full of rollers on the bed in front of her. "Did what work?"

"The ointment?"

"Oh, I forgot." She stretches her arm out, bends it, then starts stretching and bending, moving her arm and wrist—I don't know why she added the wrist in—around and around, then in a big circle. "It doesn't hurt. I guess it works. But it'll wear off tomorrow."

"And then you could use it again."

CHAPTER TWENTY-TWO
THE LUNCH TOUR

A WEEK AFTER I recovered from the cold and conjunctivitis, I still had a post-cold cough, but I was ready to start my lunch tour, which is the non-celebrity version of the talk show circuit. A lunch tour is when you go to lunch with one friend after another and tell each one what happened on your trip. I was a smash hit. I started with Mitch.

I had errands to run that morning, plus a trip to Central Market. Central Market is in upscale Alamo Heights and carries imported specialty everything and has the biggest gluten-free selection and the best cheese department in the city, so I do a pilgrimage there about three times a year. I run into a former student right away. I was standing by the Brussels sprouts, which, at Central Market are on long thick stalks, stacked in rows resting on a bank of crushed ice. I only needed two sprouts as garnish for a mashed parsnip side dish I wanted to make, and the injustice of having to buy an entire stalk had paralyzed me.

"What are you doing?" He was standing right at my shoulder.

My brain didn't engage quite right. "Hi. It's good to see you," I chimed. I have this response because after twenty years, I've taught thousands of students and they are crushed when you don't remember them. Usually, I say, 'hi' and add that I remember their face, but I am bad with names and they have to remind me what class they were in, and how long ago. Then I swing into how are they now, what four-year university did they transfer to, have they graduated, what job do they have, and generally just keep the conversation all about them. They are happy, and so am I, especially if they are doing well.

But I already know something is off. He's older, with lank gray hair. And I feel like I actually remember him, which is a bad sign because the students I remember tend to have done something strange or threatening. He says he was in my class at Bexar Colleges Downtown two years ago. Hhm. I transferred to Mirador five years ago but I keep my face frozen in a 'happy to see you' mask.

And then everything clicks into the usual routine for a while. He's a paralegal now, working in a law office specializing in immigration. "That's an excellent field," I say, following the 'compliment everything' rule. I start wondering if he's number four of the five students in my career that I have truly disliked. Is he that student from Central America who I suspected had been a member of a death squad in one of those countries that had death squads? He tells me again how helpful my class was. He takes classes online now though, because going to class is so boring since he already lived through what they're teaching, while the younger students have to learn it all.

Right. It's him. He was arrogant in class and wrote misogynistic essays. His analysis was always that the women in the stories we were covering deserved whatever tragedy happened to them because they were not modest enough or they talked too much or were promiscuous even if there was no sex in the story: he could tell, the woman was a whore.

During the semester, I suspected he was on the wrong side of a lot of Central American history and then came the final exam. Students had to write an analysis over a story called "The Colonel" where a military strongman dumps out a bag of human ears in front of two Americans asking about human rights. Instead of giving me a paragraph about how the severed ears are a symbol of the poor and oppressed in a corrupt regime, he wrote about how sad he was for the misunderstood colonel, who was working hard to bring order to the world. He made no mention of the bag of ears.

The former student digs in his wallet and hands me his card as I wrap up the happy talk. He evaporates back into the Central Market ether. I abandon the Brussels sprouts and head to the mushrooms. Two hundred and eighty dollars later, I have a cart full of organic everything; gluten free maple buckwheat cereal; goat, sheep, and buffalo cheeses; imported chocolates; three bottles of Greek wine; pitted olives and I'm done.

Mitch's new house is in a gated community that is either high-end middle class or low-end upper class; take your pick. The house is next to a forested green belt with a creek surrounded by curving trails and deer. Already talking as he opens the door, he gives me a perfunctory hug and keeps talking: he is editing an art journal that has to go to print in ten days, but he stopped giving a shit about it weeks ago.

The house has an open floor plan. I sit in the great room area. He's replaced his tattered furniture with a leather couch and overstuffed chairs. Mitch keeps talking from another room, and I see him wander past into the kitchen, typing on a laptop propped on one arm.

"The artists keep sending in poor quality photos of their paintings. The files are too small, not magazine quality. They're being artistic idiots about it all." He emails an artist and closes the laptop. "My house is a wreck," he says. "I screwed up. I didn't sign the boys up for camp, so they've been home for a week, which I love spending time with the boys, but I've got to catch up on work. I helped mom pick out a new car."

Mitch's mom, Miriam, has the boys for the afternoon. "They wear you down," he says about car salesmen. "They bring out all this confusing shit so that by then you just say yes to whatever. They should just have a touch screen menu on the table. You touch what you want and see the price for the upgrade and the total for the car and you're done, out of there with time for Costco, see. Let me change into pants."

A few minutes later, we're at the Thai restaurant on Nyla where the waiter apologizes for interrupting us each time he brings something to the table. I tell Mitch all about my Colorado cannabis shopping trip and I'm still not done by the time we've finished eating. I talk about the dispensaries, how nervous I was, the budtenders, receptionists, the smell of the shops, the music they use as part of each store's branding, security, and the prices. Cannabis ain't cheap.

Back at his house, I go over the bus ride home, the bus stations, the guy coughing behind me and the cold that I caught, adding, "You're really gonna like this," and tell him about the mucus dripping eyeball conjunctivitis.

Mitch groans, "You better not still be contagious, girly. If I get sick 'cuz of you."

I hold up the water he gave me, "Burn this glass when I leave."

"I can't believe you did it. I didn't realize you had gone already 'till I got the picture of you in the snow. Seriously, I so advised you against it. Hell's bells." Mitch pauses to admire me and my huge steaming pile of bringing-cannabis-back-to-Texas bravery. "I can't believe you went for it. What did your mom say when you got back?"

I tell him and then talk about her sore elbow and the totally effective cannabis ointment.

"Wow," he says, "wow."

Lauren was in the living room with Mom when I got home. The alternating highlights Lauren had added to her hair right before the divorce were fading, and her hair was growing long again. She was sitting on the edge of the couch, the over-sized purse looped on her shoulder. I made a perfunctory nod then slid into my room and convinced myself that I was starting some of the prep work for the upcoming spring semester.

The conversation coming from down the hall limped clumsily for a bit, then dwindled. Mom attempted to fill the gaps, complimenting a drawing Jovi had done, asking if Jovi would join the school choir again, then asking Lauren if her dress was new, but every topic threaded back somehow to the divorce which Lauren still had not directly mentioned to us, even though she knew that Tessa had told us about it. Jovi was with Wyatt for the weekend, and Lauren wasn't spending money on new dresses anymore.

"Lauren?" Mom sounded odd. "Lauren?"

"Mad at me," Lauren said, and her sudden sobs heaved

around, breaking up her words, "Everybody, blaming me. I know you don't want to see me—"

"That's not true. You know we love you."

"—yelling at me—"

"—We've been concerned about you and Jovi—"

"You want Jovi to come over but not me—"

"We want to see you and Jovi and Callie. We worry about all of you."

Lauren's voice pitched up, "Alene won't talk to me. She goes in her room whenever I come over. I know she's ignoring me."

I hear them moving past the dining room to the entryway.

"Lauren, I know you've been going through a lot of difficulties," Mom says, "been under so much stress—"

The front door opens, Mom following Lauren to the driveway, Mom's arms open. I watch through my window as Lauren opens her car door. Mom catches her and hugs her. Then Lauren gets into the driver's seat.

Mom stands in the driveway even after the car disappears down the street, and I already know what's coming when she opens my door. "I want you to start talking to Lauren again. She's having a difficult time right now. She's upset."

"Alright."

"You're hurting her feelings."

"I'll talk to her."

"And be nice."

I wasn't crass enough to wish Lauren misery, but I wasn't sure how, on a certain level, to stop being angry at her. Trying to reprogram a few more synapses, I spend the evening with *The Art of Happiness* and the notes I wrote down when I was reading anger management books. I re-walk the steps to reach empathy, starting with understanding someone else's realities. I actually have to sit quietly for a while, not quite meditating but definitely turning down the day's clatter of thoughts and distractions.

Lauren had never even dated anyone other than Wyatt. She'd never traveled alone or lived on her own. Three months after I graduated from high school, I was a freshman at UT Austin, living the first year in Jester Center's huge co-ed dorm and the next years in Sonora House. And after UT, it was Los Angeles and USC. But Lauren, after high school, had gone from her mom's house to a campus apartment twenty minutes away at Crockett State. Her first year, she and Wyatt took half their classes together. She dropped out when they got married and moved into their first small apartment.

Jovi had just spent Christmas with Wyatt and his new girlfriend, whose name was Jazzmin, Jazzmin with two 'Z's', even though she wasn't a stripper. He introduced her to Jovi as his cousin's friend, who was passing through town. Next year, it would be Lauren's turn to have Jovi for Christmas. The court had mapped out the holiday schedule for years to come.

In addition to dealing with Wyatt, Lauren also had to sort out health insurance for herself and Jovi, keep driving a worn-out car, build up her finances, and recognize that, without a degree, her payroll clerk job wasn't good enough to handle all of that. So, the ground Lauren had built her life on had given way.

Book cover Dali Llama looks at me and sighs.

Fine. I would talk to Lauren, and I would be nice. I could go through the motions, even if, deep down, I didn't really feel them yet.

Next on the lunch tour circuit was Nicoletta, a friend of mine from the University of Texas. Every few years, she had a convention in San Antonio, and every few years, I'd drive up to Austin for a concert that we both wanted to see. This time Nicoletta was giving a presentation at a conference in town but could meet for lunch afterwards. Her new boyfriend Mark would be with her.

I arrived a little late because of road construction. Señor Veggie is the epitome of a San Antonio restaurant. The building is saffron yellow and looks like it's made of adobe but with big windows along the street side. Inside, each room is painted its own saturated color: aqua blue in the main dining room; tangerine in the private party room, melon green behind the register. Only one other table was occupied, and everyone's conversations bounced off the mauve concrete floors and the Mexican tile on the walls.

"Alene. So glad to see you," Nicoletta got up to hug me as a plate of hummus surrounded by veggies and pita slid onto the table. "We were hungry. We ordered," she said.

Nicoletta is ethereally beautiful, stunningly so. The fact that she's not obnoxious makes her beauty more bearable, and dealing with Nicoletta's beauty was like dealing with Nolan's intelligence. Both lie so far beyond normal they do not create a sense of threat or competition, just other-worldliness, in a strangely everyday way.

Her classical face was a shade thinner than the last time I saw her, but the big change was that her hair was mostly gray. It had been playing with gray before, but now the chestnut brown was almost gone. Her hair was long and, as always, ringlet curly. She can't comb it. After she washes it, she can run her fingers through it exactly three times while it's still wet to give it some order, but a comb turns her hair into a gigantic fuzzball. Growing up with this affliction taught Nicoletta discipline and minimalism. She had pinned her hair half up, half escaping confinement, Greek goddess-like. Her eyes are not big, but her gaze is intense, mixed hazel and gray, continuously catching the light with odd little sparkles. I don't know how that works.

Knowing the waiter would have to come and go several times between the gap after we ordered and when the main course actually came, I wanted to wait before embarking on my cannabis adventure story. The waiter made eye contact from across the room and walked over very slowly. He stood at the table and smiled for a while, then he vaguely inquired about drinks or what have you. Again, a very San Antonio place.

Since I was helping myself to hummus and pita bread, I got empanadas to share with the table and got caught up on how Nicoletta had been doing over the last year. She worked in marketing and made safety and promotional films for businesses, and she'd just bought a house in Austin, small but comfortable.

The drinks came. Before telling my story, I wanted time to size up her new boyfriend, Mark. He would probably be safe. It seemed unlikely that Nicoletta would be dating a Texas Ranger hell-bent on enforcing draconian marijuana laws, but it seemed best to find out while I was still dipping the crudités, if I should divulge any interstate trafficking I may have recently committed. Mark—neat mustache, reddish-brown hair, friendly eyes—turned out to be a counselor specializing in rehab, addiction, and substance abuse.

I talked about Dad, his kidney tumor, belching, the herbal tea, prostate cancer, and cannabis research, followed by the Saga of My Trip to the Denver Dispensaries, resorts, hiking with Nolan, and the tedious bus ride home. I left out the eye ooze.

After our plates had been cleared, the remains of the appetizers were still on the table. Mark wipes up the last of the hummus with a slice of cucumber. "You could put the weed in your luggage," he says. "They only use the sniffer dogs that walk up and down the aisles for international flights. Or better yet, you know, next time you could just mail it home. FedEx." I must be looking dubious. "You wrap it up, put it in a box, and mail it. FedEx ships everything out at nine o'clock. So, you take it to the FedEx in Denver at, say, eight p.m. It goes straight to their processing facility and ships out at nine that night and it's waiting at your house the next morning. The tinctures don't have a smell anyway. Maybe you wrap things in one of those oven bags, seal it up, then fill the rest of the box with t-shirts or socks. Give it all a little cushion."

Yahtzee.

Friendly-eyed, not-a-Texas-Ranger Mark has spoken, although casually, with a definite air of knowledge. "So I could fly to Denver, do my shopping, FedEx it home and just fly back to S.A.? No need for a twenty-seven-hour bus ride?"

"Oh yeah."

"You have no idea how much time and stress you have just saved me in the future." Mark's mention of the oven bag reminds me of the Mylar bags, and I explain how I'd used them in my carry-on.

"Even better," he says.

"Seriously. This is great."

Mark makes a bathroom run.

Nicoletta pinches her lower lip lightly, a habit she had when we were at UT together. Because Nicoletta looks like she wandered out of an old Renaissance masterpiece, I wonder if there is a painting somewhere with a Madonna pinching her lip. She asks if I am sleeping with Nolan and, when I say no, asks why not. 'Sleeping with' seems to have become the default. 'Not sleeping with' was what required the explanation. Then she talks about Mark, how they met on a dating app because they were both reading *The Power of Now: A Guide to Spiritual Enlightenment*, and she discusses their satisfying sex life.

Mark's return to the table does not change the conversation, but he yawns: a heavy meal, a warm restaurant, and relationship conversation—even if it's his own relationship—was sedating him. We've tied up the table for nearly three hours and only stop talking because Nicoletta and Mark have to drive back to Austin. Before she leaves, Nicoletta veers to the Colorado cannabis story again saying, "You are so brave."

Hearing that actually gave me a thrill like the nervous electricity I had felt in my fingertips before I went, but without the fear and needle-like pain. Finally, she wonders if I had tried any of the treats I went up there to get for Dad.

"No?" Nicoletta arches her delicate eyebrows. Just as Nolan had no real interest in drinking alcohol, I had felt no particular interest in feeling the effects of cannabis, and I wonder if I hear a tiny trace of disappointment in Nicoletta's "Oh," as she hugs me goodbye.

Euphoric, analgesic, or hallucinogenic: actually taking cannabis did not occur to me as an experience I needed to have or as information I needed to know firsthand. And I didn't need to know it. Not yet anyway. Not quite yet.

CHAPTER TWENTY-THREE

BLACK CHERRY CHOCOLATE

My parents expected that I would die young. I had a heart murmur when I was born and in the sixties, the doctors believed it was a congenital heart defect, and I would not survive childhood. Don't get too attached, they suggested, in a not-at-all callous, detached medical way: She's not gonna be a long-term investment, tell ya' what, not gonna be a going concern. Dad's response to my impending demise was to spoil me: "Want a pony? I'll make that happen." Dad decided to make happy memories for when I was gone, partly because I was expected to die and partly because he was an alcoholic and felt guilty for days after he'd gotten drunk.

Mom, however, was a nurse and remained practical. She told him to stop spoiling me, reasoning that if I died, I died, and there was nothing they could do about it, but if I didn't, I'd be a monstrous brat by the time I was ten. "Suds aren't going to kill her, are they? So make her wash the damn dishes," she said when they thought I was in another part of the house.

And Dad did stop spoiling me, at least in the open. But

he was there in the background. Money, if I asked for it, was just handed over. Candy always. Toys if I even looked at them twice. Fortunately, I was not a very greedy child.

The doctors predicted that my parents would walk into my room one morning and find me dead. Sudden and quiet, in the night, just painlessly gone. While my parents clashed over spoiling me—Mom put her foot down and I did not get the pony—there were other things they were in complete agreement over, mainly that I was frail and sickly. My pending sudden death was evidence of this, as was tonsillitis and a parade of all of the diseases kids caught back then: mumps, measles, chicken pox, ear infections, sudden fevers, and random headaches. So I was frequently checked on. My parents would poke their heads into my room to see what I was doing—Still breathing, yes? —and sitting still for a long time invited suspicion, inquiry, and sometimes alarm. It went like this:

Mom would say, "What are you doing?"

"Just sitting here," I'd reply.

"You've been sitting quietly for a long time."

"So what."

"Well. . . Okay."

Waking up to find a parent standing next to your bed, listening intently, is not creepy when it has happened from time to time all your life, until you learn that the same thing does not happen to any of your friends. That starts you thinking.

The takeaway is that when I was young, there was no expectation of me doing any real manual labor or heavy lifting. Even when I was an adult, sometimes, my aging mom, unable to break old habits, would take backpacks off my back, and my lost-his-butt dad would take stacks of books, bags of groceries, or boxes from Amazon out of my arms with, "That's too heavy."

He has spinal arthritis and COPD. "Let me get that," he would say. Prostate cancer and Alzheimer's. "It's too much for you."

My parents never told me they thought I would die. Tessa did: "The doctors told them you'd be dead before you were two. Four, if no one startled you too bad."

Somehow or other, it explained a lot. I was nine when she said it.

❧

Before the start of each fall and spring semester, Bexar County Colleges has a week of convocation with meetings, updates and presentations. Between meetings on Tuesday, I ran home for lunch. Dad had finished his chemotherapy treatments the previous week, and as I walked in, Mom and Dad were about to leave for his first radiation treatment. When I reminded Mom about using the CBD tincture to remedy nausea, she surprised me. She had given Dad his first drop of tincture the night before. "He slept pretty well and did not toss and turn, so I slept well. First time in years he hasn't been up half the night," she said, then fussed about the jacket he'd chosen as they headed out the door.

Over the next few days, I noticed that Dad was indeed sleeping through the night, without his oboe-groan and without waking up and pacing the hallway. The immediate beneficiary of this change was Mom. Very quickly, she looked more rested and less strained. She still fussed at him, but the sharp edge came off her comments. I could hear them laughing in their room. According to Mom, Dad tolerated the treatments so well even his doctors were amazed.

By the middle of February, Dad had gone through four weeks of radiation. Jovi was spending the night on Sunday since she would be out of school for President's Day on Monday, and if she stayed overnight, no one would have to drop her off in the morning and Jovi could sleep in.

Mom had become increasingly anxious over the weekend. Prior to having each radiation treatment, Dad was supposed to drink a lot of water, so he could go into the treatment room with a full bladder. This makes it easier for the radiologist to hit the prostate cancer target and avoid other organs. But on Thursday, the wait for Dad to go in for his session had stretched longer and longer. Two patients ahead of him had problems that dragged out their appointments, and finally Dad could not hold it any longer and went to the bathroom. When he came back, it was his turn. Mom told him to drink more water and wait until his bladder was full again before having his treatment, but Dad said it would take up the whole day if he did that and went in when they called him.

The radiation nicked his intestines.

By Sunday, he had not eaten for the last three days. Mom made a pot of spaghetti, thinking that would be easy to eat, but he wouldn't touch anything. Finally, when she started to wonder if we should drive him over to the hospital, I told Mom that she should give him one of the squares from the Denver chocolate bars. The chocolate bars are half CBD and half THC, a one-to-one ratio, and THC, though psychoactive, is also the component in weed that stimulates appetite. I tell her twice what to give him and how much, but she hesitates and tells me to get the right amount and give it to him.

I get one of the Black Cherry Chocolate bars out of the glossy dispensary bag in the linen closet and take it to the kitchen, so I can cut the bar while also hiding it from Jovi. I don't want her to see the bag or the chocolate. Of course, as soon as I get to the kitchen, Jovi wants hot cocoa. Mom has to get the cocoa package, Jovi has to dig around in the pantry for marshmallows, and they both have a discussion about which mug the drink should go in. Eventually, Jovi heads back to her room, Mom starts measuring the milk and heating it up, and I find out that the child proof packaging on a cannabis chocolate bar is pretty damn difficult to open.

The wrapper is a thick plastic sleeve with a rigid sliding mechanism like a heavy-duty plastic freezer bag, but it also has a kind of lock mechanism on the slider, where two rounded teeth click into place to hold the slider shut. To open the slider, I have to grip and squeeze super hard so that the prongs on the locking end of the zipper open. Simultaneously, I have to pull the wrapper part out of the plastic rod. It's clever. The whole thing impressed me by being hard to open yet easily defeated by a pair of scissors if anyone was physically unable to move the slider.

The chocolate bar has ten squares on it, and each square is molded with '5 mg' on it. I show the bar to Mom, slice out one square, and, by pushing the slider back, I re-lock the plastic wrapper. The square of chocolate goes on a saucer, and I take it to Dad.

Dad eats the chocolate, finds a few spare flecks and dabs those up with his finger. I worry that I'd been too stingy and hadn't given him enough, but everything I read about edible dosages says to start low and see if it works. The edibles, unlike tinctures, can take two hours to kick in. If it didn't work, we would take him to urgent care in the morning.

Ninety minutes later, Dad was in the kitchen heating up a bowl of spaghetti. A thunderstorm was rolling in, and Jovi, getting fidgety in anticipation of lightning, was finding reasons to go up and down the hallway and into my room and my parents' room. Once Dad starts eating, Mom stops focusing on him enough to realize the local news is announcing that we're under a tornado watch.

A weatherwoman points at a swirling radar color palette and mentions wind rotation, and my parents clear out a space in their walk-in closet and lay down blankets in case we get hit. We watch—me on the TV in my room and my parents on the TV in their room—as the storm tracks closer, and outside the wind picks up. Mom and Dad go into the closet with Jovi and hunker down. I stay in my room, despite Mom telling me to join them. Ten minutes later, the storm has moved past us, and the weatherwoman is telling people farther away to seek shelter.

My parents had the right idea. In the morning, we find out that 100 homes in the surrounding areas and an apartment building a mile away were damaged as four small tornadoes touched down. In the afternoon, when Lauren comes by to pick up Jovi, I stay in the living room. "Are those your casual Monday spike heels?" I ask. Lauren loves shoes, and the heels she's wearing could harpoon a beluga. She looks over, unsure if I'm being chatty or critical. "They're posh," I add. "I assume something endangered sacrificed its life to get you a lot of envious stares from the women in the office today?"

"No," Lauren angles her feet so we can see the shoes' details. "They're actually really comfortable. I re-discovered these in the back of my closet recently. I don't know why I ever stopped wearing them." Lauren and Mom begin a strategic discussion about shoes, stores and sales, and I feel I've done my bit to let Lauren know I'm no longer bearing a grudge against her, even if I still am, which I can't be sure of anymore. That's something one of the anger management books suggested: practicing kindness, even if you just go through the motions, leads to kindness. Better than practicing meanness. Either way, the next visit will be easier, and I can fake it until the emotions truly become familial again.

On Tuesday night, I give Dad another square of CBD/THC Black Cherry Chocolate, and in an hour, it gives him an appetite. Two nights later, it works again. The rest of the weeks of radiation treatments go on without incident, and Dad's appetite returns to what has become normal for him.

⁂

Mom and Dad's last trip to Hot Springs was in 2015, and even then, Mom predicted that it might be the last time they ever saw Arkansas. Their old high school had a class reunion, roughly a sixty-year class reunion, but it combined four years' worth of graduates so there would be enough people attending. Even so, it was sparse. So many of their classmates had died, especially in the previous decade, that four years' worth of graduates could not fill The Arlington's Magnolia Room. After the trip, they sat on the couch, Mom reviewing who was still alive, who still 'looked like themselves,' and who'd just gotten married 'old as he is.'

Dad didn't comment much and gradually I learned something on the trip had disturbed him. Aunt Gracie and her husband were at the reunion and, besides spending time with them, my parents had also visited extended family. Dad had outlived all nine of his siblings, but he had cousins that he kept in touch with. His cousin Melvin and Melvin's wife, Alma, had been in the same nursing home for two years. Alma had died earlier in the week, and Mom and Dad stood in the nursing home day room, late afternoon sun pooling on the linoleum floor. Melvin sat at a table playing cards with another resident as my parents offered condolences. Mom talked about how smart Alma had been in school, answering questions so fast. After high school, Alma supported herself as she worked her way through college, her widowed mother unable to help. Eventually, she moved back to Hot Springs to become the first female math teacher Langston High School ever had.

Melvin slapped a card down and said nothing. Dad asked him if he knew Alma had died, that his wife of fifty years had passed away.

"Yeah," Melvin said, pulling from the deck. "They told me. She was a good wife."

On the couch in the living room, Dad kept returning to Melvin's lack of reaction. "He really just didn't care," Dad said for the second time, fixated on the visit.

"The dementia's dulling his responses," Mom said. "He loved Alma."

"She was his wife, and he doesn't remember her. Not really. He didn't feel anything. He wasn't himself anymore. Couldn't have been."

I knew now that what Dad truly dreaded was that loss of self, not just of knowledge and those worlds he shared that were now dissolving, but the personhood built over a lifetime, the emotions that tied you to love and obligations. I knew that, between the cancer, Alzheimer's, COPD and whatever else was stalking him in his eighties, Dad would rather his body give out before his mind did. Fulfilling his duty to others had been his life. Serving family, country, or God had shaped his days for decades.

If someone loses those ties, he believed, then the shell that person was in was already empty.

CHAPTER TWENTY-FOUR
SUMMER 2017

BLUE SHUTTLE VAN had gone out of business, and on my phone, the map on my newly downloaded rideshare app had a little car driving toward me and a countdown indicating that my driver, Selina, was seven minutes away. At three minutes left, I dragged my luggage to the driveway. Mom and Dad followed and sat on the bench on the porch, mentioning again that they could drive me for free. "This is how people do things now," I said.

An SUV pulled up and the driver let her window down. "Alene? I'll open the back."

Dad hefted my bag into the rear lift as I got into the passenger seat explaining to Selina that I had never used Lyft or Uber before. We talk on the way to the airport, and she fills me in on the rideshare game: She drives overnight now because the money is better. She was just coming off the end of her shift and about to go home when this one last fare came up and she was close by. She used to drive during the day and averaged about ten dollars an hour, but she'd noticed that when she worked days, things were picking up at the end of her shift or early in the morning. Gradually she started working later, then overnight and makes twenty-five dollars an hour. Much better.

At the airport, Selina has to inch her way into the Southwest drop off lane. "Okay," she says, "so I'm ending the fare." She shows me how to use the app; a second later, my phone dings and I open the text. I tap the five-dollar tip button and rate the ride five stars with another tap for a clean car and friendly driver.

Inside the airport, everything is automated. A Southwest Airline guy roves around their check-in, and if you eyeball their counter, he intercepts and points to one of the dozen kiosks dotting their front area now. The touch screen kiosk prints off my luggage tag from the boarding pass that I printed yesterday at home. I lug my bag onto the weight platform, and the check-in lady takes it with a smile but no eye contact. Minimal human interaction has been achieved.

I throw away my bottle of water at security, take off my shoes and belt, go through the scan, put on my shoes and belt and head down the concourse. A new bottle of water is four dollars and a king-size Kit Kat three.

At the gate, they announce that the plane will be nearly full up, and once on board, after I shove my carry-on under the seat, I take note of an unclear weirdness while we are waiting to depart. The plane is warm. All the windows are closed, and the weirdness is that they stay that way. Usually, when I'm at a window seat, I open the flap and watch the take off. No one on this flight does that. It's like we're in a tube underground. It's early afternoon and the plane is shadowy and quiet as everyone stares at their screens, and the guy next to the window in my row has no carry-on bag at all, just an oversized phone with headphones. He falls asleep before we push away from the gate.

Before the pilot starts to taxi, he really gives the engines a rev, ready to slingshot us up in the air, which may have something to do with the heat. The news reported that flights in Phoenix are being canceled because it is too hot to take off there. We have an odd, jouncy lift off, and since the window covers are closed, we climb with no references to light or direction. The cabin cools off when we reach altitude and a stewardess takes drink orders, and everyone for five rows orders ginger ale.

When we start our descent in Denver, the windows are still closed, and the jolt on landing is startling because I don't know when to expect it.

❧

As soon as I deplane, I find a bathroom. They all have 'L' shaped entrances now to avoid doors. I hang my purse on the hook inside the stall door. The seat is sprinkled with water from the force of the last flush and before I sit down, I wipe the seat with toilet tissue, then lay the disposable tissue seat cover from the dispenser on the wall onto the seat and pee out the airplane ginger ale like a fire hose, pat dry, and listen to the toilet furiously flush itself behind me as I adjust my clothes.

One thing that gets me about reading old books is that the authors from every bygone era always skip descriptions of the basics: those things they either take for granted or decide do not merit discussion since routine body functions rarely affect the narrative. Whether an author is writing in Ancient Greece (which they just called Greece) or Medieval England (same deal), they assume everyone already knows how and where people took a poop and do not need that bit included. But honestly, that's the part of the time capsule that I'd really like some detail about. Surely Jane Austin could have explained how Miss Elizabeth Bennet managed her ablutions at the start of a long day of being a not-yet-married gentlewoman in the 1800s. Did the chamber maid crinkle her nose? I'm not the only one who wants to know this stuff.

When you tour Greece, Rome or any other Old Place in Europe, the guide always points out baths or the latrines and explains how they were used with the water flowing underneath the toilet seats that are lined up in a row, cut into a long marble bench with no walls separating each hole. Very social time it was, taking a poop 2000 years ago. There's even a seat with a toilet hole cut into it in the front row of the ancient amphitheater in Athens, where the plays were so riveting that the twenty thousand people seated behind you would not notice your use of a damp sponge on a stick.

I went online once to figure out how Eskimos take a poop: is it done in or out of the igloo, and does it just freeze and last for thousands of years until global warming gives everyone above the permafrost an awful surprise? The only thing I found out is that Eskimos are Inuits, not Eskimos. Beyond that I could not find a clear answer or even a Wiki page with a faded photo from the 1800s of a sledge party holding a national flag and pointing at a pile.

On my first University of Texas Hiking Club hike, I asked Nolan where the bathrooms were. "The forest is your toilet," he answered. The soap dispenser in Denver International has to be pushed before the foam plops out, but the faucet is motion activated, and when I put my hands near the sink, the water that gushes out is crazy hot. I don't mind. Boil those microbes.

Denver International still has not improved its signage deficiencies, and I ignore the apocalyptic decor. I ask which baggage claim I should go to, which carousel is for the Southwest Flight from San Antonio, which way to the bus. The two-story escalator going down to ground transport is being repaired. There is no signage, but a guy in an airport vest is at the top of the broken escalator directing people to the elevators that are out of sight to the left. "Press one, go all the way down. Turn right to go to the buses." I'm guessing he's been repeating that sentence for hours.

I ask a guy in a brown uniform where the AB bus will be—he thinks it's at station number eight—and I ask which kiosk takes cash. Everything goes faster when you just ask.

I miss the 4:20 AB1 bus to Boulder by eight minutes, and since it's Sunday, the next one isn't until 5:20 and I sit alone in the bus tunnel on the slotted metal bench. The area looks clean but has an exhaust and urine smell. A sparrow hops under the bench near my feet and by the time the bus pulls up a couple dozen people are waiting for the Denver Airport to Boulder AB1.

As everyone lines up with their ticket or with exact fare, the driver loads the bags then gets people to move back as the bus fills. All the seats are taken, and people are standing in the aisle or sitting on their carry-ons. He bellows, "We can do this! Move back, one more to get on." People shuffle and he pulls out of the tunnel. "This is a happy bus."

We ease past the rows of snow breaks leaning in the brown grass and past the acid blue bronco, and an hour later we pass small rectangular houses as we head down Broadway. Nolan's waiting for me at the Goodwill shopping center with Noodles & Company.

I wait till we've both started eating before catching Nolan

up on everything that has happened since last year. He knows that I'm there to shop at dispensaries. I'd already told him how well the CBD tincture worked when I talked to him on the phone, and now, I go over how the CBD/THC piece of chocolate that I'd started giving my dad every Sunday has been working too. When I had flown to Denver in December, I had only been thinking about making sure Dad had some cannabis during his cancer treatments. Now I have to get enough to last at least until next summer since I can't keep flying up during the school year. I confess that I wish I had thought things through a little more the previous winter but did not know enough at that time to plan ahead.

Even though I've already got a Greyhound ticket, I also tell Nolan about my lunch with Nicoletta and her boyfriend's advice to FedEx everything home. Nolan considers and says it makes sense. I tell him that one more cross-country trip on a bus is good just for the experience, but after this, I'll figure out the FedEx thing if I ever need to do a shopping run again.

When I'm done explaining my shopping and transport plans, Nolan tells me about Megan's wedding. In the spring, Kinsley's mom married the HVAC tech she'd met at the Home Depot where she's a cashier, and she used the wedding to repair relationships: she'd located her brother and invited him, met an aunt and two cousins for the first time, and even reached out to her mother who'd had a drug relapse and refused to leave rehab. Her father, who was vaguely rumored to be in Nevada, could not be located, so Nolan walked Megan down the aisle, which is what Megan had wanted anyway. Kinsley was the flower girl. Nolan doesn't have any pictures of himself at the wedding since he doesn't do selfies.

And then there's a Nolan-pause. "One thing did happen

that kind of concerned me," he says. "Well, I'm not sure 'concerned' is the best word. Bothered maybe? It caught my attention." His brows do not furrow, but his face shifts in a subtle way. "So, daycare has always been a big issue for Megan. It is really hard to find daycare that is halfway decent and also affordable, and this last year, Kinsley switched to a new place when school is out and Megan has to work. I had never been there, but Megan said it was better than where she had previously been taking her. It was cleaner. They had more activities, she said. So it sounded good and she really liked it. Anyway, she was at work and one of the other workers called in sick and Megan had to stay. She called to see if I could pick up Kinsley for her, and I said sure, and I go and find the place, and it did look nice, all bright and clean, with lots of kid art up on the wall. But I go in there, and the kids are sitting at their tables, and the teacher, well, whoever she was, the daycare lady was walking around holding a big sign. And I paused in the doorway. She was telling the kids, 'What about evolution? What is it?' And she raised the sign over her head and said, 'It is a lie.' The sign had the word 'Lie' on it, in big red letters. Then she said, 'And when they tell you that animals evolved, that they changed, what do you say inside your head? That's right, children. It's a lie. Evolution is a lie.'"

"What did you do?"

"Well, I picked up Kinsley and I got the hell out of there. I mean, I guess I knew that it was a Christian daycare. I think Megan had mentioned it, but I had no idea. I was pretty shocked actually."

"What did you say to Megan?"

"Kinsley's her kid. She can put her in any daycare she

wants. But I told her that I can't pick Kinsley up from that place again. She will just have to do it herself."

I look out at the parking lot, thinking that affordable daycare comes with a price. Nolan refills his soda, and when he comes back to the table, I get to my big proposal: I looked up white water river rafting online and want to try it. If he's game, I will pay for the tickets for both of us since it was my idea and also since, obviously, he will be driving us to wherever river rafting takes place. The river rafting outfitters have half-day and full-day tours, and the half-day tour looks like it will work for Tuesday if there are still openings. Just show up, and they put you in a wet suit and a raft, with a guide. I smile, expecting some Nolan-excitement.

Nolan looks at me mildly, just like the Dalai Lama; it's one of his natural expressions, but right now, it can't be promising. Nolan has gone river rafting before, many times actually, and the water is cold, very cold. He explains that a wet suit actually gets soaking wet, all the way through. When a person is in the ocean, this keeps water against the body and provides insulation since the water held by the wet suit warms up relative to the surrounding water. But in a raft, where you keep getting splashed, the wet suit just keeps letting cold water soak through, over and over again.

Clearly, I did not understand the concept of a wet suit. I thought they kept you dry. He says that's what a dry suit does. Professional divers use dry suits, like in the arctic, but not in river rafting. And no, the river rafting company does not hand out dry suits even if you ask for one. I look at what is left of my noodles. Extreme cold is a deal-breaker for me, as Nolan expected.

The creepy prison sheets and the old, nautical comforter

are still on the bed in the basement apartment. A few dry leaves have worked their way in from the window, littering the flat pillows, and the basement is chilly from air conditioning that's blowing too hard. I do want to visit Nolan and, just like last year, I desperately want to talk, but damn if the Residence Inn in Denver wasn't sweet.

After I meditate, I think on Kinsley's mother, Megan, who'd had a hard life yet kept working to gather friends together and reknit her fragmented family. Nolan had described her as generous and naturally kind. I try to remember what all my anger management books said about being kind and generous but can't dredge it back up as my mind darts sideways when I suddenly wonder if Nolan has been to the Arctic and met any Inuits. I'll ask him tomorrow, maybe over lunch, and just as suddenly, I finally stop being pissed off at Lauren.

CHAPTER TWENTY-FIVE
SEEK AND FIND

Nolan has to work on Monday, and I have to shop for cannabis. He had told me the night before that he had to submit a project proposal by noon. I wake up early and look over the Boulder bus routes trying to map out a dispensary shopping plan. When I go upstairs, Nolan hands me half a toasted bagel with cream cheese. He has the other half. Two-thirds of the medical bills and paperwork that covered the table last year are gone, and on one end of the table is a new computer with dual monitors. Nolan is already working when I head out the door and down the hill.

The morning is shiny as lacquer as I catch the nearly empty bus to the Pearl Street Mall. I walk down Pearl Street Market, looking for dispensaries and can't find any. Google Maps says I'm four hundred feet from a cannabis store, and my little blue dot closes in on the store, and finally, on my phone, the blue dot is in front of the dispensary dot that I am seeking. I look around. Nothing. I go around the corner; maybe the map is a little off. Nothing. I go back and try the other side of the street mall. Nothing again. I sit on a bench. The map on the phone insists that I am practically in the lobby of the pot store that I am looking for, but there is nothing here. Do pot stores go out of business in Colorado?

Google Maps says I'm seven minutes from another dispensary, a block over from Pearl Street. There are people on the pedestrian mall, shopping and already going to restaurants, and there's a church on the street behind Pearl Street, with office buildings, wide sidewalks, cool shade, and no dispensaries.

I head back to Pearl Street, engrossed in my phone. I'm two hundred feet from Helping Hands Dispensary and finally, I decide to look up the address of the store as I start walking up the mall, watching my blue dot close in on the target, and watching the numbers above the shop doors: 1056, 1044, closer, 1037, nearly there, 1021—I've missed it.

I back up and see a vintage clothing shop and a gelato shop and look again. Clothing shop. Gelato. Clothing. Gelato . . . and there is a narrow walkway between them. I am staring and suddenly, like sorcery, it appears, or rather, resolves in front of the pseudo-alley. Between the clothing and gelato stores, with prominent signs, sits a small 'Helping Hands' sign that is set back above the walkway, at the end of which is a side door. I get it. The dispensaries are here. But you can't see them unless you know *how* to see them. You have to know where 'there' is.

Inside is a door for medical marijuana customers and signage with a prominent arrow to the recreational dispensary upstairs. The Helping Hands lobby is unmanned. This dispensary's theme is California surf culture, with bright Cali colors on their logo and a cresting wave painted on the wall. Weed themed t-shirts are for sale, though I have not noticed anyone in Colorado walking around in a marijuana shirt. A sign on the counter says someone will be right with me and that I am being watched. Cameras, high up on the walls, had already gotten that across.

A coffee table has magazines on it like in a dentist's office, and a magazine file on the counter is full of pamphlets. I take a Colorado Marijuana Tourism Map and, best of all, a Boulder Discovery Map just as an intercom voice says that I'll be shown back into the dispensary as soon as a budtender is free. The man's voice is chipper, and I wonder if there really is a delay or if waiting-in-the-lobby is the Boulder version of dispensary security. Customers sit around for a while, while someone inside sizes them up on closed-circuit screens.

A guy with glasses that have thick black square frames, like men wore in the 1960s, pops out of a door and slides behind the counter. "Hi!" He's so happy it's catching. He checks my driver's license and leads me through the door behind the counter and into the recreational dispensary where a couple, carrying a paper bag of goodies, is leaving. The display cases in most of the dispensaries seem to have been reincarnated from some other business. These had a previous life in an ice cream shop, with big rounded glass fronts that used to show buckets of rum raisin and now bulge out over edibles, drinkables, topicals, and flower in glass canisters.

Their selection is a little limited and I look at the various gummy edibles, trying to find something that is not sky high in THC. The guy who showed me back into the dispensary area talks me through the products but passes me off to another budtender, a woman in a long broom skirt, as a bell dings and he heads up front again. "I love my job," he blurts and bounces out to meet more customers.

A display on the wall is arranged in a sort of pyramid, and

I ask if they have some cannabis already made into cigarettes. "Oh, sure we have pre-rolls," she gestures at the display. "Indica here. Three hybrids here, which are a cross between indica and sativa, and," she points to the bottom of the pyramid, "sativa." She names the indica strains, explaining indica's body relaxing high, then sativa's more stimulating effects for mental creativity and energy: "Like if you want to clean the house or paint a canvas or go for a run." Then she goes into the hybrids.

She talks in generalisms about the highs you get from smoking the pre-rolls. The budtenders in Denver knew their product, their descriptions informed by real experience, either their own or from a cheat sheet provided by their faceless corporate masters. And much of the clientele in downtown Denver was too knowledgeable to need clarification on indicas, hybrids, and sativas, wanting instead to sample an Emerald Triangle ghost strain or a diesel with citrus undertones and delayed body lock that was so worth it. The budtender here may never have smoked a joint in her life.

One thing they do have that I had not seen before is a wall display of seeds in little cardboard boxes, running between seventy to one hundred and ten dollars a package. I forget to ask how many seeds are in each box but remember from one of my books that seeds cost five to fifteen dollars each, depending on rarity and demand for the strain.

I buy Peach Pucks, which are one-to-one ratio CBD/THC gummy candies, more CBD tincture like I got in Denver last winter, plus a CBD/THC combo tincture, and, at the last minute, two joints, a sativa and a hybrid. The cannabis books said that smoking a joint, while the most wasteful way to consume marijuana, since most of it literally goes up in smoke, was also the best way to get the fastest effects. What if Dad suddenly has pain? What if he starts having that Alzheimer's sundowner effect of restlessness and agitation at the end of the day? Which, frankly, he is already having sometimes. The most recent research states that since cannabis is neuroprotective, especially for concussions. It might also be a prophylactic against dementia. A glass of wine a day reduces heart disease by reducing the cholesterol clogging up arteries, and apparently, two puffs a day on a joint might prevent plaques in the brain.

I have Alzheimer's on both sides of my family. My mother's mother died of it when she was ninety-five, unable to swallow in the last two days of her life and no longer recognizing Aunt Gracie as Gracie sat next to her bed. And Dad can no longer remember what he ate for breakfast. High cholesterol runs in the family too. I don't have a half-dozen children and their loving descendants to surround me when I'm ninety-five, and I'm not a billionaire with a dedicated staff to attend to my increasingly decrepit needs. I'm a fifty-year-old literature professor, exhausted by decades of teaching Freshman Composition and starting to care for aging parents. All I've got is my brain. If smoking a joint on the weekends will keep me from losing my marbles before retirement, then that's just part of a practical life plan, like maintaining my car and having mutual funds.

Each joint comes sealed in a black tube with white stick-on labels.

The budtender passes me off to a guy at the register. "We're having a sale." He actually grins. "Twenty-five percent off tinctures, and the second joint is on me."

"Hooray for me." I actually grin. Two hundred and forty-two dollars. I pay in fifties.

He adds the joints to the paper bag and staples it closed.

"Remember not to open the bag while you're still on Pearl Street," he says, starting to offer me my change, but I wave it off. There is a tip jar on the counter.

I leave. The place was nothing special, but the people were cool. No matching t-shirts, no carnival show. Boulder just feels super honest.

The day is starting to warm up and I need to hit another two weed stores, but I'm tired and need a break. I catch the bus then walk up the long hill to Nolan's. My shins hurt from walking on pavement all morning, and I sit on the couch to cool down and rest.

The pamphlets fold out. On the front side, the Colorado Marijuana Tourism Map has Frequently Asked Questions like "Can I consume marijuana in a hotel room or on a balcony?" It also has a section of Dos and Don'ts: "Do Consume your cannabis in a private location. Don't Cross state lines with cannabis." The "Kush Directory: Your Guide to Legal Cannabis" is on the back side with a state map indicating the location of Premium Retail Shops and also just regular Retail Shops. Coupons line the edge of the map.

The other pamphlet is exactly what I need. The Boulder Discovery Map is a detailed map of CU-Boulder and downtown Boulder including Pearl Street Mall. Discovery Maps have little labeled buildings drawn in, including businesses, parking garages, bike trails and parks, police stations, restaurants, even tiny trees, people, and buses. The Helping Hands Dispensary is labeled with an arrow showing where it is wedged between clothes and gelato.

Nolan makes the deadline for submitting his proposal and listens while I tell him how hard it was to actually see the dispensary. "It is just like the signs in Denver Airport," he says.

"There is plenty of information on posts sticking up from the floor throughout the airport, but if you don't actually know to look at the posts, you walk right past them. Since it's not where most people expect it, it's confusing," he says. "Are you hungry?"

I am.

"Do you think you can eat some Thai food?"

I can.

Nolan has a dentist appointment, so he will drive us to a restaurant that's on the way to his dentist and close to Pearl Street Mall. After we eat, he'll drop me off so I can finish shopping while he goes to his appointment.

A few minutes later, we pull into the tiny parking lot behind Khow Thai. The Miami Art Deco exterior is the most soothing shade of baby blue, while the inside is mundane, decked out in surplus restaurant furniture with square tables and oversized laminated menus. Most of the lunch crowd has come and gone, and we sip iced tea while waiting.

Nolan has been thinking about the river rafting that I suggested the night before and worries he over-played the cold-water factor and talked me out of something that I would enjoy, or at least be able to tolerate. I had been thinking too. The rafting only takes a couple of hours. If I like it, then great. And if the water actually is too cold, then the trip won't really last that long, and I'll still be able to check river rafting off of my list of things to try. The website says children seven years old can go. How bad could it be?

Nolan says he'll go online when he gets back home after the dentist and also call Kinsley's mom to see if Kinsley can go with us—he'll pay for her ticket, though he's a little worried that Kinsley might be hesitant. He took her tubing two weeks earlier, and when they went through the chute, her head went under, and it scared her even though she didn't swallow any water.

The waitress puts our dishes on the table and the yellow curry vegetables are amazing. The vegetables are in a bowl filled with glistening sauce. Whatever Nolan ordered must be pretty spicy; he sucks in air after each bite. I keep eating even after I am full just because the potatoes and tofu in the curry are so perfect, but I can't finish even half of the order and stash the leftovers in Nolan's car when he drops me off at the top of Pearl Street Mall.

This time when I look for a dispensary, I bring up the store's street address. I watch the dot on the screen and the numbers on the buildings that I am walking past, until I reach a confluence of dots merging on the screen and of street numbers matching up in real life, yet once again, the dispensary is playing hide-and-seek. I look deep for an alley. I look up for stairs. A small sign for the dispensary is hovering over an iron barricade. Ahh. The stairs go down, and the iron bars, in the middle of an open area, are blocking each side of the descending stairs to keep people from tumbling into an open stairwell that seems to lead nowhere. Just down. Into the dark.

I descend into Native Roots, Boulder Edition. The Native Roots that I went to in the sub-zero weather in Denver was a showstopper, with a hostess tapping me through the triple layer of key code security into a vast underground white and chrome fun house.

This is not that. This. Is kinda grubby. Huh. And not well lit. Also huh. Down the stairs is the obligatory security area before I get into the dispensary itself, but once in the actual store, the place feels shady. The dispensary has three budtenders, each with a small, crunched up four-foot length of counter space. The cinder block back wall is just three feet behind me because the store has been stuffed into a space on Pearl Street, in order to be in a place on Pearl Street, but it doesn't fit. Earlier in the morning, I thought that the choices at Helping Hands were a little limited, but they probably weren't. Instead, the selection in downtown Denver must have been Premium Retail Store big, and now I am going to Regular Retail Shops on a high rent tourist boulevard. I get it.

The budtenders here are not improving the 1980s porn shop feel. My guy reeks of existentialist college student ennui. His hair is unwashed, and I get a hostile undertone from him the whole time, vague but there. He would rather be somewhere else. He would rather I be somewhere else. When I want information about a product, he tells me the price, even though I didn't ask. I go through the motions of being kind of interested in this and that. I'm not going to buy more joints, so I don't even look at flower. The one thing they have that I do want though, is the one-to-one CBD/THC Cherry Chocolate bars that I give half a square of to Dad every Sunday night. The budtender tells me they are forty dollars.

In saffron robes, His Holiness stands next to me, a bit too close because of the narrow aisle, and says to chill. I sort of do, deciding that my existentialist budtender is having a bad existentialist day since no good existentialist days have been invented.

"I'll take four chocolate bars." I pay in fifties and ask for a plain bag when he starts to open a logo encrusted glossy bag like I got before at the Denver store.

He snaps open a brown bag and staples the chocolate bars inside, uttering, "And don't open it on Pearl Street."

The warmth of the day is gone as I head to the bus stop. It's overcast, with one part of the sky looking dark enough to rain. I wait for the bus to take me back down Broadway and open two pamphlets I had picked up when I went down the stairs. Both are for Native Roots. One lists their store locations in Colorado; the other is a pricing guide.

❧

Laying down in the basement feels mellow. Nolan's not back from the dentist yet and after fifteen minutes I need to decide what to do. I still have energy but can't face another mission to a dispensary, so I'll cram one more weed store in on Wednesday morning before I take the bus back to Texas, but right now, my most desperate need is for decent bed linens, and I get up and hoof it, blocks and blocks, downhill to the Goodwill in the shopping center.

The linens are in the back corner of the busy store. It takes me twenty minutes to settle on a fitted sheet set in an abstract leaf print. Most of the comforters have been used, and even the ones that are still in packages are dreary, so I don't bother. I grab a new pillow, pay up front, and head to Noodles & Company for a bottle of water.

The sun and my shin-ache are back, and I can't manage an uphill trudge toting linens and a super fluffy poly-fill. At a table in front of the restaurant, a couple talks, with intense calm, about their sex life. She is trying to decide whether to break up; he is trying to philosophize her into thinking that things are okay, and they should just go on as they have been. After all, they both have another year in their programs, and who knows what could happen after that: They could end up on opposite sides of the planet. He is thinking about London after all.

I try to tune out their issues, but they actually bring Nietzsche into their debate, and I wonder if the Native Roots budtender is about to show up.

Can I take a rideshare just a few blocks? I open the Lyft app and in five minutes, a compact car pulls up, and I pile into the front, telling Trevor, my driver, that my destination is not far. He's pleased since he's almost out of gas and was worried he might have to fill up in the middle of a ride. Trevor, a student at CU-Boulder, makes extra money driving for Lyft and likes it; he meets lots of people.

We head up the hill and get caught by a light. In a squared-off field out of my window, I see a dozen guys milling around, about to practice for some kind of sport. It looks intramural casual. At the far end of the field, isolated by himself, is a fat guy in red shorts. I do a double take. I don't know how to say this without sounding like whatever the word is for a Goodwill bigot, but even the people milling around the linens in Goodwill were Colorado fit. This guy is built like a refrigerator with legs, thick and rectangular with shaggy hair. Huh. Well, I've finally seen a fat— He catches a ball and sprints like the wind. The other men on the field are after him and he dodges, swerves like a rotund gazelle, and scores. The light changes. My mind folds like dough thrown on a counter, punched and kneaded. It's Colorado, where even an amateur fat bastard can outpace a stallion. The heat and the tacos in Texas would kill him if he tried that down there. And, by dashing like an Olympian, he's just disqualified himself from my fat search. Trevor drops me at the door to Nolan's basement and I give him a five-dollar tip on a four-minute ride and dump my Goodwill bag on the bed before going upstairs.

Back from the dentist, Nolan is in the office attached to

his bedroom, with his old laptop open. The website for a river rafting company still has spots open for tomorrow's 11:30 a.m. beginners' tour. The outfit is an hour away in Idaho Springs and will cost one hundred and eighty dollars for the three of us. I fill in my name and credit card number. Nolan hands me a crumpled wad of cash that's "about right," to cover Kinsley's cost. I stuff the money in my pocket and don't bother to count it.

The rest of the evening, I talk to Nolan for a couple hours. I let him know that Lauren's brains seem to be functioning normally again, now that she's divorced, and that Jovi is on a gluten-restricted diet and not missing school days because of stomachaches anymore.

"Things work out if you give it some time," he said, which seemed like an odd comment coming from Nolan.

"What makes you think that?"

"Science teaches you to play the long game sometimes."

"Hhm."

Nolan's teeth look good, cleaned of all the tartar build-up that happened during the treatment for the lymphoma, but, unsure what the etiquette is for making that kind of a compliment, I don't say anything. Nolan goes to pick up Kinsley, and when they get back, she wants to watch the movie *The Mask*, for the fifth time, promising me that it is really funny. I'm glad to see her, but an evening with a green Jim Carey just can't happen, so I go downstairs, organize my luggage, seal Mylar bags around the day's merchandise, and think of number twelve of the *Thirteen Ways of Looking at a Blackbird*:

The river is moving.

The blackbird must be flying.

CHAPTER TWENTY-SIX
IDAHO SPRINGS

In the morning, Nolan is tending a skillet full of eggs, sprinkling cheddar on top. I pour orange juice, and Kinsley starts fussing that she doesn't want eggs. Nolan reminds her that he asked if she wanted eggs before he cooked them and she said yes. She says she meant 'no.' This goes on for a while, but eventually, eggs are consumed all around before we take Fia—completely deaf now—for a walk then load into the car.

Ten minutes outside Boulder, Nolan stops at a convenience store to get gas in a neighborhood that's brand new: streets are jet black with bright white striping, there's a forest of apartment complexes, and the McMansions barely have yards. Colorado is the new 'It' place, and the building rush is on. Suddenly I see her: a fat woman heading back to her car. She's lumpy all over, wearing leggings with a long shirt flapping in the breeze and sipping the local version of a Big Gulp. In Texas, she wouldn't register, but here, for the moment, she's a rare bird, part of the new people from outside the state who are moving in, without adopting the Colorado worship-of-the-outdoors ethic.

We drive through mountains gashed apart to build roads, their insides jutting like exposed bone. We get to Idaho Springs a little early and drive up the mountain to walk around, stand on big rocks, and look at the view, then go back down to Foam Water River Rafting. It's the middle of summer and they are moving hordes at an industrial level.

After we sign legally binding paperwork promising not to sue anyone if we drown, die, hit our head on a rock, die, or somehow unexpectedly die, we go inside. The outpost is shaped like two long staggered wooden triangles that are fused together halfway down. The fused double triangle part is the lobby and gift shop, and out back in the courtyard hang a couple hundred wet suits in various sizes, styles, and levels of damage. I pick out one that I think looks cool—purple and black—while Nolan helps Kinsley before grabbing one for himself. Kinsley and I head to the women's changing room to put on shorts and then wriggle into the wetsuits which are soaked from whoever has already gone down the river and returned that morning. I discover that my suit has a rip on the right knee and the left butt so that a little flap is hanging down. There are suits in better condition, but I decide I can live with a minor butt tear.

Next, we pick up purple helmets and yellow life vests and mill around on the deck running along the back of the building, waiting for the 11:30 group to be called. Kinsley starts to express apprehension: "I hope I don't drown," she says. She'd said the same thing twice in the car.

The deck is underneath the final stretch of a zip-line running down the mountain, and, every few minutes, people fly by overhead, screaming as they gain speed before braking near the landing platform. The last guy in the group lets go of his handhold and flips over, yelling, "Help!" so that we all turn to look, "I'm upside down!" He kicks his arms and legs then rights himself as he reaches the platform, laughing.

"The zip guide," Nolan says as the 11:30 group is called over to a forested path. About a dozen river rafting guides start looking us over and dividing us into groups of six or seven, immediately clumping families together then filling out the rest of their raft. Their strategy seems to be to sort rafts into even-tempered groups, while also spotting high-risk customers and spreading them around. The sign at the entrance said that rafting was for those aged seven and up, but some families have children younger than that; one girl, about four, holds a doll. Nolan recognizes the real danger before I do, "Yeah, I think we are pretty much up for anything," he says loud enough for the nearest guides to hear him. "I'd like to have a little excitement." He faces me and Kinsley. "How about you?"

"Absolutely," I enthuse.

"I don't want to drown," says Kinsley.

"You three are together?" A guide in a long sleeve burgundy t-shirt and cargo shorts, with brown eyes shiny as a bead, motions us over.

Coming down the trail behind us are four men, middle-aged but mostly fit, all wearing mirror sunglasses. "Man! I am so pumped for this. Let's *do* this river!"

Jackpot. Our guide claims them too and I realize Nolan has just helped us avoid the rafts with small children, fussy moms handing out carrot sticks, and creaky grandpas. The sunglasses guys are co-workers from a steel-and-glass high-rise in Chicago, on vacation together but traveling without their wives until they meet up with them tomorrow in Denver. Today is their last day of man-adventure stuff.

Our guide's name is Tanner, and he smiles continuously.

The guides are lean people with ropey muscles, and they all have names like 'Tanner.' Two are women—Meadow and Sierra—and one is a Sikh wearing the smallest turban I've ever seen. I wondering if the turban is neoprene like the wetsuit and also what is India's equivalent of Briscoe, Brice, Baskin, Bryce, Bryson, Lukin, or Chet.

And then it's time for river rafting boot camp. For the next half-hour, Tanner teaches us how to raft a river. There's learning how to wear a helmet (snuggly), how to wear a life vest (snuggly), how to wear a paddling jacket (medium-snuggly), how to hold a paddle, how to sit 'on' rather than 'in' an inflatable raft, how to wedge one foot in the footcup for better stability, and then there is a long tutorial on how to row the raft, meaning how to follow Tanner's commands.

Tanner will be sitting in the back of the raft with Kinsley next to him. The rest of us will row while Tanner calls out strokes as he maneuvers the raft with a stern mount almost twice as long as our paddles. We have to learn how to row in sync without banging our paddles against whoever is in front or behind us, so we practice: Forward stroke. Back stroke. Forward on the left side of the raft. Back stroke on the right side. Forward stroke, forward stroke, forward.

I can see the river, and yet I am not on the river. Forward stroke. Stroke. Stroke. Hold. Then we have Insta-training on what to do in an emergency if you end up in the water or if someone else goes in.

"Does that happen a lot?" Nolan asks and Kinsley gets attentive.

"No," Tanner says, "we haven't had a swimmer all summer."

"So, kind of boring?"

"Well," he waggles his head, "I don't want to say that,

exactly. But usually, we've had at least a couple by now. And it's been busy all season. Still, it's just as well. When someone in your raft does a swimmer, you spend the rest of the day, and I mean hours, writing reports, and that sucks. So, it's almost not worth it."

All the groups have finished their training. Our raft, bright yellow with FOAM in purple lettering on the sides, is heavy, the tough Hypalon rubber so inflated it feels hard and solid. We carry our raft to the river, waiting in the middle of the pack, about seventh or eighth, as one by one, the rafts ahead of us set off. Kinsley smiles at Tanner. "I'm really scared of drowning."

"You're not gonna drown," he says. "You're sitting right next to me, where I can keep an eye on you at all times."

We put in.

Trees shade the first languid stretch of river, and once all the rafts are underway, strung out in a long line, the guides call out commands, more to get us accustomed to rowing than because our efforts are needed: the current carries us without a fuss. The rafts have to stay in visual contact at all times but also maintain a proper distance from each other, so half of our rowing involves slowing our raft down so we don't get too close to the group ahead. I'm on a slow boat to nowhere, but the scenery is great.

The high-rise co-workers make up the first two rows in our raft. The guy sitting on the right side of the front thwart, the shortest of the Chicago four with John Belushi cheeks and a hefty laugh, is the head of their clique. Nolan and I sit on the last thwart, in front of Tanner, who is on the kickrocker, the highest panel at the top of the tube at the back, with Kinsley tucked into the well at his feet, holding onto the grab rope.

Moving into Clear Creek, we leave the quiet side tributary,

and the river widens out, sparkling. There's been a lot of rain recently, so the river is high, which means it's running smooth but fast. There's not much to do, and the rest of the rafts are nearly silent, carried along by the current. Tanner, however, is still putting us through our paces, having us speed up, slow down, and finally, perhaps to relieve his boredom as much as ours, "Forward left, back right," and we spin the raft.

"Whoa," Belushi-cheeks grins hoping for something exciting, but the first rapid is no more than a leisurely one-foot dip, and even the upbeat Chicago four cannot pretend to be thrilled. The river goes flat again for a dull stretch. On a hill on the riverbank sits a young woman staring at her laptop, glancing up as raft after raft floats by.

As we round a bend, I hear the upcoming rapids before I see them. All the rafts ahead of us have paddled away from the center of the river to avoid the thickest part of the froth. Tanner aims us right for the churn. He'd held us back so that the gap between our raft and the ones ahead has widened and now he calls the stroke, so we pick up speed and go over the dip fast enough to get a little bounce out of it, and everyone perks back up. As the trip goes on, the rapids start to occur more frequently and get larger.

Tanner calls, "Forward right, back left," and takes us over the next ledge backwards. The guides in the other rafts, laden with little kids getting sunblock smeared on their nose, radiate envy, steering their cargo to the least troubled lanes of the river. Pretty soon, Tanner has us spin as we go over each rapid, so our ride gets better than a waterpark. Even Kinsley, though still holding the guide rope, has forgotten her fear and has her head up.

Rapids are created by boulders in the river displacing tons

of rushing water, and Tanner shouts over the river noise: "You guys want to bounce off the rocks?" and we side swipe the next boulder so that it boings us out as we go past. The next whitewater is fluffier, created by a series of big rocks jutting up in a spaced-out zigzag as the river narrows. The drop is steeper, and we take it at a spin. We're getting wet, but the wetsuit works, and even though I know the water is cold, it doesn't bother me. The river flattens out again. My shoulders are aware of the effort from rowing, but they don't ache yet. My ankle, however, keeping me balanced with my foot jammed under the seat ahead, is warm from the strain.

Up ahead, the next rapid is the largest so far and stretches across the entire river. The rest of the rafts have scooched over to the left where there's a drop but not much turbulence. Perched on an overlooking hill, there's a woman with a laptop and a small truck parked on the grass behind her. It looks like the same woman as before, which makes no sense, but there's no time to think it through. Tanner lines us up in the center of the river toward the foamiest section: no spinning, no aiming for boulders, vortices swirling all around. We go over. Damn it's exciting. Damn I'm happy.

The river pancakes out, broad and smooth, and we start drifting back in line. Then behind us, three sharp shrill whistles—the signal that someone's gone into the water—come almost immediately. Swept by the current, he's already going past us by the time I look back. A big chunk of our Insta-Training earlier had been devoted to emergency scenarios. Caught by the current, a person in the water moves faster than the rafts, so if you fall out, the rafts ahead have to rescue you, not the one you fell out of.

Tanner and another guide throw ropes with weights at the

end. Tanner's lands within arm's length of the man, and the other guide's rope lands in front of him. He sweeps past without reaching out for either. Tanner had emphasized that if you go in the water, you need to "become an active participant in your own rescue." The big danger in the water is getting snagged on debris or sucked into turbulence because the river is like a sieve, and if you go into it, you become the spaghetti, trapped under the flow where there's no air.

The guides of all the rafts that are now behind the swimmer steer toward the riverbank, but we can still see the action taking place. The swimmer starts picking up real speed, the purple helmet growing smaller as he gets farther away. The rafts ahead of him stay in the midst of the river, angle to intercept, and another guide throws a rope right across his path. He runs into the rope and somehow, tangled up in it or with his hands on it, gets dragged close enough to Sikh-Briscoe's raft for three of the rafters to grab him. The swimmer does not grab the side of the raft or try to scramble in. His refusal to participate in his own rescue is majestically defiant. To drag a person out of the water and over the side of a raft, you need momentum, so you dunk them under the water and then yank hard to heave them up, out, and over in one huge effort. If it doesn't work, you do it again.

It doesn't work. The swimmer is dead weight, arms folded tight over his chest. Shouting drifts back to us. Sikh-Briscoe is standing in the stern, using his extra-long stern mount and an oar to keep his raft as balanced as possible, but it's starting to twirl. There are more rapids ahead. The three rafters trying to drag the swimmer out of the water are two men with a woman between them, and her higher pitched voice, mingled with the general commotion, is the only one where we can make out the words: “Kick your legs! Grab hold! Use your arms! Dunk him! I don’t know why! Not using his arms! Duuunk!”

It takes three tries—dunk, yank, dunk, yank, dunk—before they haul him in.

Behind us, the last raft still has not gone over the big cascade, and their guide makes them hug the riverbank and slowly slip over, avoiding it altogether. I wonder out loud why the swimmer didn’t do more to get himself into the raft, and both Nolan and Tanner explain that the shock of going in the water and the speed of the current make people freeze up. More than half don’t do anything to save themselves. The guides inch us down the river to a cut bank where we beach the rafts, and Tanner tells us we can walk around for a few minutes.

Light glints off Belushi-cheeks’ sunglasses. “An old guy, isn’t he?” The man that went into the water is tall and skinny with a mop of gray hair.

The swimmer is still in the raft that rescued him, now beached, and Meadow, the guide whose raft he popped out of, asks him if he would like medical treatment. Does he need an ambulance? Is he sure? There’s an ambulance on the hill. They can transport him to a hospital right now. Does he hurt anywhere? The questions go on and then get repeated as the guides ask about ten times if he wants an ambulance. I look up. We’re in a small canyon and perched on the lip of it is a dark truck, and a man with binoculars is staring down. The old guy is Fred from North Dakota, a retired small business owner, and his wife, frail and silent, stares into his face.

After a few minutes of Fred refusing medical attention, the rafts are put back into the water, in the same order as before. Fred is draped over the bow of Meadow’s raft, and his wife sits right behind him, gazing at him like a river rafting Pieta.

Neither of them touches an oar for the rest of the trip. The other rafts that were boring before, get ultra-cautious, and even Tanner has us go over the next rapids as sedately as possible. Then he picks it back up again, going over the final few rapids spinning, backward, and bouncing off boulders. Meadow scowls at the world.

We reach the Take-Out point in mid-afternoon, grab the handles, and all of us carry the raft up a trail to the trucks waiting on top. Even Kinsley helps, holding both hands above her head, pushing against the raft's underside. We pile the rafts onto trailers, then get into a couple of old school buses ready to pull onto the highway and drive us back to where we started. Fred and his wife are in the very last seat; Nolan, Kinsley and I sit just in front of them, and I ask Fred what happened.

"We're going down the river, paddlin' yah know, and come up on the rapids, big ones, yah know, biggest yet. And jus' as we start going over, heck, we get bumped from behind. The raft behind caught up and come too close, went over the rapids right behind us, same time we did. As we come down, they rode up over the edge of the raft on my side, where I'm sitting, and knocked me clean out the raft, flipped me in the water. I was gone. Fast, like that. But I kept my feet up. Yah know, like they said before we started. If you're in the river, don't touch the bottom, 'cause that's the dangerous part, gettin' snagged on the bottom. Don't hit the rocks, don't tangle in tree roots, don't become spaghetti. Kept my feet up the whole time."

By the end of the story, Fred is grinning, all perked up and his wife gazes at him like he just carried a baby out of a house fire. She's had an adventure too, watching Fred get swept away, passing the other rafts, and dunked underwater. Then dunked again. And that third time. Her hand moves to rest on his arm.

After a minute, Fred speaks up again: "Geez. I thought this whole trip down the river was gonna be a snoozer, but I hain't had that much of a charge since I went through basic training way back when and got pushed out of a plane. Always the way though, yah? You don't feel a charge unless you're trying something new. Little charge now and again makes you wake up and notice the world around you. That water was brisk."

When we get back to the outfitter and change back into our clothes, it turns out that the woman on the hill was taking pictures which are already available on the kiosks in the lobby for twenty-five dollars. I wonder how fast she deleted the snaps of Fred pitching into the water. I buy a picture that shows me and Nolan and Kinsley, delighted as our raft goes over the big rapids, seconds before Fred went for his swim. The kiosk emails the photo to my phone and I copy it to Nolan, who says that if I leave the tip for the guide, he'll pay for dinner.

I go to the counter, write Tanner's name on an envelope and vastly undertip him by only putting a ten inside. I don't do this on purpose; it's just, until Nolan mentioned it, I didn't know guides got tips, and by the time I think through the twenty percent calculations for me, Nolan, and Kinsley, we're already headed for the car. I promise myself that the next time I go river rafting, I'll tip like crazy.

CHAPTER TWENTY-SEVEN
G-DOG EXPRESS

INSTEAD OF HITTING another dispensary Wednesday morning, I went to Safeway with Nolan and got snacks for the ride back to Texas, then we drove up Flagstaff Mountain with Fia and went hiking. In the afternoon, Nolan, Fia and I walk to the bus stop so I can catch the Flatiron Flyer to Union Station in Denver. We sit on a bench, while two college students nearby argue politics—not current events, but political theory, circa 1350s Europe. Really Boulder?

The bus heaves into view, I pet Fia goodbye, and Nolan gives me a spine crunching hug which feels good, and I say in a rush, "I got new sheets and a pillow at Goodwill for the bed in the basement, so if you go down there and see different linens that's what happened."

"Oh. That's nice. Thanks." I get a kiss on the cheek for being so uptight that I replaced a homeowner's linens without asking.

Moments later I'm waving back at Nolan as I head up Broadway toward the plains outside Boulder, the industrial parks, and the endless apartment complexes rising out of empty fields. I get out in the bus tunnel at the back of Union Station and make my way to the street corner to catch the Free MetroRide, which lets me off a block from the Denver Bus Center.

The Greyhound Station is not packed and miserable like it was after Snowstorm Decima. There are plenty of people, but the floor is not littered with them, and no one has a pit bull roaming inside. I get my luggage tagged at the counter, then head to the row of seats near Gate Five and text Nolan to let him know I'm at the bus station, no problem. I'm two hours early; I should have loitered at Union Station or hit a dispensary on my way over, but I was paranoid about being late and didn't think to go shopping, but I don't mind. I'll sit and read and listen to music and enjoy not having to do anything.

Two women are lying on the floor by Gate Five, carry-ons propping up their heads. "My butt hurts so bad," one announces. The women missed the bus at eight in the morning and have been waiting all day. The one with the sore butt has dried out, straw-colored dreadlocks. Her hair is not really a dreadlocks style so much as hair that looks like it is half dreadlocks and half just matted from living on the streets. Sore Butt explains that she has to go get her daughter in San Angelo and come right back with her on the next bus, so she's gonna be riding the bus for more than two days straight. The other one has burgundy hair which has not been combed in days.

A stout woman is standing four feet in front of me. She wasn't there before and looks homeless, but many people here look homeless, me included. I'm wearing bus travel clothes: baggy jeans, a t-shirt, and a long sleeve shirt tied around my waist for when the bus gets chilly. She's wearing a hoodie with the hood up and baggy sweatpants the color of dingy. She looks at me, then at the empty seat next to mine, then back at me. I tip my head indifferently and she sits down, continuously staring at the side of my face. I go back to my e-book, not at all bothered, so thank you, *Art of Happiness*. Fifteen minutes later, I go to the bathroom dragging all my stuff. When I come back, she's gone and not just from the seat. I don't spot her anywhere in the station.

A flock of men in fluorescent vests in the tunnel outside Gate Six push luggage carts full of boxes with shipping labels. One opens the door, pokes his head in and shouts, "Security, security. Hey, Mohamed! Over here."

Mohamed is skinny as an Ethiopian marathon racer and moves fast without exactly running. Even before he reaches the door, a fluorescent vest worker is pointing to a woman in polka-dot leggings lying on the sidewalk in front of the bus bay. "Yeah, she just fell out. She twitching. Think she havin' a seizure."

I crane my neck as everyone in the Gate Five area tries to see past the edge of the long window where the men are clumped around the woman on the ground. I can only see part of her body.

Security Mohamed leans over her. "Can you hear me? What's your name? Your name! How old are you? Twenty-seven?" He talks into a shoulder microphone and two minutes later, we hear the sirens. The fire truck arrives first; then an ambulance pulls in close enough to unload EMS personnel carrying dry boxes. A big knot of firefighters, one of them a woman with a ponytail, wanders up, and soon the twenty-seven-year-old woman is surrounded by about twenty people.

Mohamed tells EMS that her pupils were huge and black.

EMS says she's on spice, and I hear the word 'synthetic' before the door that had been propped open swings shut. EMS gets her up and she walks to the ambulance, and that's when I notice a guy on the sidewalk in the bus bay unpacking two black lawn bags that are full of shoe boxes, which are, in turn, full of brand new athletic shoes. I think the ticket counter has explained to him that his bags full of boxes take up too much space and he has to consolidate. He's dressed all in red basketball gear like a short Houston Rockets player. He lays out boxes, opens them, takes shoes out. He tries to get four shoes in one box. Then six shoes in two boxes. He keeps arranging and rearranging before finally accepting that he can bag all the shoes but none of the boxes. The realization arrives slow and painful. All the shoes go into one large lawn bag. Then he waits, dejected, inside with the rest of us.

I make one more bathroom run, and when I come back, the two women who missed the morning bus cheer as a Greyhound pulls up to Gate Five, and they shuffle their luggage so they will be first in line.

The driver gets the luggage stowed, tickets checked, and passengers loaded and pulls onto 20th Street, precisely on time. He gives a spiel over the intercom about appropriate bus behavior, telling us there is no smoking on the bus, including the bathroom, and that if we listen to music, it must be through headphones, and the sound cannot disturb anyone else. I sit more toward the front than I did during the winter bus ride. No one is coughing and the bus is not even half full.

One thing I notice that I don't remember seeing on the bus last time is a plexiglass shield around the driver's seat, extending from floor to ceiling. Attached to the barrier is a plastic gate which closes off the driver and the front exit stairs from the rest of the bus. Anytime the bus is in motion, the gate clamps into place, so no one can rush the cockpit.

I watch the city until we are on open road, then start reading again and soon have to turn on the overhead spotlight: once sunset starts in earnest, it comes on fast, getting inky black almost instantly. No one else in the bus has their light on, but phone screens dot the seats. I hear thunder in the distance and don't believe it until a lightning strike, vertical, bisects the darkness, revealing an endless flat plain for an instant. Water lashes the bus, and giant windshield wipers slap across the front glass in a deluge lasting an hour. It lightens to drizzle by the time we get to Pueblo and pull up to a convenience store to pick up one passenger, a young woman. Her parents sit in a primer gray car nearby to watch her get loaded in. Timidly, she nods back at them, excited, I guess, that she is taking a trip by herself. They look anxious.

The driver announces that we will stop for ten minutes and adds, in an exaggerated sing-song voice, "Ten minutes. Whatever you do . . . Don't miss the bus! Ten minutes." A third of the passengers get out and start smoking; others go inside to buy bags of chips. I make a bathroom run, taking my carry on with me, and when we reach Trinidad, the same thing happens, even though there is no passenger to pick up. I think the driver is letting passengers get off at brief stops, so they won't try to sneak a cigarette in the bathroom. As we pull out, across the highway stands the triangular storefront of a Premium Retail Native Roots Store. It's closed; it's midnight. But in the dark, the store's retail beacon must shine for miles like a lighthouse on a rocky shore.

If I curl up tight, I can lay down across my two seats. I semi-sleep, off and on, till we approach Amarillo, a major hub, where we need to change buses before dawn. I sit up as we drive through the city.

"Okay, folks. We'll be stopping in Amarillo . . ." A few blocks from the bus station, the driver makes announcements, explaining which passengers will be switching buses depending on their destinations, and which passengers will continue on this bus. Even those who will continue, however, have to get off so the bus can be taken to the depot and cleaned. "If you are continuing on this bus, you can leave your belongings on the bus, but anything left on the floor will be considered trash and will be thrown away by the cleaning crew. Do not leave any belongings you want to keep on the floor. Anything you want to leave on the bus and keep, put it on your seat. For those of you continuing to Plainview, Lubbock, Big Spring, Fredericksburg, Kerrville, Boerne, San Antonio, this will be a twenty-minute stop. Whatever you do . . ." the passengers join in the sing-song lilt, "Don't miss the bus." He has used that cadence all night long at each stop. "Twenty minutes."

It's 5:30 a.m. He parks in the glow of the Amarillo Bus Center, opens the bus door, along with his security gate, and the passengers shuffle off. The guy in the seat in front of me is the Red Basketball Outfit guy that had to put all his brand new athletic shoes into a lawn bag and discard all the shoe boxes in Denver. Having slept soundly through all the announcements, he stands up, stretches, and yawns, a lumpy lawn bag on the floor at his feet. I tell him about the bus driver's announcement that the bus is going to be cleaned and anything left on the floor will be thrown away. "If you want to keep something and leave it on the bus, place it on your seat." I repeat to him that anything on the floor will be thrown out.

"Oh, okay," he says. He gets off the bus without putting his black trash bag of belongings on his seat, but, unprompted, he smiles and tells the driver standing on the pavement next to the bus's door, "It's on my seat."

The Amarillo station has plenty of room this time, but I stay standing. Many of the passengers camp out next to charging stations, feeding their electronics, and one woman in pajama pants, paces slowly near the vending machines, a cell phone pressed to her ear.

"My hair ain't red no more. It's blond. Blond. . . He loves me in his own fucked up way, I think. But he's there by himself now, so that's why I'm going. He can't be all alone out there. . . Yeah, I got a new phone. I'm talking to you on it now. . . He's got two phones. She took his stuff. . . He's sick and all. I got my benefit and fourteen hundred saved. . . You thought I was going out there broke? I'll give him six hundred for rent."

By the first gray hint of sunrise, the bus has not returned, and at some point, my legs get heavy, and I sit in one of the station chairs. I look out the plate glass wall as an antsy feeling starts catching the crowd. The bus is now overtly late, with no explanation. Passengers trickle up to the ticket counter and ask about the bus, when will it arrive, what should they tell their auntie who needs to pick them up in Sterling City at eleven; she has work at noon, should she wait? When they return to the rows of station chairs, they repeat the ticket counter woman's response that the delay was because a new driver is running late, but on his way.

An hour goes by, and I stand up because I'm getting fuzzy-headed, so I sway back and forth, trying to stay alert. I don't want to fall asleep because then I might 'miss the bus,' just like the driver told us to "Don't" do. I start feeling shaky from lack of real sleep and sit down again. Not only has my bus not arrived, but none of the transfer buses that should have come by now have arrived either, yet somehow, it seems to be getting more crowded. More people make calls, alerting relatives that they will be late—they don't know how late yet, the bus ain't arrived, don't cuss me about it, nothin' I can do 'bout the goddamn bus, I ain't drivin' it, what you want me to say? Fine. I know . . . I know all that, just lettin' you know the bus is late, so I'm goan be late, okay? Okay. Shit.

Another hour passes and my eyelids feel thick. Men walk aimlessly, people cluster outside to smoke. Passengers look around at the ticket agent, at the front bus bay, at the bus tunnel at the back, and I think about insects trapped in amber, slowly encased in thick liquid, then stuck staring out of yellow stone for eternity. I try to zen-out, to be in the now without impatience, and for little bursts it works, before the pendulum swings and the tedium of bus station hell clobbers me again. I expected to enjoy reading and listening to music for one day while traveling. But the inertia of being caught in a big noisy room destroys it. Being in motion, in transit, was what made an enforced time-out and the calm of reading or listening to music without feeling guilty possible because the bus ride itself meant that there was nothing else I could be doing.

After three grueling hours, the bus pulls into the back tunnel, outside Gate Six, and the announcements to line up for those continuing to San Antonio come over the intercom like nothing has happened, like a no-show to a dinner date suddenly sits down next to you in the theater as the curtain goes up.

We load up. I get the same two seats I had before. On the sidewalk in the bus tunnel, three cops dressed like construction workers are making light conversation. They gear up, tucking the gold badges hanging on chains around their necks into their shirts. One straps on an ankle holster, though I don't see a gun yet. Half the people on the bus don't notice them, and the others don't care. I don't care. The numbness of the three-hour wait isn't lifting, and the bus pulls off just as the cops form a line and walk into the Gate Six departure door. When I lay down across the seats and Amarillo recedes behind us, I actually do get some sleep.

Two hours later, in Lubbock, I sit up feeling better, squeeze sanitizer on my hands, and dig around in my carry-on for a sandwich and a nectarine. The driver sing-songs, "Twenty minutes. Don't miss the bus. Twenty minutes," but there's no energy in it and not one passenger lilts back.

Everyone exits and the bus is driven away again. The Lubbock station is clean and nearly empty, but everyone waits out front for the bus to come back. Lubbock is where the bus switches drivers, but I assume, since we are three hours late, the stop will be as brief as possible. It is not. It takes forty minutes instead.

When the bus returns, a new driver has taken over, and the bus gets loaded with two trolley carts of packages, plus a couple of new passengers. The new driver goes inside the station, and when he comes back, he does the count, walking down the aisle to the back. Then he walks to the back again and points at a youngish woman with a cake of day-old makeup, a pink spaghetti-strap dress and a discount boob job.

She pretends that she got on the wrong bus, then, a minute later, totters off down the street, with a sad smile. I feel so bad for her my insides scrunch. I can read about seventeen kinds of tragedy in her life so far. As the driver gets set, he barks out the rules without using the intercom and announces that we're late because there was a problem with four passengers in Amarillo. The police were called, and it all took three hours. A passenger asks what the four did.

The new driver shrugs, "Not sure. Drugs. Something."

"Something good? Musta been drugs."

A soundless ding goes off in my head. Red basketball guy is no longer traveling, and I wonder if I had told him one more time to put his bag on the seat, I wouldn't be three hours late now. On the other hand, would I really have wanted to reiterate advice to a person who seems to have kept his entire investment portfolio in the form of a lawn bag full of athletic shoes, which he leaves on a bus being taken away to a cleaning crew? Maybe it's just as well I was not insistent.

On my phone, I google Amarillo bus station, Greyhound, police, drugs, and arrest. It turns out that the police in Amarillo routinely take drug dogs to sniff the buses being cleaned, which, frankly, seems unfair. From the dates on the news articles in the *High Plains Standard*, about once every month or two, the cops score a significant hit, mainly for cocaine, heroin, or codeine: A woman busted for codeine that she left on the bus when it was taken to be cleaned; a man busted for half a million dollars' worth of cocaine, detected when Diablo, the most frequently mentioned drug dog, searched a bus when it was being cleaned; a man busted when a cleaning crew alerted police to what turned out to be meth stowed in the overhead rack; a woman busted when D.E.A. agents find $400,000 in her luggage—which I don't see how that's actually a crime—after an Amarillo PD K-9 located the money in a routine sweep of the bus station; a man busted for a twenty-pound block of marijuana wrapped in blue plastic when police were tipped off that a man with a knapsack was transporting drugs; and, Diablo again, alerted deputies to ten pounds of hydro marijuana in the luggage compartment.

A few other stories also suggested that the bus station was a great place for Amarillo cops to spot sex offenders and even the odd suspected murderer on the run. Seriously, the bus station must make it rain for Amarillo law enforcement. I am surprised about the marijuana busts, though. One, why bother? And two, I'm carrying marijuana, I guess. My mind circles around again. If you have half a million dollars of cocaine or $400,000 in cash, or enough heroin to be sentenced to three years in prison . . . take the bus? Really? Well okay maybe, but then you leave it on the bus?

Still, maybe I should climb down off my high horse. The reason I have joints and THC chocolate bars in my bag is because I can't drive in snow and won't drive two days by myself each way to Colorado. But if I had half a million dollars' worth of anything, Greyhound would not be in my travel plans. A spectral Red Basketball Guy speaks to me with the voice of His Holiness. "Don't be so judgy, Alene. And don't miss the bus."

It takes a while, but I finally wish that I'd told Red Basketball Guy one more time to get his precious bag of sports shoes off the floor, that I'd tried just a little harder and kept his precarious life situation from teetering off its narrow perch. I also wish it would occur to Greyhound to find a better way to notify passengers who are sleeping, who don't speak English or Spanish, or who are just dumb as rocks that they can't leave bags of meth, 400,000 dollars, or new shoes on a bus that's about to be out of sight and picked over. Would all that fit on the LED sign above the driver? The display does scroll, after all.

❧

Lamesa. A small desert fox runs across the parking lot of an auto parts store. Eight buzzards circle over a span of dirt, but I can't see what's dead below them, and a dust devil whirls off a dun-colored field and collapses onto a mini-mall. We're on two-lane blacktop now, the American hinterlands, and the names of the towns out here are blunt and accurate: Plainview, Brownfield, Levelland. It is plain, brown, and level, but I'm not feeling as cynical as I was on the trip in December. Some counties, especially over the Permian Basin, have crops coming up for miles in serpentine rows of green, half-grown corn or rust colored sorghum.

In some towns, the Greyhound stop is no more than a pick-up point at a convenience store. One or two people stand in a parking lot with a piece of luggage, a waiting-for-the-bus look on their faces, and a ticket for the driver to scan. The driver gives everyone five minutes so passengers can hit the restroom and the smokers can take enough drags to hold them through the next stretch. When I come out of the store, there's a short line as people re-board, and a young guy in khaki shorts is talking energetically to everyone or no one depending on how you look at it.

"Hey man, dressed all in black, looks like you're going to a funeral." He offers an older man help getting up the stairs, but the old man declines, while continuing some conversation they must have started earlier.

"I did ten years," the old man says. "The reason I'm going

to Abilene, I got a trailer there. So I'm all set." Stiffly, he pulls himself up using the hand rail.

"Johnny Cash, the man in black," the younger guy bounds up behind him.

By now, I'm tired of reading, and once we get underway, I put on my headphones. Two women traveling with well-behaved children are in the seats right behind the driver. The row in front of me is empty, but across from it, is a hefty woman with dramatic stretch marks on her belly, visible because her shirt doesn't quite cover her stomach and her pants are low enough to show the top of her butt crack. She had draped an old blanket over herself overnight while she slept sort of splayed out all over the seat, but once awake, she's spent every moment scrolling Facebook on her phone. The row behind her, right across from me, was empty until the talkative guy in khaki shorts leaves the back of the bus and suddenly sits there. He's on his phone, still talking, but I have Led Zeppelin's *Kashmir* on repeat play, trying to pick up nuances that you only hear with headphones.

Eventually, I have to take my headphones off, and I move my phone to the seat next to me while I dig in my carry-on so I can take a few bites off of my day-old sandwich. The guy in the khaki shorts talks incessantly to the woman whose parents watched her board the bus back in Pueblo. She is now in the seat behind him, and she's polite enough to look at him while he's speaking.

"My mom killed my doves while I was in jail. The male dove attacked the female, so she hung it and that just left the female. Guess what she named it then? Lonesome dove. Then it escaped out the cage."

At the next stop, Sore Butt from the Denver station is

still with us, and when I head into a three-stall bathroom, she rushes into the stall next to me, starting to unbutton and de-pant herself before getting the door closed.

"God, I gotta pee so bad." She sighs repeatedly when she's finally able to let her bladder go. "I didn't know if I was gonna make it to the next stop, and I sure didn't want to use that one on the bus. It smells back there. Stink-hee. I think somebody must of gone to the bathroom back there. I mean really gone." Her sighs morph into a contentment moan. "That one woman kept going in there a couple of times, so, you know. Plus, they're drinking back there; that old man is stumbling, nearly fell down."

Big Spring. The endless parade of small towns is interesting for two contradictory reasons: their sameness and their random distinctions. The sameness is in the ubiquitous Burger King, Dairy Queen, McDonald's, two-story Best Westerns, squat brick municipal building in the town center, and the occasional Kubota tractor dealerships. The houses, ranches, and faded strip malls are all so alike the towns looked cloned. And then there's the bizarre anomalies like the incredibly specialized niche store which might find sufficient demand in Gotham, but not wherever it's been dropped off the map here. What is north Texas Nowhere doing with a Window Emporium, a Sushi restaurant, antique toys, or a miniature Statue of Liberty in front of the Big Spring Municipal Auditorium?

I stop listening to music and just gaze out of the window. New green life coming out of the ground changes open range Texas so that it feels more humane, and the enforced inactivity I was seeking starts working for me around the tenth replay of *Kashmir*.

"Yeah, it's my fault." Mom-Killed-My-Doves-While-I-Was-

In-Jail guy is back on his phone. "I put the wrong fuel in it . . . Diesel. I already talked to Kurt about it, and I'm gonna touch base with him tomorrow and work it off . . . Yeah, Mom."

Okay, that surprised me. I had assumed that after the dove killing and all— oh wait. He has more: "No, I did it. But I've never done that kinda work before . . . Shoulda given us more instruction. . . I'm just sayin'."

Okay. So, he put gas into a diesel truck, and I wonder how he managed it since the fuel nozzle that goes in the tank won't fit the wrong kind of tank. It's dummy-proof. He must really have been determined to fuel it up.

"I mean I told Kurt it was my fault. I can't believe he would cuss at Pedro like that. . . Reuben wasn't there when he was talking to Pedro . . . I mean, yeah, Kurt was mad and I can understand that, but he just fucking lost it. . . And so fucking disrespectful, in front of Pedro's wife and everything. That weren't right."

So, Mom-Killed-My-Doves works for Kurt and put the wrong fuel in some heavy industrial vehicle. Kurt owns his own business, a family business, and Pedro was supposed to be supervising Mom-Killed-My-Doves but had not watched him closely enough since, understandably, Pedro figured that Mom-Killed-My-Doves knew how to put fuel in a vehicle without, and this is according to Mom-Killed-My-Doves' report, "someone holding his fucking dick for him." The entire call went on long enough for Mom-Killed-My-Doves to work himself up then calm back down. He had already gone through the whole story with his wife, plus an unnamed someone else, in back-to-back conversations. "I mean, I told Kurt it was my fault. So I'll square it with him and Reuben tomorrow. . . Yeah. I'm on the bus to San Antonio right now. The Alamo City, right. . . No, never been before."

Sterling City. At each row of seats, the bus has two electric sockets on the ledge running along the base of the window. After listening to music for a couple of hours, the battery level started to dip, and I had plugged in to recharge the phone. But now, I think I've got enough juice to last the rest of the ride. Mom-Killed-My-Doves politely asks if he can borrow my converter plug. He asks that the moment I take the plug out of the socket, which means he's been watching, waiting for me to do just that.

"No, thanks," I say. Up close, he has a freshly crusted scratch on his leg and thick scab on his knee.

Ten minutes later, he has re-friended the young woman from Pueblo and borrows her charger as soon as she is done charging her phone. "It's okay if you're still using it. I can wait," he concedes. She hands it over. "Thanks. My phone's dead. Right as I was texting my wife. I really appreciate this."

In San Angelo we let off several passengers, including Sore Butt and Butt-crack woman. When the driver gets back on, he walks the aisle to do the count. When he gets to the back, he raises his voice to the old man dressed in black that did ten years. "Sir, get your shoes on. There's no drinking on the bus; this is not your house. You drink again on this bus, you're off. I don't care if we're at a stop or not, I'll put you off, and keep the aisle clear. Feet do not extend into the aisle."

Back up front, the driver says something about mixing Budweiser and Jack Daniels, then switches into Spanish as he climbs into the plexiglass cage.

Now that the Butt-crack woman is gone, the row in front of Mom-Killed-My-Doves is empty but doesn't stay that way.

The Pueblo woman asks him for the third time if she can have her charger back. He unplugs and hands it over to her, "Oh yeah, of course. Certainly, I mean it's yours. I know it's your charger, thank you so much. My phone was completely dead; you really helped me out." A man from the back of the bus suddenly sits in the empty row. He's wearing jeans and sunglasses and is texting with a frown. Mom-Killed-Doves occasionally speaks to him, even though he doesn't talk back, which doesn't matter; Mom-Killed-Doves is back on the phone. "I mean I told Kurt it was my fault. So I'll square it all tomorrow. . . Yeah. On the bus right now. The Alamo City. . . No, never been."

I'm certain that Mom-Killed-My-Doves-While-I-Was-In-Jail will not figure out that Kurt, Reuben, and Pedro will definitely kill him when he meets with them to 'work it off.' The truck he ruined was clearly expensive since there are no cheap industrial trucks at the center of an independently operated family business. It's not until we're going through the Hill Country, past Fredericksburg, that I suspect that the man in the row in front of him is actually Reuben and not just a second-string, deliver-a-bad-worker-to-his-own-death guy. He pointedly ignores Mom-Killed-Doves but seems to be updating someone regularly on their location and estimated arrival time.

As we enter San Antonio, Mom-Killed-Doves gets excited, reading highway signs and announcing, "We're getting close now. Remember the Alamo. San Ann-tone."

At 7:30 p.m. we pull into the Greyhound station downtown, two hours after our scheduled arrival time instead of three, so the driver really humped it, as much as you can in a fifty seat, stretch Greyhound cruiser. There's already one bus in the tunnel so, standing between buses and breathing exhaust, I grab my stowed luggage. I should Uber or Lyft it, but there are three taxicabs next to the sidewalk, and the immediate convenience of a taxi crushes frugality and common sense.

I get into the first taxi's backseat and see Mom-Killed-My-Doves talking steady, headed for a dark, king-cab F-150 across the street. I had noticed the truck when I came out of the bus bay because it was parked at an odd angle, the back tires against the curb, but the front of the truck stuck out in the street like a cop car that's just rolled up on a domestic. The tint on the windows is too dark, and the guy who might be Reuben is right next to Mom-Killed-My-Doves, and shifts him toward the back seat, opening the door, then sliding in close behind. Maybe they'll just shoot him instead of beating him to death. Either way, once the sun gets low, his timer is on countdown. They probably borrowed a tractor with a loader. Kubota?

My cab driver gets in. He has a melodic accent, and by the time I give him my address, the F-150 has disappeared. During the ride home, I find out my cab driver is from Somalia or *was* from Somalia. He's been in Texas sixteen years and still feels it's too hot here, since he was from the cool part of Somalia, but he loves Tex-Mex and loves the music scene here and in Austin. With a tip, it costs forty-five dollars for a twenty-minute ride home. The Greyhound economy fare from Denver to San Antonio was one hundred thirty dollars. Once again, a cab ride is just the cost of bringing edibles back to my house. But, as I get out of the cab, I know one thing: I am never taking the bus from Denver again.

No matter what, I'm flying back. And I'm bringing a lot more cannabis with me.

PART THREE

CHAPTER TWENTY-EIGHT
ZEN

Mitch calls after I get off work. I'm at the grocery, loading jugs of distilled water into my cart since I don't drink fluoridated water out of the tap. "How are things going with you-know-what and your dad?"

"It works," I say. "Better than expected. Great even, and that's the problem. Now that I know it's the real deal, I'll have to keep getting it forever because it's actually effective."

"It's risky," he says. "If you lose your job, Alene, that's your retirement gone, health insurance gone, everything. And we're starting to get up there, you know. It's not like you could just pick up and start a new career at our age. I would still recommend against what you're doing."

"I know, but I don't have a choice. It's making a difference. Dad is sleeping and he doesn't seem to be in as much pain; he even walks around more."

"Still though. He would not ask you to do this."

"You're right, I know." I wedge another distilled water next to the carton of goat's milk. "If I don't do this, there's no one else to do this. I have to take the risk."

Like me, Mitch does not speed or tailgate. He's my only friend who's a careful driver. Even Nolan, who is ultra-rational in every other way, careens his ancient Jeep down mountain roads, passing up 18-wheelers. He passes on the right so I can look over into the yawning abyss that awaits any little miscalculation. On my first visit to Colorado, driving with Nolan, my ass was so tight leaving the Rockies it could have suction-cupped me onto the seat. I don't know why my friends are smarter than me, more creative, more popular, and also maniacal drivers.

I end the call and put the ninth jug of water into my cart. One other improvement I thought I saw in Dad was that he was more attentive to detail, especially when talking to Mom. Nothing reverses Alzheimer's or brings back memories lost to dementia. Nothing, so far, stops names and faces from winking out. Nothing brings back those stories at dinner with details the history books don't have, like watching federal agents, lost for hours on the mountain, searching for moonshine stills, then just searching for the trail back down, mopping their foreheads with soaking handkerchiefs, wandering by, unaware of the little boy behind the blueberry bushes growing over the copper pipes.

On Friday, I don't have any classes to teach, so I get up early enough to hit the gym, go home and shower, then go to my office for an hour before running to my monthly massage where the therapist says that my back is "really angry," as she leans her elbow into a knot. After the massage, I sit in the parking lot typing 'Go With Green' into the car's navigation system. The store was on the local news a few weeks back, plus Mitch texted me about it after a friend told him that it's where she goes for CBD topicals. Places that carry CBD have started popping up in Texas the last couple of months, ever since the 2018 Farm Bill made hemp production legal in Texas, but there are not many of them yet, and they don't have much of a selection. Go With Green is up I-35 in New Braunfels.

Fifteen minutes later, I take the exit and drive past a gigantic Buc-ee's truck stop, to reach the stretch of access road that I need. I don't know how strip malls divvy up rental space, but Go With Green seems to have a half-sized store allotment. One customer is leaving as I go in.

Go With Green has gone with beige walls and brown trim for the decor. 'CBD' in wooden hobby store letters is on the wall behind the display case. A woman with silver eye shadow is behind the counter, and her mother with silver eye shadow is next to her, and two male relatives are puttering around in the back, moving boxes. After the over-the-top stylings of downtown Denver, this place is just dowdy. I'm not being mean. I give them credit for having enough grit to trailblaze through whatever inane regulatory hoops Texas requires to open a CDB shop, but the stores in Colorado had music and scented air, pork-pie hat wearing budtenders and murals on the wall. Just sayin'.

The mom behind the counter asks what I'm looking for in a CBD product today. Something to help me relax? Flavored terpenes for vaping? They also have lotions, body butter, and massage oil.

"Analgesics," I say. "Edibles."

"Oh." True sympathy softens her glittery eyes.

I scan the display case and don't recognize any of the brands. None are the same as in Colorado. I'm not interested in the CBD infused lollipops, so she shows me the sweet-and-sour gummie armadillos. The package has four armadillos in it, each one more than an inch across. The package says two hundred milligrams, and even I realize that fifty milligrams per armadillo is way up there. One time, I accidentally gave Dad a thirty-milligram dose of CBD, when I squirted an entire eyedropper-full of tincture into his cranberry juice instead of his usual three drops. It made him dizzy. She concedes I would need to cut the armadillos into smaller pieces.

There's also a four hundred milligram bottle of forty Comfort Frogs, and next to the register, packages of CBD infused Squirrel Nut caramels. Together they set me back ninety dollars. She asks for an e-mail address or cell phone, so she can text me a receipt: "The whole store paperless," she swells with pride, but I decline. "I hope you feel better," she adds as I leave.

When I get home, Jovi is on Mom's computer watching a video of a woman searching a house for a cat. There is no woman in the video, just her voice as she asks, "Are you under here? How 'bout here?" Jovi is mesmerized as the camera and voice poke around in hampers and under beds. I try to get her to practice the piano with me but she says she's eating and drags a cold French fry through a smear of ketchup. Lauren picks her up an hour later. Mitch's boys practice piano with him every day before they go out to play, and they performed in their first recital two months ago.

I lay down and look at the gummie frog and squirrel caramel packaging closely. There is not even a trace of THC, and the cannabis books said that, in order to work best, the CBD needs some THC to get it going. The Colorado CBD edibles won't get you high, but the small amount of THC in them will 'turn on' the CBD. The squirrel caramels are gluten-free, tree-nut free, peanut free, non-GMO, and Kosher, made from pure hemp CBD isolate. The back of the package talks about 'enhancing our body systems.' The products from Colorado talked about serving size, dosing levels, ninety-nine percent purity, health risks and extraction methods.

I spend Saturday grading essay papers online all afternoon, and that evening, when I'm too tired to see straight and give up on grading, I cut one of the ten milligram Comfort Frog gummies in half and give it a chew, since I should know what I'm planning to pass off to Dad. The frog tastes bad, a flavor I've never had before, and I wonder if bong water tastes like that and read the package some more. The pectin gummie frog has no sugar. It is also sort of tacky, sticking to the other frogs in the bottle. Months ago, I tasted a tiny sliver of a CBD Peach Puck that I brought back from Colorado. Lightly encrusted with sugar crystals, it was candy.

The frogs and squirrels have a lot of strikes against them. On the plus side, however, I do not have to fly to another state to get them, and, on Sunday evening, when I give a half frog to Dad, he eats it without complaint. I start giving Dad four drops of Colorado tincture in his juice two days a week and half of a local gummie frog two other days a week. A month later, the local news features a shop in town that sells CBD, and their glass cases have more products than the shop up the highway. Also, about this time, I wonder why I was being so stingy with the gummie frogs. I decide to just give Dad half a frog every day and skip the tincture in his cranberry juice altogether.

Most teaching is not actually teaching anymore; it's not even prep work or grading. Instead, over the years, teaching has morphed into ten-hour days of committee work, department meetings, college meetings, tech training, or generating data: turning in reports to prove somehow to someone that somebody is learning something. My days are so squeezed that the time spent in a classroom feels like a side gig. Still, twice a semester, instead of holding class, I schedule in a week of conferences to meet with each student to go over their writing, find out what they want to accomplish in life, and give them advice on how to get started.

Even in brief meetings, when you talk to students one-on-one, you learn odd things about them, like suicide attempts made way back in high school, a whole five months ago; bouts of homelessness, abuses they have suffered, that they're on the spectrum, have dyslexia or hyperactivity disorder or bipolar disorder, and all of them have anxiety. Our college counselor tells faculty to assume that every student has anxiety, as though anxiety is like a default setting on a new phone.

One student wants to cure brain cancer because when he was twelve he saw his cousin die from it, another wants to harness fission and solve the world's energy needs, another is driven by bitterness to succeed because her parents told her she'd never amount to anything and one day soon she's gonna shove her success in their face. And some have no ambition but were told to get off the couch, go to school or get a job, and school seemed the easiest of the two.

I also use the conferences to practice the lessons in my Zen books and be 'fully present" when the students use my office as a drive-thru confessional. This go around, however, one student's poetry essay was so incomprehensible I wasn't able to get to the part of the meeting where I asked her about her goals. Instead, I told her to rewrite her paper and come back for a second consultation later in the week. She arranged to meet during her lunch break, the only time she could leave work that day. Millie, the student already scheduled for the same time, had to wait for ten minutes while I worked with the student who had taken Millie's slot.

When I called Millie in, she was fuming and determined to show it. But I was super-considerate, friendly and kind and ignored her pissed-off-ness. Being in a good mood, out of reach of someone else's bad attitude was a bizarre pleasure in itself and yet completely free of malice. I was telegraphing to her that I was going to be upbeat and enjoy the rest of the day and life in general and she could join in or not, but either way, I was fine with it. All of this radiating felicity quickly had a second effect as I reviewed Millie's paper with her. She forgot to be angry about the ten-minute wait.

Zen: Achieved.

In October, I study the calendar but can only find one possible November weekend where I could fly to Denver after work on a Thursday, be in a hotel Thursday night, shop on Friday, FedEx twenty bars of chocolate home, then maybe hang out with Nolan on Saturday, fly home on Sunday, and be back to work Monday morning, assuming that my shipping, my luggage, and my person are not impounded along the way. Nicoletta's boyfriend had told me that I should go to the FedEx store at 8 p.m. because FedEx has to get everything out by nine. That way, the package doesn't have time to sit around.

Though I've gotten a couple of flat envelopes from them, documents I needed to sign, I've never actually used FedEx to 'next-day' ship a package, and I decide I better do a dry run. Aunt Gracie has a birthday coming up, and she won't mind getting a random present from me. So over the weekend, I bought a toiletry travel bag as a gift.

The nearest FedEx is nestled in a strip center across from The Shops at Old Mesquite Hill, a massive outdoor mall on a rise behind Stone Landing subdivision. Six employees in black and purple FedEx uniforms are in the shop, customers coming and going at a steady pace. Tamara is at the counter. She has big ringlets of glossy black hair, one ringlet braided with gold thread. And inexplicably, like the budtender at Helping Hands or a Southwest Airlines employee, she couldn't be more delighted if she tried. She immediately picks a FedEx box off a shelf, pops the toiletry bag in, adds some brown paper packing, and types my aunt's address in the computer, all while having three conversations at the same time.

The customer who came in behind me, wheeling boxes on a hand truck, greets everybody and complains about a rude customer he saw in the store yesterday. "Man, I just wanted to cuss that guy out. I know you can't say anything to him 'cause he's a customer and all, but I was about to tell him, 'They are here to help you, guy, not serve you, yer majesty.'"

"I know, right?" Tamara says, then adds to me, "Driver's license?"

"Seven-eight-one-four-nine." I wasn't listening.

"No, driver's license. We have to check it now. Ever since, you know, at the Amazon Fulfillment Center in Schertz."

I do know. Two of my students were working there last year. The package bomb did not go off, but the fallout is that Tamara at FedEx has to eyeball my ID so I can send a present to Gracie. I'm annoyed at how compliant I am about showing my license to her.

"Phone number?"

"I prefer not to give that out."

"It's in case there is a problem with delivery and they need to call you."

"No, thank you."

"Okay. Estimated value of the items to be shipped?"

"Eighteen dollars."

There's more typing on the computer. Meanwhile, Tamara's co-workers are clustered around a big package on the floor behind the counter. The box is about two feet by three feet and looks battered like it's been kicked down a street. What concerns them is that it is heavy but also saggy and feels sloshy, like there is liquid inside. Battered or not, the cardboard is intact—there is packaging tape all over it—but they are unsure what will happen when they pick it up. It's heavy but just in the middle.

"Okay," Tamara stops typing. "That comes out to one-seventeen and fourteen."

She's talking to me. "What?" I'm pretty sure I was not listening again.

"One-seventeen and fourteen."

"Dollars?" I say, like maybe drachmas are an option.

Tamara breaks it down in terms I can understand. "One hundred and . . . seventeen dollars and . . . fourteen. Cents."

"Jesus Christ. I had no idea it costs that much. I thought FedEx was like UPS, just faster."

"Yeah, that's the part they never tell you about. How expensive it is. You did say you wanted it there tomorrow."

"I'm not sending an eighteen-dollar present for that much."

"Two-day shipping is sixty-six."

"Do you have a chart or something that I can see the choices and how much they cost?"

They don't. The cost depends on how far the package is going and how fast you want it there. I can go online and put in the destination and delivery times and the website will tell me the price. Tamara says there's a United Parcel store next to Panera Bread, so I pay the two dollars for the FedEx box that Aunt Gracie's gift is now inside and leave as Tamara and the remaining customer join the debate about what to do with the squashy box behind the counter.

Outside, it's gray and drizzling, so I skip United Parcel and head home.

When I hit the FedEx website that night, I see that FedEx is really expensive but worth it if you are shipping something even more expensive—like art, heirlooms, or golf clubs for your fabulous island vacation. Also, the bigger the box and the more it weighs and the faster you want it delivered, the more it costs. So, if I mail a medium, not too heavy package from Denver and want it in San Antonio the next morning—as Nicoletta's boyfriend suggested—then it costs one hundred ten dollars. Ouch. If I'm not picky about what time it gets delivered the next day, I'm down to seventy dollars. Two-day delivery is thirty. Not too bad. Doable, in fact.

I check other websites to figure out the best way to ship twenty cannabis chocolate bars and maybe a couple pre-rolls with the least risk of detection. Twenty bars is the amount that should take care of Dad for more than a year: I'm planning on one square, twice a week, and in the days in between, it's CBD frog-time. After a year and a half, I'll run out of chocolates again, by which time, I hope, the law will change, and I can buy the cannabis chocolate here in Texas.

Eventually, I end up on Leafly's website and read an article that warns me not to do anything illegal, not to ship cannabis through the mail, and especially not to ship cannabis across state lines since interstate commerce involves federal crimes and the DEA. But then the site goes on to explain that, to open a package, the United States Postal Service must have a warrant, while FedEx explicitly says it can open a package just 'cuz it feels like it. Leafly phrases this more uptown than that, but I get the gist. Then the article explains how to package items so that they do not resemble bombs—which *are* of profound interest to USPS—and that millions of packages are processed each day: USPS about fifteen million a day, and FedEx about 3.5 million. Screeners have less than five seconds to decide whether to flag a package as suspicious.

Twenty bars of chocolate wrapped in a sweatshirt seems doable, and honestly, I'm not afraid of arrest, so much as I'm worried about theft. Twenty Black Cherry Chocolates would cost north of eight hundred bucks. Plus, theft would ruin the whole point of the trip, which itself will cost eight hundred dollars, and require days of effort, the hassle of a flight to Colorado, plus, apparently, a visit to the Denver post office instead of the Denver FedEx.

The next day, I bop over to the local USPS and mail Gracie's present for fifteen bucks. It'll get there by Friday. I keep thinking about the article on Leafly's website, and that USPS needs a warrant—which means they first need probable cause—in order to open a box, while private companies, what the Supreme Court calls third parties, like FedEx, UPS, DHL and Greyhound, do not. Greyhound Package Express even specifies that you need to show up with your package open, so it can be inspected, and then Greyhound will kindly tape it shut for you.

Two weeks later, I leave my office mid-afternoon and go

over to the college's library to search the web as anonymously as I know how. How to mail weed, is the question of the day. Like Leafly, all the best marijuana information sites agree that the U.S. Postal Service is the way to go. The websites are clear about the private carriers: Not only can they open a package, they have outright employee theft of shipped marijuana, since no one will complain about a missing package full of weed.

So, private carriers are out, and USPS is in. To mail weed, a parcel needs to get past x-ray machines and sniffer dogs, while it also avoids getting too many 'flags', the term for a suspicious attribute. What makes a parcel look suspicious—which creates probable cause, then a warrant then an open package then arrest—are things like way too much tape or way too much postage. As I read, I make a list of flags: No return address, a hand-written address, a poorly typed address, a fake return address, a misspelled address, a known drug den address, and using nonexistent zip codes. Apparently, drug enthusiasts are not good at addressing.

The rest of the dos and don'ts are a mix of the really obvious, a little common sense, and hmm, I hadn't thought of that: Avoid reusing boxes. Avoid old, beat-up boxes. Avoid boxes with stains or oil spots. Avoid restrictive markings such as "Do Not Open", "Do Not X-Ray!" and "Personal!!" Avoid strange odors by triple sealing the goodies in bags that are washed and dried between each sealing—meaning seal it, wash with soap, allow to dry, then seal that bag in another bag, and wash and dry. Do not use masking odors. Sniffer dogs are not fooled, but your postal carrier will notice if a box reeks of rose perfume, coffee grounds, or Lysol.

Pay with cash. Do not use your real name, even if you are mailing the package to yourself. Use names that are not connected with either address, but don't make the name too generic nor too outlandish, so John Smith, John Jones, John Snow, John Terwilliger Esquire the Third, and John Mickey Mouse are out. Ross Busch is in.

The package should not make noise when shaken. The package should not be lopsided. The package should not have an uneven weight distribution, and the package's weight should not shift around when the package is moved. Basically, packages should not make FedEx Tamara and friends wonder what could be inside.

Do not ship more than twenty-eight grams which is one ounce. Fines and jail time go way up for more than that, and shipping more than four ounces kicks you up to drug dealer realms.

Then the websites explain other risks: USPS employees also steal, but then they send you an "Out of Delivery" message afterwards, so you'll know that your package is never going to show. It's hard to tell if that's surprisingly polite or just dickish. They can also get a reward for information that leads to a conviction for mailing illegal substances. One of the websites warns people who want to mail weed, not to get complacent. One thousand people are arrested by postal inspectors a year for trafficking through the mail. The risk is low, but it does exist and mailing weed is a crime that can lead to an expensive shit show involving fines, jail, and federal forfeiture laws, so ship it properly. USPS ships fifteen million packages a day. One thousand people a year get arrested. I hate math, but even I can cipher that the odds of arrest are low. I've played the lottery several times and never won. Why should I get snagged on this?

A couple of websites mention that edibles and concentrates are harder to detect than actual weed, and since I'm not interested in whole marijuana buds, this, I guess, is a bit of good news, though I don't know what the equivalent of twenty-eight grams of weed is when translated into chocolate and gummies. Anyway, I'll type up some shipping labels before leaving for Denver.

Late in December, a day after the semester ends, Mom takes Dad to a check-up. There are no detectable levels of prostate cancer. The treatments are done, and the doctor is surprised at how well it turned out. Dad will have to be monitored, and the doctor emphasizes that it's essential that he get up, move around, and exercise. Dad is lying on the couch as Mom tells my sister Tessa this over the phone.

My next trip to Denver will be in January. I had started planning for it during the middle of the semester, determined to avoid returning by bus. I'm flying back. And at least twenty Black Cherry Chocolate bars are coming back with me, along with Peach Pucks, THC tincture, and maybe a handful of joints.

CHAPTER TWENTY-NINE
JANUARY 2019

I GOT UP early, put half my money in envelopes and repacked the suitcase, hiding money in various places: taped into the lining of my luggage, inside my makeup case, in a shoe, in the pocket of a pair of jeans folded under my pajamas. I spread the rest of my cash around my person: a hundred in my jeans' pocket, two hundred in my purse, and, for the first time in years, I hung a silk money bag around my neck, sliding it under my t-shirt. It had hundreds and fifties so that I could use them at the dispensaries. One of the websites I'd checked said to keep the bulk of your money on your body, not in your luggage.

Jovi was on Christmas break and was sitting on my parents' bed, harassing Dad who was still trying to sleep. Mom was on the computer. I handed her a copy of the flight itinerary. "I'm headed out."

"Have a good time. We'll see you Monday night."

"I'll be in late. Leave the porch light on."

Jovi looked over. "You're going somewhere?"

"Colorado." I kissed her and waved goodbye to Dad as he gave up trying to get more sleep.

The closest of four Lyft rides was two minutes away, and by the time I put on my puffy jacket and got to the driveway, the car was pulling in, and half an hour later, I was passing through the scanner at San Antonio International. A Transportation Security Administration agent who looked like a teenage girl gave me an ankle pat-down before I put my shoes back on. I bought water then waited for my flight. In my carry-on, I had two books on advanced teaching methods, and couldn't bring myself to give a shit about either. At the gate, a man with a wiry-haired dog was making his way down each aisle of seating, explaining that the Belgian Malinois was a therapy dog to help passengers reduce the stress of traveling. No one looked stressed. But folks gave the dog a pat anyway.

"Don't TSA dogs get trained in San Antonio?" asked a man with pock marks on his face.

"Yeah," said the dog's handler, "I think they do." The bored Malinois sniffed me as I stroked his back then headed to the next row.

When the plane landed in Dallas, it was supposed to take on passengers heading to Denver. Instead, they announced an unscheduled plane change and told everyone to deplane, go to Gate Three, and re-plane there. I bought a sandwich on the way, then scored a window seat on the new plane since they let everyone who had been on the old plane board first. During the flight, I left the shade up and looked down at the sluggish brown serpentine rivers, the khaki and bone mottled land, and the wind farms that I had grey-dogged past the last time I was heading back to Texas.

Once you go zen and make the anger change, it seems so

obvious in retrospect. You wonder how you didn't figure it all out sooner—all that energy and time spent on trivial discontents. We fly over huge plots of caliche and black, cut into square grids by roads. I think about the fury inside the skulls of people. If someone in the seat next to me is seething, are they crazy? Or foolish? Do they have any idea of the pointlessness of it? If I am neutral, is that better? Or should I sit here with love in my heart for those sitting around me in this hurtling cylinder? If I don't, am I crazy?

The bleached out wastes below shift into a pattern of brown, drab green, and rusty granite red. I look up into the slate sky deepening into the cobalt stratosphere, sipping ginger ale the steward brings me, listening to Led Zeppelin and Tom Petty, with the down jacket stuffed in the carry-on getting saturated by the smell of a club sandwich, and I wish for a Height of Civilization Moment, but don't feel it. Those moments are crystalline in their perfection. When they hit me, I know. Kings of Olde didn't have to do their own laundry, but they stank like goats and died of infected bug bites. One thousand or five hundred or even a hundred years ago, could anyone imagine such luxury as a flight covering nine-hundred miles in a couple of hours and of it becoming so mundane?

Out of the left window are flat plains at the beginning of their stretch to the wheat fields of the mid-west, and out of the right are the Rockies, where a thick haze hangs over Denver as we land. Christmas decorations are still up in the airport. I've got the layout now and follow the flow, boarding the People Mover, passing the astronaut holding his gold helmet, getting to baggage claim, heading out to the light rail platform, buying a ticket for the A-Line, hoisting my luggage into the rack on the train, then watching the dead grass slide by. A bell 'dings' through the PA system and a jolly, Regional Transportation District auto-voice says, "Welcome to light RTD Rail. Do not cross tracks when lights are flashing."

Out of the train window, shrinking patches of snow cling to the shadows on the ground, and ducks walk around on a frozen pond sunk into a gully.

"You a security?" As we're gliding through the warehouse district, a man with wild gray hair stands in front of a man in a black uniform, who had been slumping against a grab pole in the center of the train car. He adds some muttering: "Social security . . . toxic waste . . . three hundred per week."

The officer squares his feet a bit. "I've got no idea what you're talking about." He listens to more muttering, then says, "I don't know what you're asking me to do." Rapid muttering. "I'm not writing my name on anything."

"I'm legal," says Gray Hair, louder now. "They can't hold me here. You're the law."

"I'm not the law. I'm a security officer."

"Tennessee. All your commie jails. What happened to Saudi Arabia. Al Capone. Look who New York. How in the hell did I learn all this? Right in prison. They hang 'em there. Paper is murder. Money is paper. Money is murder."

"I'm not gonna have a political conversation with you. Have a seat."

'Ding,' the PA chimes in. "Peoria Station."

Gray hair shuffles his Denver Broncos shower sandals over to a seat, and the Security Officer stays in our train car all the way to Union Station watching him.

Now that I'm no longer overwhelmed by a trip to Denver, I look around. Union Station is opulent. Across the top windows, big Christmas wreaths are high up on the walls, and a row of gilded Beaux-Arts chandeliers hang over the dark wood tables in the Great Hall. I inhale the Union Station food and coffee and holiday spiced tea smells. Then I head outside. I've timed everything right. It's after four o'clock, so I won't have to wait to check in at the hotel, but it's still light, the sun setting, streaking the sky copper. It'll be dark by five.

The MallRide is at the corner in less than two minutes, and as I heave my bag on, I see the lock on my luggage is missing and my stomach sinks. I get off at Curtis Street, which turns out to be a block or two too soon but start heading toward where my mind map tells me the hotel that I picked should be. I zig-zag up a block and over a block.

"Draggin' a lot o' stuff." It's chilly enough for a jacket, and he doesn't have a jacket. Or all of his bottom teeth. I look at him, frown, hold the stare for a long moment, but keep walking without changing my pace. "You that mean?" he says.

"I am."

"That's why you draggin' a lot. You self." He had been walking past me but has turned to follow. I watch his reflection behind me in the glass of the storefronts, then stop and watch him till he passes, continuing now that I'm behind him. "Cuz you mean," he adds as he angles off across a parking lot.

I cross at the corner, go up half a block, and find the car entrance to Aloft. The hotel is supposed to appeal to the young and hip crowd, so the front desk is not grand. Two young hip guys in dark jeans and plaid shirts are working. Both are bearded. Blackbeard is handling a middle-aged mom and her teen son, so Rustbeard greets me, tells me know the hours for breakfast and happy hour, and hands me a key card. Residence Inn was thirty-five dollars more a night. So Aloft it is.

The room, an efficient one-bedroom facing a busy street

one block off 16th, feels like it has been cleverly folded on itself. As I enter, the bathroom with the sink, toilet, and shower are to the right, and past the bathroom is a room with a king-size bed facing a desk, a long bench, windows, and a flat-screen TV on the wall. I put my luggage on the bench and start taking everything out. The lock has been neatly cut and left inside. None of my money is missing. There is no note from the TSA, but I guess the cut lock is the note.

I go on Google to figure out why my bag was searched, and also, maybe, why a Belgian Malinois was sniffing me while I waited at the gate at San Antonio International: It could have been a random search, or the hair curler, Swiss Army knife, and Mylar bags could be the culprits creating suspicious shapes on the scanner. Blow dryers can also trigger a search and, oddly, lotion and books. I'll have to get an extra box and mail home anything that might get the bag searched on the flight back when I plan to have more bars of edibles than ever before.

The overnight noise pollution turns out to be serious. I'm on the second floor, and the L, H, and D-Line all run down Stout Street, right under the windows. Each light rail rings bells when it crosses an intersection and the rail runs late and early. Well past midnight, a nightclub nearby has a house band that only seems to know three chords. Two little boxes of foam earplugs sit next to the desk lamp, along with a letter from the Manager thanking me for my stay and gifting me the earplugs to make my stay as comfy as possible. So, the hotel knows the street is noisy, and instead of pretending there is no noise, it hands out earplugs and a note that essentially says, "Don't come to the lobby and complain about noise that we can't do anything about. We acknowledge the problem. Here's a solution: Orange earplugs." Being forthright as a strategy? I like it.

I decide I can zen-out the noise: it will not bother me if I decide it will not bother me. The noise outside my hotel room is a small thing, and if I really think about it, I'm in a pretty luxurious state, well-fed, laying in a massive bed, under a white duvet. This is practically the best of all possible worlds.

The light rail's clangs are followed by a cop car siren. I flip on the light and read the directions on the earplug package.

CHAPTER THIRTY
BLUE BEAR

A TINY DOG named Meeko, wearing dog shoes and an argyle jacket, stands in line ahead of me. The Aloft check-in desk is in front of an area that's a combination convenience store, snack bar, and grab-n-go breakfast window, where five breakfast pods are on the menu. The Hearty Pod has Tuscan beans, roast pork, and enough kale to satisfy Aloft's Young Bohemians, who don't have time to sit and eat. A lady, dressed in what looks like layers of scarves, floats over to the dog holding her place in line and gets a pod that arrives in an Earth-friendly paper cup-bowl with a recyclable fork. I get tea and a croissant and sit in the computer station work area, which is also a lounge area, and watch the street traffic, light rail, and homeless people carrying blankets pass by. Steam rises out of manhole covers like vents on a waking volcano as three tattered college students with backpacks, two guys and a girl, march out of the lobby headed for new lands. I'm too stodgy for this place. I want my Residence Inn big ass breakfast buffet, newspapers, and 14th-floor suite looking across the city.

More people on scooters fly by. A year ago, that wasn't a thing. Now it will exist till sidewalks move. Back in my room, I take out the Free MetroRide map that I printed at home, marking the locations of my hotel, some restaurants, and weed dispensaries, so I can plan out the day.

☙

On my way over to 16th Street, a street guy sits on the edge of a large planter and yells at the building in front of him. "Are you out of your goddamn mind? . . . Kill all of you muthers. . . Yes, I mean you."

Either I've gotten better at recognizing dispensaries, Colorado has changed its dispensary signage rules, or the signs have become more uniform with their big cannabis dispensary green crosses, making them easier to pick out.

I take the MallRide to Tremont and spot Euflora. The dispensary's door opens right onto stairs going one floor down, and there's no line. The guard inside stands up to check my ID then gestures me in. Budtenders dressed in black wander the floor in case anyone has questions, but otherwise, after an initial greeting, they hang back while customers mill around.

The store is laid out with half a dozen tables, each with half a dozen iPads. Each iPad is next to a clear plastic sphere enclosing a cannabis bud, and the sphere and iPad are attached to the table with cords like at an Apple store so that you can pick them up but not walk off. The spheres have rows of holes drilled into one side and a rubber cap that comes off, so customers can smell the flower inside while the iPad next to each bud displays information: the cannabis strain, its THC percent, price per gram, per eighth, per quarter or ounce, and whether the strain is sativa, indica, or hybrid. The top third of the display plays a video that explains the strain's traits and recommends activities.

I start at the hybrid table, sniffing my way around it, but I'm too much of a novice to smell much difference until I get to Banana Kush which, along with the odor of pot, has a strong yummy smell of banana. I move to the G-Train Funk, Hybrid, twenty-two percent THC, Silver Price Tier: twelve dollars a gram, thirty for an eighth, sixty for a quarter, and one hundred eighty for an ounce. "Uplifting and euphoric for creative projects, with a sweet and sour taste and skunky aroma." The video suggests playing board games with friends, working in my garden, or eating food, as this strain will enhance those activities.

The edibles are in light boxes recessed into the wall. Each box shows the products from a particular brand; one is for Dixie Synergy, another for the 1906 brand, with milk chocolates labeled 'Chill' to help you relax, 'Midnight' for sleep, and 'High Love.' Farther along, an entire alcove is dedicated to vaping. I don't bother to look at the table full of waxes, dabs, and other exotics. Budtender Kevin sees my quizzical head tilt, drifts over, and shows me the case, which has the Incr*edibles* bars. I want to get the cherry-chocolate that I'd been giving to Dad last year.

Taxes on two hundred and ten dollars of assorted chocolate edibles is fifty bucks, plus I slide a dollar into the tip jar next to the register. The bag that they staple shut has a green "Euphora" logo on it, which I hold logo-side against me, so no one will know I just bought weed, as I'm coming out of the weed store. When I get to the street corner, the 16th Street MallRide is just arriving and four minutes later, I'm back at Aloft.

I head to Rocky Mountain High Dispensary next, and, on

the MallRide, listen to locals complain about two of their favorite restaurants closing. The rents on 16th have gone through the ceiling, and the owners couldn't hang on any longer. Family restaurants don't have a chance.

Even though my plan is to stay focused and get to three dispensaries in one day, I spend a little time walking around LoDo, the Lower Downtown area on Blake, Wazee, and Wynkoop streets close to Union Station. The district is full of buildings from the mid-1800s and my *Walking Denver* travel book wants me to admire the architectural details. While I'm walking around LoDo, another street guy is yelling at air. The day is mid-fifties and blue-sky perfect, and, like everyone else, a lot of the street folk are out and about, enjoying the weather that is twenty degrees above normal.

Rocky Mountain High Dispensary is boutique small, and the wood and glass storefront entrance is in keeping with LoDo's historic atmosphere, but otherwise, the store is nondescript. There is no line; just an ID check, then straight back into the dispensary. When I go in, there's only one other customer, and he's not buying. Instead, he's explaining to a budtender that he's homeless and has no money, but this is his favorite dispensary. He just came by to check a price. Twenty-six dollars. That's all he needed to know. Give him half an hour and he'll be back with twenty-six bucks.

He leaves.

I ask about CBD edibles and find out they don't carry CBD products. They're just a recreational store, not medicinal, so almost everything they have is THC. After I've taken two turns around the shop—I do find some random CBD watermelon gummies and a one-to-one ratio CBD/THC bar—Budtender Michele pulls the edibles I've picked from behind the counter and staples them inside a brown bag with the store's logo which is so subdued I don't need to hide it in my jacket. A tip jar is next to the cash register, and I ask her how much should a person tip. "Is it a couple bucks or a percentage? I'm sorry for asking, but I'm new to this and just don't know. Is it like at a restaurant?"

"Usually, it's a couple bucks," she says. "So, we're called budtenders, like bartenders, so like you tip at a bar. But if a budtender spends a lot of time with you, or you need a lot of help, then maybe you tip a little more." I put two dollars in the jar.

On my way back to Aloft, I grab a sandwich and meander up side streets. There's a blue bear staring into the second story of the glass wall facade of the Colorado Convention Center. The bear is standing on hind legs, its front paws up to the glass, helping it look into the building. Some taller trees reach the bear's waist and I walk under the blue groin, between its legs.

On Stout Street, I spot the source of the bass-heavy night music: a strip club next to the hotel. After I eat in my room, I head to Native Roots. I had decided to save it for last since it is right around the corner, less than a block away from Aloft. And it's huge. It'll have it all.

Only it doesn't. When I get to Native Roots, instead of the huge storefront with the separate down-to-the-basement and go-back-up staircases, the door opens immediately onto the stairs, which had previously been the one-way exit stairs. The storefront is one-third the size it was before. I go down, getting my ID out.

"Oh, I don't need to see your ID." says the man near the counter. "This is a CBD only store, so no ID is needed." Three frat boy types ahead of me are already clunking back up the entry-exit. *Native Roots Wellness* has no music, no line, and no long L-shaped counter with six budtenders, just a man and a woman, who are not wearing sweater-vests but are still giving off a sweater-vest help-you-with-your-ailment vibe.

There is a soft couch and a coffee table with reading material extolling the benefits of CBD, and shelves of ointments, lotions, massage oils, patches, and CBD only gummies. The far wall displays bacon flavored CBD sachets for dogs with joint pain, stiffness, or chronic itching, plus sachets called 'Calm' for the pet that is so stressed out by modern life that he can't take it anymore and just might do something crazy when you leave him alone, all all alone in the house.

A woman that came in after me has a swath of ombre pink hair, like a soft swirled Mohawk and speaks with the CBD-tender. I'm still over at the pets' wall and just hear fragments including 'eczema' and 'lupus' until I head back toward the counter. She wants to know how long CBD can be detected in your system during a drug test. Her workplace is obsessed with drug testing and she needs to take CBD every day as a maintenance dose or else she gets flare-ups. But they fire people who test positive.

The CBD-tender switches into consultation mode. "It depends on the person and on the type of test: urine, saliva." He starts explaining variables, studies, and test accuracy like he is a wall chart then concludes, "But I'm not an expert. Anyway, it's not usually CBD that's being tested. It's THC they look for."

I buy CBD Strawberry-and-Cream bars and transdermal patches. The CBD-tender shows me where he puts a patch on the top of his foot—they go on areas like a foot or wrist with lots of veins close to the skin's surface. He does distance bike riding, so he uses the patches regularly to reduce pain and inflammation. Then I ask about the Native Roots Premium store, "You know. The full store."

"It's now at our Highlands location." He staples everything in a brown bag with Native Roots Wellness stamped on one side. "Just a short Uber ride away."

So, dispensaries are no longer packed with long lines and wait times. The stores seem smaller but more ubiquitous, with one or two on every block, and they are niche-focused: all recreational, all medicinal, CBD wellness, laid back and take your time, or full-service premium store showstoppers. Clearly though, the boom-and-bust legal weed business cycle, while not quite a bust, has moved past the boom in downtown Denver.

❧

The Walgreen's on 16th has a market in the store with a guy making fresh salad and sushi wraps. Not once have I seen a Walgreen's in Texas with a salad maker inside. Or a salad. I get a box to mail home my hair curler and other items that might make the TSA rummage my luggage, and also get a cheap bottle of lotion for the dry-ass Denver air.

The Walgreen's has eight registers, and it's busier than any of the dispensaries. My cashier is bent with osteoporosis, but she has perfectly coiffed, 1950s Liz Taylor hair. While I'm at the register, I hear a high-pitched laugh as the manager rushes a disheveled man with a hysterical expression out of the store's automatic doors. When the manager steps back in, he thanks the doughy faced girl at Register Three for alerting him.

"Yeah," she says. "I saw him up the aisle there. I know he ain't let in here no more."

On my way back up Stout Street, a woman in a purple

jersey and matching cap is perched on a planter and as I pass, I catch a whiff of candied apples and sweet cherry, countered by more tame earthy notes. Space K Andy? By the time I reach the corner to cross to Aloft, she's sweeping the sidewalk again, dumping debris into a trash bin, her joint out of sight. She must be old school; young bohemians are vaping now.

Who wakes up every morning wanting to despise each of these people, people whose lives echo out of their bodies, their eyes, their bones? Me, maybe, a few years ago. Being angry is a deflection. Casual contempt is an easy way to ignore the human condition and the human. Actually seeing their struggle saps emotional energy.

In the hotel, I lay down for a while, then look over receipts and purchases to sort out what I will mail home, what I will take back in my luggage, and what I've forgotten to buy. I listen to the news with cardboard boxes, money, and edibles spread out around me. I've spent less than four hundred dollars, though I'd meant to spend a lot more, so I'll have to do more shopping.

The weatherwoman talks about the great days we've been having, unseasonably warm, then mentions high winds that will hit on Monday and, in passing, says 'hurricane strength' and 'warning.' I glance up, but they've gone to commercial.

CHAPTER THIRTY-ONE
SHOFU-EN

EITHER SATURDAY NIGHT in Denver is not as noisy as Friday night or I was actually able to zen-out the noise and sleep through the din. The gray of Sunday morning overpowers the street lights, still on at 7 a.m., and I look out at sidewalks, empty except for a few people draped with dirty blankets. The D-Line dings as it trundles by. Residence Inn, where I stayed when Snowstorm Decima hit, is only three blocks away. Cities are stunning when they are draped in so much snow you can't actually see the people dragging bundles of belongings around, screaming at skyscrapers, returning in a half-hour with twenty-six dollars, and squatting, in every sense, in alleys.

The breakfast pod named 'The Original' has seasoned fries, a poached egg, bacon bits, and cheddar sauce. I eat at the desk, looking onto Stout Street until the fries start to cool and the sauce congeals. In addition to gifting me earplugs, the letter next to the desk lamp also says I should not leave valuables lying around. The closet, tucked into the bathroom area, has a small room safe. I type in a code and put my edibles and extra hundreds and fifties inside.

Nolan arrives at 10:45, the old red Jeep pulling into the lot across the street. By the time I get there, he's parked and meets me halfway, so that we hug one-sided while walking back to the car. Kinsley moves to the back seat as Nolan looks at a map on his phone and sets it to give directions to the Denver Botanical Gardens. When we talked on the phone yesterday, he had consulted with Kinsley, and decided that they would spend the day hanging out in Denver instead of having me take the Flatiron Flyer to Boulder. As we go up 15th Street, the phone map says, "Turn Right. Turn Right."

"That cannot be right," says Nolan. "I'm sure it is this way."

"Turn Right."

Three cars across three lanes are coming toward us. The car in our lane toots his horn and shifts one lane over. Nolan stops. "I hate driving in Denver," he says, making a U-turn so we are going the right way on the one-way street.

The Botanical Gardens are four minutes away and Kinsley gets in free. We wander through some easy trails lined with herbs that have not been killed by the snow that fell a week earlier and still dusts the ground. Their sage is doing better than mine on the patio in Texas. Another trail meanders past boulders and a frozen creek, where I take pictures of Kinsley with the stream of ice as a backdrop. Her long hair is parted, combed, and evenly trimmed; and Kinsley's shoes, pink sweatshirt and gray fleece jogger pants are not faded or threadbare. She looks like a back-to-school tween fashion ad and chats about the plants growing along the trail: her class had a field trip here.

Neither Kinsley nor Nolan wear jackets, but on a fifty-degree day like this, Nolan has on his *heavy* khaki shorts and the Red Rocks sweatshirt that I got for him after my first visit. The ponds in the Japanese garden are frozen and surrounded by trimmed evergreens. It's tranquil and no one talks. So here's the deal. Nolan is buff. Like when we were in college. That level of buff. I suspected it during the half-hug before I got in the car. The weight he gained back has hardened up and gotten properly distributed on his frame. His teeth are shiny, and he mentions that his new haircut is bothering him because it's too short in the back and feels funny on his neck.

Nolan says Japanese gardens have names and we have just left Shofu-en, the Garden of Wind and Pines. Then we top a hill where an elongated lattice and glass mothership has landed: it's the greenhouse dome of the Tropical Conservatory. Along one side, the entrance is lined with poinsettias, dozens of different varieties: white, pink, green, yellow, peach, speckled, and fuchsia. Across from them is the orangery, a long row of large pots, each with a citrus tree heavy with fruit: lemons, limes, and a Buddha's Hand citron with a dozen yellow fingers splayed open. We enter the tropics. Streams flow through the multi-story forest, and level by level, we wander up the stairs into the canopy, lush and humid. Ducks paddle around in the pond below.

We have lunch in the cafe after.

The Denver Museum of Nature and Science is only five minutes away, but we park at least half a mile from it, at one end of Denver's City Park, and hike down the massive green with broad walkways, past a boathouse and a lake full of geese walking on the patch of ice covering most of the water, sliding a bit with each step. The museum is at the top of a hill, and by the time we reach it, we've been passed by a dozen scooters.

Kinsley has gone on alert, desperate to ride one saying, "That's my scooter, mine," each time someone cruises past, "I should be on that scooter." Several are parked at the bicycle U-racks in front of the museum. Nolan has a Lime app and unlocks a scooter which we wheel over to the sweeping walkways that curve around the hill, on the side of the museum which faces the park.

The Denver skyline is the park's backdrop, downtown skyscrapers jutting up before the long gray line of the Rockies, capped in white. Stepping onto the scooter, Nolan takes off fast along the walkway, stretching the length of the museum. He curves up the hill, across its top, then back down in a wide canted oval.

Kinsley hops up and down as Nolan shows her how to kick off. She pushes off, has to stop to regain her balance, takes off again and doesn't stop for the next ten minutes, accelerating, going up and down the hill, turning in wide circles. Unsurprisingly, for a nine-year-old who free climbs boulders in flip flops, she has no helmet and no fear. We watch her in silence. I'd been wanting to talk to Nolan all day, grown-up talk about my dad and how his prostate cancer was undetectable, but the Alzheimer's was getting worse, and about how Jovi was doing much better. My niece, Lauren, still had not studied Celiac disease, but once Jovi had been diagnosed, Lauren became a self-taught expert at cooking gluten-free foods. Plus, she was incredibly circumspect: Jovi had not had a gluten exposure in over a year, which, for a kid her age was remarkable. I also wanted to ask Nolan about himself. Earlier in the car, he'd mentioned that Fia was the same, old and deaf, but still chasing Frisbees, but that was the only update he'd given me.

Just as I give Nolan a summary of Jovi and Lauren, Kinsley,

winded, pulls up to us. So now, it's my turn. It takes me three tries to push off fast enough to get the Lime motor to engage. I go down the walkway, step off the scooter, turn it around and ride back. Then I try the big oval circuit that Nolan and Kinsley have been zipping around. Up the hill is not too bad, though I start to drift and have to get off the scooter and adjust its direction. Along the side of the museum is a straight-away, but coming down the hill, I start to pick up speed. I'm afraid to squeeze the brakes on the handle too hard, worried that a sudden stop will pitch me over, plus I'm not matching the curve of the walkway. As I propel toward the grass, I freak out and jump off, landing hard on one foot, jarring my ankle, but nothing creaky and old down there snaps. I walk the scooter down the rest of the hill then ride it back to Nolan and Kinsley who is shouting for me to "Go! Really Go! Fire it up!"

"This is as fired up as I get," I said. Other than my impending sudden death, my parents never had to worry about me much while I was growing up. I was never too much trouble. My sister Tessa was adventurous. I was steady, reliable, seemingly made for college and late-night study sessions. Tessa wouldn't hesitate to ride a scooter for all it was worth, go with her gut, follow her heart, lose her head. In the moment, it always felt right for her to do so, inspired even, and only later came regret, retrenching, even retreat.

I start to hand the scooter back to Kinsley, but she jumps up and down yelling, "Fire it up, Fire it up," like a cheer, pauses, then jumps again: "Go, go, go, go, go!"

I don't know why, but I take off along the straightaway again and rev it, curving up the hill, managing to stay off the grass, zoom across the straightaway along the top of the oval, then start to slow for the downhill curve. But I don't. Instead,

I run two trains of thought at the same time: I'm not wearing a helmet. If I fall and bang my head, get a concussion, end up with massive medical bills, miss work, and become a speech-impaired and no-longer-able-to-teach burden to my family, it would be my own fault. Going fast would be foolish. Don't be reckless, Alene. You are not that type of person. Walk the scooter down the hill.

Those thoughts run parallel to hearing old Fred—the river rafting swimmer—on the bus as we headed back to the outfitter, and how delighted he was to feel a 'charge' and suddenly the scooter is picking up speed. I turn the handle and follow the curve and I'm doing this; I'm riding a scooter and wind tousles my hair, hair streaming behind me, and I see a peripheral blur as I make it to the bottom walkway and vaguely note that a man on a bike has swerved away from me as Nolan and Kinsley get larger very fast.

I stop with a skid a few feet past Nolan and hand the scooter to Kinsley, who takes off full speed. My face feels tight. I'm grinning, maybe? I'm not sure. I force myself to blink.

"You are okay?" Nolan asks. "You screamed a little."

"Did that come out of me?" The grin absconds. "It was involuntary."

"I assumed as much."

"I heard something," I add. "Didn't realize it was me."

When we take the scooter back to the racks, Nolan closes the app and the scooter goes comatose, though he tests the scooter to make sure the session is over. When he tries to ride it, it gives a "No, don't steal me" beep, until he leaves it alone.

"Not bad," he says, checking his phone: the twenty-five minutes costs 5 dollars.

Inside the museum, families are everywhere, all of them

toting kids, but the promise of dinosaurs keeps me moving. I pass the animal dioramas—moose, wolves, mountain goats, bison, bears, brown bears, polar bears, more bears, and a manatee. The diorama habitats are excellently staged, though I wish there was a disclaimer that all the taxidermy animals died peacefully in their sleep.

The Native American exhibit has a real adobe house, and the dinosaur exhibit is the best I've ever seen, with so many dinosaur skeletons the halls seem full of them. Kinsley takes us up to the second level, where below, the dinosaurs look like a herd migrating across a plain before us. Hours later, when we're walking the half-mile back to the car—all of the scooters that we come across have dead batteries—it is too late to go to the movies and still get Kinsley back to her mom before Kinsley's bedtime.

"What time do you have to leave for work," Kinsley asks. "Nine, right?"

"That is about right," says Nolan.

"You're not working from home anymore?" I ask.

"No, not for months now."

We go to a Mongolian Grill, where Nolan and I manage to have coded conversation about my dad since Kinsley is at the table. I let Nolan know that my dad no longer has detectable levels of prostate cancer but that the progression of the Alzheimer's has sped up lately.

The drive back to the hotel is quiet. Nolan lets me out in the parking lot across from Aloft and gets out to hug me. This time it's not a half-hug while we're walking. I hang on way too long, like a full minute past a normal hug time. "Things will work out," he says, referring to my dad.

"No," I say, "they won't."

Nolan squeezes me extra tight, and I wonder if he has taken up sledgehammering or anvil tossing or something else requiring iron musculature. The day has been so packed that we have not actually talked much. I head across the parking lot to Aloft, and Nolan's Jeep is easing the right way onto the one-way street by the time I go in the lobby which is full of Bohemians socializing, sitting near the electric fireplace, and having drinks at the work area that is now a bar. Music is playing and the place has a vibe. I don't stay.

The news that night keeps returning to the anticipated windstorm, the weatherman sounding wistful: "We did have a beautiful day today, but you know, it's been a long time since we've had a big windstorm and people forget that this *is* the time of year for them. Powerful jet stream. The warning area includes the Front Range, Urban Corridor, the Foothills, and the Plains. Fifty mile an hour winds gusting over seventy-five to near one hundred miles an hour. So, folks, it's not just the mountains. Mountain passes will be closed. Expect zero visibility in the High Country with that snow getting picked up and blown around. For a full list of closures, check us out online. The Front Range will experience dangerously high winds, so hold on to your dogs tomorrow. Everyone will be affected by this. Power outages are possible with these types of conditions. Big rigs, don't even try it. Askin' for trouble is all."

The street noise doesn't bother me now. Like trains in the distance or the patter of rain, the bells of the L-line sing an abstract refrain.

CHAPTER THIRTY-TWO

USPS

I WOKE UP early but stayed in bed watching the weather report. Winds would be peaking at ninety miles an hour in the mountains and then hit Denver mid-morning, but unlike monster snowstorms, they don't name hurricane-force windstorms. Yesterday, the crane on the high rise being renovated across the street was lifting concrete slabs.

In the lobby, I make sure that a late check-out at 1 p.m. would be okay and get my tea and croissant. I packed my luggage then put everything I thought could trigger a TSA search into one mailer box and all the edibles in the other. I stuck on the fake return address labels and the address label with my home address but a made-up name then taped up the boxes. I carried the boxes around my room. The walk to the post office on 20th would only take ten minutes, but the boxes were too bulky to carry that far so, at 10:30, I take a Lyft to the post office for six bucks.

The United States Post Office on Curtis and 20th has a dull, functional design. "Five pounds, twelve ounces." The postal worker weighs the larger box. "Denver to San Antonio. Priority Mail Express, that's one day. It'll arrive tomorrow, sixty-one dollars and fifteen cents. Two day is fifteen dollars."

"Two-day delivery is fine."

"Fifty dollars of insurance is included. Do you have anything worth more than fifty dollars in the package?"

"No," I answer. "Nothing of value." The smaller box, with the chocolate bars and my paisley pajamas for padding, is three pounds, two ounces and fifty dollars for one-day delivery. I cheap out and get the two-day delivery for thirteen bucks, and no extra insurance on that one either, even though it has three hundred dollars' worth of edibles in it.

On the walk back from USPS, I pass the Greyhound Station which, in the cold bright light, seems less grungy than it did a year ago. The streets are full of people: the rich and the desperately poor. Construction crews and cranes are still working on the tops of buildings as I stop by Native Roots Wellness, deciding to buy more CBD bars and transdermal patches to give as gifts back home. While the same CBD-tender from Saturday is stapling my purchases into a plain brown bag, I ask why they moved the big premium store that used to be here.

"The new Colorado Director of Marijuana Coordination. The store was eight feet too close to a school, so she enforced the regulation and closed us down, the recreational side anyway, but the CBD store is surprising everyone with how well it's doing because people are discovering the benefits of CBD."

After I get back to Aloft, I decide to make one more trip to Euflora, and, once I get to the corner on 16th, there's a one-minute wait for the free MallRide, two minutes to get to Tremont, twelve minutes in the store, and eight minutes back to my room. I line six edible bars in my cosmetics bag, put another two bars in a sock, and close up my luggage with the spare lock I brought. I didn't quite reach the twenty Chocolate Cherry bars that was my goal, but I've got more than I brought back last time. As I'm zipping up my bag, it occurs to me that my flight goes from Denver to Phoenix, where I have a plane change and an eighty-minute wait in Arizona. A quick search says Arizona's legal for medical and prohibited for recreational. Good enough.

Just as I check out, the high winds hit Denver. Debris flies down the street like a witch on a broomstick and when I step outside, the wind tries to mug me and rip my puffy jacket off. Construction crews are standing in clusters on the sidewalks and the cranes on top of buildings are locked down. I make it to the corner, catch the MallRide to Union Station, feed eleven dollars into the ticket machine on the platform, then duck back inside for a sandwich. The A-Line Commuter Rail from Union Station to Denver International runs every fifteen minutes, and by the time I finish eating, I'm ready for the 1:30 run. Just as I board, settle my luggage in the rack and take a seat, I get a text: "Your Southwest flight from Denver now departs at 5:50 p.m. We're sorry for the delay."

I grab my suitcase and jump back off the train before the doors close. I've got an extra hour now, but opulent Union Station is not a bad place to burn time. I start with The Terminal Bar and start with a Manhattan. The bar looks very fin de siècle—1899, not 1999—with cushioned booths, carved and polished dark wood paneling, gold filigree, and brass plaques on the edges of tables. The bartenders wear black vests, ties, and starched white shirts.

Later and lubricated, I get on the three o'clock A-Line and notice, for the first time, that it passes a prison with a guard tower in the middle of the yard, surrounded by a fence topped with razor wire. We also pass a field of little boxes: tan rows of McMansions and townhouses. I'm still buzzed from the bar and enjoy the slight rocking of the commuter rail, admiring the dozens of graffiti murals on the backs of warehouses, as I hope, in a detached way, that I won't be humiliated and jailed by the end of the day. At the far end of the train car, a Really Important Business Guy talks loudly on his phone about clients, deal structures, and incentivizing some funds that could be made available. Mercifully, the Manhattan floats me up and away.

Beyond a field of solar panels, Blucifer rears at the top of the highway, maniacal red eye blazing as we pull into Denver International. I ride the escalator up to the terminal, then head to kiosks in front of the Southwest counter and key in my confirmation number. Then key it in again, each time getting an error message. On the fourth try, a Southwest Air guy materializes at my shoulder and looks over the confirmation page in my hand.

"Yeah," he says, "come with me." A ticket agent does some super-fast typing as Southwest Air guy explains. "The windy conditions have affected the schedule. Your flight was delayed, which means the connection in Phoenix won't connect, so you've been re-booked on a later flight." He's talking to me; the agent behind the counter is talking; someone is handing me something; my bag is being weighed; it disappears behind the counter; I've been maneuvered away from the counter, "This is your baggage claim. Your baggage claim. You need to keep this," I'm walking with Southwest Air guy, "Your flight leaves at 8:20." He tells me the flight number and the gate. "It's nonstop, Denver to San Antonio.

"Eight-twenty? Okay. Wait. That's four more hours?"

"Non-stop."

"Okay." I zen it. I'm walking, "I guess that's not bad. It gets into San Antonio almost the same time, not much later anyway. Non-stop is good." Southwest Air guy has evaporated. I'm talking to air, holding a baggage claim ticket, heading to security screening.

Four hours in the late afternoon, easing into evening at a major air hub is butt-loads better than three hours in a bus station in Amarillo at 5 a.m. I sit, eat, people-watch, walk around, let the moving sidewalks walk me around, use the toilets that flush themselves, wash my hands under the faucets that turn themselves on and off, and listen to music on my headphones. Enforced non-productive time without a cross-country bus ride is so doable.

The pilot warns us that the take-off will be choppy because of the high winds but vastly understates it. The ascent is so steep, my sphincter checks in and asks, "What's up?" The butt-clenching ascent is followed by a quiet flight back to San Antonio. By the time we touch down and I grab my luggage off the carousel and figure out which Lyft circling the pick-up lanes is mine and not the Lyft for the guy next to me or the Lyft for the couple next to him, it's after 11 p.m. The Lyft driver looks like she's nineteen and she plays hip hop on low volume all the way to my house. The ride costs seventeen dollars, less than half what I paid last year for the cab from the bus station.

The lock on my suitcase has not been cut, and the cosmetics bag is just where I packed it, still full of cannabis chocolate bars, so Yahtzee Colorado. Yahtzee. Now all I have to do is wait for the United States Postal Service to bring my boxes to the door.

Two-day delivery and I'm set for a year.

CHAPTER THIRTY-THREE
RECITAL

On Wednesday, I work in my room all morning with the television on. The window faces the front yard, and I can see the intersection. At noon, the local news starts with a 'drug deal gone bad' report about two men dead in a car, shot in the back of the head, over marijuana they were selling or buying or stealing or something.

The next story says that ten million travelers passed through San Antonio International Airport last year, a new record, and I get so preoccupied with trying to calculate how much unsearchable, inbound luggage from Denver that amounts to that I almost miss the report on a woman arrested for fraud and identity theft. Surprisingly, it is not her porcelain pallor and long black hair that takes me back to that classroom three years ago; it's the perfect lack of emotion on her face as she is perp-walked to a squad car in front of a clinic.

Ivy Ruelas, the student who I yelled at so crazily one morning that I had to call Nolan to cope with the stress of flipping-out during class, did not fulfill her avaricious plan to become a nurse. Instead, apparently, she learned medical coding, started working in a pediatrician's office, and used her access to patient files and physicians' accounts to embezzle money, siphoning nearly a hundred thousand in less than a year. I replay the story and note how Ivy looks untroubled by the handcuffs on her wrists.

The mail arrives at 12:30, a USPS truck pulling up to our box on the curb. That's how old the neighborhood is: a mailbox in front of every house. The mailman slides letters into the box, then starts to pull away and I sigh, but then he stops, blocking the driveway, walks around the cars carrying two packages, and I'm already heading to the front door. I have to be the one to get them, so Mom does not see the fake name on the address labels.

I scurry back to my room and open the box that has all the flotsam that could have gotten my suitcase opened on the flight back then open the box with the bars of edibles. All are accounted for and the box was not stolen and cops are not kicking in my door and the feds are not taking me away and TSA is not explaining what a strip search involves. Win-win-win.

"I don't want you to give Dad any more cannabis," Mom says in the kitchen later that day. "He's been sleeping too much. Yesterday he was in bed all day. Didn't even get up and get dressed. Just wakes up to eat, drink some juice, and go to the bathroom."

"I don't think the cannabis is making him sleep all day," I say. "I'm just giving him a maintenance dose. It's anti-inflammatory and analgesic, but it's not enough for that kind of sedation."

"He's becoming bedridden. He hasn't left the house in nearly a week. He won't go anywhere. He won't do anything."

"Plus, I give it to him at six in the evening so that he can be comfortable at night. The edible may help him sleep at night without waking up over and over, but it is not causing him to sleep constantly all day."

"That could be right," Mom says. "This could be a progression of his disease. He could be sleeping so much because of the Alzheimer's. Let's just try going without the cannabis for a while and see if he wakes up more and is more active. Just hold off for now."

After such a successful cannabis run, I wonder if Mom believes Dad is sleeping because of the Alzheimer's or because of the cannabis or if she just doesn't want me to risk bringing edibles back to Texas. Even though I have never explained how I'm bringing the goods back, she knows I'm not waving a magic wand. And it's not like I work construction. If a construction worker gets arrested with weed in his luggage, it's a court date; if a college professor gets arrested, it's the lead on the local news. Academic Freedom means I can say any crazy crap I want to in a classroom, as long as I remain an upstanding member of society: teachers work under a morals clause, and I'm guessing the District would find muling weed into Texas a bit of a gray area. That evening, I leave two books, *Brave New Weed* and *Cannabis Pharmacy*, on the recliner Mom uses for reading and hope she'll reconsider.

Mitch calls two days later. His mom fell and broke her wrist. Miriam was on a step stool in her house, getting sweaters off a shelf. She's already had a wrist procedure, he says, and her arm is propped on a cushion. So is her foot but he's not sure what's up with that. He needs information about CBD. Does it work, what to get, and how much does it cost by the way?

❧

Mom comes into the kitchen in her pajamas while I'm getting ready for work. It's been two weeks since she put the injunction on me giving Dad any more cannabis, and initially, I had wondered if she might be right, not because he suddenly started sleeping less, but because he was still able to sleep at night. When Dad first tried a few drops of CBD tincture, the first effect was that he was able to sleep without waking up over and over, and without making his oboe-groan. Because of that, Mom was able to get a good night's sleep too. When I stopped giving him cannabis—the daily CBD and the twice-weekly THC—there was no sudden change. Dad kept sleeping at night, but he also kept sleeping a lot during the day, so maybe the edibles didn't really matter.

It took three days before I started hearing the oboe-groan again, at first just once or twice a night. Then noticeably during the day. But he was still spending all day in bed. A week after that, he was waking up at night, oboe-groaning a lot, then getting up a couple of times a night.

I put an apple in my lunch tote. "So, I was thinking I should start giving Dad his cannabis again."

"Yeah, go ahead and start giving it to him." Mom loads silverware into the dishwasher. "He was bouncing around all over the place last night. I just thought maybe he would get out of that room some more. Be more active. But. He just. Yeah, I think it helps."

Classes have started and I don't get home until six that evening, but by six-thirty, I'm getting my cosmetics bag out of the closet and looking over the Cherry Chocolate bars. The hard to open, press and simultaneously unzip wrapper thing is gone, and instead, there is new packaging that does not require brute strength or a pair of scissors to open, just multiple steps: there's a paperboard box enclosing a plastic tray with a peel-back cover that reveals the chocolate bar, in a plastic wrapper. Even the arthritic could manage it.

I give Dad a whole chocolate square since he hasn't had anything in two weeks, and I figure he could use the analgesic, and he and Mom could both use a rest. I hear him wake up and talk to Mom once that night around eleven. I can't make out what they're saying, but she chats back, and their voices don't sound distressed.

I get home late the next day and give him half a CBD gummie frog, deciding that I'd go ahead and use those up before giving him the Strawberry-and-Cream bars from Native Roots Wellness. Mom and Dad watch *Cast Away*, and Dad stays awake for the whole movie then sleeps all night without a chat, thermostat adjustment, or oboe-groan.

On Saturday, I go over to Mitch's house and take transdermal CBD patches plus two CBD Strawberry bars. I make him responsible for explaining them to his mother, so she doesn't make a mistake and eat a whole bar. The boys are doing fine, running around, burying their old toys in the backyard. It's something they started doing a week ago: bury a toy truck, dig it up a day later, and bury it somewhere else. They've also recently had their second piano recital, and I listen with envy when Mitch tells me about it.

Jovi watches videos online after school, and lately, I've been too tired to teach her piano when she comes over. I try to remember how many recitals I played in before I rebelled and tried to quit taking lessons when I was eleven. It didn't work. Mom insisted that I continue to play. She always wanted to learn to play when she was a girl and never got the chance. Eventually, my teacher, Adelaide Shelp, a local concert pianist virtuoso, told Mom she was wasting her money: I didn't want to play, I didn't practice, and there was no point in Ms. Shelp trying to teach me anymore. Frankly, she found it too futile to keep trying. She used the word 'futile' instead of 'depressing' and the lessons stopped.

My reasons for teaching Jovi the piano are not that I wanted to take lessons when I was a girl, but because learning to play the piano will help her with math, will make her more rounded, will teach her persistence. Kids that can do things like play piano have more confidence, better thinking skills, and they don't take drugs. They get first chair in band, go on band trips, make friends, ace college, and land a job that does not involve standing behind a register for hours, while their feet swell. Swimming lessons or gymnastics, Saturday morning soccer or Brazilian Capoeira, San Antonio Youth Choir or playing piano is what middle-class kids do, and I don't want the family to slide into the poverty my parents worked like ten dogs to keep us out of.

Knowledge is a possession: Once you can swim, you can swim. Once you know that five times five is twenty-five, you know it forever. My hands still know Sonata in 'C' Minor. In a darkened Trinity University auditorium, a year before my piano lesson rebellion, an audience of Adelaide Shelp's students, their friends and families, applauded as I walked into a spotlight, curtsied in my empire waist gown and patent leather shoes, and sat at a grand piano. Getting into the car after the recital, I saw tracks in Mom's make-up from the tears she cried as I finished playing Mozart in front of three hundred strangers. No one will applaud Jovi for searching a virtual house for a virtual cat, and I silently vow to hold onto enough energy to give her piano lessons every Friday when she comes over after school.

I find *Brave New Weed* and *Cannabis Pharmacy* on my bed, where Mom has left them without telling me if she read them or not. If you can keep your shit together enough to play Mozart from memory into the murmuring darkness when you're ten, you can keep it together enough when you're fifty to pack weed in your luggage, get drunk in a bar, and fly back to Texas in the middle of a windstorm so your parents can get a decent night's sleep, despite Alzheimer's, arthritis, and radiated prostates.

It just stands to reason somehow.

CHAPTER THIRTY-FOUR
HOT SPRINGS

The Hedge Trimming Follies are on again, late in the summer, and I stand around, waiting for Dad to get tired. It takes longer than expected, but he eventually needs a break and I take over, determined that I won't stop until the hedges are subdued. Anyway, how hard could hedge-trimming be?

Extremely. Extremely hard, actually. The electric trimmer is heavier than it looks and the cris-cross snicking blades are longer than I'd realized. It's like hefting a broadsword that bites. Hedges, peevishly, do not want to be trimmed and they grab at the trimmer like an *Alice in Wonderland* hallucination come to life. Repeatedly, the trimmer gets hung up on the thicker branches. My shoulders bunch up. Mom holds the extension cord, her lips beginning to moue at my lack of hedge trimming skill.

"Make sure you can see what you're cutting." From the bench on the porch, Dad starts coaching. "And keep track of your feet; don't get tangled up."

I take a step. There's enough extension cord to go all the

way across the yard, but it's gotten hung up on something, tugs me back, and I feel a catch around my ankles and an off-balance trill in my gut.

When my grandfather, Lennox, built my grandmother Ella's house in Hot Springs, he built it without hallways: the door on the right side of the living room led directly into their bedroom; the door at the back of the living room led directly into the boys' bedroom, which led to the kitchen at the back of the house. By the end of his life, in an age before power tools had safety shut-offs, my grandfather had lost parts of half his fingers. My mother learned to drive when she was eleven. If he cut off one of his fingers, my grandfather would need someone to drive him to the hospital, and my grandmother had never learned. He would wrap the end of what was left of his finger, and whichever kid was nearest at hand would perch on the edge of the driver's seat of his truck. Once, my aunt Gracie had to work the pedals while my mom steered. Lennox needed the hospital to stop the bleeding and stitch things up. Of course, the finger, back then, was just gone.

My finger comes off the hedge trimmer trigger as I lose balance. I never topple completely back but do scrape my shoulder across the brick on the front of the house. A segment of extension cord is wedged under my SUV's front tire, and a pile of hedge trimmings has pushed against my ankle, not really tripping me but making me step away.

I kick the debris so I can see my feet, tell Mom to let out more cord, and see that Dad's face has gone immobile, his reaction when he tenses up. He's been watching, seeing me nearly trip. He's about to stand and take over again, but I start the trimmer back up and finish the hedgerow.

When I go inside, I rub sports cream on my neck, arms,

and shoulders. It doesn't work, but I lay around enveloped in a haze of menthol with a warm sting on my flesh. Then I remember the THC/CBD lotion I got in Colorado and later, after the menthol smell has faded away, I try it. It has a smell too, not as strong, more medicinal, and the lotion goes on cool. I lay down to watch TV and two hours later, the aches have faded so much that I only remember them when I get up to go to the kitchen.

❧

Eleven years older than me, my sister Tessa was born in the '50s, grew up in the '60s, hit college in the '70s, then dropped out within two years to be part flower child, part reporter. Tessa's downfall was her undeniable beauty. We have pictures of Tessa in the house of course, but the frozen images cannot match what her actual presence was like by the time she was fifteen years old. Inside the family, we were immune to her, but, as a child, I saw others feel a tangible loss when she left the room. The air around her seemed iridescent; when Tessa's large eyes landed on you, they swallowed you. Strangers in the street would stare at her, turning as though a gazelle had just strolled by. My friend Nicoletta has the unearthly beauty of a Renaissance Titian, but she never let the attention it attracted boggle her common sense. To Tessa, however, attention had always been her due until she woke up alone one morning in Dallas, flat broke and exhausted, with no rent and no plan for the future.

After she dropped out of UT Austin, she got a job at a Houston newspaper, but in just a year, when she forgot to change the oil in her car and the engine caught fire on an overpass, she walked away without bothering to give notice or pick up her last paycheck, deciding the flames were a signal to move to another city and change her life up. Tessa wanted to be a radical without putting in the detailed work of actually picking a particular cause, and she ended up flitting from one worldview to another. That worldview was always adopted from whatever boyfriend she had at the time. The first one she brought home for us to meet was an astrologer who sold crystals at flea markets and hoped to study with 'the shamen' but didn't know any authentic ones just yet. The boyfriends got stranger after that until, in front of one of them, my mother railed at Tessa for dropping out of college and associating with lowlifes and libertines, which was the only time in my life I heard 'libertine' used in 20th century speech.

The last boyfriend declared himself an Anarchist and talked passionately at dinner about why governments needed to be overthrown, while Dad, an officer in the U.S. Air Force, asked in a flat tone if he wanted more mashed potatoes. Mom asked the Anarchist what kind of career he wanted and got a miasma of screed and historical mash-up of the crimes the United States was committing in Central America.

At the height of their careers, my parents had thrown parties, some formal sit-down dinners and others just a houseful of people dancing, drinking, filling ashtrays with cigarette butts, and eating food speared with cocktail forks from a buffet, spread down the dining room table. Dad had a reel-to-reel tape deck so music could play for hours. Mom had crystal dishes full of cashews or candy, depending on the season. Two glass trays were designed just for holding deviled eggs. They were perfect hosts.

When the Anarchist paused, Mom produced her tightest smile and handed him a basket of dinner rolls, wrapped in a cloth to keep warm, as Tessa beamed at him for sounding so clever in front of her parents who, unlike him, *had* actually been around the world.

On a warm afternoon five months later, the Anarchist parked in front of a bank in Austin and walked inside while Tessa sat in the passenger seat, with a foot propped up on the dash so she could repaint her big toe. A pedestrian on the sidewalk did a double-take—her beauty, you know, that and the foot, but she was accustomed to stares and did not notice him. She also did not notice her boyfriend running until he jumped in the car as the bank alarm went off. The high-speed chase headed up I-35 South, attracting cop cars like a magnet collects loose bolts.

The 35-corridor was not built up back then. It was a straight-away, open ribbon cut through farmland, so it took the boyfriend, going ninety-five in a faded Chevy Nova, some time to lose control. The skid blurred into a roll, down an embankment and into a ditch, which, in an incalculable way, absorbed much of the energy of the crash. Tessa went through the windshield, breaking an arm, a leg, and sustaining a concussion. The glass gashed open her ankle, the back of her wrist, her forehead at her hairline, and the space between the top of her lip and the bottom of her nose on one side of her face. She was rushed to a hospital back in Austin since nothing closer had a decent trauma center.

It was hours before my parents got the call and, stone-faced, drove seventy miles in darkness and silence, unsure whether they would have to claim a body when they arrived. A week later, when they brought Tessa home, helping her hobble slowly to her old bed, I hid in my bedroom doorway, afraid of her casts, her bandaged head, her wounds that were still weeping, as she lay in a room full of brown shadows, with the curtains drawn.

The Anarchist did not go through the windshield. He was half-ejected from the car, which rolled on him, fracturing his skull. He never spoke again. His vegetative state, combined with the pedestrian's statement to the FBI that Tessa seemed "untroubled and oblivious" as she sat in the car while her boyfriend robbed a bank, meant the boyfriend could be blamed for everything. The vanity of painting her nails kept Tessa from doing twenty-five to life. Gradually, her hair grew back and covered the stitches above her forehead, but the cut on her face turned into a ragged scar two inches long. She sat in front of the mirror and cried for days. Then stopped.

In a few weeks, she was hopping around the house on one leg—it was faster than using the crutches, she said. And when the casts came off and the threat of prosecution for bank robbery ended, she decided that the only place to be was in Dallas. She had friends there, and against all advice, she left. The outcome was predictable to everyone but Tessa. Her friendships may have been genuine at one time, or they may have been based on using her as decoration. In any case, her college reporter buddies had moved to the next rung in their lives, either sliding off the map into obscurity or maturing into steady job holders who were not interested in the randomness Tessa towed with her.

Despite having cried for days in front of a mirror, on some level, she had not understood that her power base, the radiant good looks she relied on like a sorcerer's gift, were gone. That morning in Dallas, when she truly realized what was lost, her sense of herself was lost with it. For the first time since high school, she did not have a boyfriend or clique of groupies.

Unable to bear coming home and facing Mom and Dad, she called Aunt Gracie, who wired her the money to take a bus to Hot Springs, where Tessa emptied her heart like an old purse onto Gracie's kitchen table. For a few weeks Tessa did nothing. She sat on the back porch and stared at the base of the mountain that rose up behind Gracie's backyard and turned twenty-two.

Four months later, Tessa enlisted. For four years, she was a model soldier, trained in engine repair, thriving in the structure of Army life and planning a career. Then she met Reid. He was getting a divorce and was six months away from getting out of the army. Tessa was pregnant before either was done. They got married, had a baby girl, Callie, got out of the military, and moved to Rockford, near Reid's brothers and cousins. She had Lauren two years later. A month after Callie and Lauren's babysitter, Mrs. Kerns, died of a stroke, Tessa put the girls in the car and drove a thousand miles back home.

I was in Spain at the time, yelling at Mitch in El Escorial's little cafe.

A few weeks before the fall semester, I took stock, dragging out all my remaining edibles, pre-rolls, and oil, to figure out how much was left. CBD shops had sprung up in San Antonio, including franchises, but the quality of their edibles was not up to Colorado's. I didn't care, so long as I could get them in town. And I did not let myself think about the eight-hundred-dollar yearly cost for a supply of CBD gummies in Texas because getting THC chocolates was the real problem. When I had last gone to Denver and brought back edibles, I estimated that I was getting enough to take care of Dad for a year. But gradually, I started giving him more of the chocolates, a whole five milligram square each evening, because it helped him sleep better than the CBD alone. By cannabis-user standards, that dose wasn't much, but it meant that a Cherry Chocolate bar only lasted ten days now, so a year's worth of chocolate would be close to forty bars and around a thousand in cash. My current supply was getting depleted.

I put the problem out of my mind, unable to find the will to go on another Denver run or even plan one. Going to Denver no longer felt like an adventure and instead was tinged with a little grubbiness and an itchy worry that my luck would run out, especially if I tried to really *really* stock up in one trip. I shouldn't have to fly two states up to get medication that I could easily, albeit expensively, purchase there, just so I could grift it back to Texas. Trying to avoid a pressured-filled trip to Denver that would burn money in airfare and hotel costs, plus hundreds in cannabis, helped me slide into a sort of magical thinking that somehow a solution would appear and things would just work out.

Each day that passed meant I was coming up against the clock, just when I needed to get ready for fall. With seventeen days of chocolate squares left, I looked at the calendar. Convocation week had started and I was in my office between meetings. Zero-day would be on the 5th of September and then Dad would be up six times a night and confused the next day and exhausting Mom. The only way to fly to Colorado now would be over the first weekend of the semester since Labor Day was coming up. I could fly up Thursday night, the 29th of August, shop on Friday, mail back a couple boxes on Saturday morning, fly back on Sunday, and still have Labor Day to get my shit together for the rest of the work week.

I checked Southwest Air. Shit. I'd already waited too long. The cheap seats were gone. And without the supersaver fares, I was looking at a stiff four hundred dollars each way. But that's the price of being slow. Now I started playing around with the flight times. If I left on Thursday, after my last class, no, that wouldn't work. Screw it. I'd need to leave early on Friday, fly to Denver, get to my hotel, shop Friday late in the day and also probably Saturday morning, then mail boxes home. The bigger problem was that the best flights—the ones that were non-stop and arrived while I could still drag my luggage to a hotel in the daylight, meaning before 7:30 p.m. at the end of August—those flights were selling out.

I closed the website and headed to a meeting. I'd figure it out tomorrow or the next day, when there would be even fewer choices, and I hadn't even looked at what price Aloft charged on short notice.

☙

I had insomnia that night: falling asleep, waking up, falling half asleep, waking up. At four in the morning, I woke up fully: Tessa was in Hot Springs.

After Tessa had moved back home, she worked as a paralegal for a mega-sized law outfit, climbing the ladder until she was the top paralegal in the firm. She went to school at night and on the weekends, while Mom watched Callie and Lauren. Tessa got her bachelor's, then a master's degree. To drop some of the weight she'd gained over the years, Tessa trained to run a half-marathon, and, an hour after she ran her first and only race, sweaty and euphoric, celebrating at a bar with the ladies in the office who had cheered her on, she met Jeff, a co-worker's cousin who was in town on vacation in his Luxury Motorcoach.

Six months later, she sold her house in Winter Forest, climbed into his RV, and moved to Jeff's ranch in Arizona.

And now, Tessa was married to the Arizona rancher who, though retired, still kept a few head of cattle and got up every morning before dawn to take care of them with Tessa by his side. Jeff was a hard worker. At fourteen years old, he'd quit school to help support his family and could fix anything from a gate to a hot water heater to the cracked concrete that was starting to separate my parents' patio from the rest of the foundation of the house.

Tessa's beauty was back, but not with the stupefying stun gun power she used to wield. Over the years, she had aged into loveliness, and the scar above her lip had flattened and faded. She could have hidden it with make-up now but didn't bother, focused instead on helping Jeff maintain the property on the ranch.

August was their slow month at the ranch, so Tessa and Jeff had been traveling around the country in the RV, stopping at national parks on the way to Branson, Missouri. Jeff's first wife had died of cancer, and his grown sons, also ranchers, took care of his property when he and Tessa were out of town. After Branson, they were planning to stay in San Antonio for two weeks as the last leg of their trip before heading back to Arizona, but then on a whim, they left Branson early so Tessa could spend a few days with Aunt Gracie.

Mom had told me about it last week, and at four in the morning the solution tallied up: Arkansas had medical marijuana, and Gracie had a medical marijuana card. The surgery she'd had twenty years ago to relieve her chronic back pain had given her a reprieve for a time, but her back had deteriorated and she had to use a walker now, just to slowly shuffle around.

She also had emphysema, from a pack-a-day habit. She had called me when the first cannabis shop opened in Hot Springs to find out what worked best for pain. My mom had told Gracie about my trips to Denver, which made me the family expert on all things weed related, and I spent an hour explaining buds and budtenders, pre-rolls, edibles, and topicals to her.

Convocation week was still underway, and I'd had four back-to-back meetings, each in a different building on campus, before I walked across the green in ninety-five-degree humidity back to my office. The Arkansas dispensary websites looked homemade. Hot Springs only had two dispensaries and the pickings in each were slim. Neither had THC chocolates and the only THC edibles were gummies: ten count packages in grape, mango, or lemon for forty-five dollars. I looked at the milligrams per gummy and did minimal arithmetic. I'd need six of the ten-packs to get Dad to Christmas.

An online newspaper review of the newly opened Hot Springs dispensaries said that, of the two, Green Haven, the one that was closest to Gracie's house anyway, was the best. Apparently, it looked more 'finished' the article said, clean and bright. And, since the owner of the place walked around the lobby with a chrome-plated gun holstered on his hip—that's Arkansas security for yah—as he welcomed customers, it seemed more secure than the other dispensary as well.

I called Gracie when I got home. Tessa was at Gracie's kitchen table. In the background, I could hear Gracie's great-grandbaby, Lissa, making noise, and Jeff talking to Gracie's husband about home repairs. After explaining what I wanted to Gracie, she had me re-explain everything to Tessa, who could write it down for her more easily. Depending on Arkansas's cannabusiness tax rate, the gummies would run between two-seventy and three-hundred-and-fifty bucks if Gracie could get six packages for me, which she said would not be a problem. Tessa would give her the money, and I'd pay Tessa back when she got to San Antonio.

And then I could do Denver in December. Just like magic.

⁂

Tessa wouldn't take my money when she handed me the six squat jars of gummies five days later. She and Jeff had parked at an RV campground a few miles up I-35 and driven a jeep over to the house. Over dinner, she told us that Gracie was frail and dragged oxygen around with her on a little cart everywhere she went.

I had considered the frog shaped CBD gummies that I got in New Braunfels to be low-rent compared to the sweet Colorado edibles, but if Texas frogs were low-rent, the Arkansas gummies were downright primitive. They looked like Jello gone bad and came in a jar with a label slapped on at an angle. If there was a way to ruin a good thing, the Hot Springs dispensary had found it. I ran out of squares of Cherry Chocolates three days after Labor Day, and on the fourth day, I opened a jar of Arkansas gummies, grape or mango—I didn't know which. Both flavors were a murky blackish-violet. The gummies had merged into one mass. I tried to figure out how the blob I was looking at was ten pieces of anything. I pulled on it and eventually peeled off an oval shape that I suppose was one-tenth of the rest. Now I had to figure out how to dose Dad.

The label on the bottom of the jar said that each serving was ten milligrams of THC. So, I would have to cut each gummy piece in half and combine it with an edible from the Texas CBD I already had. I cut a sliver off the oval; it was tacky and slightly melted, feeling not quite solid at room temperature. And it was gritty. Some of the granulated sugar it was made with had not fully dissolved. Zen or no zen, I was pissed off. I pictured Gracie hobbling around the Hot Springs dispensary past the gun-totin' owner, oxygen tank propped up on her walker, getting six jars of this muck for Dad with his Alzheimer's and arthritis. The country's been sliding toward legal cannabis for years, and I've been to Colorado three times just to shop for edibles, and the best that the next state over can do is this? Dammit.

I cut the oval in half, get it un-stickied from my fingers, then divide a CBD frog and put them on a saucer together.

"What's this?" Dad asks.

I sort of explain, and he takes it, having to tug a little at the Arkansas gummie, which leaves a purple stain behind. The gummie tries to escape by climbing onto the back of Dad's fingers, but he wrangles it into his mouth and asks what it is again.

Alright, I resign myself. I would start looking at Southwest Air's schedule again. And Aloft. Plan ahead and look for discounts. Maybe take a Thursday off from work, I don't know. But a trip to Denver was back in the works. At least Tessa had covered the cost of the six-jar debacle. I had to thank her for that.

After work the next day, I sit at the desk in my room with the Arkansas jar of gummies, which are like jelly, and use a spoon and fork to separate each jelly-gummy from the blob, laying them out in a row on a sheet of wax paper. The blob had left a slick of syrup in the jar. I slice each oval in half and find that although they are all the same shape, they vary in thickness, so they are not uniform. Each half jelly-gummie gets wrapped in a square of wax paper, then stuffed back into the jar.

When the jar is full it goes into the fridge. The whole process is strangely meditative, and I feel calm once it's done, which is good since I'll have to do the same thing every twenty days whenever I open a new jar.

The next evening, I take one of the chilled wax paper packets out of the jar and put the THC gummie on a saucer along with half a CBD frog. The gummie is still a little tacky but not the mess it was at room temperature. When Dad eats it, he asks if it's Jello, and I decide I can hold off on the trip back to Denver. Wax-paper-packaging and chilling the gummies is not ideal, but it is doable, so I'll do it till Winter Break, then fly to Denver, take a Lyft to the big premium Native Roots on Highlands, and stock up on easy-to-dose chocolate bars. And this time I swear I'll plan ahead.

Mitch calls after work the next day. He's getting married.

CHAPTER THIRTY-FIVE
DECEMBER 2019

A YEAR AFTER I had stayed with Mitch in Spain, right before we started graduate school, Mitch came out as gay. In the '80s, this was brave, defiant, and honest, even if it might seem dated now. I have boys in class with henna designs on their hands; girls named Finnegan, Flynn, or Darien, and a few students—Schafer, Garza, or Freeman—that go by last name only. A male adjunct in the science division wears a dress about once a week. No make-up, jewelry, or explanation. Just a day in a pedestrian frock and old loafers.

In grad school, Mitch had his first of three boyfriends, Glenn, a funny and charming farm boy who fled Idaho for college in the big city. Glenn also drank too much and got crabs twice. I flew to Wisconsin to visit Mitch over a four-day weekend. They broke up a week later.

While working on his doctorate, Mitch started what became a six-year relationship with Brian, a high-level civil servant, bland as low-fat mayo. Brian owned a small mansion that had been in his family for four generations, had relatives in

Milwaukee and a job with a phenomenal retirement package. When Mitch graduated and got a job in San Antonio, Brian refused to move. They're still friends.

Being a professor, curator, and grant writer meant that Mitch had to do a lot of hobnobbing. Sean collected art, was an important guy in finance at Ruttman Bank, and had a high-rise condo in downtown San Antonio with a modest view overlooking Earth. He was not out and never planned to be. They lasted three years. They are not still friends.

The engagement surprised me. In a phone call during the summer, Mitch mentioned that he'd gone to a convention in Ohio and had dinner with Patton, an old friend from his undergrad days at Harvard. That was all Mitch said about it. In August Patton came for a visit. In September they got engaged. And in October, when Patton was in town again, we all had lunch together, along with the boys, at the Thai place on Nyla, everyone ordering a dish but then eating communally, picking from all the entrees in the middle of the table.

Immediately, I knew Patton was a truly cool guy. After graduating from Harvard a year behind Mitch, he worked for a non-profit helping refugees or oppressed somebodies or the especially needy in Eastern Europe for years. He was actually much more specific when he recapped his life, but the Blackened Noodles and Green Curry Vegetables were killing it, and I still had two spring rolls left, so I missed a lot of detail. By the time the spring rolls were gone, Patton was a specialist in ergonomic workplace and industrial design, with his own business in Ohio, and it was going to take more than a year for him to fully transition to San Antone. He would need to spend months flying to Ohio for two weeks so he could complete ongoing projects, then fly back to San Antonio for a week or two to spend time with Mitch and the boys while setting up his office in town. Mitch's boys liked him, and Mitch had his Mitch-grin going.

I snapped my fingers in front of Mitch's face to get his attention. "You want to land the helicopter already?" I said. Throughout lunch, he'd been nagging the boys to eat this, put that down, use a fork, sit up straight, wipe your mouth, with a napkin. "Let 'em be for five minutes. You're at a table with two adults; talk to us for a while."

"They're constantly squirming or poking each other—"

"Stop hovering."

"And when one of them spills water across the table?"

"Mitch!"

During our fussing, Patton scooped the last of the noodles onto his plate. I add a chilled-out temperament to his list of attributes. I liked him, and I liked him for Mitch and the boys. The wedding would be in March 2020.

COVID-19? We'd never heard of it.

When I go through security at San Antonio International, I put everything in my pockets into the tray, but I don't take the money bag from around my neck. I have five hundred in my checked luggage, but the money bag under my shirt has nine hundred cash, and not putting the bag in the tray earns me a special screening pat-down. The screening lady's blue latex-gloved hands slide down my back and legs. By rote, she says that she'll use the back of her hands to check under and between my breasts and asks if I want to be screened behind a partition. I don't. I don't care, and neither does anyone else. Then she runs an electronic wand that ends in a black, spoon-shaped disk over her hands and monotones that she is testing her hands and then she will test mine. I ask what she's testing for.

"Explosive residue." She yawns, checks my money bag, hands it back to me, and reminds me to put everything in the tray next time to avoid a special screening.

At the gate, I search 'How much money can you take on a plane.'

Flying within the U.S. there is no a limit, but anything over ten thousand needs to be declared. The websites, however, are not telling me what I really want to know, which is 'how much can I carry without the TSA deciding to care?' The sites do tell me never to put money in checked bags since they are out of sight for too long. Instead, put money in a carry-on, not on my body, and if the carry-on is searched, state that I have money in the carry-on and want to keep it in sight while it is searched—because a TSA agent will love hearing that. Then transfer the money to a money belt in the restroom after I've gone through security. Also, I need to state 'honestly', the site says, why I am carrying a large amount of money. I get stumped on a reason to carry fourteen hundred in cash since "I'm honestly going to buy weed in Colorado," doesn't sound best.

This flight, I'm struck by the idiocy of having to spend a day in transit, flying to the middle of the country with fourteen hundred in cash stuffed into nooks, crannies and a moneybag dangling around my throat, to buy an overpriced product that grows for free and then 'smuggle' it back to retrograde Texas in luggage and the U.S. mail.

There is no snow on the ground in north Texas, and the vista is drab brown under a blurry haze, with dried up rivers twisting 30,000 feet below like dead snakes. I feel irritable, like I'm being forced to attend a boring convention. Yesterday

I was hassling a freshman to turn in an argument essay late so he could scrape through my class. Today I'm off to the land of edibles to re-supply Alzheimer's Dad, who will spend the next three days asking, "Where's Alene?"

The flight attendant, a guy with a receding hairline up front and a ponytail in the back, hands me a ginger ale just as I realize I forgot to stuff my tennis shoes into my luggage.

The sun is behind us as we descend, the plane's dragon-shaped shadow zooming closer and closer until plane, shadow, and ground all connect when we touch down in Denver. Under the haze, the Rockies have a flat, paint-by-numbers look. When I come down the stairs from the concourse, the People Mover train is arriving and I hop into the first car, sit in the very front under the bubble-shaped window and get to see the guts of the tunnels underground. When I yank my bag off the carousel, I check that it still has a lock before heading to the airport's rail platform.

The sun is setting as the train pulls away from the airport, and when it gets dark outside, my reflection hovers on the window. My face looks puffy-soft. I have end-of-the-semester exhaustion bags under my eyes like my mom used to get decades ago when she would come home from work and lay down for thirty minutes, slowly smoking a Virgina Slim, letting the day drain away. After she quit smoking, she would put a straw in a can of Coke so she could sip it instead.

Union Station is warm and crowded, shadowy and sparkly bright all at the same time. I walk out through an arch made of light bent into the shape of a Christmas tree ornament and take the Free MallRide, which is warm and crowded too. Women stand in the handicapped area, and one young woman offers her seat to a lady with purple walking braces but gets declined because, "It's too tough to get back up again." The young woman then offers her seat to an older lady who declines with a vigorous, "No, no, I'm standing, standing." She's also holding a poster board. They all just came from a political rally. "Took me all day to make it," she says, angling the poster, which is elaborate and creative with too much written on it to read at a distance. But maybe reading it is not the point.

At Champa, I walk a block to the hotel, dragging my luggage past a blanket pyramid, swirling up like the frosting on a cupcake and topped with a dirty puff-ball knit cap. Inside the whirled mound of blankets is a homeless someone, head bent forward into the top of the blankets so not even a face is visible, wrapped for the night on the low wall-extension of the hotel's street-level sign. I go in the lobby with the check-in desk, except there is not a front desk. And what should be a lobby is a large, blue-lit space filled with dozens of tables seating men in black ties and women in black dresses being served drinks from waiters with white towels draped over their arms.

Tiny white Christmas lights are flickering on the tables and walls. My puffy jacket does not match the decor. On one side is something like a podium with a busy young man giving directions to the wait staff, talking into his microphone headset, and greeting me with a toothpaste commercial smile and a 'just-one-moment' gesture. His hair is twisted into Bantu knots, laid out in a ruler-straight grid pattern all over his head, and his bolero half-jacket could have come off a runway in Milan. He clicks a silver button on the headset and plates of food glide in.

"I'm looking for the check-in desk?" I say.

"This is check-in. Can I have your name?" I give it to him and see a tablet on the podium. After soft clicking on the keyboard, he asks, "Could it be under another name?"

"No," I glance around. An older couple has lined up behind me, the woman's frosted hair bouffanted into a beehive. She is dripping with opals. "I've been here before but this does not look like it did—"

"Are you looking for the Residence Inn? This is Renaissance. No worries. Happens all the time. We get theirs; they get ours. It's okay; we're all in the Marriott family. Residence Inn is a little further up Champa; let me show you." He reassures the couple behind me that he will be right back, waves off a staff member trying to intercept him and leads me across the dinner gala, through glass doors and onto the sidewalk under the Doric columns of the Renaissance Hotel facade. He points across the street as the 'Walk' signal on the corner turns green. Past the upscale hair salon, wafting out the smell of weed, I see the Residence Inn sign.

Their front desk is unmanned, and a "Notice" sign reminds Valued Guests that this is a non-smoking hotel. The bottom of the sign has a slash through a cigarette, a vape cartridge, and a marijuana leaf. After three minutes, the check-in guy appears. His Marriott jacket is too small to button. He offers a been-a-long-day smile, asking if I prefer a low floor or a high one, then puts me on fifteen. Tippy-top.

When I unlock my luggage, I find a 'Notice of Baggage Inspection' slip inside from the TSA. They appreciate my understanding and cooperation and sincerely regret if the TSA officer inspecting my bag was forced to break the locks on it, and yet they are not liable for any damage to my locks resulting from this necessary security precaution during the search for prohibited items which is done to protect me and my fellow passengers. The reverse side says the same in Spanish.

❧

By now, I have a script to follow, a mental map of Denver City Central or at least the parts connected to 16th Street, with favorite restaurants, dispensary preferences, and a puffy coat to camouflage me in with the locals. The morning news is chipper: "Thirty degrees in Denver, warming up to fifty today, so a lovely, mild day." I go down to the free breakfast spread that tipped me over into choosing Residence Inn this trip over cheaper and hipper Aloft, and when I get back to my room, I figure out which bus will take me to Native Roots on Highlands.

The fastest, easiest way to get there would be rideshare. But I just can't bring myself to do it, partly because I know a bus will be much cheaper—three dollars—and I feel like I ought to be able to navigate Denver by bus now, but overwhelmingly because I'm too embarrassed to tell someone to take me to a weed store and simultaneously embarrassed to be so uptight. After a quick run to Walgreens to get packaging tape, cheap lotion, and a box of tissue for the nose bleeds I'll get in a day or two, I head out to catch the 44 bus and discover that the bus stop for it is just across the street from Aloft, under a street sign with nothing but a large white "Y" on it. A block away, there is another sign with an "X" on it, and for the first time, it occurs to me to actually see the signage I've been oblivious to. The streets are a cacophony of information, if you know how to listen. Until I was standing under one of them, I'd never synapsed that the big white letters affixed on posts were bus stop indicators.

Lots of handicapped people are out and about, partly because it's sunny and warm but mostly because in Denver, they *could* be out and about. There are buses, trains, MallRides, and light rail, and the guy in the wheelchair on my left is missing the bottom half of both legs and chats with me about the great weather. Kudos to places where you don't need legs to leg it.

Since I've gotten so used to the Free MallRide's instant appearances, the five-minute wait for the 44 bus feels like a personal offense. Google Maps says the bus ride and the additional walk to the dispensary should only take twenty minutes. The 44 bus rolls through Platte River Valley Park. It's an area past LoDo and Union Station, with a creek, stone amphitheater, Centennial Gardens, the Downtown Aquarium, and the Museum of Contemporary Art Denver—all of which I'm keen to see. The bus drops me off on Tejon Street, a steep hill in a quiet neighborhood, about two blocks from the dispensary.

Tucked between two restaurants, Native Roots Highlands is just a regular Native Roots store, not a premium location, and, though I'm disappointed I'm not walking into the big show, it's good enough for my needs. My plan is to buy four of the one thousand milligram bottles of gummies that I saw on the Native Roots menu online. I've calculated that four thousand milligrams will carry Dad through 2020, and once I have that base amount squared away, I'll spend the rest of my edibles money on the chocolate bars he likes.

At the counter though, I don't see one thousand milligram jars of anything and ask the budtender about them.

"Oh, that's only for medical cannabis." She nods at the door leading to the medical section of the dispensary. "Medical card holders can get higher doses. Purchase limits are higher, and there's no strength cap on THC. The prices are also lower for medical. Twenty percent off. Ten percent more off for veterans." The part of the store that I'm standing in is just for recreational, and recreational purchases have a limit of eight hundred milligrams per day.

Shit.

Shit, shit. Visions of Platte River Valley Park's creeks, gardens, and aquarium vanish. I focus on the gummies in the case in front of me. There are actually more choices than there were eleven months ago last January. The Blue Raspberry and the Tropical Punch gummies are THC only and cost eighteen dollars for a hundred milligram bottle. The Pineapple is a one-to-one CBD/THC combo with one hundred milligrams of each and cost twenty-three dollars, so that's more cost effective, I guess. But then again, I can get CBD in San Antonio, and then again, the combo would be easier to give to Dad in the evening, but then again . . .

I can never make decisions when I'm standing in a store. I agonize over the gummies, the other edibles, the eight hundred milligram limit and the awareness that now I will have to hit multiple dispensaries for multiple days. Finally, I split the difference and get four of the one-to-one Pineapple gummies, two Blue Raspberries, and two Tropical Punch. I'll think through my decision after the fact, back in the hotel, sitting on the bed and looking over all of the day's purchases closely, doing all the CBD, THC, dosage, and cost calculations slowly in my head.

Two hundred bucks later, I tip the budtender three dollars as she slides my eight jars of gummies into a glossy Native Roots gift bag, which I slide into a Walgreens bag as I step outside and walk to a bus stop on the 'return-to-Denver-City-Center' side of Tejon Street. A bus sign labeled 'The Ride' lists both the 32 bus and the 44, and Google Maps says the 44 is supposed to show up at 1:20, which comes and goes. Over the next forty shitty minutes, I loiter under the bus sign in front of an apartment block, watch people take dogs to the dog park across the street, and see two 44 buses go up the hill. Neither one comes back down on a return trip. Eventually the 32 bus comes by and, being profoundly stupid, I do not get on it, thinking the 44 will roll to my rescue at any moment. The 32 bus driver seems surprised but closes the doors and pulls off. I don't make the same mistake when the next 32 bus comes by, which drops me off on 17th and Champa.

I've wasted an hour getting back to the heart of City Central and it takes a while to drop off the gummies, shake off the aggravation, and find my zen. When I look over Google Maps to do a postmortem on my bad trip, it turns out that the bus stop was less than a block away from Simply Pure, a dispensary I'd seen on TV and wanted to go to. Crap.

I head to Euflora.

In electric blue and green, the electronic display over their entrance proclaims Happy Holidays, We Love our Veterans, and Let's Go Nuggets! I spend a few minutes at the bud tables sniffing the strains of sample nugs before perusing the edibles wall. In addition to the unvarnished smell of weed, the store has a low steady background of the best, very serious rap music on continuous play, with explicit lyrics on life, diabetes, and social injustice.

Plus, there's a new trend: the gummies and chocolate bars come in the regular edibles bars like last year—the Incr*edibles* Strawberry Crunch, Vanilla Affogato with espresso beans and caramel, Monkey bar with coconut and banana, or the Dixie Straight Up Dark Chocolate—but now they also have chocolate bars '*made with high-quality* INDICA *oil*' and some '*made with high-quality* SATIVA *oil.*'

The Blue Raspberry and Tropical Punch gummies that I got earlier at Native Roots Highlands also had 'INDICA' in block letters on their bottles, and the Pineapple gummies boasted that they were 'made with pure CO 2 oil' which is supposed to mean that the natural terpenes in the plant have not been stripped out of the oil distillate when making the edible. Indica is the type of marijuana that helps you sleep, and I decide that, even though he spends most of his time in bed laying down, since I give Dad the THC chocolate at night, indica is the way to go.

At the register, I ask for two boxes of one-to-one Mixed Berry Mints, a box of Relaxing THC Peppermint Mints, a Vanilla Affogato White Chocolate Latte bar, and six bars of the Dixie Milk Chocolate Indica bars. The register tells the budtender that I've reached my eight hundred milligram limit as she tries to scan the last two chocolate bars in. So, eight hundred per store, per day it is. I drop them off on the 15th floor and just have time to make one more stop.

Native Roots Wellness has no other customers when I go in, and Tony, at the register, explains that the store is just for CBD and only gets off his stool once it is clear that I intend to stay. Colin, the other guy, shows me around. At first, he is so vague about the products I think he's been told to avoid even the most remote suggestion of sales pressure, but soon I realize he's just an airhead. When I pick up a box of CBD dog treats, he tries to talk about a dog he used to have, gets lost in the midst of his own story, and gradually stops before reaching any clear point. Maybe it's his first week on the job. Maybe it's his generation. Maybe, like most of us, it's the best he can do right now on an average Wednesday. He reconnoiters with Tony and lets me be.

Native Roots Wellness does not have new products since my last visit, and CBD does not have a buy limit. Even though I can get CBD in Texas now, the CBD gummies in Colorado are half the price they are in San Antonio, so I figure I'll stock up a little. One bottle of six hundred milligram Mixed Berry Hemp Gummies is only sixty bucks, and even the Strawberry-and-Cream Bars that Dad likes still come out a bit cheaper than the same amount of CBD edibles back home, so I pick up six of those.

Two spry old guys, tourists, come in as I am leaving, and as soon as Tony tells them it is CBD only, they leave, ticked off. As I hike back to Residence Inn at sunset, my lips are dry and cracked like I am dehydrated, but it's just Colorado's dry ass air sucking the moisture out of my body.

I already have the 'Do Not Clean This Room' magnetic card stuck to my door, so I put eight hundred dollars of purchases in the closet and lay down. My legs ache and I feel slightly short of breath from the mile-high altitude as I fall asleep and slide into a hazy nightmare about bad 44 bus signage on Tejon Street, where I wait on a sit-next-to-a-sculpture bench for a bus that never comes. The sculpture is a homeless man, swaddled in a cupcake swirl of blankets, faceless and motionless, but yelling nonetheless.

CHAPTER THIRTY-SIX
DOOMED

THE FIRST NOSEBLEED of the trip shows up before I shower in the morning. Then I hit Euflora up for two Strawberry Crunch bars, two Birthday Cake bars—white chocolate with rainbow sprinkles—two Milk Chocolate Indica, and, on a whim, two Milk Chocolate Sativa. Two-hundred and forty-five dollars. On my way back to Residence Inn, I stop by the Target on 16th Street to buy mailer boxes, packaging tape, and bubble wrap. Since my luggage keeps getting searched, even though it's just when I leave San Antonio, I've decided to mail everything home instead of splitting it between my luggage and the post office.

It's the first two-story Target I've ever been to, crammed into a narrow space, probably having bought out a small business or two that used to be there, maybe a family-owned restaurant. The place is crowded, like people are gearing up for the end of days. I spend less on three boxes in Target than I spent on one box in Walgreens. I get lost inside the store as

I'm trying to leave and end up on an escalator but eventually escape back out onto 16th.

It takes a while to un-flat the boxes, tape them into three dimensions, add address labels, line the boxes with a double-layer of bubble wrap, arrange edibles, and tape it all closed. Then, it's a two-block walk to the Post Office on Curtis to stand in line, go to the counter of a postwoman, and for eleven dollars a box, mail three boxes of federally prohibited goodness home. Fuck da gov'ment.

Mission complete, I walk around the city center to see what some of the official-looking buildings are. They're federal court-houses, U.S. Marshals offices, and the Board of Geographic Names, which is real and exists for some reason. A block farther down is the 18th and Stout Light Rail Station, an elongated stretch of concrete with an arched covering, ticket machines, D, F, H, and L-Line departures, and boards listing destinations. Like much else in public transportation, the boards assume that people already know how to use the system. Even though I'm not trying to catch a light rail to Littleton-Mineral, Ridgegate Parkway, or 30th & Downing, I get overwhelmed by the color coded, numbered, and time divided charts. They are a study in complexity made complex.

Nolan sends a text around 7 p.m. We meet in the hotel lobby and walk down 16th Street to an open-air Christmas market full of booths selling beer, bratwurst, and ornaments, and across the street from it is an outdoor ice-skating rink surrounded by Christmas trees. Both the market and ice rink are lit by thousands of blue and white lights, some twinkling, some not. The air, in the thirties, is brittle, but it's puffy jackets all around, and my feet are stuffed into wool socks which are stuffed into Sorel boots, so I don't have to care about the cold. It's the holidays; everything is warm and sparkles, and the streets feel like life. We end up at Cheesecake Factory, which is piping in the best Christmas mix tape I've ever heard.

Nolan is practically chatty. Without prodding, he gives me an update on Fia, whose eyesight is still good enough for her to navigate; on Kinsley's mom, Megan, who is expecting a baby with Kinsley's new step-dad; on the step-dad, who is thinking about moving his family out of their apartment and into what Nolan calls a 'starter McMansion'; and on Kinsley, who has adjusted to having a step-dad and thinks a baby will be nice to hold but hopes that it won't cry too much at night. I give an update on Jovi, order a drink, and finally remember to ask Nolan my in-or-out of the igloo Inuit poop question, and also about Arctic poop preservation in general. Seriously, the first people crossed to Alaska fifteen thousand years ago, so those melting glaciers must have more than just woolly mammoths and fresh water locked up in them.

Besides saving me from death while hiking on mountainsides, Nolan's had many tremendously unusual experiences. They tend to come about through improbable sets of Nolan-circumstances. He buttered a hunk of bread: "As it happens, a year after my first doctorate, I was returning from a conference in Copenhagen using the trans-arctic corridor—the way one does when the magnetic field is lateral at solstice—when our Citation X unexpectedly soft-crashed or hard-landed, depending on how you look at it. Anyway, Nukilik, the leader of an Inuit hunting party who witnessed our plane's fall from the sky, kindly offered me, the pilot and visiting Professor Gulliksen, shelter during the remaining two months of Arctic night.

Luckily however, Nukilik's cell phone finally got a signal, and he called snow-Uber-mobile—they don't have Lyft—to pick us up, but not before explaining the proper indoor-outdoor arctic igloo pooping etiquette. It all depends on the strength of the prevailing Front Range winds you see, but first, there are three things about traditional Caribou parkas you need to know."

That was the sort of answer I was expecting. Shockingly, however, he had no idea.

"But you're an Eagle Scout, Nolan." I searched his face. "So there's no arctic poop badge?"

"No," he said. "Just wilderness survival."

"Seems like an oversight." By the time we get the appetizer, I've meandered around to talking about being a prepper and my top ten list of the most likely ways that society will collapse and the world-as-we-know-it will end. "Environmental collapse, economic collapse, pandemic, hit by a killer asteroid, or massive solar flare. Personally, I'm betting on a collapse of the electrical grid with or without a solar flare."

Nolan does not contradict me. Instead, he agrees and actually has better information on one of the ten end-the-world-as-we-know-it potential disasters. "Craig Venter wants the old, slow, expensive process of synthetic biology to be changed. He wants to use his biotech genome company to do for biology what Gutenberg did for books and make bioengineering a fast, accurate, affordable process. He wants to develop a machine attached to your laptop that can print out synthetic biological compounds in every home. That way, flu vaccines can be sent wirelessly to everyone."

"When the invention of the printing press made the Bible widely available, it kicked off two hundred years of religious wars," I say. "And when someone sneezes on a petri dish, it'll bubonic flu us all to death, right?"

"Well, I assume there will be a sneeze guard over the growth medium, but yeah. We're doomed," he says mildly. "Also, the technology could be misused to create illicit drugs, poisons, all kinds of things. The only real point of interest is what will get most of us first. A guy in California is trying to alter corn DNA with a bacterium so the corn becomes sterile and also spreads its sterility to other crops."

"Won't that have adverse effects when it inevitably gets out of the lab?"

"Well, the lab is a table in his garage, and yes, it will kill us all. Except for some hermit out in a desert, but he'll die out eventually too, so yes, it will kill us all."

Jesus. And all I want is some weed for Dad without a quota filling narc trying to snatch my SUV or Mom and Dad's cracked foundation house. I forget to ask Nolan how he knows about some random in Cali brewing up pathogens in his two-car home hobby space. So that guy will kill us all. Or someone like him, with a combination of somewhat smart and extremely stupid, uninterested in considering consequences. I hold up one of the poppers Nolan ordered as an appetizer.

"You know what this tastes like?"

"Jalapeño and cream cheese, wrapped in bacon?" Nolan says.

"No." I shake my head. "It tastes like the end of western civilization. Like Rome before barbarians tore down the gate." Our entrées arrive.

Nolan has to go in early to work in the morning, so we walk back to Residence Inn around ten. We kiss in the lobby. Warm and fuzzy like Sorel boots. Twinkly like the holiday lights.

CHAPTER THIRTY-SEVEN
KLIEG LIGHT

IN THE MORNING, I head to Euflora at 9:15 a.m. Denver's air is at nine percent relative humidity, lower than a desert. The temperature is in the 30s and wind cuts through my jeans.

A Santa in a wheelchair greets me cheerfully at the corner on Champa. Do I want a hug or a free high-five? I decline and walk up 16th Street since I don't see a MallRide on the way. The population at this hour is sparse, but half the people who are out are homeless. The rising sun has reached a low angle so that it sits, an egg-yolk disk, at one end of a canyon of buildings, hitting 16th Street with Klieg light ferocity. A woman in a motorized wheelchair, shrunken legs propped up and her small feet tucked into quilted slippers, converses with a man holding a "Please Give" cardboard sign. A MallRide scoops me up.

The guard inside Euflora gives me a nod as he checks my driver's license, recognizing me from the last two mornings, and today my eight chocolate bars totaling eight hundred milligram of edibles costs only two hundred-and-ten instead of the two hundred-and-forty-five dollars they cost yesterday.

My purchases are being rung up before 10 a.m., qualifying for Euflora's fifteen percent Early Bird discount. If I had been a half-hour earlier yesterday, I could have saved thirty-five bucks. Next time I'll pay more attention to the specials the dispensaries run, I think, walking down the street, already laying down the structure of a future trip. For now though, I still have to box up these last eight bars, get to USPS, pack, check out by 11 a.m., get to Union Station, and take the rail to Denver International early enough to get through security and catch my 1:30 flight, as the holiday travel rush really gets underway.

In an alley near Stout, brake lights come on as a truck, with a round oil tank on it for sucking up restaurant cooking grease, starts to inch past a dumpster. Strung across the alley, thirty feet in the air are a stack of giant air fresheners, the kind that hang from the rear-view mirror in a car. If I eat my Cheesecake Factory leftovers just before I head to Union Station, I won't need to eat again till I get home—

The fuck? I head back to the alley. The air fresheners are ten feet tall. The one on the top of the stack is green; behind it are purple, blue, red, and yellow. The green one says 'Alley-Freshener' and I look at the dumpster, which is full to the brim. No one else on the street is noticing that there are giant air fresheners. And alleys do smell, so this is actually a good idea, good use of tax dollars, especially in a tourist area. Perhaps it is a new trend to reduce urban stinkiness—

It's art. You idiot. Denver art. Like the giant blue bear, the giant chair, the giant maniacal, red-eyed bronco, the giant fucking Rockies.

Wheelchair Santa is still on the corner when I get back to Champa, only now a woman is sitting on his lap and taking a selfie. She gets a hug. Back in my room, I line a box with bubble wrap, tape it all up, and jog-walk the two blocks to the post office, glancing at the Greyhound Station across the street, looking all innocent in the morning sun. There could be five riots and a car fire going on in there, and from the outside, you'd never know. The line inside the Post Office is not bad, only four people ahead of me, but a woman at one window is delivering a complicated complaint about State Department documents that have not arrived, and a man at the other window has a dozen boxes and also wants to buy 700 stamps, holiday themed.

Seventeen minutes later, I mail edibles box number four then run back to Residence Inn.

On the way up, the elevator stops on the parking level and a man gets on, avoiding eye contact, reeking of weed. He went out to his car to toke up and now heads back up and gets off on the thirteenth floor. Also, I know words like 'toke' now. I grab my suitcase and carry-on, feel heartbroken as I throw out the leftovers from Cheesecake Factory, then check-out a few minutes late and head to the Free MallRide, which, bizarrely, takes ten minutes to show up. It is absolutely stuffed, and I squeeze on anyway, shoved up against my luggage, clinging to a pole for balance.

I've entrusted all my boxes of edibles to USPS five days before Christmas and suddenly get plagued by a superstitious feeling: I should have given money to the homeless "Please Give" man; somehow that would have ensured my good luck. My lack of charity tugs at my mind as the MallRide disgorges me at Union Station, where the train to the airport pulls off thirty seconds before I get to the platform. I stay out there and wait fifteen minutes for the next one, paranoid that if I go back inside, I'll miss it. Denver International is crowded, but security is barking orders at the throng, and the serpentine lines move fast. At the gate, they announce the plane is full, and anyone on standby will be booked on another flight. I am the last one to board.

San Antonio is cold, foggy, and gridlocked as my Lyft driver, Marcello, takes me home during the evening rush, silent for most of the drive so he can focus on the slick road. I spend Saturday and Sunday digging blood crusts out of my nose, and I spend Monday, two days before Christmas, reading on my bed and watching out the window for the mail. Three boxes arrive at three o'clock. Back in Denver I had numbered each box on an inner flap, and box number two is not in the mix. Box number one has a three-inch gouge on the front, just like one of the boxes from the last time I went to Denver, just like Amazon packages. The gouges on boxes have happened so often I assume a postal worker is trying to see if a package is theft-worthy, but I had double bubble-wrapped the contents.

I sit on my bed that evening and do the math. Southwest Airlines round trip, three hundred and twenty dollars. Three nights at Residence Inn, four hundred fifty dollars. Lyft, trains, and buses, seventy. Eating in Denver and in transit, that's another eighty. Plus USPS shipping adds fifty. And, of course, the edibles came out to twelve hundred bucks, just on their own. I've spent over two thousand dollars on one single Denver trip, plus packing, unpacking, and wiping nosebleeds to get edibles for Dad that won't even last a year. This is just not sustainable. I'm looking at four grand to do this twice a year plus the exhaustion and risk to get something that grew on the side of the road, in ditches, for free.

Right.

Online, I find grow tents starting at seventy dollars. Ultrahigh end grow boxes go for over two thousand. Some grow boxes look like a mini-fridge, some like a safe, and one is designed to look like a boring old filing cabinet. The most expensive ones boast that they are fully automated and can be controlled by an app on your phone. They even have a camera inside the box, so you can watch your weed grow from work, on vacation, or while riding on a Greyhound bus.

Grow tents are cheaper than grow boxes, but I don't know anything about growing cannabis; I don't have the time, energy, or brain space for a steep learning curve, and I need this home grow to work the first time I try it. Grow boxes are basically pre-assembled grow tents with a container, hydroponic system, nutrients, fan, grow light, and importantly, a carbon filter that keeps the odor from seeping out onto the streets of Winter Forest. Under LCD grow lights, cannabis plants mature three times faster than in the wild, producing bud in three to four months. The various tents and boxes state how many plants they can grow at a time and even give estimates of how much bud you can produce every three months and how much to expect annually.

I had already watched shows on how to turn bud into cannabutter or canna-oil and then into medicated brownies, so I knew I could make my own edibles.

The weed seed companies have web pages that can filter a seed search by plant height, by sativa, hybrid, or indica, and by growing temperature: cool or tropical. My garage in Texas in summer? Tropical. I need short plants that'll fit in a compact grow box, and I need a grow box that will fit in a cluttered garage, which will take me a couple days just to get a corner free of junk.

The carbon air filters in the grow boxes that eliminate

the weed smell are supposed to last a year, but I'm suspicious. Closet space in the house won't work. All the closets are packed, and I can't use my own closet because I can't stroll into work with the scent of ganja on my blouse.

The final USPS box from Denver shows up the day after Christmas, the postman leaving it on the porch, in plain view, not bothering to ring the doorbell, and I'm glad that I waited around, watching out the window for the delivery. The gouge on the front of the box is two inches long, and I thank bubble wrap for its ability to deter probing fingers. The mail-yourself-weed websites said that one sign of a suspicious package is too much tape around it, but I'm starting to think that, as far as clear packaging tape goes, there is no such thing as too much tape for a USPS package.

That realization is actually a bit late, however. I don't know it yet, but I will not fly up to Denver again. Not next year or the year after that, and I am holding the last USPS box of edibles that I will ever get from myself.

PART FOUR

CHAPTER THIRTY-EIGHT
EMPIRICAL METHOD

Two days after I get back from Colorado, I use up the last of the bad, sad Arkansas gummies and switch Dad back to the Straight Up Dark Chocolate bar for his evening THC. The bar is divided into twelve squares, eight milligram of THC each. The CDB gummies that I got at Native Roots Wellness are twenty milligram each. So, each morning he gets a half gummie and every night I give him the other half of a gummie along with one chocolate square. When the dark chocolate bar runs out, I open one of the Milk Chocolate Indica bars, the kind that the budtender told me helps with sleep.

Dad wakes up at midnight having a nightmare-dream-hallucination thing. He insists that the window blinds are open, and wants Mom to close them. From my room, I hear her tell him, "Look, they are closed." He insists he sees the limbs of the pecan tree in the backyard, swaying in the wind. He wakes again at three in the morning and wants to know where the orange ball on the floor next to their bed came from. He has

Mom sit on his side of the bed so she can see it and she tells him there is no orange ball.

In the morning, Mom wonders if the hallucinations are a progression of Alzheimer's, though she can't recall seeing hallucinations mentioned in any of the books or support group meetings. I don't say anything about the "Made with high-quality Indica oil" chocolate that I gave him, even as I face the fact that I am basically running an experiment on my dad, where I randomly try this chocolate or that gummie at various dosages and at times of day that fit around my work schedule, to see what will happen. I've thought for a while that I probably wasn't giving him enough cannabis to make him as comfortable as a higher dose would, but I have no idea how much an effective dose would be, and, on a practical level, the more I give him, the faster it will run out. I switch to a regular THC Vanilla Affogato bar and Dad goes back to sleeping through the night.

When the weekend comes, at 8 p.m. I pop an eight-milligram square of Dixie's Straight Up Milk Chocolate Indica bar in my own mouth, deciding that I should see if the indica oil chocolate whacks me out before giving it to him again. I bought six indica bars, plus 4 bottles of indica gummies, and if it turns out that Dad can't tolerate them, that's more than three months of THC that I can't give him, which will immediately poop-up the timeline where I do not have to go to Colorado again for a year. The edible is velvety with a sudden tang like a waft of weed, as the creamy chocolate melts on my palate.

And nothing happens. Unimpressed, I keep working on updating a syllabus, and then it starts at 8:45, an almost-tingle in my fingers then hands then gradually becoming a relaxation heaviness up my arm and into my shoulder, spreading across my body. My toes do some type of warm, vibratey tingle that goes up my calves and thighs. My face feels glowy-puffy. I can feel my lips touching and my throat is dry. Lying down would feel nice right now, and the semester is days away. I decide to lay down and a little TV. This sensation needs to be focused on. My hands are heavy. I've done enough for the day. I'm okay with that. That I've done enough today. So. It works. The indica. Working.

At 9:10 I get uncoordinated, and laying down is no longer a matter of choice, plus the sensations are not uniformly agreeable. I feel jittery, my stomach a tiny bit queasy. My sense of time becomes stretched out or compacted; I'm not sure which. I think I've been lying down for an hour, maybe two, but each time I check the clock, only ten minutes have passed. I feel like my thinking has been sped up. Images flash in my mind and immediately link to the next idea and the next. Genius ideas, but they slide by to be replaced by something even more vivid and then that too is lost.

At 10 p.m., I hear Mom in the kitchen emptying the dishwasher, plates clacking as she stacks them in the cabinet. But it's late, and she unloads the dishwasher in the morning, not at night. I'm unsure if I really hear the plates being put away or if I'm just imagining it, and then I am sure I really hear it, as clinking utensils slide into the drawer. At 10:10, the TV's sound annoys me, so I mute it. My hands feel shaky and heavy at the same time, and the light from the TV presses against my cheek, so I turn it off. It's 10:30 and there is a pit of heat in my chest, then my groin as my dense body is melting into the bed. Thirsty.

At 12:30 it's over. I wake in the dark, uncertain if I was actually asleep. But I can tell for sure that I am awake and that the effects have passed, though I still feel relaxed and unwilling to get back to work on anything as horrid as a syllabus. I flip through TV channels for a while, but that's boring so I go back to lying in the dark, and it's okay. Perhaps the indica edible is just double strong. Next time I'll try Dad on half a piece, four milligrams, instead of the whole eight milligram square.

The following Saturday, I try one-fourth of a piece of indica oil chocolate to see if I can get the dosage right to relax without getting knocked down, and an hour later, I think I feel something, but I'm not sure. I get a little bit thirsty, sleepy, and relaxed, but it's late, so why wouldn't I? Maybe half a piece next time will be the sweet spot.

A week later, I try half a piece. It takes longer to hit, eighty minutes, and it doesn't hit as hard as the whole piece had. I can still control my limbs, but they tingle, and I feel relaxed, but not flattened. Still thirsty though.

The experiment the following week is with a Mixed Berry Synergy mint, which is a one-to-one combination of five milligrams CBD and five milligrams THC. I take it with the idea of 'taking the edge off' a long work week. The cannabis taste is strong and 'blah' and minty. The onset takes a long time and is so gradual, I don't notice right away that it has started, like the Doobie Brothers' "Minute by Minute" where the song fades in and you're never sure what moment you hear the music.

The mint turns out to be a very slow burn. I feel thirst, but it's not overwhelming, and my toes, ankles, and arms are heavy-ish and thicker but not weighted down. I can still sit up, enjoy reading and sip water. Over ninety minutes, the effects get stronger but remain manageable. I'm not really euphoric, not quite tingly, but I'm there, with a feeling in my body, a hum in my mind. I fall asleep, and in the morning, my balance is a teensy bit off for the first thirty minutes that I'm up.

Finally, I take half a square of the Straight Up Milk Chocolate "Made with high quality Sativa oil," which is supposed to make me energized and creative. Fifty minutes later, I start feeling it, without being knocked over. I watch TV, feel a bit uplifted, bubbly even, and not sleepy. Another fifty minutes go by and it kicks in, more tingly. The sativa gives more of a pleasant mind feeling than the indica did, but is not nearly as body relaxing. indica felt like being sedated or taking a muscle relaxant. The sativa pleasantness continues to gradually intensify for another hour. Overnight, I drift out of sleep periodically, but it is not annoying like insomnia. It's more like surfacing, an enjoyable mindset still fizzing about, then sliding back into agreeable dreams. Sativa turns out to be mental detox. Or maybe mental floss.

The next night I give dad his CBD gummie and, remembering the hallucination weirdness that happened with an entire square of indica, I give him just half of a square of sativa. The next day, Mom says that he woke up and talked about his siblings' children for a while, trying to remember where they were living, what they were doing now, but she gives no reports of orange balls on the floor or tree limbs swaying out the window.

So, half a square of indica or sativa it shall be.

CHAPTER THIRTY-NINE
SHELTER AT HOME

January starts off the way that Januaries start off now. I rested up after the trip to Denver, got ready for classes, got a massage, got my teeth cleaned, got a mammogram, got my hair trimmed and the gray covered up, ran by a friend's to drop off a late Christmas present, went to the gym a little more often, and slept in before the semester started.

One evening I laid around watching *Thor Ragnarok* and wondered how no one had noticed that a major character sells innocent people into slavery where they are then murdered in public, but because she's an attractive alcoholic Valkyrie suffering from PTSD ever since she tragically lost all her Valkyrie sisters in a battle, this is okay? Despite living for thousands of years, she has not developed any other job skills and sending innocents to their grisly death is the only way she can earn a buck? She decides to join up with Thor so she won't be afraid anymore and then, to cure her PTSD, she battles hordes of resurrected dead Asgardian soldiers and re-kills them by fighting alongside some of the slavery survivors who she was complicit in enslaving? I watch the movie again to be sure that this is an accurate take on her storyline—which is played laughs—as she flirts with the Hulk who murdered the people she sold into slavery.

Huh.

Every meeting during convocation week is a drag. Even the training for an Active Shooter on Campus gets tedious as a District police sergeant defines 'running' and also 'hiding' to an auditorium of professors staring at their cell phones, then the sergeant explains how to file a report if a student displays a gun in class.

A professor wearing gray crocs interrupts. "Regardless of what the governor says, surely there is some way we can prevent students from having guns on campus, regardless of whether it's concealed carry or not," he says, attempting, for some reason, to start a discussion doomed to resolve nothing.

"It's Texas," responds the District sergeant, cutting him off. "Even my dog has a gun."

Dean Fuentes looks over, "Your Rottweiler has a gun?"

In between meetings, I sit in my chilly office with a forbidden space heater under my desk. I hide the space heater in a filing cabinet when I don't need it.

Classes start and the parking lots are packed. By late February, I spend days having conferences with student after student, then stay late, doing committee work. For years I'd served on the committee that put together the annual pedagogy conference for the college, but the previous year I'd become the committee's chair and had to work with public relations on marketing and with the dean's office for the budget. In less than a month, the college would host dozens of presenters and hundreds of conference attendees. By the time I get home, all

I do is eat, bathe, and go to bed. On the weekends, I catch up on the grading that has piled up.

After I get home Monday evening, Deacon Turner and his wife come over to visit my parents. I've already disappeared into my room, but I hear them in the living room as the Deacon discusses passages in the Bible. Dad has stopped going to church, no longer able to sit up through an entire service. Everyone laughs at something Dad says, his natural sociability coming out even now, then the Deacon and my parents pray together, before he and his wife leave, and my mom brings me a plate of the appetizers that are left.

After work on Tuesday, I run by the grocery store on my way home, hustling across the parking lot at sunset, noticing, without actually paying attention, that the store is busier than it should be on a Tuesday at the start of March. When I step inside, the ground sinks. There are too many people moving too quickly, their eyes too alert with the frisson in the air. The click that happens in those few moments when you know that you will remember where you were when it happened, that click, experienced less than half a dozen times in a lifetime, thunks through me. I was on a shuttle bus heading back to my co-op from the UT campus when I overheard a frat boy behind me say that the Challenger Space Shuttle had exploded. I was getting ready for work, wearing my favorite orange silk blouse, making breakfast with the TV on in the living room when the first plane hit the Twin Towers. My mom was picking up a cake for Aunt Gracie's surprise party when Kennedy was shot.

People had started to panic buy. The reports about the spread of a lethal new coronavirus had been building throughout February. When I see shelves where rice should be, all the prepper books I read come rumbling back. Rice and beans, peanut butter and pasta. Staples are being depleted. There's still some rice, but not my brand, still some bags of dried beans, but the shelves have bare spots. 'Product Availability Update' signs hang over bottled water, and then: 'Bath Tissue Multipack: Limit one item per transaction.' And the shelves for toilet paper are empty. A woman who must look frazzled in the best of times turns in the middle of the toilet paper aisle. "Get Kleenex," her teenage son hisses at her. "We just need to wipe our asses. Grab a box."

Cases of bottled water are nearly gone. I loiter in front of the empty shelves because I've never seen them before. About one in ten people is wearing a surgical mask.

Cash is King. I stop by my bank's drive-thru and withdraw hundreds as beginner prepper training takes over. When I get home, I call Mitch and tell him to keep cash in the house and top off his gas tank, text the same information to Callie and Lauren, then work on conference preparations till midnight.

The next morning, Bexar County Colleges cancels all travel and student gatherings, but my dean assures me that the conference is still a go, since the administrative big wigs had a special meeting, she says, where she told them how much work—and money—had already gone into the planning.

The week-long Spring Break holiday starts on the 9th of March, and I take a break from conference work to make chocolate mousse with Jovi, who stays in her pajamas all day, having decided that she's officially on vacation. Then the dean calls. With less than two weeks left, the conference has been canceled. She fought for it, she says, but there was nothing she could do. I call the keynote speaker, a psychology professor, who takes the news stoically. His presentation was going to be about 'Kindness: The New Teaching Strategy.'

On the 11th of March, the stock market crashes, Bexar Colleges extends Spring Break making it two weeks instead of one, and I take more cash out of the bank. By now, all the channels are talking coronavirus all the time, and I have a formless, free-floating anxiety for a day where I lie in bed, stare at the ceiling, wander around the house, try to read but put favorite books back on the shelf without opening them, stare out the window, then end up lying in bed again, tense and restless.

A national emergency is declared on the 13th. Travel is restricted. People are told to avoid close contact with anyone not in their own household. Non-essential businesses are closed. I spend the afternoon putting fresh potting soil in my herb pots on the patio. When I go back in the house, Dad is on the phone, talking to somebody, which alarms me because I assume some scammer has gotten hold of him, and I pick up one of the other phones. It's Mitch. He's in the middle of telling my dad that he's getting married on Sunday.

"That . . . that's great," Dad says. His hand trembles. Months ago, Dad thought he'd had a stroke when he had trouble speaking one morning and his limbs were uncoordinated, but Mom had him sit on the edge of the bed, raise each foot, touch the tip of his nose with each hand, and she determined he had not. Some days were worse than others, and now Dad had days where he couldn't balance well or walk down the hall without keeping his hand on the wall. Today he had been stuttering all morning, and as he talks, he fumbles for the word, "Congratulations. Congratulations."

"Thank you." I can hear the little smile in Mitch's voice.

"Alene has picked up, so I'll, I'll let you. Go. Turn it over to her. Congratulations, again," he says. "God bless you." Dad hangs up.

"Hey."

"Hey, yourself. Your dad doesn't sound too bad. So, I'm getting married. We're gonna have the big wedding and all that next November, but we're gonna go ahead and do the actual marriage on the fifteenth like we planned. We already had the inside of the rings engraved with the date."

"Cool. So where? How?"

"In the green belt behind my house there's this big tree that's amazing. We'll do it in front of that. We're gonna Face-Time it. The boys have the biggest job; they're gonna hold the phones."

On Saturday, it takes two hours for Mitch and Patton to figure out how to use multiple cell phones to video chat with me, Mitch's mom, Mitch's brother, Patton's mom, Patton's brother, Patton's best friend, plus the woman who will actually conduct the ceremony. The reason it takes so long to sort everything out is that to end a FaceTime call, everyone has to hang up their phone: the person who called and the people on the other end. Everybody. But the phone doesn't tell you that so you walk around with your phone still connected to a call that ended an hour ago.

On Sunday afternoon, I sit on the back porch and watch Mitch and Patton, in matching gray suits with pale yellow ties, walk into a strip of forest and stand under a hundred-year-old oak, as Lewin holds up the phone containing the minister, who is standing in her own yard somewhere across town, as she leads them through their vows. Halfway through, Archie gets a little bored, and the happy couple drifts out of the center of the picture. It all takes less than fifteen minutes. After the ceremony, Mitch sends everyone pictures of the Wedding cake.

❧

Faculty report on Wednesday. Report. That's what it's called when District tells you that you have to be somewhere. During the additional week of Spring Break, the colleges gear up to 'go remote' and I go to campus early so I can stack books, folders, and my office laptop onto a cart and wheel them out to my car. Then I go to Remote Launch, the training sessions being run back-to-back all day, to get the faculty ready to convert all their face-to-face classes to Online Remote Learning. My district goes with the Zoom app, and I spend an hour in a computer lab learning what Zoom is and how to be a host. Every alternate row in the lab is left empty, and signs commanding us to stay six feet apart have already been taped on the walls.

There's cake at the English Department meeting that afternoon. Each professor sits at their own table in the large double classroom on the second floor. Gibbs, who works with me on the Conference Committee, volunteers to take down the promotional banners we had hung around the campus weeks ago. He eats a piece of cake while the department chair briefs us, then wraps two pieces in napkins to take home. The building will be disinfected and sealed when we leave, so any cake that we don't take will be thrown out. I wrap up two pieces for Mom and Dad as the department chair assures us that we will be back on campus in about a month.

On Monday, I set up a card table and teach a class from the corner of my bedroom next to the closet. The shelves behind me are stacked with books, herbal teas, and old DVDs. I flip around the books on cannabis so the titles don't show as I lecture into a thirteen-inch screen, fumbling through a PowerPoint presentation and a midterm review and then I teach a second class right after the first one. The students are patient and tell me what to click on when I get stuck. When the second class is done, I lay down, sweaty, and realize I've blurted out 'fuck' at least four times that morning. No one complains.

At the end of the week, about the time I realize that I left two notebooks I needed back in my office, the District decides to go remote for the rest of the spring semester and sends out expanded instructions to 'Work Safe from Home.'

The department chair's prediction that we would be back in a month will turn out to be wrong, of course. I won't work in my office again for another year and a half, after half a million Americans have died from Covid-19.

CHAPTER FORTY
LEMON THUNDER

My BIGGEST CONCERNS about growing weed had always been the smell and lack of space. Marijuana smells pungent and distinctive, and you need to grow it out of sight. Our garage, I learned during more cannabis research, would get too hot to grow marijuana which doesn't like temperatures over eighty degrees, and there is not an empty closet anywhere in the house. So I had shelved the whole idea, plus I didn't have time to deal with it anyway.

Until COVID.

I drove to the gym to cancel my membership and found the gym had already closed without sending any notification. A man swollen with muscles stood at the locked and chained glass doors staring inside at the weight machines.

At the end of my first week of teaching on Zoom, I pulled an N99 face mask from my bug-out-tote and headed for the grocery store, which was one of the few businesses still open. The face mask was too big. After putting together my emergency supplies in 2016, it never occurred to me to test anything.

I'd never worn a respirator mask before and didn't know the default size was for a large male construction worker, not a small woman grocery shopper. I went in the store, repeatedly tugging the stiff nose bridge and paper dome away from my eye sockets. The panic buying that had started two weeks earlier had intensified. Staples were gone. Aisles of beans, rice, flour, cereal, bottled water, toilet paper, and paper towels were bare.

In the 1980s, my parents had a room built onto their bedroom to use as a home office, and by mid-April, Mom is sitting at her computer, conferencing on Zoom with her Lunch-with-the-Lord crowd. On other days she meets her Caregivers Support group, Alzheimer's Information Network group, or her Church Seniors group, all on Zoom. Before the lockdown, she hadn't been to any of the meetings in person in months, and now she clicks 'unmute', amazed to find herself socializing again. Ten feet away, Dad lies in bed and watches from the sidelines, looking at the computer screen full of faces. On Sunday mornings, church services are streamed online, and I hear gospel music and a sermon coming from their room.

Mom and I walk in the park at the back of Winter Forest. The playground is closed, blocked off with orange and white traffic barricades. The swings are tied together so they can't be used, and yellow caution tape is wrapped around the gazebo that families reserve for parties.

The abnormally quiet street was still. On Saturday afternoon, I have a Zoom meeting with my old clique of four high school friends that I usually go out to dinner with once or twice a year. Piper refuses to turn on her camera: she hasn't been to a hair salon in weeks, so her voice floats into the conversation from a black square on the laptop.

In mid-May, I get my last box of edibles out of the closet

and count up the remaining stock of THC candy bars, mints and gummies. There's about 150 days' worth left, and then, once again, I'd be in a bind. In a grow box, a cannabis plant takes three months to grow from seed to harvest. So, I need to order a grow box. And a seed.

I pull out *Cannabis Pharmacy* and *Leafly Guide to Cannabis*, go to Leafly's website and find 'Seeds' under 'Cannabis Products.' The filter on the seeds page has a drop-down menu that lets me select by price, rating, companies, and strains and I check mark all the strains that match up with Dad's various ailments. The first search gives me twenty clickable choices. I read through each seed's description, genetics, plant height, days to harvest, and customer reviews. The larger seed companies have a page that explains how easy or difficult the plant is to grow, including its susceptibility to pests and mold. There is even a panel of 'Similar Items' just like on Amazon.

I spend the evening looking for the perfect match. Most of the packets of ten seeds fall between thirty and sixty dollars. Some strains are over 150, and one strain is only ten bucks, but the one-star review calls it Mexican Street Weed. I have to look up 'SOG' in the descriptions to learn that a Sea Of Green means you can grow a lot of plants close together.

After running another set of choices through the filter and getting side-tracked by interesting sounding names—Chocolope, God Bud, Zookies, Dirty Taxi, Blunicorn, Low Flyer—I settle on CBD Purple Kush: autoflowering feminized seeds, fifty-five dollars, grows wide rather than tall, one hundred centimeters high, beginner level of difficulty, high mold resistance, matures in eight weeks outdoors or seventy days indoors, Sea Of Green, produces seven hundred grams per square meter, good for bliss, euphoria, relaxation for pain and stress, from Weed Seed Express, a company from Amsterdam with a catalog of three thousand strains.

I hit the 'Buy Now' button.

And, it's out of stock. Plus, because of the pandemic, international shipping time has stretched out to twenty-five business days. My eyes are bleary from looking at bud and I go to bed. The next afternoon, instead of writing a letter of recommendation for a student's university application, I go through the search all over again and decide to shop domestic, U.S. and Canadian only. Two hours later, Lemon Thunder is the winner: the strain is a high CBD and sativa dominant cross with Alaskan Thunder Fuck and Lemon Pineapple, with an ACDC and Cannatonic lineage, producing a one-to-one CBD to THC ratio. The sativa dominance in the Lemon Thunder strain creates an uplifting high used for depression, anxiety, fatigue, and chronic pain. Mold and pest resistant, it takes ten weeks indoors and it's good for beginner growers, by Premium Seed Market. With a three-dollar flat rate for shipping, a packet of ten seeds is forty bucks.

As I place my order, their web page lets me know that the billing on my credit card will show up as "Oregon Market." All the seed companies had promised to be discreet, but their privacy policy states that they share my information with Google. So only the entire world knows I want to grow weed. Now, all I have to do is clean out a closet, get a grow tent, assemble it, and wait for my seeds to arrive. Oh, and learn how to grow marijuana.

Ten days later, my seeds show up.

The guy who answers the phone at the hydroponics store in San Antonio says that they are only doing curbside business right now because of the 'Rona, so I look at the website for New

Braunfels Hydroponics. It invites me to "Come learn how to grow hemp."

Come indeed. I'll go out there, see if they have classes, read books, study till I'm an expert.

No. Wait. Already I'm finding a way to over-think, over-plan. I just need to grow some weed. Hell, stoned-out dancing hippies could manage it. I order two books in the Grow-Your-Own-Weed category and decide that once they arrive, I'll order whatever grow kit seems best and harvest Lemon Thunder by mid-September, a few weeks before my Colorado edibles run out. This will work if I just get out of my own head.

An Amazon fulfillment center is ten minutes up I-35 and *Cannabis: A Beginner's Guide to Growing Marijuana* is on my porch the next day. After reading the whole thing, I have to admit that at least some of the dancing hippies must have been intelligent and anal-retentive. Growing weed in a grow tent involves keeping track of grow cycles, soil mediums, nutrients, pH levels, lights, filters, fans, and temperature, plus mold and pest control. There's also a chapter on harvesting, drying, and curing the buds. I'm sensing a serious learning curve. Maybe flying to Denver was easier after all.

I spend the next afternoon watching videos on YouTube, starting with how-to-grow-weed-using-a-grow-tent. Unlike shaky-cam videos that I've watched on how to grow asparagus or poblanos, the how-to-grow-weed videos are good quality, easy to follow, and closed-captioned, in case I'm deaf. Some growers even make a series of videos documenting their entire weed growing journeys and material expenses, so the days of needing a pot-growing buddy to teach you all of his grow room secrets are long over. Oddly, the websites for hydroponic stores from San Antonio to Austin are unforgivably crappy, and I can't tell exactly what they stock, so I start sorting through grow tents on Amazon, Home Depot, and Walmart. The kits come with a tent, exhaust fan, carbon filter, timer, and 300-watt LED light. But my book says I need 600 watts.

A week later, after I've measured the closet in the small room across the hall, I spend an evening comparing grow kits, not completely satisfied with any of them. The closet is small and my choices come down to a 16 by 16 by 48-inch kit for 270 dollars, which, I guess, will grow one Lemon Thunder plant at a time. Or, for 350 dollars, there's a 24 by 24 by 48-inch kit which will grow at least two plants but will barely fit in the closet.

I go through my weed books again—by now I have three—make a list of everything I need, then start looking up the individual items instead of whole kits. The 24 by 24 by 48-inch tent by itself is ninety dollars, and I can get the 600-watt LED grow light for seventy, a six-inch inline duct fan and carbon filter for 125, and a timer for ten bucks.

Even though I'd promised myself I would not get slowed down by over-thinking, it still takes me three days to finally order everything I need to get started. I did save myself fifty bucks by ordering each item alone rather than in a kit, and I scored the 600-watt LED light instead of the 300-watt light that the kits included. As I'm placing the order, Amazon tells me that the product's packaging reveals what is inside the box. Would I like to hide it inside an Amazon box for free?

The grow tent arrives in a box that is inside a box, and that box is a yard long and almost too bulky to handle. I flip it up on end, then ease it over to get it into the house. The inside box does not have a big label that says "This is for Growing Weed," so I could have avoided the box within a box thing. I shove it in my room, into the lane between my bed and the dresser, and stack the LED light and the carbon filter on top of it when they arrive.

And Finally. I'm ready.

Time to grow some weed.

CHAPTER FORTY-ONE

REVISIONS, DECISIONS

By the middle of summer, the only times I leave the house are to go to the grocery store or Walmart, and to go on walks in the park with Mom. Having upgraded to a softer N95 mask for children, I haven't been out of the house without a mask on since March, but as I head into Walmart, I notice the family walking in front of me: a mom, dad, and two teen kids. None have a mask and all are proud of it as they stroll past the Walmart guard, an old man sitting outside in the heat, near the carts. He starts a "Hey, you have to wear a—" but they are already inside, and the guard does not even try to stand up. I buy trellis netting and the heavy-duty mechanical timer and head home.

When I tell Mom that I want to clear out the closet in the small room so I can grow cannabis, she says, "No, Alene, definitely not. It's too dangerous. We'll make do without that."

And I don't say anything because this is the part that I thought would be the easiest.

The news is all COVID, all the time. Every evening the local news starts with numbers: how many dead nationally, how many dead in Texas, how many dead in San Antonio, how many hospitalized, how many in the ICU, how many on ventilators, and the seven-day rolling average of the numbers of dead. States across the country are declaring their own travel restrictions and quarantine requirements, and since Texas has high numbers of infections, no one wants people from Texas dropping by to say 'hi.'

Colorado has a mandatory two-week quarantine for anyone entering the state. I doubt that if I flew there, Aloft or Residence Inn would tackle me if I tried to walk in and out of their hotel, but that hardly seems the point. Air travel is down by ninety-five percent. Hotels are virtually empty, and coronavirus outbreaks are emerging not only in nursing homes, prisons, and factories, but also in random pockets like the downtown Denver postal distribution center, which Denver Public Health has ordered closed. Trips to stock up on edibles are done.

In August, I start preparing for the fall, revising all my classes which will be taught remotely the entire semester. I get permission to go to my office to retrieve books that I left behind in the spring. On campus, the signage, including arrows taped to the ground, direct me to a lobby check-in area, where I have to fill in a questionnaire that asks if I have been around anyone who has tested positive for COVID, if I have traveled outside of the country, or if I have a fever. The lady who normally checks in media equipment reaches her arm around a plexiglass barrier and aims a digital thermometer at my forehead like she's lining up a shot in a pentathlon. The Science Division dean sits behind another panel that has a slot cut out of it.

"Most people with COVID are asymptomatic," I say, "and a fever isn't always a symptom even for people who get sick."

"I know," she says, sliding a blue wristband through the

slot. The wristband shows that I've been cleared to be on campus. "But we have to do something."

The third floor is deserted, and my desk has a trace of dust. I check the cabinets to make sure that I'd taken my stash of oatmeal cookies with me when I left in the spring, then grab the books I need. Before I go, I look out the window at the empty sidewalk surrounding the green, next to the Student Commons. Three deer graze on the field.

Revising my classes so that I can teach them over a computer screen from a corner in my bedroom takes weeks. All the meetings for convocation are held over Zoom, and I catch myself going to the kitchen for a snack when the District reports get dull, so I go through my curriculum again, looking for my own boring trip-to-the-kitchen sections where I'd lose the students' attention.

At the end of the day, Mom comes into my room, closing the door behind her, to tell me that Dad's kidneys are starting to fail. "I want you to stop giving him the marijuana," she added.

"I don't think it's harming his kidneys."

His evening CDB gummie and THC mint were already on a saucer on my nightstand. To make the THC edibles last longer, I cut down on the amount I gave Dad each night to about three-fourths the dose I'd been giving him at the beginning of the year. This way, he would have enough to last through December.

"Well, he's got an appointment with a nephrologist this week, and they've got to do more tests and figure out what's going on and, and I want them to be able to do that without anything interfering in the test results."

"Mom, I don't think—"

"Just stop giving it to him, Alene. Let's just give it a break for now." I put the gummie and mint away.

Two mornings later, Mom has changed her mind. "He was up all night. At least five times, he woke up and went to the bathroom, then he sits on the side of the bed and drinks water. An hour later he's awake again."

I wait till September to bring up the idea of growing cannabis again, and this time I fill in the details: I can't fly to Denver, and even if I could, the trips cost a lot, plus the edibles themselves are expensive, including the CBD gummies that I now get in Texas. If I grew the cannabis myself, it would be—well, not free—but a helluva lot cheaper. Oh, and organic. I top all this off by explaining that there have been technological advances so that the plant is out of sight, easy to grow, and inside a ventilation-controlled enclosure. The bottom line is that if I don't grow it myself, we'll run out by New Year's Day. And Dad won't be able to sleep.

My delivery is flawless, but all I get is, "Well. I don't know. I'll think about it, I guess." She thinks for a week, then finally asks me what's in the boxes that have been stacked next to my bed since July. I explain the grow tent, LCD light, and the carbon filter and fan. "And you can't get your money back? Maybe if you called Amazon—"

"No, Mom. I'm sure I can't return it all now."

"And you really think it's safe to do this?"

"I'm sure Mom. Everything is automated. LCD lights don't generate heat, and the carbon filter keeps the smell from getting out of the tent."

"Okay," she sighs. "But I don't want Jovi to know."

CHAPTER FORTY-TWO
SEA OF GREEN

THE FIRST STEP to having a Home Grow was clearing out the closet in the spare room. My parents have a walk-in closet that is packed full. Half of the clothes will never be used again: uniforms, tuxedos, and suits that no longer fit are on Dad's side, and on Mom's side are skirt suits that have become out-of-date since she retired. The closet in the spare room held evening gowns, a Singer sewing machine, and a set of never-used towels. To move everything out of the spare closet, we had to sort through everything in the walk-in, and this took days. Mom got stalled as various items triggered memories and stories. Dad watched the closet clean-out from bed, objecting when we wanted to throw out jackets he hadn't looked at in decades.

I spend an evening watching videos of people unbox new grow tents while they explain the tent's features, ease of assembly, and the time it takes to complete the tent and install the lights, fan, and filter. The next day, I open the box and spread out the poles, end connectors, the tent, and the support bars to hang the light and carbon filter from. The tent is all one piece that zips up into a rectangular fabric box around the frame that you snap together. I put together an Ikea dresser once in grad school. The grow tent is easier, though it takes me longer than the guys in the videos.

I make the mistake of putting the tent together in the living room and then need Mom's help to maneuver it down the hall and awkwardly into the closet. The grow lights are a single panel with big, clearly labeled buttons that say things like "On-Off" and "Hi-Low," so, yeah, good signage.

The step I worried about was installing the carbon filter and fan. The fan and filter weighed twelve pounds, and, while everything else was dummy-proof, the fan and filter combo had to be mounted together, positioned correctly to the tent portal, and connected by a ring clamp to the long silver tube of ducting that would channel out the filtered air. It took a while, and I had to rewatch a video just on this step.

The trip to the plant nursery on Loop 1604 the next weekend felt a little surreal. Fox Farms products are formulated to grow weed. Just weed. And loading the bottles of Fox Farms Liquid Plant Food Trio, smart pots, and Fox Farm potting mix was bizarre, not because I was advertising what I was doing, but because I didn't care that it was so obvious.

After the nursery, I run by Walmart to pick up the rest of the home grow tools on the list I made. The guard standing there is in his twenties, alert and mobile, and you can't get inside Walmart without a mask now. Carts are sprayed with disinfectant, the handle still dripping as I push the cart inside.

⁂

By October, I'm all set. Even though I only plan to grow two plants, I put three seeds in starter cubes, so I'll have a backup if one fails. Then I wait. In mid-October, cotyledon leaves from all three seeds peek above the soil, and I plug each starter cube into a smart pot in the grow tent. The first true leaves only have two lobes and do not look like marijuana, the next leaves only have three lobes, and I look at the plants with the magnifying glass I store in the grow tent tool bag.

The hand shovel, hygrometer for measuring humidity, calendar for tracking plant growth, and other supplies are spanking new, and the non-stick bonsai tree pruning scissors that I'll eventually need for trimming the buds are high end, the nicest Amazon had. My reasoning behind the lack of frugality was that I'm so boring. I have no uncontrolled vices: I don't lose money at the track, trophy hunt on safari, or collect Louboutin handbags. My hobbies are hiking and growing herbs to cook with. If I'm going to grow organic weed in the closet across the hall, I'm gonna go classy and enjoy it.

It takes a week before the first leaf that actually looks like pictures of marijuana shows up.

Cannabis has two stages of growth, vegetative and flowering, and during the vegetative stage, the timer keeps the lights in the grow tent on for eighteen hours a day to simulate the light a plant would experience as it grows outdoors in the summer. One of the buttons on the LCD light panel is for the vegetative stage of growth, and blue light floods the reflective interior of the tent. In one corner of the tent is an oscillating fan providing wind, since plants do not develop strength without movement, and the branches have to be strong enough to support mature buds which, on cannabis plants, are heavy.

By the middle of the fall, I can teach, go to meetings, and have consultations with students from the table in a corner of my room, all day long. My back hurts and my ass feels flat.

Even with the foreknowledge that the entire fall semester would be remote, teaching online still turns out to be a monster battle of adapting assignments and revising teaching techniques, constantly sifting for the most effective way to turn on the lights in someone else's house.

The weed grower books, which I'm reading obsessively now, all say that the biggest mistake beginners make is to over-water and over-fertilize, and I resist the temptation to do those things each time I open the tent. Instead, I make unnecessary micro-adjustments, moving the lights up a fraction of an inch, checking the undersides of leaves for insects, and scanning the dirt, thinking that tomorrow it will need just a little sip of water. In November, I finally get to prune a few lower leaves, which is supposed to improve air circulation and force the plants to develop a better canopy.

All three plants are still growing, and I can't bring myself to destroy whichever one is the spare. I watch videos for two days before I top off my first plant, making a single snip to take off the top of the main stem, which will force the plant to develop more branches, which will then produce more colas. And in mid-November, I press a button on the light panel to switch from the blue light used eighteen hours a day during the vegetative stage, to the twelve-hour red light that triggers the plants' flowering stage. I start training the branches so they will spread into a Sea of Green using the netting, string, and stakes to hold them up, so they won't break when the colas develop and become too heavy for the smaller branches to support.

Aunt Gracie calls. Mabel, my great-uncle's wife, has died at 102 years old. Great-uncle Quinby died at least a decade ago, and they did not have any children, so Whitney, one of my cousins, had to drive to New York to make the arrangements and be the executor for Mabel's estate. Mabel once had a career as a radio talk show host on the East Coast, and her husband owned real estate in New York. But my mother and Aunt Gracie wonder who was with Mabel at the end. Did she die in their New York penthouse all alone?

A week later, Mom watches Mabel's funeral on Zoom. The service starts with a half-hour of people walking past the casket, but there are not many people. Because of COVID-19, only ten can attend the service, and they have to sit far apart. Funeral home attendants move about in the background. In a Zoom square, Mom sees her father's sister, her aunt Annie Mae. She is the last of my grandfather's generation and sits propped up in a bed in a nursing home, a woman on staff entering the frame, adjusting her pillow. Certain that Annie Mae would not understand the chat feature on Zoom, Mom holds up a piece of paper with a greeting on it for her. In another square, Annie Mae's son waves back. Then the funeral service begins as a woman, without a choir, sings to a recorded church organ.

When I get home from my weekly grocery run, Lauren is in the living room, and once I put the food away, I sit in there with her, expecting her usual frittery chatter, but instead, she checks her phone repeatedly, distracted. "You guys want dinner?" I offer, thinking of the leftover taco fixings in the fridge and wondering if I should explain that I made the taco filling with a vegan meat substitute.

"Oh, Jovi's not here," Lauren replied. "I was on my way to pick her up at Wyatt's, but he texted he's running late, so I came over to visit. I've texted him back twice, but he doesn't answer."

After dating Jazzmin with two 'Z's' for the two months

around the Christmas just after his and Lauren's divorce, Wyatt had a series of girlfriends, all with names spelled in some fashion that required a short tutorial: Charrdonay with two 'R's'; Laurah with an 'H' on the end; Hanna without an 'H' on the end but with three kids and two ex-husbands; and Siouxzie Rose, not a stripper.

Twenty minutes later, Jovi walks in, followed by Wyatt, and Lauren sniffs, quivering her nostrils like a coyote catching a whiff of lameness in a prairie dog. "Where have you been?"

I'm not sure whether she's addressing Wyatt or Jovi as both are still paused where the entryway leads into the living room, but I sense what Lauren sniffed about. Jovi's hair has not been combed in a day or two, and she's frowning as she goes up the hallway to her room.

"Out and about," Wyatt smiles. "I lost track of time."

"You think I won't say anything to you because I'm at my grandmother's house. That's why you're dropping her off here instead of having me pick her up at your apartment. Where was she?"

"She didn't miss any school. She had her tablet; she remoted in on time every day. I made sure."

"I didn't ask if she missed any school, which she did, today. Mrs. Chiba-Garcia called to let me know that the school had resources if Jovi needed assistance or hot meals. She said Jovi remoted in on Monday from a front porch somewhere, and there were 'sounds of chaos' in the background when Jovi unmuted to answer questions in class."

Mom, in the middle of wiping off a pan with a dish towel, was now suspended, pan in one hand and dish towel in the air. She was listening as stealthily as someone holding a pan and a dishtowel, in an avocado green kitchen with pineapple print wallpaper, is able.

"You took her to Houston. In the middle of a pandemic. It's ridiculous enough that you can't keep yourself at home, knowing she comes over to stay with you, and you're out in the streets getting exposed to COVID-19 and UK COVID and new COVID variant they haven't even named yet."

"I wasn't out in the streets. I was at the big cabin with my cousin."

"Which cousin?" The tone Lauren used when she asked this told us that which specific cousin was about to be named was as relevant as the nuclear launch codes. And then, Wyatt hesitated.

The reason public executions, frequent and popular in the Middle Ages, were stopped, was because the crowds enjoyed them, reveling so much in the 'theater of horror' that the massive gatherings became raucous and uncontrolled. The ritualized spectacle of executions, supposedly to deter the great unwashed from crime, were themselves a threat to public order. They weren't working. So executions were moved indoors, out of sight.

Lauren had the supernatural skill of dialing her cell phone without actually looking at her cell phone, so she stared at Wyatt, while the fingers of one hand tapped away. Mom moved forward holding her breath, but Lauren's phone was on speaker, so we all heard: "Go for Grant."

"Hey Grant, this is Lauren. Hope you don't mind me calling, but we can't find Jovi's tablet. Do you know if she left it there? She needs it for school, and we really need to track it down."

"Lauren, umph. Yeah, I don't know. Still cleaning up. Trash can's full of pizza boxes and beer cans, hhrm. I'll look around, but in case I don't find it, uh, you might check with Marshall. He was here all weekend. Maybe he picked it up? Not sure where he's got to now though, uhm. Wyatt, I think, left already?"

Lauren's thumb shifted and the call ended.

Little zings thrilled through my fingertips.

Wyatt attempted a casual gesture, a man on the gallows nodding to the crowd. "You know that every year we have a party for Marshall's birthday. All the cousins get together. We always have. The family can't change that. It's tradition." And the trap door dropped.

"Don't give me that! What you've always done. What you did when you were fifteen, or twenty, or twenty-five. It's not a reason to do it now. How is it a tradition to go to a birthday party in a pandemic? How has it not crossed your mind to break with tradition? And I know you went to Miami over the summer. You went there because the nightclubs were still open when we were already on lockdown here in Texas."

Emerging from the hallway, Dad tottered into the living room in pajamas, with thin old socks, rumpled, around his ankles. "Hey, Wyatt. Thought I heard your voice. Haven't seen you in a while."

"No, no. It's been a while."

So, the cause of the divorce was not drugs and not drinking, even though Wyatt seemed to drink too much and too often, and it was not gambling, which we had long suspected was behind their inability to save money when they were married. The divorce was because he just would not grow up. A year after the divorce, he lost the house and moved into an apartment, then moved to another apartment and another, each shoddier than the last.

"That's it." Lauren inhaled deep and slow, the way the yoga teacher at the gym told us to summon our 'Ujjayi, the Ocean Breath.' "You are not my responsibility; I'm free of you. It's taken this long, but it's gone now. You were the only boy I ever loved, and I thought my feelings for you were gone before, but I'm sure now. You're on your own, Wyatt. I'm taking care of me and my daughter now and that's it."

"Look Lauren—"

"No, you look. You think because I didn't want to argue in front of Jovi, it was because I couldn't, but you're wrong. It was a choice. I chose not to argue because it was best for her. But you are not taking my daughter anywhere without my knowledge and without my permission. You went to Houston because you were bored and wanted to hang out with your stupid useless cousins for the weekend. If you think I won't argue about you taking my daughter somewhere without my say-so, you are out of your mind."

"Out of your mind," Dad added pleasantly.

"Come on out of there," Mom said, but Dad didn't move. Instead, he stood steadier than I'd seen in a year.

"Guess you'll be going now," the smile stiffened on Dad's face as he stared at Wyatt.

All this time, Wyatt had been half-lounging on the small couch, in a way that annoyed me, and now he rose, awkward and slow. As he left, he called down the hall, "See you next week, Jovi," and I saw her loitering in her bedroom doorway, listening to everything.

Jovi came into the living room as the front door closed. "So," she looked at Lauren. "Are we in our best mind and making good decisions? Did we breathe deep, count to ten, and check with our calm voice of wisdom?"

"You don't need to be a smartie," Lauren said.

"Did we look with the inner Eye of Consequence or whatever?"

"Alright little girl," Lauren smirked. Dad sat down, looking as though he wasn't sure why he had been standing there, and Jovi sat next to him.

Holy crap. The conversations Lauren and Jovi must have had for Jovial to snark off like that rolled over me, and then Lauren turned to Jovi and actually said it: "Jovi, I'm sorry that I spanked you."

What?! I'm not expecting this. My family doesn't do this.

"You probably don't remember—" Lauren continued.

"I remember," Jovi cut in.

"Well," Lauren blinked. "I'm sorry."

I wasn't sure where to look. I wanted to look at them both and was uncomfortable looking at either one. Jovi, as thoughtful as I'd ever seen her, was focused on Lauren.

"Okay," said Jovi, and not in the way that children forgive everyone for everything because children don't understand and don't have a choice, but the way someone who knows what her mother had gone through—divorcing a husband, losing a house, and health care, losing all she had counted on and then losing control—the way a person who's witnessed all that and more, could forgive.

For a minute, I didn't know what to do. My family doesn't do feelings and forgiveness right out in the open like this. I felt surprised by my own presence, as though I should have been rows away, watching from a distance. Mom, waving the dish towel like she was dancing, brought Lauren a glass of iced tea she hadn't asked for. Lauren had laid it all out there and hadn't even dropped an f-bomb, or eight, and without knowing how it happened, I hugged her like she was Superman and had just punched an asteroid about to hit my house, back into outer space.

❧

I've been growing herbs for years, but never with the kind of intimate attention I lavished on the marijuana. Growing weed turns into my new meditation, the grow closet across the hall my new nirvana. I have to avoid checking the plants too often. Is the greenness too green, I wonder, while also dreading any hint of yellow in the leaves. The plants fill out, becoming bushier, and the pistols, flower clusters, and first white crystals appear.

I have a jeweler's loupe for looking at the calyxes. Orchids are legendary for inspiring obsession in people who grow them. Tulips and bonsai too. Three weeks before she died, my grandmother Ella, who could no longer remember her children's names, still trimmed the tea roses along the front of her house. She had been tending them since before her first child was born, and even when Alzheimer's took away her connection to the events going on in the world, caring for the roses kept her moving and alive. I put the jeweler's loupe back in its case, beginning to understand her lingering habit a little, even as outside, my potted herbs are starting to flounder as the autumn light slants low across the patio and December draws closer.

On Tuesdays and Thursdays, I have a gap between classes that is just the right amount of time for me to eat lunch, lay down for a few minutes, then get set up to teach again. The light in the spare room is on as I come up the hall, balancing leftover potato soup and a sandwich. Dad is looking at the sliding closet doors.

"Your mother said there's something in there, but I can't remember what it was that she said not to bother."

I slide the closet door back, pausing for a minute as Dad looks perplexed, taking in the flat front of the grow tent, the silver vent hose snaking out the side. I put the food on the dresser, so I can give a flourish to unzipping the tent but end up standing awkwardly sideways as I do it. Dad sits on the end of the bed.

"That's marijuana," he says. "I don't smell anything."

"The plants don't smell until they start to mature a little more and grow flowers."

"You're growing marijuana. In the closet? Gonna burn the house down?"

"No, Dad. The lights stay cool. They're LED lights; it's all modern. When the flowers get large enough, I can harvest them and turn them into chocolates and gummie bears." I adjust the oscillating fan a bit. "I can't leave the tent open too long, so bugs don't get in." Dad nods his head and I start to zip it up.

"This is for me?" he says.

I slide the closet door closed. "Yes Dad. For you."

The marijuana aroma shows up in December during Finals Week, weedy and lemony, as the pistols begin to color and the trichomes swell. The carbon filter works, but I get Ona Gel to neutralize odor when I open the tent. A week later, after I've turned in grades and paperwork, the buds are plump, trichomes full of resin, and the smell has intensified. I open the tent one afternoon and gasp: I've lost a cola. One of the branches has broken. In response, I tie so many support strings, the plants look like marionettes.

When you're ready to harvest, the books say to wait a week,

but the books are not living under lockdown and running out of edibles from Denver.

"The time has come," the Walrus said, "to talk of many things: Of shoes and ships and sealing wax, of cabbages and kings. And why the sea is boiling hot and whether pigs have wings."

Time indeed.

CHAPTER FORTY-THREE
WINTER HARVEST

ONLY AFTER I read it in one of the books do I realize I don't have to harvest an entire plant all at once, so on December 21st, I cut off the end of a branch and harvest just two colas. The topmost buds closest to the lights are the most mature, with cloudy amber trichomes, resin glands shaped like tiny mushrooms. I've moved the card table from the corner of my room to the spare room, where I can use the bed as a seat, and I place the branch in one of the two trays that I have for trimming. Even though I'm not harvesting much today, I decide I'm going to learn everything the right way, step-by-step, and the book says to have two trays: one for debris and another to hold the trimmed buds and the good leaf pile.

I cut off the fan leaves then start snipping off the smaller leaves with crystal on them, the sugar leaves that are saved. Then I cut the buds off the stem and take off my disposable gloves. Everything has already been set up in the kitchen to make the cannabutter—the 240-degree oven, already preheated. If you eat a raw cannabis bud, you can get some anti-inflammatory benefits, but nothing exciting will happen. The plant has THCA and CBDA in it, and to convert those into the analgesic CBD and the euphoria creating THC, you have to expose it to heat, to decarboxylate it. Exposing a dried bud to fire when you smoke it does that. But to make potent edibles, breaking the fresh buds onto my parchment lined casserole dish and baking them for an hour works too.

When the cannabis is cool enough for me to handle, I go with the simplest method I could find in the cookbooks and put the sugar leaves into a canning jar with two cups of butter, then break up the decarbed colas even more and scrape those in as well. I seal the jar and stand it in a pot of simmering water. It'll take a couple hours before I can strain the butter through cheesecloth and into a silicone mold to make new sticks of cannabutter, ready to cook with.

I had a digital scale in the kitchen to weigh the cannabis before adding it to the butter but forgot to use it. In theory, I should be able to weigh the buds, estimate the CBD and THC level based on the strain, and, using the science of Math, calculate the strength of the cannabutter produced. In theory. In reality, not only do different growing conditions create variables that affect cannabinoid levels, the levels also vary due to how mature the buds are when harvested and even where on the plant the buds are located. Without a lab, it's all guesstimation. Three hours later, I wring the last of the hot melted butter out of the cheesecloth that I've strained it through, leaving the plug of spent plant matter behind. The butter comes out tinged a deeper shade of chartreuse than the cannabutter pictures in my cannabis cookbook.

The silicone mold goes into the fridge, and I spend the

evening comparing fudge recipes, looking for one that requires a lot of butter.

Though it's been decades since I made fudge from scratch, I remember that whenever I made it, I would always replace the milk chocolate with combinations of bittersweet and semi-sweet chocolate and add in more cocoa and vanilla than the recipe called for. I make two pans of fudge on the 23rd and, worried about a repeat of Dad's orange ball hallucination thing, decide to test a sample to see how strong it is.

On Christmas Eve, I have a piece of fudge. The fudge is creamy and dense, with the burnt cocoa overtones of dark chocolate but also with citrus and weed accents kicking in underneath. Oddly tasty. Even artisanal if I want to get pretentious about it, and why not? Christmas concerts are running back-to-back on PBS television, and I settle in, just as angels we have heard on high are sweetly singing. Lemon Thunder's sativa dominant, one-to-one CBD to THC ratio suggests that the evening's slow, smooth tabernacle ride will be fine and mellow.

It starts during 'Here's A Pretty Little Baby.' Then Lemon Thunder's uplifting high observes and floats over a solemn 'Noel Nouvelet.' My mind is awake but not racing the way it was when I tried the sativa THC chocolate the year before, and now I feel pleasant, buoyed along with 'Bring a Torch, Jeanette, Isabella.' The homemade fudge does not hit my body super hard, but I feel it comfortably in my limbs and back. Just three months ago, I had never grown weed before, and now, Hallelujah, Hallelujah, Hal-le-lu-jahhhh.

Jovi has ended up spending Christmas with her dad. Once she turns twelve, she can declare which parent she wants to live with full time, and Wyatt is realizing that she's gotten old enough to understand he's unreliable. In the living room, the presents we have gotten for her wait, stacked around the five-foot, light-up angel that we snapped together this year instead of dragging the artificial tree out of the attic. I got her some sketch pads, watercolor paints, and charcoal pencils. Before the pandemic, I'd finally taken her to the San Antonio Museum of Art, and over the last year, Jovi started drawing again, brilliant abstract sunsets that look like rippling textiles.

COVID Christmas is as basic as I can remember Christmas ever being. Mom doesn't even buy a full turkey, just a turkey breast and a spiral-cut ham. Lauren and Callie drop by in the afternoon to pick up presents and plastic containers of Christmas dinner, so that, as Mom says, "Even if we can't eat together, we can at least share a meal."

Callie only has one day off from work before she has to spend the day after Christmas in a rehabilitation outpatient clinic doing observations on two new hires, so her plan is to go back to her house, eat the dinner Mom made, then spend the rest of the day sleeping and playing video games. She gives me and Mom polarized sunglasses that we can wear while walking in the park but refuses to come into the house because she's been around patients and won't risk exposing Mom and Dad to anything. The girls loiter on the front porch in the cold, and Lauren mentions that Jovi will be back with her next week and that she thinks this will be the last holiday they spend apart, but other than that, Lauren doesn't talk much.

That evening, I give Dad a square of fudge and he sleeps all night without getting up and without seeing tree limbs swaying in the wind or orange balls on the carpet. I had gotten down to the last five pieces of Colorado edibles and now I can make my own edibles at home, without flying to Denver and dragging my luggage down Champa after sunset, and without having to buy another grow tent, grow lights, or how-to-grow-weed-for-beginners book. The economics of edibles has just become extremely reasonable. So Yahtzee, edibles. Yahtzee.

The rest of Christmas weekend is spent harvesting the rest of the cannabis, taking down each plant in V-shaped branch sections, so I can do a wet trim, then hanging each branch, using the 'V' as a natural hook, to dry for a week inside the grow tent, with the LCD light off but the fan and carbon filter still running.

Trimming weed has a reputation for being a chore—professional trimmers earn sixteen dollars an hour—but I don't mind it. After months of complex thinking, curriculum redesign, and teaching into a little camera, the mechanical feel of cutting off the large leaves, clipping the glittery sugar leaves with the tips of the scissors, shaping the buds, and cleaning the sticky buildup off the tools is a sort of meditation. I take my time and lean into the repetition of movements.

Mom pokes her head into the spare room only once. As an excuse to open the door, she asks if I want her to warm up a plate of leftovers, then watches for a bit, assessing the buds, citrus-ganja scenting the air. I offer the magnifying glass in case she wants a closer look, but she shakes her head, noticing the glass jars lined up in the top of the closet, where the buds will cure once they are dry, then she backs out of the room, closing the door.

Once I start giving Dad the homemade weed fudge, I realize that, because I had worried so much about running out of the Denver edibles, I had gotten pretty stingy about giving them to him. Spinal arthritis is progressive. It can get worse quickly or slowly, but it always gets worse over time, and Dad was having more and more trouble moving around. On New Year's Day, I put the dried buds into mason jars so they could start curing, keeping one bud out to make a jar of canna-oil. A canna-oil citrus vinaigrette goes on a salad for Dad that evening, but it does not go over well. He's accustomed to chocolates or gummie frogs, and explaining to him that the salad is his evening medicine takes a lot of effort. He looks at the salad like it might speak. I flip through my cannabis cookbook again, go online and order candy molds, deciding on silicone trays with little fish shapes pressed into them.

Lemon Thunder fish gummies turn out to be easier to make than fudge and easier to dose than vinaigrette. I dye the first batch blue.

❧

January 2021 starts. The gym is still closed, I've gained twenty pounds since last January, none of my jeans fit, and my bra is too tight. I wear stretchy leggings and a t-shirt. My hair has gone gray at the temples and hasn't been cut in a year. I remember to burp the curing jars twice a day. The distribution of the coronavirus vaccines that start coming out in December is so slow it's estimated that it will take half a year before people who are not frontline medical workers, high-risk patients, the elderly, nursing home residents, or inmates can even get in line for a vaccination. Talking heads predict a new normalcy should solidify sometime in 2022.

My students are more depressed than they were in the fall. When the pandemic lockdown first started, they were energized by anxiety and novelty, but by the fall, they were tired, cooped up, and antsy. Now they are marking time, and there are fewer of them: enrollment has dropped ten percent. When I first started teaching in '93, I printed out transparencies for the overhead projector, wrote on a chalkboard and even bought my own box of colored chalk, so I could get all fancy. To show *Hamlet* in class, I wheeled in a television with a VHS player, and I had to rewind the tape between class periods.

Now during lockdown, I teach a literature class online in the morning: I lecture while screen-sharing slide presentations with embedded videos, then teach the same class two hours later. In a classroom, teaching the same class twice in one day remains interesting: you make micro-adjustments as you sense which students are lost or distracted. But teaching into a screen is like performing the same play without an audience, over and over. If a student misses class, he just watches the Zoom recording later that night while heating up spaghetti.

Traditions are made to be broken because as soon as you call something a tradition, you're admitting that there is no reason for still doing it, other than that you've done it before, like spanking kids, restricting cannabis, or teaching classes the same way they've been taught for a thousand years, even if it is on a laptop with video cut-ins. Tradition.

At the end of the first week of classes, I review my retirement date calculations, knowing there is no way, after all this, that teaching is going to be the same profession in three or four years. Realizing that the way I taught was now just a tradition? That one hurt. On the other hand, Brave New Online Learning meant I could soon take a course in physics when I wanted, at my own pace, sitting in my pajamas in bed.

At the end of the month, Jovi sits alone in a small white room and answers questions from a family court judge on a monitor. The judge is sitting in a wood paneled room somewhere else in the city, maybe downtown, maybe in a corner of his house, and Jovi tells him that she wants to live with her mother instead of having to split her time between her parents.

When I was a kid, the fanciest restaurant on Treece Road, the long commercial strip running between all the nearby subdivisions, was the San Francisco Steakhouse. My parents would go there for anniversaries and come home talking about the woman on the velvet swing that hung from the rafters inside. After the steakhouse closed, the restaurant was resurrected as a family buffet for a decade. But in February, when I stand in the parking lot, the building—still the same shape as the steakhouse, with a neon steer above the entry—is now painted lavender. It does not have a sign on it, but there are cars in the spaces.

The smoke shop's website boasts that they sell pipes, papers, posters and erotica. Booths still line the area that used to be family dining, and the air is heavy with incense. Two cats lay on the counter and the one next to the register lifts his head as I weave around the racks of new-age calendars, tie-dye t-shirts, and pot leaf bumper stickers proclaiming, 'The Law is the Crime.' Marijuana is illegal in Texas, so the selection of chillums, pipes, and bongs are sold as novelty items rather than drug paraphernalia. The grinders seem to be hidden, and after two turns around the shop, which turns out to be erotica-free, I pause in front of the neatly dressed owner. "Do you have three-chamber herb grinders and rolling paper?"

"Right there on the wall," he says, a question in his voice as though my question was not quite sensible. He leads me over, waiting for me to tell him what I want. "What brand do you usually get?"

"I don't. I've never been in here before."

"Hm. Most people get regular paper. All of them burn fairly slow, but I use hemp paper. It's a little thicker."

A booklet of fifty is the size of a packet of gum. He points me to the grinders next, a few plastic ones for less than ten bucks and others shiny as stainless steel. I pick one with a Captain America shield enameled on its lid, go with the hemp rolling papers, add an odor-proof cigarette case, and remember to ask about a crutch as he's ringing me up.

"Filter tips?" he says, giving me the correct local lingo.

Dad's back causes him pain even when he rolls to the edge of the bed to get up, but the buds have cured now and wait quietly in the top of the spare room closet. I lay the accessories out on the card table. The grinder is heavier than it looks, a cold, dense alloy, sturdy enough to pass down through generations. The diamond-shaped teeth hang down inside the lid and, in a maze-like pattern, interlock with the teeth sticking up in the first chamber.

I press a rolling paper into the bend of an index card bent into an 'M' shape, lay the filter on one end, then load flower into the grinder and give the lid a twist. I get the consistency right, breaking the bud into fragments without turning it into powder, then line the rolling paper with the cannabis.

Rolling the joint turns out to be the actual 'skill' part. I drop it, crush it sideways, roll it lopsided, drop the tip, roll it too skinny, and spill the weed out of the end. The smoke shop sold jars of pre-formed cones, but I had disdained them. Part of the reason I enjoyed making Dad's herbal tea is that the process felt a little mystical, and rolling a joint, ritualistic and elemental, feels outside the structure of my rigid days, the days that I'd cycled through for decades without interrogation, the patterns I had not veered from. Concentration clears the mind. Eventually, I get the movements right, or the movements get themselves right. In addition to being the fastest way to feel marijuana's effects, smoking it is also the best way for a person to control their own dosage.

I roll my first inelegant but satisfactory joint, and Dad's days get much more comfortable.

One afternoon when Tessa had visited the previous year, she and I sat at a picnic table in the RV park, having a beer. She had already asked me if Lauren and I were getting along again, and I said that we were 'all good' and Tessa had nodded and sipped her beer. Her face, calm and lovely, was unreadable. "Everyone spends their thirties fixing what they did in their twenties," she said. "You're not like other people, Alene. You make a plan and follow it your whole life. You're the only person I know who has never had to clean up their past."

During Spring Break in March, I plant fresh herbs and also start several Shishito Chile Peppers, the new food trend, so I can give them to Callie, Lauren, and Jovi. They like spicy food. I also spend a day laying on my back, staring at the ceiling: I've had enough. I give it five years before half of all college classes are taught as interactive videos that any twelve-year-old can download, and why not? If you're twelve and can master non-Euclidean geometry at a desk in your living room from a near-real teacher who patiently constructs Platonic solids as many times as you need to hit rewind to understand them, you should.

When I was an undergrad, my calculus TA threw an eraser at me when I asked him to explain homework problem number eleven for the fourth time. Videos don't chuck erasers at your head. Not yet anyway. I decide that in the summer, I'll do some research on careers in vertical farming, hydroponics, or solar energy and figure out what classes I can take online. Someone somewhere must teach hydroponic vertical farming using solar energy. I don't need to earn another degree. I just need to learn enough to get started. Also, I failed calculus.

I carefully prepared for the meeting with my HR guy. I already knew him well enough to like him, since each semester, for years now, I made a pilgrimage to Mirador College's Human Resources Department and reviewed my Educator's Retirement Plan, defined benefits, and the retirement contributions that were being matched by the District. This was the first time I'd met with Damarian on a screen.

He was Zooming from his dining room table, a China cabinet visible behind him. We went through about one minute of the usual niceties and lockdown chit-chat, so when I flipped out, it happened quickly enough to not waste any of his time. I had been thinking all morning about Colorado: the mountains, the sweet air, the vast sky, trips to get edibles, old Fred feeling 'charged' when he got knocked out of his safe, slow river ride, Kinsley jumping as she urged me to "Fire it up" on the scooter.

"I quit!" I said suddenly. And loudly. And in exactly the way that I had not planned on doing.

Damarian heard me and pretended that he had not. "What was that?" he asked.

"I quit," I said again, less intensely. Many of the teachers in the District worked more than a decade past retirement, several each year at District convocation were presented with their forty-year pins, and I'd heard of three who had actually died on the job, one while grading history essays in her office. "I was planning to ask you what would happen if I retired early in two years instead of waiting till I reached full retirement in four years, but two years might as well be two hundred. So, I quit. At the end of the semester, I'm done."

"I'll start the process for your separation from the District and check back with you in a week to confirm that you want me to continue."

"I won't change my mind, Damarian."

"I understand," he said. "It's happening all over, you know. It's the lockdown, the pandemic. Everyone's tired, but everyone's also been thinking, making choices, I guess. They're calling it the Great Resignation."

"How many have you had so far?"

"Teachers? You're the third. Admin and staff? Nine and counting."

When I leave Damarian's dining room Zoom office, I breathe deep. I have no idea what I will be doing in a year. For the first time in decades, I feel awake like I'm hiking a fresh trail, alert like Fred doing a swimmer as he sped down the river, alive like Kinsley taking off full tilt on a scooter the first time she stepped onto it.

CHAPTER FORTY-FOUR
QUIET TOGETHER

I DIDN'T DIE in childhood as doctors predicted when I was born, but I was sickly, and long past the time when I did not die, Mom would sleep on the floor next to my bed whenever I got sick so she could hear if I 'went into distress.' During fevers and flu, mumps, measles, chest colds and sore throats, she put down a comforter and pillow and lay there till morning.

When I was five, I learned to ride horses in Arizona when we were stationed at Brinstaff Air Force Base. Bible school was Sunday mornings, but I would leave class a little early to get to the stables in time, trotting around the corral in line with a half-dozen other kids. Dad would take me, and after the lessons, Dad and I would sit on the black leather couch in the stable owner's shadowy office that smelled like cigars, and he and my dad would talk. Dad had a habit of stacking leftover change in towers on his dresser at the end of the day, and so did Mr. Tarrent, the owner. He had 50 cent pieces and silver dollars on his desk, and I would restack the coins into towers of different heights. I never listened to anything Dad and Mr. Tarrent talked about, too preoccupied with the dull coins, warm heavy disks of gravity.

Dad drank a lot back then, but he wouldn't admit it for another decade. Saturday was our time to go riding together, but about one weekend a month, he had a hangover in the morning and couldn't go. He would lie on his back while Mom harangued about his drinking, her voice pounding through his head. When we did go to the stables, after greeting Mr. Tarrent, we took out Colonel and Molly, the mounts he always reserved for us. Then we rode for hours in a loop from the stables, across fields, along a narrow trail, over a metal bridge that the horses didn't like, and onto the Base. Tracing around the edge of it, we would ride right to the back of our house, which was in the very last row of low, one-story duplexes. We would stop and give the horses water, then continue riding past the kennels where they trained the security police dogs, then back to the stables and Mr. Tarrent's office. It took up half of the day.

Before we reached the trail to the metal bridge, there was a long broad field surrounded by trees but open at one end like a horseshoe. It was perfect for racing across. I would play Lone Ranger, getting Molly up to galloping full speed, then hook the loop reins on the saddle horn, so I could shoot imaginary guns straight up with both hands. On the far end of the field was a 45 mile-an-hour farm-to-market two-lane, and one pastel morning, midway across the field, the reins slipped up Molly's neck. I held onto the saddle horn with one hand and reached for the reins with the other.

Dad saw it happen and spurred Colonel, a larger, faster thoroughbred, so he could catch up with me, grab the reins, and slow Molly down, but when Colonel started closing behind, Molly, instinctively, put all she had into it and ran hard as she could. Even at six years old, I could work out what this was leading to and started flailing for the reins, lying flat out, trying to stretch up Molly's neck, but the reins had flopped all over, worked their way up and gotten hooked on her head and ear. Dad inched closer, but it was clear that even if he caught up, we could never stop short in time. The vehicles on the two-lane couldn't see us coming: three were cars, one was a delivery truck. At this speed, even if we could make it through the traffic somehow, as soon as she went from grass to asphalt, worlds would fly apart. I was fifty yards away from the pavement.

Dad did not catch the reins, and he didn't stop the horse. Ten yards away, as he brought Colonel parallel with Molly and then got a fraction ahead of her, he turned Colonel to the right and Molly, frenzied out of her head, also curved to the right and pounded up the edge of the field, running along the road instead of flying across it. Dad was on the outside of her, between me on Molly and the speeding cars. Molly was crazed now but spent and frothing, and Dad grabbed her by the mane, then managed to get my reins in his hands while still controlling his own horse and gradually guided both horses to a stop, in the strip of clearing bordering the highway.

We sat there a long time, Molly tossing her head for a while until she finally gave that up and stood quiet, while cars zoomed by and wind brushed the evergreens. He handed the reins back, an inch-wide strip of warm leather, tanned on only one side like an old soft belt. If Dad had hesitated, I would have been killed. If he had tried to catch Molly and failed, he'd have died with me.

"Don't ever do that again," he said. I nodded 'okay', staring at the sweat-darkened hide on Molly's neck. Dad let a breath out and shifted in the saddle. "And don't tell your mother."

We never spoke of it again.

After I finished teaching my literature class remotely for the day, I went to the kitchen and quartered an apple, but because the apple was so big, I took two of the quarters to Mom and Dad's room. Mom was lying on the bed, half propped up on pillows, holding Dad's hand. He was looking over at her, staring in her eyes, her face. Her checkbook was out, and there were bills scattered at the end of the bed. She must have been in the middle of paying them. He must have said her name. I sat in the blue swivel recliner. Dad's thumb stroked the back of Mom's hand, and her other hand reached over and covered his.

For weeks, in the corners of my mind I had been terrified that there would be pain, fear, and struggle, then sirens and EMS. But Dad got what he wanted; his body was giving out, but his eyes held Mom's eyes. He was still in there; he knew Mom and me and himself. He remembered he had daughters, granddaughters, a great-granddaughter. An hour after I sat in the recliner, Dad died in the afternoon, and it happened quietly. And I was grateful.

Mom still held his hand and told me to call Tessa at the ranch in Arizona and Callie, who was at work. Callie could drive back to her house and pick up Lauren who was working remotely at Callie's dining room table, and Jovi at her desk upstairs, going to fifth grade on Zoom. Mom didn't want Lauren to drive once she knew. Lauren was emotional, but Callie would keep her eyes on the road.

When my great-grandmother, Maggie Brown's husband died in his sleep, her son, my great-uncle Lowell, who was a doctor, happened to stop by her house late that morning. "Mama," he said, "Daddy's been dead for hours. Why didn't you call anyone?"

"I knew as soon as I did," she said, "there would be a big fuss and the commotion would start and people filling the house for days, and this would be the last time I would have with him, quiet together."

Callie was still wearing hospital scrubs when they arrived but changed into some clothes she had grabbed at home. Lauren was crying with abandon and holding a whitewood basket, long and shallow, with a handle. The rest of us were tearful and calm. Jovi stood by the bed and put her hand on Dad's cheek, then on his hand, which Mom had lain on his chest.

I went to the living room to start making the calls to Arkansas. The harvest basket was a present Lauren had gotten for me but hadn't had a chance to bring over. It sat on the coffee table, lovely in simplicity, looking brand new and ancient at the same time.

When I went back into the bedroom, Jovi was sitting next to Lauren, her arms wrapped around her mother, and Lauren, calm now, had stopped crying. We sat there, all of us quiet together, for a long time.

~

I called Nolan late that night to let him know. He'd only met my dad a few times. Mostly I called because when Nolan had dropped me off at Aloft in Denver, he'd said, "It'll be alright," and it turns out he was right. I did not feel numb exactly, but knowing that Dad would never tell me more about his worlds of experiences, the finality of that, even though he had not really been able to remember those worlds for some time now, left a hollowness, like the sound after an echo stops, and all you have left is the wind moving across the canyon.

Nolan also had news: Kinsley had compared the algae that grew in different ponds around the CU-Boulder campus and won first place in her school's science fair. I know Nolan enough to know that he wouldn't do any of the research for Kinsley, yet I detect him in the shadows, steering a little: Not many twelve-year-olds spontaneously decide to study the adaptive characteristics of pond scum. "That pond has a lot of algae in it," Nolan must have said one morning, retrieving a strategically thrown Frisbee from Fia. "But the pond we just came from, the one with lots of turtles in it, did not. I wonder why."

And Nolan had passed a checkup and was officially recovered, no longer at an elevated risk of non-Hodgkin's lymphoma. He also had added another patent to his name. During the COVID lockdown, while I was learning to grow weed in the closet across the hall, Nolan had developed a cheaper, faster way to clean things on a very small scale, like on a nanoscale, which he explained was "sort of a big deal in high tech industries."

"Wow," I said, adjusting a blanket. "That's nice."

There was a Nolan-pause. "So, I've been thinking about doing some river rafting when things open up again. Do you think you would be ready for a medium-level river trip? There are rafting tours that actually last a couple of days, going down river all day, pitching tents and camping at night, in places where you can pick out features in the Milky Way. The tours cut through some pretty spectacular canyons."

I told him that a trip sounded perfect, and I would be up for it, once tours and trips and traveling was a thing again.

Mitch came by the next day, sitting in the living room with his mask on, reminiscing about my dad for a while, before spiraling into conversation about Lewin and Archie. The boys were thriving, and Patton, Mitch's husband, had persuaded Mitch to cut back on the boys' activities. They still had music lessons on Zoom instead of in-person, and Brazilian capoeira outdoors now, instead of in a dance studio. Archie was turning out to be a phenom at soccer, and Lewin did math two grades ahead of his class. Then, as Mitch was in the midst of explaining that the family was having more family time instead of racing from one team or tutor to another all week, he stopped. I thought he was about to say something more about my dad. Instead, he asked, "Am I boring?"

One year when Mitch and I were undergrads, he spent the summer in Berkeley, living in a frat house. The fraternity members were gone for the summer, so renting a room there was cheap. Half the rooms were empty, and half were occupied by other random, non-frat guys, mostly Berkeley students picking up a summer class and a few students like Mitch from other colleges, who were just hanging out in San Francisco.

The frat house provided no services: the kitchen was closed; the trash wasn't being picked up regularly; the place was a sty. I went to visit him for a week, absolutely unnoticed going up and down the carved wooden staircase, and even sliding down the balustrade once. The public transportation system was stellar, and Mitch and I rode the Bay Area Rapid Transit under the bay to San Francisco, hopping buses to tourist spots: the Presidio, the Golden Gate Bridge, Fisherman's Wharf, Chinatown.

One afternoon, he detoured to an industrial zone. The warehouses went on for so many blocks I couldn't see the end of them. Streets were vacant; there were hardly any cars parked in the area, and between the warehouses was white concrete so desolate it felt like it might echo. He counted warehouses as we passed them then went down the broad space between two of them.

The windows were too high up. We had to roll a metal trashcan underneath one. Mitch said to be really quiet. I held the trashcan steady as he climbed up and peered in through the hazy glass. He had heard, at Harvard, about the sweatshops. He climbed down and pointed to where he wanted the trashcan positioned next. Farther down, some of the windows were propped open and he peered through an open one, while I watched the courtyard. When he climbed down, he asked if I wanted to look while he held the trashcan. "They're in there," he said. "So many."

We had been out there, exposed, for a long time, and I wondered where whoever was inside was going to emerge from, then we walked the blocks back to the nearest bus stop. I always regretted that I didn't peek inside, that I was too timid to be a witness and be able to truly report the hardship of others.

Years later, in my early days of teaching, I had my community college students write about the Hero's Journey that they were traveling on in their own lives, how a trauma they had experienced, or a hardship overcome, had set them on a path to college. And college was preparing them—as modern scholar warriors possessing the magical gift of education—to serve something beyond just themselves. Clearly, I took literary theory pretty seriously in those days. Many of my students were the first person in their family to go to college, and I felt that, for some, just getting there had been a helluva battle.

On the couch in the living room, social distancing slips Mitch's mind, and he scooches closer, reaching a hand toward me. "I used to worry about big things," he confides. "Art and culture.

Justice and politics. Now I'm checking that Archie diagrammed all ten sentences, in some language arts homework of his, that I couldn't remember how to do anymore if you forced me to at knifepoint. Linking verbs? Predicate nouns. You kidding me?"

"Mitch, are you happy?"

He sinks back against the couch. "I am."

"Then do you care if you're boring? You've done a great job with Archie and Lewin. The boys'll hit college in six, seven years; you can get interesting again after that." The relief that floods his face pleases me in some odd way, and we talk for another hour.

In the mythic stories of cultures worldwide, at the end of the Journey, the Hero that survives his adventures returns to his own land and distributes gifts to strengthen his tribe and to permanently weld his bonds with his companions. I had two pans' worth of Lemon Thunder weed fudge in the freezer which I had cut into squares. I gave Mitch some to dole out to his mom, who, in her seventies, had various pains and an ache in her wrist from when she fell off the step stool. And I saved some to give to Tessa. She and her husband, Jeff, were loading up the RV to drive to San Antonio for Dad's funeral.

Over the phone, Tessa told me about getting a flat tire one night when she was still a freshman at the University of Texas at Austin. She had called home, though I don't know how or from what phone, and Dad told her to lock herself in the car and stay put. He got out of bed, drove ninety minutes to find her on a dark, back country road, and made her change the tire. That's the part she hadn't expected. She didn't know how to change a tire, but he talked her through it, taking three times as long to get it done than if he'd changed it himself. It took her years to realize that he wasn't doing it because he was ticked off at having to drive to another city at midnight—he was—but because changing a tire was a skill he wanted her to have for the day when he was not close enough to change it for her. Then he drove back to San Antonio, got up and went to work on time the next morning, and decided to pay for her to get Triple-A.

Outside my window, the hedges in the front yard are getting a little shaggy, but the trimmer is in the garage, and I know how to even them out now.

The last pan's worth of square fudge blocks in Ziplock bags was under the frozen spinach. They would stay there, waiting till I had a hard day and needed to take the tension out. Mom had never tried any of it, not CBD frogs or Cherry Chocolate bars, THC mints, Lemon Thunder fudge, or blue fish gummics. But if she changes her mind, I'll open the freezer or get a jar of bud from the top of the closet and lay it all out there.

❧

It's been thirty years since I was at the University of Southern California, and my writing teacher and friend, Tom Maslin, told me to risk revealing what I was afraid to reveal.

Don't be mean. That's the fourth thing this book is about.

Weed should be super-legal everywhere and a helluva lot cheaper. You should grow some in a pot on your patio or in a closet until the patio becomes a non-jailable option.

Don't hit kids. Ever.

Don't be stupid.

And don't be mean. In fact, even if you are stupid and you could care less about weed, just don't be mean, and that will solve most everything else.

I wish you well.

AFTERWORD

SNOWMAGEDDON

In February of 2021, Texas was slammed by two massive winter storms, and San Antonio, which typically gets less than a half-inch of snow once in twenty years, was blanketed twice in a week. Temperatures dropped to 9 degrees in a city that can go a year or two without even a light freeze.

Unlike the rest of the United States, Texas has its own power grid. It is poorly maintained. To keep the entire system from collapsing under the energy demand, ERCOT, the Electric Reliability Council of Texas, began rolling blackouts, plunging millions into freezing conditions inside their own homes and apartments. The state shut down. Schools and universities, already teaching remotely because of the pandemic, canceled all classes for a week, as everyone just tried to survive. Without power, online classes could not happen anyway.

Roads were iced over, and cities like San Antonio halted public transportation. There was no place to go since businesses closed, including grocery stores. Gas stations cannot operate without power, and without the trucks to resupply them, they don't have any gas to sell. Without trucking, grocery stores are empty warehouses. As power outages lengthened, millions of Texans no longer had water because pumping stations could not pump. Once water began to be restored across the state, everyone was under a boil water notice.

This event is not represented in the book; a few neighborhood in San Antonio did not lose power or running water. Because of the prepper planning, I had already stashed jugs of potable water all over the house, and, when the power outages started, I filled one bathtub so that if we did lose power and water, we could flush the toilets using a bucket. My main worry was that if we lost power and the house got cold, Dad would not be able to tolerate the conditions. Hotels that still had power were already full with people whose homes were freezing, and by the time the city thought to open warming centers, the logistics of doing so took several more days. This meant that the warming centers were largely pointless.

For three days, Callie's house lost power for hours, then had it back on for 15 minutes before it would go off for another three to five hours. Mitch's situation was worse; his power came back on for two minutes instead of fifteen. When I first started my prepper craze, I nagged Mitch to store jugs of water until he finally did it just so I would stop bothering him. The boys said the bottled water they drank during the freeze tasted like plastic. But they had water. Many didn't.

Over five days, San Antonio stayed below freezing for 107 hours, which had not happened for at least seventy years. When the temperatures rose and power was gradually restored, many homes suffered massive water damage from frozen pipes that had burst, even though the home owners had wrapped their pipes before the storms hit. Supply chains were so smashed, grocery stores could not restock and even when they did get deliveries, they imposed purchase limits, especially on diapers, milk, eggs, water, bread, and other staples like rice.

More than 200 people across the state died, most from hypothermia, freezing to death in their homes, some from carbon monoxide poisoning as they tried to heat their homes, and others when their medical devices failed from lack of power.

DAD'S COMPLICATED YET VERY EFFECTIVE HERBAL TEA RECIPE

Get a mug and a cup with a spout, like a measuring cup. Boil distilled **Water**.

Into the mug, put 1 tablespoon raw organic **Apple Cider Vinegar**. Cut a 1/2-inch piece of fresh **Ginger** and slice off the thin peel. Using a garlic press or a ginger press, crush the ginger over the mug to get the ginger juice, then put the remnant of the crushed ginger into the cup. Cut 1/4 of a **Lemon** and use a lemon press to squeeze the lemon into the mug. Then put the remnant of the pressed lemon peel into the cup. Add 1 organic **Chamomile tea bag** (or Mint, Sage, Green tea, or Hibiscus tea bag) to the cup. Add 1 teaspoon organic **Honey** (to taste) and 1 teaspoon organic **Maple Syrup** to the cup. Take two **Cardamom** seed pods and crush them a little. Try using the back of a spoon if you don't have a mortar and pestle. You can substitute a pinch of Aniseed (not Star Anise) or a pinch of Celery seeds or you can use any combination of the three. Put the seeds into the cup.

To counter Dad's Alzheimer's, I also put three threads of **Saffron** onto a saucer, crush them with the back of a spoon and then tap them into the cup. And I add two leaves of fresh **Sage** to the cup.

Pour about 2/3 cup of the hot distilled water into the cup, enough to cover the ingredients. Stir the mixture to fully soak the tea bag, muddle the lemon peel and sage leaves, then cover the cup with a saucer to keep the volatile oils in. Let the mixture steep for 4 minutes.

After four minutes, spoon the dregs out of the cup, put them into the lemon press and squeeze the dregs into the cup carefully since they will still be hot. Then discard the pressed, spent dregs.

Place a strainer over the mug and pour the cup into the mug through the strainer.

Drink the mug of tea while the herbal tea is warm. Add more honey or maple syrup if the drink is too tart.

The drink tastes like a combination of wassail and lemonade. It is soothing. Have one cup each day. By the fourth day, it reduces chronic belching.

A DENVER ITINERARY

Go online and Google Denver sunset times. Check-in at hotels is at 4 p.m. and give yourself two hours to get from the plane, through baggage, to the airport commuter train, to Union Station, onto a MallRide, and to the hotel lobby. So, if getting to the hotel while it is still light outside is a concern, plan to land in Denver three hours before sunset.

Go online. Get a round trip ticket to Denver International Airport. Southwest Airlines Gotta Get Away fares are the cheapest. Checkout at hotels is 11 a.m., and give yourself 90 minutes to check out, catch a MallRide to Union Station, wait up to 15 minutes for the light rail, take the light rail to Denver International Airport, and get to your airline's check-in counter. Plus, you have to arrive two hours before your flight to go through the TSA security lines. Checking out of the hotel at 11 a.m. will give you enough time to hit a dispensary or two on the morning that you fly out, go back to your hotel, box up the edibles, mail them at the USPS on Champa, and still get back to your hotel in time to leave by check out.

So, decide on when you want to arrive in Denver and when you want to depart, and how many days you want to stay for dispensary shopping and maybe some vacation activities like Union Station, the Denver Art Museum, the Downtown Aquarium, the Denver mint, the Botanical Garden via Lyft, the Natural History Museum and the Denver City Park, etc. You can reasonably get to three dispensaries a day, four or even five if you stay focused and get up early or stay out later in the day. There is an 800 milligram edibles limit per day, per dispensary.

Go online and google 'Downtown Denver City Center' map. Print out a map with hotels on it, and choose a hotel within a two-block proximity to 16th Street. Anything with 'Grand' in the hotel name is too expensive. The map will also have the post office, restaurants, and some dispensaries on it. While you are at it, print off address labels with Denver addresses and a fake name and print labels with your home address and a fake name.

Go to the App Store on your phone. Download Lyft and Uber for free onto your phone. You need to have a credit card to do all this and an account in an App Store. To get an account in an App Store, you need an email account. You can get those for free from Google email. Google a video on how to do each of these steps if you don't know how.

The day you are flying out, get a Lyft or an Uber to the airport. Remember to take the Downtown Denver City Center map that you printed out. Fly to Denver. Take the People Mover train to the terminal—just follow the crowd. Get your luggage at baggage claim. Face the nearest windows. The nearest windows look out at parking. Turn right and walk down and exit. Turn left and go down the escalator. Turn right and walk a short way. Put $11 into the ticket vending machine and get an A-Line Commuter Train ticket. If you don't know how, there's a little building with a train guy inside who can help. Pick up some light rail and bus brochures while you are there. Go to the platform, and once the train is there, get on the train. There are metal racks to stow your luggage.

Google RTD Denver. It's the Regional Transportation District in most of the Denver-Aurora-Boulder area, and their accurate information, correct routes, and current prices will be more up to date than this is.

Ride the train to Union Station. Pick up some light rail and bus brochures while you are on the train. When you arrive at the back of Union Station, walk through the building (it's beautiful and sells good sandwiches) and go out the front. Turn right and go to the corner. Catch the Free MallRide down 16th Street. Get off on the corner nearest your hotel and walk the block or two to the hotel and check in.

Do your dispensary shopping and pay attention to the discounts and specials for each dispensary, like the early bird discounts, the Edible Tuesdays discounts, and things like that. Check out the restaurants that are a block or two off of 16th Street. They have good food and not all of them are chain restaurants.

Go to Target on 16th Street and buy mailer boxes, clear packing tape, bubble wrap, and cheap scissors. Save the big bag that Target gives you. To assemble your mailer boxes, line them with two layers of bubble wrap, put your edibles or other goodies inside with extra bubble wrap cushioning, and close it with packing tape. Put on the fake Denver return address (in the corner) and your home address label (in the middle) with your fake name.

If you are close enough and don't have too many boxes, put the boxes in your big Target bag and walk to the USPS on Champa and 20th Street. Or take an Uber. Mail the boxes home. Be nonchalant. Keep the slip of paper the USPS person gives you. It has the tracking numbers for your packages.

When you are ready to leave Denver, check out of your hotel. Take the 16th Street MallRide to Union Station. Catch the light rail for $11 back to Denver International Airport. Follow people to the escalator. Go to your airline check-in counter and check in your luggage, then get in the TSA line after that. Fly home.

When you get home, follow the progress of your packages by using the tracking number on the USPS website so you can bring in the boxes as soon as they arrive. Watch for the mail delivery. Porch pirates do not deserve a windfall after all your work.

STUPID THINGS THAT NEED TO BE FIXED

Toilet floor mats are too small.

Headlights on cars get foggy after years of driving because of tiny debris hitting the plastic and scuffing it up. Headlight polish doesn't work, so car companies should make headlight covers that can be replaced when they get cloudy.

Get rid of all the dings and bells in the car when something is wrong. Just have the car actually tell me to put on my seat belt, or that I left my headlights on, that the door is not locked, and that the car is still running as I'm walking away holding the key fob, which, by the way, should have a battery that is easier to replace. The car can also just tell me if the transmission needs a tune-up and why it needs a tune-up, instead of giving me a transmission shaped light that I have to decode like a hieroglyph. And, while you are at it, back up the car voice with an informative scrolling LCD display.

The same goes for the smoke detector in the house. When the smoke detector's battery is low, random beeps don't make me change the battery. Just have the thing say, "The fire alarm battery is low. Replace my battery by Friday or I will beep at you all night." Also, during a fire, the fire alarm should scream,

"The house is on fire. Wake up. Grab the kids. Leave now! Call 911." Or whatever the alarm company decides is most effective.

And, as long as we are talking about cars, they have gotten so complicated that the dashboard looks like a cockpit and the owner's manual is three inches thick. Car dealerships should have new car training sessions using interactive car simulators, like in an arcade. The guts of all the cars from the same manufacturer are pretty much the same, so sitting in a training simulator for a Toyota Corolla would be about the same as it would be for a Tundra or a Rav4. When I buy a new car, I don't want to read a book. But I still need to know how to work the lights, the radio, satellite navigation, the voice-activated coffee maker and the hand sanitizer dispenser. So, a new car purchase should come with 4 hours of new car simulator time, broken into 4 one-hour sessions. One more thing. Why does the seat warmer get its own dedicated button, but operating headlights and windshield wipers requires blindly fumbling for knobs jutting behind the steering wheel? Sort that crap out.

Along those same lines, iPhone should have free downloadable classes that teach me how to use my iPhone without a buttload of stress, without videos of obviously talented people dancing with their iPhones, and without snarky insider smarminess. In fact, they should have three programs, and the first one is "How to Use Your iPhone for People Who are Not Really Into Having an iPhone."

This idea is grafted from Dr. David Laude's video (*Everybody Can Get an 'A'*) where he predicts that pretty soon, college courses and other curriculum will be bought and played the way video games are bought. Why move to another state, sit in a class that you might fail, and spend thousands of dollars to learn Chemistry 1, when you can download a program that can teach it to you for $29.50, with a 95% pass rate, and with as many attempts at the interactive gamified quizzes as you need to go through to figure out cobalt variances? And yes, I know this means my days as a traditional professor are done.

If you are having hot flashes, get two clip-on fans and clip them onto each end of your headboard pointed in at you. And lay a terry cloth towel between the fitted sheet and the flat sheet. The towel will absorb the moisture when you sweat, so you won't have a wet spot waking you up all night.

The packaging on blocks of cheese is not resealable, even though it would be easy to make it resealable so the cheddar doesn't dry out and get hard.

And Apple, you can stop creating artificial scarcity by having too few Apple stores in big cities forcing people to make an appointment and then wait two hours just to ask a question about an iPhone or iPad that they already bought. And put the stores in regular outdoor malls, where people can actually get to them easily. Seriously.

So, if the electricity goes out in the winter because the grid is overtaxed during a hard freeze, how has no one invented a little indoor warming tent that you can set up in your living room. The tent should be just big enough for a family of four with a dog or cat to sleep inside. It needs to run on a battery pack, have vents, a low profile and Mylar lining to reflect body heat back in.

And Amazon, invest in better packaging technology, especially for bigger boxes. Cardboard boxes get torn and gouged before they get delivered. Maybe a reusable plastic jacket that the delivery guy could slip off the box right before bringing it to the porch? Then the cardboard box wouldn't need to be so thick in the first place, and it wouldn't end up with holes and damaged contents.

And finally, marijuana. Make it legal.

I got more on my list of stupid things that need to be fixed, but those are the ones that wake me up at night.

ABOUT THE AUTHOR

Denise Stallins taught literature for Alamo Colleges in San Antonio for more than 25 years. She earned her bachelor's degree from the University of Texas at Austin and her master's in Professional Writing from the University of Southern California. Denise likes to travel, hike, garden, cook, and walk small bossy dogs. *Laying It All Out There* is her first novel.

See pictures from Colorado on her website at
denisestallins.com

www.ingramcontent.com/pod-product-compliance
Lightning Source LLC
Chambersburg PA
CBHW022021300726
48970CB00003B/987

9798985558029